PACK ICE
ICEDANCE SEA
PERMAFROST LINE
ERLINMEYER
PIRATE ISLE
SUNGSONG SEA
HAIN
TURNSHIRE
TURN HALL
KINGSKEEP
THE VICEROY'S CASTLE
SALT CRYSTAL CAVERNS
GWILFIFESHIRE
MOONCALL SEA
LOST LIBRARY
LONG POND
VALLEY OF TOMBS
STOAT FOREST
URLAND
SWORD'S HEARTH
THE EYERIE
GADOT
CINCH MOUNTAINS
SKIPPING LAKES
CROW'S NEST
BRYSTOL
QUEEN'S DREAM
RAINSLEEP SEA

The Forgotten Tale
Book Two of the Accidental Turn series

Cover design by Ruthanne Reid and Rodney V. Smith
Edited by Kisa Whipkey (2016) and Donna Frey (2024)
Book design by Brienne Wright
Map by Christopher Winkelaar

Electronic ISBN: 978-1-7778107-9-5
Paperback ISBN: 978-1-7381485-0-9

PRAISE FOR THE SERIES

"Being a part of a family, however unconventional, is an integral theme of Frey's clever, adventurous, and endearing Turn novels. [...] The thought-provoking story discusses the stereotypical role of women in fantasy novels, but more focus is placed on the characters' struggles with their familial roles and relationships, creating depth and commonality."
—Publisher's Weekly

"I started reading and was captivated. This superb novel grabbed me from the opening sentence, and never let go. [...] The whole tale is several clever twists on the oh-so-familiar fantasies we've read before. I want more. *Books* more".
—Ed Greenwood, *Forgotten Realms*

"Let me start by saying [...] that I think that J.M. Frey's *The Untold Tale* is the most important work of fantasy written in 2015. It may be the most important work of fantasy written this decade, but I'll have to get back to you on that in 2020.
—Dr. Mike Perschon, *The Steampunk Scholar*

"INSANELYAMAZING! The Untold Tale tears apart the tropes of heroic fantasy and gives back what we need: true heroes, true love, and the astonishing realization that yes, real people are magical."
—Julie Czerneda,the *Night's Edge* and *Trade Pact* series

"This story is nothing short of fun, unexpected, and a little bit queer. If you're interested in a Science Fiction/

Fantasy undertaking with all of the ingredients of a queer anthology, *The Untold Tale* is for you."
—Dallas Barnes, *Pink Play Mags*

"It's easily the strongest I've read in the last year. [...] The fictional world = real world trope isn't the only one Frey twists, however. She also plays with the ideas of the hero and heroic adventure, feminism, gender roles, and the role of the narrative itself, in innovative – and occasionally cheeky – ways. This novel has the potential to appeal to a great many readers, across genres.
—Violette Malan, PhD, *Dhulyn Parno* Series

"If I could mark this as 10/5 stars, I would, but that's impossible, so 5/5 it is, with much hearts and swoons. [...] *The Untold Tale* is delicious, each word meant to be savoured, breathed in, nibbled at, full of hidden delight and wonder. Frey has a beautiful writing style - all at once slightly old-fashioned and delectable, whilst also being modern and quick-paced. It's tongue-in-cheek and it's serious. It's like an epic fantasy and a modern YA all in one. It is a book for every bookworm or geek [...] But most of all, it is a book for writers - and Frey delivers."
—Ana Tan, *A Tsp Blog*

"John Scalzi did Redshirts. He poked fun at a beloved symbol of geekdom, and we loved it. Frey has done the same for the sacred fantasy tropes and it's fantastic. An empowered woman of color, thrown into the chauvinistic world of the epic fantasy today's geeks were weaned on, serves as the perfect narrator for a critical and wonderful look at fantasy in the modern world."
—Leah Petersen, *The Physics of Falling* series

THE FORGOTTEN TALE

J.M. FREY

To Dr. Jennifer Brayton, my MA thesis adviser,
who showed me that being an avid fan and being a
passionate academic do not have to mean being a
divided writer.

Sleep now, my baby, and hear my sweet rhyme:
The Writer will come to us all in his time.
The books, they all close,
Our tales all conclude,
We're all for the shelf, asleep and sublime.

So dream now, my child, of adventures to come
Of laughter, of starlight; the moon and the sun.
Our children, our sequels
Spin out 'cross the years,
To continue our stories when our chapter's done.

STORM

he air above the barn rips apart, wind against wind, power thrust into the multitude of skies, raking through the void. Feet braced apart, bracketing the barn's peak, a slight woman reaches into the sky and slices again.

The world shrieks.

Thunder rumbles around her head; clouds heavy with the woman's sorrow sop up her tears and absorb them, gray as grief. Between her fists, lightning arcs.

"Where is he?" the woman howls, and her voice is the hurricane.

On the other side of the rip, the Readers' eyes are closed, cast away. They do not see. They did not see. None answer. But the Readers have *never* answered.

"Where is he?" the woman—or rather, the woman-shaped thing—demands again.

Laughter dances through the void, shivering like silver bells.

"Sisters?" the woman-shaped thing calls. "I hear you! Fetch me back to our realm!"

"We cannot." The silver laughter drips, words sliding like mercury through the rip, weeping down the pane of the sky and pooling in the woman-shaped thing's ears. The words are clashing music, a hundred thousand voices singing at once in a chord that is just the uncomfortable side of atonal. "You are sullied."

The woman-shaped thing tears her hands apart and the sky crackles and booms.

"By no fault of my own!" she howls.

"But sullied all the same."

"Then aid me in my search!"

"We cannot."

The storm swirls and bucks around the woman-shaped thing like a wild-born stallion, refusing to break to her bit.

"Tell me where he is, at least!"

"We cannot," the many mouths say. Some sound gleeful; others are filled with despair. She is, after all, their sister. Her sorrow is their sorrow. Or their enjoyment.

"He has passed beyond the veil of the skies! I cannot see him. He has left this realm for another, and I will know which!"

"Sister, we cannot."

"Tell me!" the woman-shaped thing snarls, and around her the clouds turn black, the sky bleeds to amber and green, the winds rotate around her body. Hair the color of the night sky, threaded with silver that winks and peeks between her locks like stars, is tossed and plastered to the side of her head by the force of her own displeasure. "In which realm does he now dwell?"

"Sister..."

The sky screams again.

"Then I will find him myself!" the woman-shaped thing screeches. The lightning crackles out from her hands, striking the thatch roof all around her, setting the decades-old straw alight in a showering spray of sparks. Fire jumps and hisses at her feet, but does not dare to lick at her skirts. "Even if I have to tear each and every realm out of the sky and crack it between my jaws, I will find him!"

"Let him go, sister," the voices cry, and now there is

panic in their sound, the liquid words splashing against the clouds. "Sister, forget him!"

"No!" the woman-shaped thing says. "You banish me because a human man tricked me into binding myself into flesh against my will. You will not aid me, call me sullied because he *raped* me! And now you tell me that I must forget the only good thing to ever come from my imprisonment in flesh. Well, I will not! And if you will not aid me, then I will tear through you to get to him!"

"Sister, peace!"

"Sisters, *war!*"

"Sister—" the voices beg, but the woman-shaped thing is incensed. She claps her palms back together, and the rip in the world slams shut.

The storm, however, grows stronger. Clouds circle and churn. The woman-shaped thing's eyes shine gold and fierce. Triumphant. Master of her own life. Of her own *body*. Finally. Free at last. After so many years, at *last*.

And at last: revenge.

The tornado comes down, landing in a precise crater, blotting out the old crumbling well she despised hauling water from every morning. The funnel chews across the hated, horrid potato field where the woman-shaped thing spent thirty years in backbreaking mortal labor. It throws tubers and tender green shoots into the air, tosses them like stones against the side of the tool shed, the barn. The funnel roars and growls, alive with the woman-shaped thing's fury, crawling and raking gouges out of the earth. It snaps the laundry line, sucks the costume of a peasant woman and her farmer husband away, gone forever, destroyed as finally as the lie that was the woman-shaped thing's life itself.

And then the tornado falls upon the rude stone cottage. It slaps away the roof, reaches inside, and sucks the hand-carved furniture, the rusting pots and pans, the linens, the *lie* down its gullet.

The last thing to fly into its stormy maw is the corpse of the woman-shaped thing's husband.

Dead but ten minutes, the man's flesh is barely cool when it is ripped away from bone.

ONE

"—And then the blue cable goes here, into this port." I lean back so my daughter can make out what I am doing, should she decide that it is, indeed, fascinating. Apparently, it is not. Right now, she is more occupied with trying to stuff Library's face into her mouth. The sodden lion plushie looks long-suffering—if a toy can have an expression—but otherwise content to be the source of her comfort.

And *I* am content to be second-best to a drool-encrusted collection of fake fur, stuffing, thread, and buttons. Let Library have her now. Soon enough she will want a bottle, and the coziness of her father's embrace. I take satisfaction in the knowledge that she is the most fascinating part of *my* day.

Alis Mei Piper entered my life eight months and some two weeks after her mother and I defeated a crafty villain, outwitted a Deal-Maker Spirit, deciphered an ages-old riddle, and tore a hole in the veils separating our realities with a bit of parchment, a metal quill, and some salt water. Alis was heralded into the world not as a lordling's daughter and heir ought. But she was well loved, and well come all the same. Gifts from colleagues, neighbors, Pip's students, and our mutual friends were abundant and generous.

Had we been in Turn Hall, my serving staff would

have aided us in the early, sleep-deprived days of new parenthood. Here, Pip's workmates brought us ready-made frozen meals to eat swiftly while the baby napped. Pip's own parents gave us the rare ability to sleep and bathe alone in those first few weeks by coming over every other day to watch our newborn. My own parents are long dead, and though I wish Alis's paternal grandmother could have known her namesake, I am glad that her paternal grandfather is not present.

Elgar Reed, unfortunately, is. He sent us a very large bouquet of flowers and some celebratory wine, along with a startlingly large painting of Turn Hall looking, well, exactly as it ought. It was signed in the bottom corner by one of those fellows who worked on the *Lord of the Rings* film designs, and was Reed's first, but sadly not his last, foray into breaching the tight-knit tapestry of our family.

I wish he would just go away. He wishes I would call him *father*.

Since the Lady Alis's grand and squalling entrance, it has been another ten months. I have been a resident of this realm for nearly two years, and Alis is now strong enough to hold herself upright if she can cling to something. Soon she will be making the first swaying, drunken motions toward walking, and then, if she is anything like my brother was, the Writer help us. Even though I am the younger son, I can still recall Kintyre bashing into the sides of tables and knocking over chairs, tumbling down small flights of stairs and coming back home with half the covey forest stuck in his hair, or a great portion of the fish pond leaking from his boots. Alis has my watery gray-blue eyes (not green, thank the Writer, not *green*), and my mother's thick, curling auburn hair, though of a shade much closer to Pip's black than that of the former Lady Turn. Alis also has my mother-in-law's nose, and

Pip's Asian facial structure. But the look in her gaze when she is plotting mischief is all Kintyre Turn.

Right now, Alis is bouncing gleefully in a romper attached to the lintel of my office doorway, smashing a sodden Library against the edge of the harness each time her chubby little feet leave the carpet, and practicing three of the four words she has—*book*, *Da*, and *no*. *Ma* is the fourth word, but she's clever enough to have attached it to Pip already, and Pip is downstairs. I can tell, with one look over my shoulder, that Alis is unhappy, and that she fully intends to throw Library at me the moment I stop talking to her.

Which—why on Earth would I ever cease to talk to my daughter? Silly, dear thing.

"And then we turn the drive back around, like this." I demonstrate. "And this is the on button. Do you see, my dearest? Right here. Click! On it goes, and Da's server is now online!"

"Aaa-aaah!" Alis compliments.

Downstairs, a pan rattles and the oven door slams. Alis startles. She looks down at Library, as if to ascertain that he too heard it. Library is silent on the matter, and so Alis chooses to follow suit.

The people of Hain celebrate the longest night of midwinter with feasts and light, for it is the turn of our calendar. And downstairs, my wife is trying to recreate it for me. I tried to help prepare the finger foods, and was instead banished to my office. Lucy Piper brooks no incapability in her kitchen, and I am a man who grew up with a cook and a wait staff.

In Lysse, it was my habit to invite the people of the Chipping—farmers, merchants, tradesmen, travelers, nobility, and all—to a feast at Turn Hall. The gathering brought my Chipping together for three days and two nights. Our little affair here will be smaller, only a single night, and starting in...

"Oh," I say, glancing at the clock in the corner of my monitor. "I do think it is time for your dinner, my lady Alis."

Alis kicks her feet in an uncoordinated jig, and I pull my bones up off the floor to give her a cuddle. Alis drops Library and reaches out for me, pleased that I've abandoned my boring old computer for her. I scoop up her compatriot and tuck him between our bodies, for, like his namesake, he doesn't like being left behind.

"Hush, though, sweeting," I caution Alis. "There is a dragon in the kitchen, making all sorts of smoke, and we daren't anger it."

"I heard that!" Pip calls, but there is humor in her voice. I cannot help the grin that curls over my lips in response.

"Perhaps if we sing to soothe the beast?" I ask Alis, and she pops her fist against my chin to indicate her assent. "Very well. Ready?

> *Ah! The fields are dappled over, my love,*
> *And the spring sings high and sweet!*
> *Ah! The fairies flit and spin, my love,*
> *And so it's time for us to meet!*
>
> *The sun sinks ever lower, my love,*
> *It marks an end to play,*
> *So come straight to my side, my love,*
> *Now at the close of day."*

Together we go down to the kitchen, where Pip has left breast milk in the fridge, and Alis smacks my shoulder in time with the children's song. Pip herself is in the dining room, putting something onto platters out of our view.

"Come not through murky forest, my love
Where trolls and goblins bide,
Come not o'er standing pools, my love
Where kelpies wait and hide.

Come not through vasty deserts, my love
Where sun and djinn are cruel,
Come not through the icy wastelands, my love
Where reflections baffle fools."

It's a song meant to teach children the dangers of the unknown world, though it is surprisingly catchy. I push the buttons on the microwave in time to the beat.

"Come not past cavern mouths, my love
When they issue smoke and steam,
For those are the homes of dragons, my love
Where they hoard things bright with gleam.

Heed not to the call of sirens, my love,
Nor any creature of deep,
For they long to sing away children, my love,
To hold, to drown, and to keep.

Go not through the lofty halls, my love,
Made of fir, or ash, or pine,
For those are the realms of the elves, my love,
And to trespassers they are not kind."

The bottle sufficiently warmed, I pop the plastic nipple into Alis's obliging mouth and with her tucked warm and sweet against my hip, we spin in the kitchen in a gentle waltz.

"When you come to me, my dear sweet love,
Come safe, come sure, and come true.
For adventures are all well and good, my love,
But home is now calling for you.

Come only to the parlour, my love,
Come only down the stair,
Come to the fire with me, my love..."

"...and sit with your family there!" my wife finishes behind me. Alis and I pause in our waltz to drop kisses onto Pip's cheek. Well, I kiss. Alis smacks her face off Pip's, making a loud "MUAH!" sound that she learned from her *wai po*. I abandon the now empty bottle in the sink, earning a sideways look of reproach from my wife.

Ah, yes, I do sometimes still forget that I have no servants here.

"All set up?" Pip asks as she puts the offending bottle in the dishwasher. Alis makes grabby hands at both me and her mother, clearly unsure about which of us she is more excited to touch. I make the choice easy and step up to sandwich her between us. We both get thankful pats on the neck with fat baby hands.

"I have the server hooked up and the modem working. Tomorrow, I shall calibrate the Netflix."

"Neeeerd," Pip teases.

"Indeed," I agree. "And you love me."

"That's true."

"Bah!" Alis adds.

Then we head into the living room. With Alis tucked against my shoulder, I begin the lengthy process of selecting music to play softly in the background. Were we at Turn Hall, I would have hired Turnshire's resident musicians, but here, I must select a list of songs from a fiddly little box.

Very slowly, I am learning to use the magic of this realm—the wirelesses, and the microwaves and Bluetooths, and the wands that are boxes. In short, all the things the people here take entirely for granted. For Pip, navigating a website is as effortless and instinctive as breathing. For me, it is a fascinating, and sometimes infuriating, challenge. Or at least it was, until I fully understood the knack of navigating with one's fingertip.

But now, my paperwork has all been sorted, and I am a fully recognized Canadian citizen, even though I had to issue the certificate myself. I was introduced to the concept of hacking quite early in my relocation to Pip's world; generally, at first, as I learned the interface upon which all transactions and the acquisition of knowledge was based, and then more specifically as my interest in the Internet and its uses grew. From there, I spent every waking hour between my job shelving books at the university library and caring for my increasingly pregnant wife reading coding handbooks, consuming technical manuals, and lurking shadowy Internet forums with an increasingly parsable slew of code terms and jargon.

Information is my addiction. Spy work is my passion. And the easy acquisition of the skills required to attain both is *literally* what I was created for. My Writer wrote me to be adept, quick-witted, adaptable. I am, as Pip puts it, a "scarily clever sponge".

Learning computers has therefore been, if I may dare brag, *simple*.

The one thing I did not falsify was a license to drive, as I would not endanger my wife or daughter by pretending that it was a skill I could lay claim to. I learned the slow way, by attending courses and terrifying my father-in-law one two-hour jaunt through the suburbs of Vancouver at a time. I hear that is the traditional method.

He is a very good sport, that Martin Piper. He reminds me of Rupin Pointe, Sheriff of Turnshire and one of my only real friends in Lysse. The paternalistic camaraderie, the gentle ribbing, the support, those are all the same. And of course, Martin knows what it's like to be a newcomer in a strange country, to be confused by a new culture. He lived in China for several years before returning to Canada. But where Pointe would have made ribald jokes about our love life, and would have offered advice and opportunities for me to become a good husband and lover, Martin likes to pretend it isn't happening, and that Alis's conception was a sort of chaste miracle. I am content to play along with the fantasy when he is within earshot. The alternative being that I bring attention to the fact I am sleeping with his daughter.

Once I have the music queued up, Alis and I count her toes. "One wee goblin, and one maid o' the lake. One small dwarf, and one big krake. One fairy, one centaur, one elf tall and wise, and here is one dragon, king of the skies! That leaves just two, love, this one and that, one for your mother, and one for your Da!"

Alis giggles as I blow raspberries on the arches of her soft feet. Pip arrives, holding two glasses of red wine, and makes a sort of soft, sad sound. I accept the glass she's holding out to me with a questioning look.

"Yes, *bao bei?*"

"Just thinking..." Pip sips once, then smiles softly. "Alis is going to go to kindergarten with absolutely no familiarity with all of our culture's nursery rhymes and children's songs. She's going to know all these rhymes that none of the other kids know."

"You must teach me some, then," I say. "So her education may be balanced. Are there books?"

"Yes. And, speaking of books, all these stories and rhymes you're teaching Alis—I should write them down.

They're from your own childhood, and there's probably no record of them anywhere." Pip gets the familiar far-away look in her eye of an academic lost in thought.

Ah, yes. The one thing I am never able to forget is that my wife is, above all else, a scholar. Recording the rhymes is a good idea, but the thought of other people reading my personal childhood memories like so much invasive fan fiction is unappealing. Pip catches the way my nose scrunches and shakes her head—she won't press the issue. Although, I fully expect that I will catch Pip scribbling them down in one of those leather-bound notebooks she's such a fan of, even if I do not give per-mission. Pip has a passion for words that sometimes su-persedes her understanding of what might be the proper course of action. So, as a compromise, I suggest:

"You can write them down, so long as they stay in the house. I would like Alis to have a collection, for her own children. But I do not want Elgar Reed to read them, nor his fans."

Pip brightens. "Okay. Thank you."

Reed is a bit of a difficult point for us. In all practical ways, he is my God. He thought me up, made me, molded me for my role, and crafted of me the perfect foil and support for my brother, Kintyre the Hero. In other ways, he is like my father, so much in appearance and manner of speech the late Algar Turn that the first time I saw his photograph, I nearly fainted.

And to him, I am, by rights, a perpetual fascination.

But I want no relationship with him. My life, my history, my memories, my joys, and my pains are my own. Perhaps he set our world into motion, and perhaps it was his conscious choice to create of me a scholar, a spy, and a coward. But I am more than Shadow Hand and foil for my brother. I have a favorite food, and verbal tics. I have preferences, and opinions. I have favorite songs, favorite dances, favorite ways of buttoning my opponent in a duelist's circle, and favorite ways of tying my cravat. I can drive an automobile. I want to be a hacker who uses my powers of spy-mongering and data-hoarding to do good things for my new world.

My life is my own, not fodder for more of his wretched books. Nor for the ungainly television series he has told me is in development.

And yet, at least once per month, we receive a phone call or letter from Reed, asking my opinion on a script note, or requesting information about the sorts of fabrics that decked Turn Hall, or inviting us to visit his home. I have replied to none. I will not be his back-story, his resource, a thing he can mine and use up.

Perhaps, if he were a different sort of man... if he had treated Pip differently, or treated his fans differently, perhaps then I would have been willing to forge a relationship with my creator. But as it is, he is dismissive, misogynistic, racist, and frankly, an appallingly ungracious elf-cock to the people who have lined his pockets. He patterned my father off of himself, and the ego to do such a thing—to write oneself into one's own books as the father of the hero—is appallingly telling.

I did not like my father. I do not like my creator. And I will not have my daughter exposed to him.

I owe Reed nothing. Not even the knowledge that had the Viceroy—his ultimate, overarching villain for the book series—made his way into this realm as he had planned, he would certainly have tortured Reed to death for what he perceived as the deliberate injuries to his plans, power, and person that Reed knowingly perpetrated. I'll admit, the idea of slicing Reed a new breathing hole was appealing when I realized that it was by his deliberate choice and malice that my mother was taken from us in the prime of her life. But for all that he was the author of all of my life's misfortunes, I cannot hold him accountable for every terrible moment of it, nor can I revenge myself on him for them.

Reed was also, unfortunately, the author of all of my—admittedly few—childhood joys.

No. I am simply satisfied to shut him out.

My agitation must be apparent, for Alis stares up at me with large gray eyes. I take a quaff of my wine. "How about a Pip rhyme, darling girl?"

My wife laughs. "Is that what we're calling them? Pip Rhymes and Syth Rhymes?"

"I like it."

"I sort of do, too. All right." Pip sets down her own wine, touches her fingertips together, and sings: "*The itsy bitsy spider went up the water spout. Down came the rain and washed the spider out. Out came the sun and dried up all the rain, and the itsy bitsy spider went up the spout again.*"

"Ah, teaching persistence," I say. "I like that one."

Alis seems to have liked it too, for Library smacks into my chest.

"Lord, you love that kid," Pip says softly, smiling as I kiss my daughter's temple. "You dote."

"Of course I dote," I say. "I don't know about the men of your world, but in ours, we cherish our wives and children." I bend to kiss her temple as well.

"I know, *bao bei*. And good men do here, too." She rolls up on her toes to give me a spicy kiss. "Man, what did I ever do to deserve a guy like you?"

"You were you," I say.

"You old romantic softy," she scolds, and kisses me again. "Mmmm. People are going to be here soon."

I cannot say that I have *forgotten* that guests were due, but losing myself in the warmth of Alis in my arms and Pip against my mouth is certainly distracting. Were we in Hain, this would not have been an issue, as my staff would have dealt with any interruptions. We also would have already done our duty as hosts and welcomed our visitors into the Hall the evening before, leaving us free to entertain ourselves in the small, quiet moments before the feasting and dancing began in whatever manner we saw fit.

On the first day of Solsticetide, the house would be opened and aired, and each room turned into a billet where whole families would pile onto the beds and floors. Save for my own, of course, the servants' rooms, and my mother's (which had remained shut up until Pip's arrival). Even Kintyre's rooms would have been lent out, if he had not indicated that he intended to be home for the festival.

This had, of course, been the source of one of the many rows I'd had with my brother while he was on the road and I was, in his eyes, nothing more than a silly, crumpled book-mouse. He had come home for the holiday one time to find his rooms let out, for he had not replied to my letter inquiring if he was returning. Bevel had said that he received it, though.

I'd put them up in my personal study, which usually remained locked to guests due to the quantity of expensive books and heirloom bric-a-brac I kept on the credenza. So, of course, that was also the year that Kintyre smashed our great-grandmother's Sylph Crystal sherry decanter and three of the matching demitasses, the uncultured swine.

I should have just made them sleep in the ballroom with the rest of the Chipping, which would be lined with the blankets and sleeping rolls of everyone who could fit that first night, though it was given over for dancing on the second. Nobody slept before dawn on the longest night anyway, and most even forwent sleep in favor of heading home to their own beds in the first light of the

New Year. Those who could not fit at Turn Hall went to Law Manor. Still more brought covered caravan trailers, which they parked on the dormant lawns. The merchants in town opened their doors to farmers from the out-flung areas, and the schoolhouse became a sea of children allowed to stay overnight without their parents. They told ghost stories, and roasted apples.

On the second day of Solsticetide, which Pip and I were now attempting to replicate, Turn Hall's kitchens and courtyards became a hubbub of culinary activity. My kitchen garden was raided for the last of the herbs, the brush that my gardener had been hoarding was piled high in the dry bowl of the fountain, and the goats, chickens, and sheep that my people had brought along were slaughtered. The outdoor oven was fired, and those who had brought flour and grain made breads and pies. Fruit was poached, wine mulled, and ale kegs tapped. Children played games of chase through the covey forest and ran along the rock walls that separated the fields. Mother Mouth held court in the morning parlor to tend to burns, scrapes, cuts, and tears.

When the sun set on the last day of the year, it was my duty and pleasure to raise a toast to the Chipping. The Chipping then raised one back to me. And we defied the longest night of darkness by lighting torches in the courtyard and lamps in the ballroom and foyer. We put candles in the snowbanks, and the children raced around with sparkling twigs, writing their names against the blackening sky.

When dawn came, parents separated their children from the pile that had inevitably formed as the wee things dropped off in the kitchen, next to the warm stone of the oven, and bade each other a good new year. Neighbors, family, and friends wished each other all the luck and joy of the season, and every face turned upward and said,

"It can only grow lighter from here." Each took home a torch lit from the embered remains of the Solsticetide bonfire to light their first hearth-fire of the year.

And when Turn Hall was finally silent, Pointe and I would sit on my front steps and share a pipe, along with the last of the winter sherry. We would watch the sun come up, and the longest night end. We would make our New Year Wishes. We would laugh and tell one another of all our hopes for the new year.

Pointe had first told me his wife was with child in the rosy-orange glow of a fresh year's dawn. The next year, Lewko had been asleep in his father's lap, his head cradled on my thigh, and I had brushed my fingers through his curls and told his father how dearly I wanted a child of my own.

Now, six years later, it is Solsticetide once more, and my own child is lolling against my shoulder, my wife pressed against my front. And I cannot share my greatest joy with the man who had been my greatest friend.

"Hey-o, what's this?" Pip asks, leaning back.

In an effort to hide the shift in my mood, I walk Alis into the dining room to show her the array of small tasties Pip prepared. I target the platter of wine-poached pears that have been quartered and stuck with little plastic forks.

"This looks excellent. What do you say, sweeting? Shall I have a taste?"

Pip made them to Cook's recipe—as best as I could remember it, anyway. I pluck one up and pop it into my mouth.

Pip follows me. "That's not an answer, *bao bei*."

I chew. She waits. *Blast.*

"It's nothing," I say.

"Liar."

I set the plastic fork down on the plate meant for

trash. "It really is trivial."

"You look like I kicked your puppy."

"It's not you."

"Then what?" She looks around the living room, which is decorated in a sort of mash-up of Christmas and Yuan-Xiao, with the abundance of candles that are required for Solsticetide threaded throughout. "Is it not right?"

"It's perfect."

"Well, no bonfire."

"I'll build a fire pit in the backyard this spring, so we may have one next year."

"Then what is it?"

I pet along Alis's back, twine my fingers through the fine curls of her cap of silky hair, and know that my wife has me cornered. She will not continue with her party preparations if I do not answer, and then she will be cross with me that she has not finished everything before our guests arrive at sundown.

"I miss Pointe," I say finally. "It's ridiculous, but... every New Year Morning, we would sit on the steps and... make wishes."

Pip puts her lips against my neck, her arms around my shoulders. "I'm sorry," she says.

"I don't regret—"

"No, I know that. I meant that I'm sorry we couldn't invite him. That there's no way for him, and Lewko, and Dorthi to come to the party."

"I would have liked him to have met Alis," I say.

"Me too, *bao bei.*"

A piercing beep from the kitchen jostles Pip and she vanishes with a curse of "Fuck, the dumplings!" My daughter blinks, opens her mouth to wail, and then apparently thinks better of it, looks up at me instead as the fire alarm is shut off by her mother.

"Good choice, sweeting," I say to her. "Ready for a bath, and your brand new Solsticetide pajamas?"

"Da-aah!" she agrees, with a tongue-curling yawn, and Alis and I go upstairs to deliver on both promises as Pip wrangles the last of the preparations before the sun sets.

When we come back down, our hair is damp from my daughter's splashing. Alis is clutching Library and wearing a fluffy onesie patterned with lightning bugs, and I am in pressed Turn-russet trousers and the matching waistcoat. I have decided on the more flamboyant Sheil-purple silk shirt for underneath, and have my sleeves rolled up over my elbows to concede to the casual nature of our open-house event.

Pip smacks a kiss off my cheek and careens upstairs to our room to change into the Turn-russet sweater-dress I surprised her with as a Solsticetide gift. Which means Alis and I are alone when the doorbell rings.

Most of the melancholy of missing my friend is swept away in the joy of welcoming my parents-in-law and *wai po* to our home. They are very impressed by the lights set up before the mirror above our mantle place, and *wai po* immediately blusters into the kitchen to poke at Pip's last morsels and suck air in between her teeth when she finds Pip's culinary focus to be lacking. I don't bother to intervene—I know that Pip and her grandmother have the same bullheadedness about food.

Instead, I draw Martin and Mei Fan into the living room. I drop Alis into her grandfather's waiting arms—for here is another man in this realm who dotes—and pour each of us the closest thing I could find to a winter sherry. Pip is back down the stairs in a flurry, cackling with laughter and squawking with indignant pride as soon as she catches her grandmother with her cooking chop-sticks in hand and her face over the dumpling basket.

The next few hours leave me no room for sorrow as

I facilitate the entry of each of our guests. Colleagues from the university mingle with neighbors and the parents of the children Alis and I have managed to cultivate as friends at the local park.

In Hain, it is custom to bring some edible thing to share to Solsticetide. Where I had expected cheeses and wines, breads and haunches of meat, the people of Pip's world come from more different cultures and culinary traditions than I can name. We are therefore met with hummus and crudités, beer and vodka, souvlaki, home-made onigiri, and a platter of olives and pickled onions. There are samosas with a sweet chili dip, and tatziki and pitas, salted watermelon, jerked chicken, and a feast of cookies, pies, and loukoumades still dripping honey. Adding Pip and Mei Fan's traditional offerings, like mooncakes, it is enough to make the dining room table groan and each face split with a grin of delight upon seeing it.

I am making my second round of grazing with relish, putting a sample of each treat on my plate. I am the Lord of the Manor, after all, and so I must not refuse any of the offerings. It is tradition, I tell myself. It is polite. And I resolutely do not contemplate my waistline, or the way the lack of a sparring partner has turned me into an inconstant swordsman.

My vanity can wait for tomorrow. Tonight, I feast.

"You know," says one of the neighbor's lads as he helps himself to the spread. "This is almost like what they do in those books. The Turn books?" The boy is just beginning to sprout facial hair, and is exactly the sort to be reading my brother's adventures and be entirely absorbed by them—be it in a tavern where Bevel happened to be recounting them, or here where they are bestselling paperbacks.

Just after Alis's birth, Pip accepted a position to teach Critical Literary Theory and Gender Studies at the

University of Victoria, on Vancouver Island. We sold our little condo in the city of Vancouver itself, and traded up for a small house with three bedrooms, a bit of greenery, and framed copies of the concept art for *The Tales of Kintyre Turn* all around the living room. The lad now points to the artwork nearest to us in demonstration—a painting that depicts my brother engaged in battle while on horseback, two armies clashing in the distance. It was in that battle that Stormbearer, the great stallion depicted, was slain.

"Oh?" I say to the lad, and pretend very hard that I don't already know what he is talking about.

"The midwinter thingy." The lad grins, spotty and pleased to have someone to converse with. He is affecting a pose of adultness, and I can see that he very badly wants to impress upon me that he is no mere child. That he is sophisticated and can hold a conversation about books.

Along with another round of treats, I had come into the dining room to fetch myself a glass of wine. The first desire met, I pick up a bottle and fill my glass, then offer a small pour to the lad as well, silently accepting the pact that I am to treat him as a man, not a boy.

"Solsticetide," I correct him softly.

"That's it!" he says, accepting the glass. "Have you read the books?"

"Yes," I lie. I have yet to pick them up off the bookshelf. But if I were to say no, then I would have no explanation as for why I am as familiar with Kintyre Turn's adventures as I am.

"Cool!" the lad says, and then obligingly chimes his wine glass off mine. "Uh, don't, uh, don't tell my Mom I'm drinking, okay?" he asks, shamefaced.

"Should I have not poured for you?" I know there are laws in this world about who can and cannot purchase alcohol, and at what age it is suggested that children begin to drink it, but I had not thought that they were so rigidly enforced. It is custom in Hain for children to drink watered wine at dinner, the refreshment gradually becoming less and less watered the older they grow. It is a way to teach responsibility and accustom them to the effects.

"No, it's cool... she just..." He shifts furtively, which explains all I need to know to make my conjecture:

"Ah, alcoholic sibling?"

"How did you know?"

"Just a guess," I say, knowing that the observations of a former spymaster are not always welcome.

The lad shrugs.

"Very well," I say. "Your secret is mine."

"Thanks, Mr. Piper."

The lad finishes the wine and leaves the glass on the credenza, clearly hoping to get a refill later, so I let it remain where it is. I then go out into the living room to make toasts, facilitate introductions, and revel in the fuss. Alis is now in the hands of her great-grandmother, and *wai po* is speaking to her in Mandarin.

Pip and I both hope that our child will grow up bilingual. Pip had very little interest in a second language in her youth, and regrets now that she cannot speak it fluently. I am a polyglot, of course, but Dwarvish or Goblinese is of very little use in this realm. So I pay careful attention to *wai po*'s lessons as well.

Stuffed with delicacies and delight, wine and wonderful company, I feel like the very spirit of good cheer, just as a lordling celebrating with his Chipping ought.

Right up until I open the door to Elgar Reed.

SHOES

The woman-shaped thing travels first to the grand and exotic Kingdom of Brystal. Located in the narrow waterways between islands in the warm Mooncall Sea, Brystal is an accumulation of the great southern archipelago. Each isle boasts its own city-state, and though it has a capital in Queensdream, it has no real rulers to bury among the Hainish, Gadotian, and Urlish kings in the Valley of Tombs. Every city-state is backed by jungle and mountains; every window faces the salty, blood-warm water; every larder is full, and every flagon overflowing. And the Brystalians reason that, with bounty like this, who needs a single king?

In the resort town of Ariail, the woman-shaped thing folds herself down into the form of a courtier so as to be able to pass amid the crowds untouched. She was a rude farmer's wife for so long, her lips and hands chapped from laundry and cooking and gardening, that it is a luxury to have soft, smooth skin and shining hair again. The woman-shaped thing takes smug enjoyment from the way the humans regard her with lust and covetousness as she passes them. It is her due.

These are people who would sell their souls for a night between her legs. People who will be willing to make a Deal, and that is what the woman-shaped thing needs most.

She makes three Deals in Ariail, manipulating each of the dumb animals as she shakes their hands, so that their desires match her own. Creatures like her cannot Speak Words, but she can barter for them, can kiss and suck and lick them out of a human mouth, if the human is willing to let her.

Each of the three stupid mortals whimpers "Thank you, Mistress Solinde!" as she steals away their magic, twists the three new Words into spells of seeking and revelation. She casts them back into the air immediately.

That bitch-fairy, Luck, is on her side, it seems. That for which she searches is on this very island.

She finds the first totem in a cobbler's shop.

The shopkeeper is proud of his craft, despite how impractical shoes are when they're made of anything but leather and wood. Dancing slippers crusted with silver leaf, and crushed ruby powder, and sharded glass glitter on his shelf. They are meant for the courts, for the mistresses of those who claim royal blood—an overabundance in Brystal. They are meant to be danced in only briefly, meant to glitter under chandeliers, and then sat in carriages, and at tea tables, and to whist. They are not meant for the streets, for chores. They are not meant for farmers' wives.

Solinde despises them.

That night, when the cobbler and his offspring are fast asleep in their beds above the shop, Solinde sets fire to it. She is not allowed to kill mortals, by the laws of the Deal-Maker Spirits, so she is compelled to knock on the proprietor's door and alert him to the conflagration, though there is no rule saying how *loud* that warning must be. After all, it would not do for anyone with the talent or skill to remake the totem to live.

Solinde turns away from the burning building, slipping through shadows and the reflections of flame in nearby shop windows. She pauses in an alley and looks up, to be gleeful witness to her handiwork. Far above the veil of the skies, a realm burns.

TWO

I don't see his face at first, shadowed as it is by his cold-weather cap and the way the porch light shines onto it. The chill breeze of the evening bites the wine-flush in my cheeks, nipping at the heat and most likely making my nose redder. I always did gain such a motley, unattractive blotching when slipping into my cups, and in this world, the wine is never watered.

"Come in, come in!" I say, turning to open the closet door and fetch a hanger for his snow-sodden coat. "Well met, and well come."

He enters, doffing his cap and stuffing it into his pocket. Then he shuts the door behind him and raises his head. I turn around. His smile is gratified and hopeful, and a very great shock to see.

The sound of the wooden hanger clattering to the tile is bright, and abrupt enough that several pairs of eyes turn from their conversation in the living room to peer at me. I don't recall backing up the staircase, but when I blink again, I am three steps away. And Elgar Reed is standing in my foyer, dripping melting snow on the tile and holding an enormous bottle of wine tied with a ribbon dangling mulling sachets. He holds the bottle out, a clear offering. And one that he equally as clearly expects me to accept.

Oh, the *fool*.

"N-n-no," I say, as firmly as my tripping tongue allows, though whether the denial is for him, or for me, I am not certain. All I know is that I will not stand by the door and welcome Reed into my home on Solsticetide, bad luck for turning away a guest on the Night of Light be damned. A little bad luck is well worth the price of keeping Elgar Reed away from my family.

"Hello, my boy," Reed says, and it is stiff sounding. Tentative. Hopeful. He is clearly under the assumption that he can bludgeon my rebuff into nothingness with the force of his cheer. His cheeks are also red, but from the cold, and his jowly face is covered with a thinly cultivated beard. He looks like the fat spirit of cheer that is summoned to homes on Christmas.

"N-no," I say again, in the face of his blind and selfish hope. I gesture as sharply toward the front door as I can. "L-l-leave."

He toes out of his boots and puts one socked foot on the lowest step, extending the wine toward me, cradled in two hands now as if it were a sacrificial offering or a white flag of peace. Neither of which I was willing to accept from the likes of him. "Come now, my boy—"

"I am not your b-boy!" I hiss, keeping my voice low for the sake of our guests. The very last thing I want is for Martin or Mei Fan to come see what is wrong, for them to get sucked into Reed's persistent delusion that I think of him as part of my own original family, or that I want him involved in my new one.

If Pip's parents come into Reed's orbit, the sly old bastard will introduce himself as my father, and then I will be *stuck*. Worse still, they would probably bring Alis with them to the door, and I have done my utmost to keep Reed *away* from my daughter.

Elgar Reed has ruined enough Turn lives. He will have no hand in Alis's.

I scan the crowd in the living room quickly, but no one seems to be paying us any mind for now. Good, we have not made enough of a mortifyingly obvious scene for that—yet. All the same, I wish Pip were here with me. While I am perhaps more elegant, the viciousness of her crasser vocabulary is to be admired, and she deploys it so very well.

"Leave," I say again, catching myself backing up the staircase, step for step at pace with Reed. I force myself to stop, to stand my ground. This is *my* house. I will not be chased into a corner like a mouse. "You are not w-welcome here, and I believe I have m-made that c-clear b-b-before."

"Forsyth!" Reed pleads. He stoops and leaves the wine on the step beside him when I do not release the banister to take it from his hands. "Please."

I cannot shove him back down the stairs and out the door, not bodily, not the way I wish. Not without attracting the attention of my guests, which would lead to having to lie to cover up Reed's presence. In my time as Shadow Hand, I learned that it was best to avoid having to speak at all, rather than accumulating lies and having to recall them all later. But I also cannot let Reed into the living room, among our friends.

Defeated, I turn my back to him and retreat up the stairs. Reed follows, just as I knew he would. His footfalls are heavy and deliberate behind me, and it feels like nothing so much as having an ill-wish riding my shadow.

The door to my office, the first room on the landing, is open, and it is here I lead my maker. Though the master bedroom is furthest from my guests, and perhaps the better choice in terms of choosing somewhere where the argument that is inevitably about to ensue will be most muffled, I cannot bring myself to invite the man behind me into the most intimate place in my home. The place of greatest vulnerability in my life. And of course, I will never allow him into Alis's nursery. That leaves only my office.

Were I feeling polite, I would wait by the door for my guest to enter first. But I am not feeling polite, and Reed is not my guest. I walk into the room, picking up the scattered toys that Alis and I left on the floor and depositing them into the small playpen in the corner.

Then I pace to the center of the room and turn to face him. Reed takes a tentative step over the threshold, as if, for the first time, he's uncertain of his welcome. Uncertain in his *belonging* here, amid the detritus of my existence. He has always behaved as if he had a right to occupy the domestic spheres of my life, as if that which belonged to Syth Piper by default would also belong to Elgar Reed. As if my own wishes and my own right to privacy were moot.

In my indignation, I nearly forget that the whole point of getting the lug upstairs was to keep our argument secret. I have an itching desire to cross the room again, shove him backward, and slam the door in his face.

"Close th-the d-door," I say, coldly, instead.

Reed kicks the door shut behind him, and I can't help the way my nose wrinkles at the uncivilized motion.

"Your house is nice," Reed offers into the following silence. His fingers fiddle with the edges of his coat, clearly uncertain if he should remove it or not, the gesture nervous and extremely telling. My maker would be either the worst or the best person with which to play poker, depending on how full one's wallet was.

"How did you f-f-find us?" I ask. "We *m-moved*."

"The university had Lucy's address on file—"

"You *lied* to her administrator?" I gasp, agog at both his boldness and his temerity to address my wife by her given name.

"I told them I was a friend, that I needed the address for tonight." He shrugs. "The receptionist is a fan, did you know?"

"So you did lie!" I snarl, my stutter burned away in the heat of my anger.

Reed's smile quivers, even as it tries to widen. "Am I not your friend?"

Unbelievable! I feel my hands curling into fists. I am no Kintyre, to throw punches or smash breakables when in a rage, but for the first time, I can see the appeal. If there were anything in my office that I did not value, I would surely be tossing it at Reed's head right this moment. "No, you are not!"

Reed blinks, surprise and hurt and denial chasing their way across his features. "Really now, Forsyth," he cajoles. "Do you honestly want nothing to do with me, son?"

"No!" I snap. "Not that! Absolutely n-n-not!"

He steps forward, hands out and palm up, like a supplicant or a child trying to appease a snarling dog, too stupid to know that he should not approach. "But I—"

"I had *one* fa-father, Elgar Reed," I interrupt, standing my ground, refusing to let him back me into a corner, refusing to cringe. "And you know *damn well* what sort of an experience that was for me! I shan't have another stepping in, especially not *you*."

Thankfully, Reed stops. He drops his arms and huffs a great sigh, as if I were the one testing *his* patience. "Forsyth, be reasonable. You're the closest thing to a son that I'll ever have."

"And of that I am quite glad! I cannot even begin to fathom what torments you might enact on a flesh-and-blood child!"

"Now, that's not fair," Reed blusters, hauling as much of his impressive girth upright as he can and thrusting out his chest. "I wouldn't hurt a real kid."

"But I do not qualify as 'real.'" I snort. "You made the man who sired me *beat me* for daring to get between my *mother* and his drunk fists."

"You weren't a person then—" he begins, hands once more raised in supplication, in defense, but I cut him off.

"*Enough!*"

He is startled into silence. He blinks at me with my father's rheumy blue eyes, reddening around the rims, not from alcohol withdrawal, but from hurt. I take the respite to breathe deep, to rein my temper in, to remember that I was once the Shadow Hand of Hain, and I can *keep my head*. Eventually, I sigh and force my fists loose. I gesture dismissively, forcing myself to keep my gestures measured, gentle.

"Enough," I repeat, softly. "We have had this conversation before, and I won't have it again. Now please, take yourself away, and do not return."

But Reed isn't looking at me. He probably, as per usual when I request that he remain far away from my family, isn't even listening. He is snooping around him. In the time I've taken to compose myself, he has moved over to my server bank and is staring at it with the same sort of horrified wonder that I had seen only once on Kintyre's face: when he watched me murder Bootknife, my wife's torturer.

"What... what *is* all this?" Reed asks, eyes wide as he takes in the wall of monitors, the banks of hard drives, the long desk filled with precisely organized file folders, the toy wastepaper trebuchet that Pip gifted me with. "It's like something out of a cyberpunk book."

"It is my *office*," I say, impatient and annoyed that he has ignored my demand that he leave in order to gawk. "It is where I work."

Ah, and *now* I have his full and complete attention. Reed turns to face me, eyebrows furrowed and mouth slightly ajar. He looks stunned, as if he hadn't anticipated that I would need employment in this world. Of course I would. How is a man meant to support his family with no vocation? All men must work—even one who was made up.

I scoff at Reed's surprise. "It's not as if I can draw a wage from the king as Shadow Hand, nor tribute from my tenants! Here, I must buy my way, as any other citizen. And so I work. Do not look at me as if doing that which is beneath a lord's son offends you!"

He gawps, goldfish-like and infuriating. "But what do you even *do*?" Reed breathes, and I can hear it in his voice, the small and subtle glee, the *interest*. I can all but see the wheels and cranks of his imagination creaking and clicking to life. That great mind from whence I was hatched is warming up, and just knowing that he is *thinking* about my life, about Hain, horrifies me.

"No," I say. "No more stories. Leave my brother alone to live his life. He is *happy*, for once. Let them be."

Reed does not pout, but a dampened mood settles over him. "Wandering the roads forever?"

"Obviously not," I snort primly. "He is managing Lysse like a good eldest son ought, I assume, with Bevel by his side. *So leave them be*," I snarl.

Reed shakes his head, clearly startled by the news. "Kintyre? Staying in one place? Being *domestic*?"

"More than once he expressed that he was feeling too old and tired for the wandering life. What he ran from when he was eighteen no longer frightens him. Lysse will do them both good. Leave them be."

Shrewdly, Reed narrows his eyes. "Then tell me what you do."

"Are you *threatening* me?" I snarl. "*Do not think* that I will acquiesce to blackmail, Elgar Reed."

"No, no," Reed says, hands up, placating. "That's not

what I meant, I just... Forsyth, you fascinate me. You have to understand that! I just want to *know* you."

"I will not be your experiment," I counter.

"I don't want to *experiment*," Reed protests. "Just talk. I just want to be *let* in."

On the surface, it is not an unreasonable plea. But Reed's mere proximity makes all the lovely Solsticetide treats I've consumed roil and curdle in my gut. To stand beside him feels *unnatural*. It itches under my skin, a prickling burn that I fear I cannot dispel without tearing off my own flesh. It would take a heroic act of intellect to become comfortable in his physical presence, and I am unconvinced, at the present, that such an act is worthwhile.

I have spent my whole life uncertain about whether or not I believed in the Writer, in the way the scholars claimed that Authorial Intent ruled our destinies, and that our lives all end in the Final Chapter. And yet here I am, standing before my maker. And he is flawed, and selfish, and rude, and so very *human* that I can barely stand it. This is no great, omnipotent, and kindly god. This is a man: self-important, without introspection, narcissistic, and cruel.

My hatred curls around my lungs, squeezes them tight, so that in order to speak, I must wheeze around my disgust: "And in return, you will vow never to write another word of my home world?"

"I promise," he agrees, far too quickly for me to be able to trust his honesty. "Not another thing. No novellas, no short stories, nothing."

He puts out his hand to shake. I fold mine behind my back.

Reed's hand drops, a small sadness pulling his smile down, but I do not feel sorry for him. I *cannot* touch him. I simply *cannot*. I did so once, and it felt like grasping an angry electric eel. I will not grasp in friendship those hands, those fingers, which tapped me into existence on a battered old typewriter.

With words tasting of bitter almonds, I say: "I hack."

Reed's sadness dissolves into confusion. "Hack what?"

"Whatever the Canadian Security Information Service tells me to," I answer with a shrug, being deliberately glib. "I learned of hacking quite early upon my arrival here, and it was easy enough to read the many volumes available regarding coding. I am a polyglot, you recall—you wrote me that way. JavaScript and C++ are just another set of languages to perfect. And it was the easiest way to set myself up with a legal identity."

"But..." Reed blusters. "Computers?"

"Of course. It is not so different from the work I did as the Shadow Hand," I sneer, raising my hands to indicate the walls covered with wires and screens, and the small bookshelf overflowing with programming books, Alis's favourite board books, and stuffies. On the wall above my main console, Smoke has been hung on a cherry wood plaque board. "I investigate, I read, I synthesize data, and I return recommendations and command actions. And just as before, I have found a way to ingratiate myself to the governing body of this nation."

Reed's jolly fat cheeks drain of color. "But you're a *scholar*."

"And in this world, libraries are digital and computers are books," I say, stunned by his lack of comprehension. I scowl. "I was no mere book-mouse," I push. "You *know* that."

Reed staggers back a step, reaching out blindly behind him and crashing into the wall, clutching at my desk chair to remain upright. "I don't... I didn't..." He gasps for air, sweat pearling on his forehead.

His reaction startles me. Derision, I expected, but not this shocked horror. Unless...

"Reed..." I say slowly, horrified in my own right. For how, *how* can a Writer create a character and not *know* all of their nuances? How could he have... *put this in motion* and not realized it? "You do *recall* that I was the Shadow Hand, do you not?"

"I... I do," he mutters. "I just... when I set it up, it was a... a bit of a throwaway, really. It was such an offhand comment. I didn't... I didn't expect you to..."

A *throwaway?* The most important aspect of my life, the only part of me that I felt made me worthy, and honorable, and *good*, the thing of which I was proudest and which redeemed me from being, I felt, a spoilt younger son, and my creator tells me it was a *throwaway?* Barely remembered, hardly thought about?

Insulting! Beyond the pale!

"What I do here, it is the same!" I insist. I cannot... this is untenable! "This is *meaningful.*"

"But... *computers,*" he repeats. "I just... I expected more... I don't know... bafflement?"

"I have lived in this world for nigh on two years," I snarl. "How simple must you think me? I am no Kintyre, to bash around, and bull ahead, and understand *nothing.*"

"Hey now," Reed says, rising to defend his greatest literary achievement.

"Spying is the same no matter where it happens. I can learn all I need about a target by following their social media accounts, tracking their IP, watching their online spending habits. It is identical to my old duties, only I need to send out no Shadow's Men, write no blackmail expense slips, take no in-person meetings with the king. Here, I need not even don the Shadow's Mask, or Cloak. Here, I need not even change out of my sleeping clothes, if I so desire," I add with a derisive snort.

My dark amusement rubs Reed the wrong way, and his hackles rise. "But being Shadow Hand wasn't important! It was such a secondary feature of your character that I..." He trails off, eyes falling to his feet, shamed and confused. "I only put the Shadow Hand in one book."

"Secondary. *Secondary?*" I hiss. "After Lewko the Elder was tortured by Bootknife, you chose me for Shadow Hand because, what? It was *convenient?* Because I was *nearby?* Being the Shadow Hand of Hain was my whole *life!* It was the only thing that was *mine,* truly *mine!*"

"Forsyth, I—" He swallows hard. "You're just Kintyre's little brother. You're not supposed to—"

"Ah!" I snap. "And there is the crux of the problem! I am no *hero,* and so I cannot have a passion, have a desire to help? I am a citizen of Canada now, am I not? Do I not owe it to my kingdom to serve her best interests?"

"But it's beneath you!" he shouts, his ire rising to match mine.

His disapproval surprises me. I expected him to understand. I don't know why I did, because every conversation I've ever had with him has given me evidence enough to assume that he would *not.* Call it blind hope. Maybe, I thought, if I could make him understand, make him see it from my perspective, maybe we could have... reconciled our differences. Maybe we could have found the friendship he so clearly wants. Maybe, secretly, deep within the part of my soul that was born of his typewriter, I had wanted... Ah, but it is pointless to wish for that which one cannot have. Reed will *never* understand how much he doesn't know about what he has created. So instead, I gawp at him again, a protest and a sound of surprise tangling behind my larynx and coming out as a scoffing squeak of fury.

"You're a gentleman," Reed presses. "I only wrote you to be the Shadow Hand because I needed an excuse for

Bevel Dom to learn about the Iridium Crown!"

"Well, whether you intended it or not, this is what I am! I take pleasure in it, and you *shan't* take that from me!"

"I could sponsor you," Reed says, standing upright, a plea on his face. "You're meant to have the life of a gentleman of leisure. I have the money, especially with the TV series coming. I could—"

"Absolutely not!" I snarl, recoiling at the thought of it. "I'll take nothing from you, especially not the gains from your stories!"

"Forsyth, be reasonable," he wheedles. "You have a daughter. You need to provide for her. You need to raise her like a Turn."

"And in taking employment, I do! I am her father, not you! I shall see to her welfare!"

"But I could—"

"And what would be your price?" I demand. "Access to her? Weekly dinners?"

"That'd be nice." He hooks his thumbs into his belt loops, pleased, thinking he is winning.

And that is it. That is *enough*.

"You ruined my childhood," I say, low, dangerous. "You shall not ruin hers. I have kept my part of the bargain and told you of my occupation. You *will* keep yours and write of Hain no more. Now leave. And if you try to return, you will find a restraining order placed against you. Trust that I hold enough power with my new government to make that happen."

Reed pales, jowls wobbling, and reaches out to try to take my hand, or touch my shoulder, or somehow press his skin against mine and force acceptance through my flesh.

Before his hand even lands, Smoke is in mine.

To him, perhaps, it looks as if the sword has simply

leapt off the wall and into my grip, but it did not. The magic I know, the spells I could once weave, the Words I could Speak, these things do not work in Pip's realm.

No, I am simply fast.

"Forsyth!" Reed yelps, and then jiggles backward as I level Smoke's tip at his neck. He snaps his mouth closed, wavering, eyes jumping from the point, to my hand, to my face. Fool— he should be watching my shoulder if he wants to track my intent. "No... no need to get violent," Reed chatters.

"There is *every* need," I said, willing my teeth to un-clench. "I have requested, peacefully and repeatedly, that you do not harass my family. And now I learn that you have not only disregarded my request, but that you have stolen information through trickery. I do not even know how you knew of our party tonight. I assume spying can be added to your list of crimes."

"It's December twenty-first! I assumed you'd be hav-ing the... Forsyth, I'm not a criminal!"

I snarl, wordless and irritated, and poke the plastic button on his cardigan-covered belly lightly and delib-erately with the sword. He sucks in a breath and jiggles some more, this time shaking in fear.

"You wouldn't," he whispers, aiming for defiance and settling on stubborn terror.

"To protect my family? I most certainly would. And do not forget, Mr. Reed," I hiss. "You wrote me to be *extremely* proficient with the Shadow's Sword."

He gulps, takes a step back, and then another. I steer him toward the door and let the press of the blade push him back against the wood.

"Now," I say, affecting my Shadow's Voice—low and deadly. "Out."

Reed scrabbles behind him for the doorknob, and the moment he has it under his hand, he is flying down the stairs, slamming into his boots, and disappearing into the Canadian winter like a siren into the depths of the sea with a victim under her arm. I watch from the top landing of the staircase, Smoke turned behind my body so that my guests do not see it. Several have crowded around the bottom of the stairs, attracted no doubt by the shouting and Reed's hasty exit. Among them is Pip, her mouth a sour line, her eyes narrowed in the direction of our front door.

"I'll be down in a moment," I call to the crowd, and they all make vague nodding motions and noises of assent, turning back to their conversations or returning to where they were before. I back into my office.

I replace Smoke on its plaque, and then return to the party. It is noticeably quieter in the house, now, but as I make my reappearance with a reassuring smile plastered firmly in place, the volume of conversation slowly bubbles upward to regular volume. I pause on the stairs to readjust my waistcoat and smooth back my hair. I also take a deep breath, schooling my face into the even, placid expression of a lordling.

Pip is still waiting for me in the foyer, and has been joined by her father. She looks grim. He, merely confused.

"Who was that?" Martin asks, looking up through the rails as I pass him on my way down. Martin is holding the bottle of wine Reed brought as a gift in one hand and Alis in the other.

I relieve him of my daughter, pull her up against my neck to inhale the safe, sweet milky smell of her. She pats my face, somehow sensing my distress, and tries to soothe me with a very soft string of "Dah dah dah dah."

When I look back up, I meet Martin Piper's eyes and tell him the truth.

"He was nobody important," I say.

RINGS

In Osgili, the far-flung island on the southernmost tip of the Brystal Archipelago, it is a ring. And it takes nearly a week for Solinde to locate the totem, lost as it is under the silt of a river. Even though her power can hold back the water, it cannot keep her boots from sinking in the sun-warmed muck.

When she finds the dratted thing, sweaty and matted with algae and bedevilled by biting instincts, she nearly calls down the lightning and does away with the horrible totem right there. But no, there are too many trees closing in over her head, suffocating and holding the fetid, humid air close to the ground. She must be the tallest thing in a clearing for the lightning to come to her hand. Even she cannot circumvent the laws of nature to call lightning where it is not wont to go.

There is a town nearby, and a defense tower with a spire. But that would mean humans, and Solinde carries too much hate for their kind to willingly venture into their midst just now.

No, Solinde desires silence.

With the ring pulled snug over her thumb, she walks for a full day and night to the southernmost tip of the world. She stands on the gray, reaching finger of rock that arrows out over the sea, on the promontory the sailors call the Astrolabe.

She slides the ring off her thumb and kisses its unremarkable gold curve, hoping.

And then she calls down the storm. The rain washes her hair and clothing clean. It is cool and refreshing, and if Solinde weeps with the sky, there is none but the sea to witness. The lightning, when she summons it, leaves her skin untouched, but turns the ring in her palm to ash and dust.

In the sky, four more stars flare and burn out. Solinde stands on the crest of the chalky cliff, waiting. She lays a hand over her heart and waits for the tug that will signal the return of that which she seeks. She waits, and yearns. She waits, and despairs. She waits, and weeps. She waits.

He does not return to her.

Her anger is the storm. Below Solinde, waves rage, flung at the rocks as if to sacrifice themselves, to be free forever of Solinde's harnessing misery.

THREE

On Christmas morning, Alis is entertained with the paper which wrapped her presents, the boxes in which they came, and the sticky side of the bows, which she cannot shake off her fingers. She is not so concerned with the gifts themselves. Which is a shame, as my daughter has been absolutely spoiled. Her splendid hoard of toys and books is even more abundant than I ever remember Kintyre's being on his birthday. Of course, there is no Christmas in Hain, and any gifts given at Solsticetide are food or drink, unless given between spouses, pairs, those who are trothed, or lovers. So to be confronted with the pile of tokens gifted to my daughter by her grand- and great-grandparents, as well as our good friends, is quite startling. Pip laughs and calls it consumerist nonsense for a baby who won't even remember, but even she is not immune to the romance of plying our daughter's first holiday with overabundance.

Worn out by all the preparation that had gone into our Solsticetide festivities and heartily sick of the leftovers, Pip decides that our Christmas Day feast will not consist of turkey, but take-away. Pip closes her eyes and plucks one of the flyers out of the fan I present to her. Indian. That sounds good.

"Mmm, curry!" I tell Alis, who is snugged in her mother's arms, her wee cardigan covered over with festive bows. She fusses if we try to remove them.

She says "Mmm!" back, as if she has any idea what curry is.

Then I trade Pip our daughter for the phone. "Will you please order?" I ask. Telephones still give me anxiety if I'm not mentally prepared for a conversation with a disembodied voice, and I end up stuttering more often than I like. It annoys the people on the other end, which in turn makes me more anxious, and prone to worse verbal fumbles.

"One of these days, we're gonna have to actually figure out where the nearest grocery store is," Pip says, taking the menu and flipping it over to find the phone number before she dials. "If only because my father can't keep driving to Victoria to give us his leftover root veggies and baby care packages."

"I like his taste in diapers," I say, patting Alis's superhero-patterned bottom. "Besides, we have the Internet now. We can order groceries in."

"You really hate the snow that much, eh?" Pip turns away from me then to talk to the person taking her order, not waiting for my answer. One isn't required, anyway.

Lysse Chipping was a fertile bowl-valley, perfect for growing stone-fruit and large families, famous for its cheese and horses. Our winters lasted maybe three or four months, and the snow never went past my knees. This is my second winter in Pip's world, the first outside of a large metropolis, and already the snow is deeper than I have ever seen in my life. She tells me that while Victoria is temperate, it does still see snow, and that the accumulation will most likely be worse in the next few weeks. I cannot even begin to fathom what that must mean. In Hain, I never went further north than Kingskeep, though my brother has been to the Dark Woods at Erlenmeyer, and out over the pack ice pans in search of the Bear

Prince. I now have much greater respect for Bevel Dom, that he managed to keep the headstrong Kintyre from freezing to death up in the Northlands. Winter is harsher, the cold more unrelenting, than I could have ever anticipated.

Luckily, in this world, there exists such a thing as forced air heating, and hot-running water. Otherwise, I would be packing up my family and moving us closer to the equator. In a nation by the name of Japan, they apparently have things called *kotatsu*, and the moment my home office is complete, I plan to turn my considerable scholar's mind toward recreating these little tables with built-in heaters and blankets for our living room.

While Pip orders our dinner, I take Alis into the living room and set her down amid the torn and crinkled paper she has hoarded. When she caught us tidying it away, she burst into fat, rolling tears, and would not be consoled with anything less than the paper snowing down over her head and drifting around her feet.

Alis returns now to the joy of crumpling and crinkling, while I make for the bookshelf. Each of us has a selection of our favorite books on the living room shelf, and there are two squashy chairs before the fireplace, each with their own lamps hanging above them to encourage our mutual love of reading. Between the two armchairs is a new, third chair, scaled to a child of perhaps ten and sporting its own festive bow. This was my gift to Alis—a reading place of her very own. It is too big for her now, but she will grow into it. And, I hope, grow to love it.

"Pip?" I call, scanning the bookshelf beside the mantel for the book I had been reading to Alis the night before. It has vanished. "Have you seen *The Wizard of Oz*?" The book is not on the floor, nor any of the chairs, nor on the coffee table.

"The what?" Pip asks, coming into the room.

"*The Wizard of Oz*. I can't find it. I could have sworn I put it back on Alis's shelf, but it is not here. I can't find the book anywhere in the living room."

Pip wrinkles her nose, thinking. It is an adorable habit. "*The Wizard of Oz?*" Pip repeats, lingering over the title as if it was exotic. "No, I haven't seen it. Is it new?"

"New? No, it's your old book, the big one? With the watercolor illustrations?" I reply, focused mostly on searching under the furniture now, so much so that I miss the little inflection of genuine curiosity that shades Pip's answer.

"My old book?" Pip asks, coming to stand beside me. "Can't have been. I've never heard of *The Wizard of Oz*."

"*Bao bei*," I reproach. "Honestly."

"Honestly," she says, and for the first time, the lack of humor in her voice catches in my brain and halts my search. I straighten, and see that Pip's expression of confusion is genuine. She is not having a laugh.

"Pip," I say slowly, standing from where I had crouched to peek under Alis's chair. "*The Wizard of Oz?* Dorothy and the silver slippers? Traveling the Yellow Brick Road with an animated scarecrow, a tin woodsman, and a cowardly lion? They're going to the Emerald City to beg boons from the Wizard?"

Pip frowns. "Are you sure this is a book from my world? This isn't a Syth Story?"

"No," I say. "No, it's definitely not."

Pip shrugs. "Well, I've never heard of it, and I don't know where the book is. Read her some Hobbit, if you want a quest-narrative book."

I feel my fingers curl into the back of my reading chair and a cold, mercurial horror slide into my gut. Something, though I do not yet know what, is deeply, terribly wrong.

~~~

The cold dread spreads upward all through dinner, wrapping tightly around my throat. Even the heat of the curry fails to dull it, making it hard to read to Alis. As Pip suggested, I read Alis the first chapter of *The Hobbit* after her bath, and then put her down to sleep. My wife remains downstairs, tidying away the wrapping while Alis is out of visual range with the hope that she will have forgotten the bounty of crackling paper come the morning. But my unease is far less easy to forget.

Lucy Piper loves *The Wizard of Oz*. She promised that once I finished reading the storybook to Alis, we would rent the musical film version. She sings "Somewhere Over the Rainbow" as Alis's lullaby. She had even once dressed as the witch on Halloween because a girl in her school told her she wasn't white enough to be Dorothy, and Pip, in her stubborn righteousness, had then adopted the witch as her favorite character because she was convinced they were both mistakenly outcast; they weren't "normal" like other girls.

So how, suddenly, did it come to be that she is convinced the book does not exist? Either something is horribly wrong with my wife (please, Writer, let that not be the case), or something is wrong with this realm. It is easier to check the latter than the former with an internet search, so that is what I do.

It feels wrong to be relieved when I find exactly zero search returns for *The Wizard of Oz*, but the terror releases my throat all the same, and whooshes out of me in a sigh.

It is not Pip. Thank the Writer, it is not Pip.

But if it is not *Pip*, then what is it?

~~~

Several days after Christmas, Pip has an appointment with her therapist. She is scheduled to see the woman once weekly, and has done so since we returned to her world; the traumas of her time in mine made it impossible for her to sleep or feel safe in her own home. Sometimes, I attend the sessions too, which has helped me understand the ongoing process of coming to terms with my own part in Pip's ordeal, and with some of my own feelings and insecurities as well.

Sensing an opportunity to go into a library without Pip hovering and becoming suspicious, I suggest that Alis and I accompany her downtown, on the promise of a lovely family lunch once she is done. Pip agrees, and we all set off, bundled tightly against the winter chill.

The weather is obliging. Though the snow is deep, the sky is clear, and the light crust of ice covering the snow banks glitters in such a way that I am reminded of the wings of the fairies who unwisely used Turn Hall's fish pond for a mirror. Alis and I slip and skid our way to the campus library after leaving Pip outside her therapist's office, ostensibly to browse the shelves for an illustrated copy of *The Hobbit*. Alis seemed to have enjoyed our reading the night before, and I certainly enjoyed the story, for though I have never heard of such a creature as a hobbit, I find the notion of a culture so wholly devoted to the wholesome pleasures of home and hearth appealing. Besides, Alis always prefers having pictures to peruse while she listens to her Da's voice.

Of course, my ulterior motive for this outing is to question the librarian on duty about the sudden and inexplicable disappearance of *The Wizard of Oz* from social consciousness.

But when I ask, the young woman at the desk protests that she'd never heard of the book, nor the author, nor of the film or stage play, though I was certain there had been both. There are photographs of Pip dressed as the Wicked Witch of the West in the albums on our bookshelf—I know this for a fact; my questions about her green face paint had been the whole reason she had produced her battered, well-loved copy of *The Wizard of Oz* storybook in the first place.

Alis has begun to pick up on my distress, and starts fussing in her carrier, arching and wriggling so that the crown of her head bashes against my chin, frustrating us both. The clerk gives me the sort of pitying look that men with young children often receive in this realm—the expression that says, "*Oh, your wife is too busy?*" Which infuriates me even more. I heartily do not understand this mentality that men are incapable of being supportive co-parents. Why, by the Writer, would I ever want to foist my daughter solely onto my wife and have no involvement in her upbringing? She is my *daughter.*

"*The Wizard of Oz*," I repeat, pulling the library clerk's attention back to my inquiry, instead of my parenting abilities. "I am certain that is the correct name."

"And yet the system says no," the clerk replies. She gives me an insolent little smirk. If she'd been *my* apprentice, I would never have allowed her such cheek.

I am starting to wonder if I should be saving my breath to blow away pixies.

I long for a good searching spell, and perhaps the Lost Library, or, failing that, Words of Revelation so I can at least comprehend the full scope of this weirdness's weavings. I sigh, rubbing first my brows, and then my abused chin, and then finally the top of my daughter's head.

"Very well," I say. "Forget about that book. I would like a copy of *The Hobbit*, if you have one that is illustrated."

The clerk frowns, straightening from her casual

slump, and types what I assume is the title into her computer. "Hm," she says, returning to her slump. "Don't have that one either. But the kid's section is that way." She points, clearly ready to dismiss me entirely and eager to be rid of my troublesome inquiries.

I sigh again, annoyed to have been stymied yet again. "May I leave my name, so you may call me when the book is returned?"

"No," the clerk says. "We don't *have* one."

"No illustrated copies at all..." I muse.

The clerk thumps her hand on the desk to emphasize her reply: "No, we don't have *The Hobbit*."

The way she says it gives me pause. "But... surely you... I am told it is one of the great modern classics of children's literature. You mean to say this library does not have *any* copies?"

"Can't be much of a classic if I've never heard of it," the clerk says. "I major in children's lit."

"*The Hobbit*," I insist, a sweep of déjà vu pricking up my spine. "Recently adapted into a film trilogy? About a young creature of the kindly west traveling with thirteen dwarves and a wizard to reclaim a kingdom under a mountain from a dragon?"

"No," the clerk says stubbornly. "I've never heard of it. Sounds a bit like the *Narnia* books, though, if that's what you mean."

"It is not," I say, my ire mounting to the point where I know I am being rude but cannot help it. "And you cannot be much of a scholar if you've never—"

"Hey!" the clerk says. "Buddy, *chill*."

Chill, I snarl to myself. *In the face of incompetence? Hardly!*

But knowing that a fit of temper would do me no good, and sensing that the clerk's patience has now reached its end, I thank her for her time between clenched teeth and take Alis and myself off to the Children's section. I waste several minutes searching for J.R.R. Tolkien's work and find no trace of Middle-earth on the shelves. I do, however, find the first of the Narnia books, illustrated with small black-and-white ink sketches, and check this book out for Alis's bedtime reading.

That evening, after our daughter is abed, I cannot find our copy of *The Hobbit*. I left it, open to the second chapter, on the arm of Alis's chair, of that I am *certain*. But a thorough search turns up nothing, and prompts my wife to ask me if I am feeling perhaps a bit ill, as I am forgetting things recently.

I wonder if the lost books are due to a spate of bad luck—bad luck I earned when I turned away a guest on Solsticetide? Perhaps I should not have threatened my Writer with Smoke, after all. But that does not explain why the librarian, majoring in children's literature, would be entirely oblivious of the books' very existence.

I shout that I have forgotten nothing, and that I do not appreciate being patronized. My reply is so heated that it startles Alis awake, and above our heads, our daughter wails. Pip stares at me in reproach, disappointed to have been on the receiving end of what was clearly— to her—an overreaction. When I attempt to walk around her to go up to Alis, she blocks my path.

"You're in no state to take care of Alis. I'll do it."

Fear high, and anger roiling, I force myself to stay still, unclench my fists, and *breathe.*

I let Pip go up alone. I have far too many memories of my father, similarly angry and puce-faced, blowing like a bellows above my bed, looking for a reason to punish a little boy when he had done nothing more than cry out in his sleep. I will not give my own child similar memories.

⌇⌇⌇

The next morning, I log onto my computer and hack. Delving deep into the darkest parts of the Internet, I search out any schemes, cyber-attacks, or viruses that could be causing these books to be removed from the vast expanse of the interweb. Though this would not, of course, explain the way they have also been lost from library shelves and the memories of people. In my quest, I realize that not only are *The Wizard of Oz* and *The Hobbit* missing, but so too are all of their derivatives and sequels, as well as the various and many dramatic adaptations.

The cold, mercurial panic returns, and to combat it, I do what the Shadow Hand does best —I make *lists*. I make a list of every missing work, as far as I'm aware, with a paper and pen, not trusting my computer, in case this is some sort of elaborate, digital virus. Then I make a list of every book we have in the house, as well as every film and television box set, and from there, I add a grid and every other tale I can recall having read or watched with Pip. I fill every line, as Pip once showed me how to do when she was compiling the Excel for our quest. Then I begin the cross-referencing Internet searches.

Cinderella has vanished, as well as the Grimm Brothers' fairy tale *The Red Shoes*. So has Thackery's *The Rose* and *the Ring*, and Wagner's *Ring Cycle*, an opera of which I am quite fond.

Shoes and rings.

It could be more than shoes and rings, but without a full survey of the vanished tales, I have no way to see the pattern, to know if anything else is lost. I rack my brain, but I cannot decipher what the connection may be. Then another thought, worse than the first, occurs to me: there is no way to catalog what is missing in its entirety.

Were I in Turn Hall, or Kingskeep, I would have had

the power not only of the Shadow's Mask and the magical knowledge preservation within it to be able to create a fairly encompassing survey of the literature of Hain, but also the Shadow's Men on which to rely to gather information from the libraries and private collections all across the kingdom. But here, I have no Mask, no Men, and more books are published annually in this realm than could fit within the Lost Library.

What infuriates me most, though, is that in not having been reared as a denizen of this realm, I have no clue what other stories are vanishing, stories that I have yet to encounter or hear. Stories that, now, I will never know.

Pip told me once of the Great Library of Alexandria. She had been emotional from the pregnancy, and a great maudlin, melancholy mood had settled upon her like a damp, woolen blanket as she recounted the ingenuity of how the Greeks had seized books at ports and copied them. She wept that night for the stories the world had been made bereft of, the scrolls and books swallowed by flame and ash, for the truths and knowledge and wonders her realm had lost forever in a single night.

Now, I am near weeping for the same reason, myself. And Pip appears to have no idea that it is happening.

〜〜〜

When I return to my office after stepping out for a quick lunch and a cup of coffee, there is a gap in my list.

Something shifted in the fabric of reality while I was downstairs finishing the last of the Indian-food leftovers. Judging by the context of the titles listed around it, I realize that the missing book is *The Magic Ring*. I look to my list of vanished books and, noting that none are missing, decide that whatever strange power is pulling tales out of existence must only erase information that already exists, is already set down, and that the process is slow. It takes time for the fingers of whatever power is doing this to leak into all the corners of this realm.

Taking up a red pen, I rewrite *The Magic Ring* onto the master list. It does not fade away, though I watch it for what must be full on twenty minutes while my coffee goes stone cold.

So, whatever is happening only affects that which exists physically. It does not take my own memories away, does not re-erase the information after the original vanishing. But it can steal the memory from others, from the denizens of this place, like Pip and the children's lit major librarian. What an odd spell. If it is indeed a spell, in this realm of no magic.

A ghastly thought occurs to me: what if this is common, in Pip's world? That stories regularly fade out of existence? Perhaps there are others, like me, whose realms fracture and dissolve when they cross the borders of reality? But no, that's ludicrous; *The Tales of Kintyre Turn* have gone nowhere.

And the world would certainly be more populated with other fictional characters, like myself. Though, it's not as if we have a support group or private message board online in which to discuss the woes of coming out of a book. I have no way of *knowing* if there are others like me here in the Writer's realm.

Aggravated, and without anywhere to turn for answers, I decide to join Pip and Alis downstairs, where they are currently making an unholy racket with one of the electronic noise-making toys our neighbors gifted Alis. How Pip can mark papers through the din is unfathomable.

Alis lights up when I walk into the room, bounces Library's face off the blanket, swings him in the air, and shouts, "Daa!"

"Wow. Look at that poor plushie swing," Pip says, looking up from her stack of paper, her red pen balanced on her upper lip like a comical mustache.

"I see more of Kintyre in her each day," I admit.

Pip snorts so hard the pen drops. "Now *that* is terrifying."

"Come on, sweeting," I say to Alis. "Let us see if we can't override those destructive Turnish tendencies and make of you a proper book-mouse?"

"'Ook!" Alis agrees as I scoop her up and away from the dreadful noise-maker and move over to the book shelf. Nothing seems to be missing this time, for which I am grateful. Alis paws at her shelf, where we keep her board books, but nothing she pulls out seems to satisfy her. "'Ook!" she shouts, louder and louder, getting frustrated when each book she inspects fails to meet her standards.

"Darling, darling," I try to hush her, moving away from the shelf, but she just screams louder. I step back up to the shelf, and she sweeps every remaining book off with all the dramatic flair my father had while raging. Oh, dear, there is *such* a lot of Turn in Alis.

Alis wriggles to get down, and I set her on her chair. She immediately scoots off that and over to the pile of books, tugging them each out of my hand as I try to re-shelve them and sobbing, "No, no, no!" And then she says a word I've never heard her use before: "Toto!"

Stunned, I drop onto my own rear end, on top of the pile of books, and stare at Alis with dawning horror and comprehension.

"Are you looking for *The Wizard of Oz*, s-sweeting?" I ask. Alis, miserable and frustrated, nods her head and sobs louder.

Oh, thank the Writer. I'm not the only one who remembers. I'm not going mad.

But then, what in the name of all that is wholesome is going on?

I can't help but rage silently. Nothing makes sense. It makes my skin itch, and my teeth hurt, and my lungs clench. It makes me irritable and short of patience. I am a man written to be physically uncomfortable when I do not understand something. I literally *need* my world to make sense, and with this knowledge missing, gone, I am not only uneasy, I am in *pain*.

I *must* get to the bottom of this.

"What'd she say?" Pip asks, abandoning her marking. "Toto? What do you think that's supposed to be?"

"It's the d-d-dog," I say, breathing deep to try to calm myself. "Fr-fr-from *The Wizard of Oz-z*."

"Forsyth—" Pip begins, setting aside her stack of papers and red pen. She stands, scoops Alis up, and then juggles her against her shoulder in an attempt to calm our child. Pip looks like she's going to say more, but instead she just shakes her head and sighs, long and frustrated.

"It's re-real!" I snap, surging to my feet. "I'm n-not ma-mad! It is a-a-a re-real book, and th-there was a f-f-film adap-ta-ta-tion, and a musical p-play!"

"I don't remember this book, Forsyth," Pip says back, trying to keep her expression to something passive and even, but I can see her frustration bubbling up in the way she widens her stance, as if preparing to lunge or dodge. Her mouth thins, and her lips go white.

"Y-you t-told me it was your fa-favori-te-te s-s-story as a child because you always w-wuh-ished to be swept away into a magical re-realm. You told me t-this, Pip!"

"Yeah, well, look at how well that wish turned out for me." She purses her lips and rolls her eyes.

"D-don't laugh!" I grab her arm, turn her toward me, and get close so she can see just how concerned I am. "*The Hobbit h*as v-vanished as well. And *The Lord* *of the Rings. Cin-cinderella.* Pip, b-books are *dis-disap-pear-ring,* and *you will believe me!*" I roar.

Pip goes entirely still, all the color draining from her face in an instant. Her gaze flickers down to where I've got a hold on her arm. Pip swings away, putting herself between Alis and my anger, and hisses: "Stop shouting!" She covers Alis's ear with her free hand and presses the other side of our daughter's head against her shoulder. "Let go!"

I take a step back, all fury extinguished in a cold splash of realization and dread. My knees and fingers shake as I unwrap my hand from around Pip's arm. Her shirt is sleeveless, and I watch with sickening, nauseous horror as the skin where I was grabbing immediately changes from a bloodless white to an angry, abraded red. It will bruise, of that I am certain.

I have hurt my wife. I look to Alis, whose face is turned into her mother's neck, and finally register that my child, my baby, is screaming. I have scared my child.

"Oh," I say, small and weak, devastated. My legs crumble and I drop into my reading chair. "Oh, Pip. I am f-f-foul. I-I-I am so-so-so-sorry. I am... how *c-c-could I?*"

For the one thing I have always promised myself is that I would not be my father.

Pip bundles Alis closer to her own chest as she takes a step back. And then, furious, she shakes a sharp finger in my direction. "This is the second time you've lost your shit over things that don't exist. So you either need to figure this out or you need to go take a really long look at yourself, Forsyth! I don't know if all the men from your realm go batshit when they become fathers, or if this is a Reed thing, but you are never going to fucking threaten me or Alis again!"

Perhaps Alis is not the only one of us with too much Turn in them.

I swallow hard, nodding, and feel desperately like I want to both vomit and sob at the same time. Alis whimpers and squirms, and Pip puts her down on her blanket with Library before coming back to kneel in front of my chair. She places her hands firmly on my knees and looks up into my face, concern and hurt written large in her brown eyes, and that is it, that is enough. I cannot hold back the wave of self-loathing and reproach.

"Oh, Pip!" I say, reaching out to touch, gently, the red mark on her arm. Her name crackles and hitches in the middle when the tears come.

"Okay," she says softly. "Okay, c'mere." She rises up and I fold down. She wraps her arms around my waist and it is perfect. It is home.

She does not forgive me, for what I did was unforgivable, and I do not ask for it. But in her arms, with my nose in her hair and my mouth against the little puffed scar shaped like a leaf on her neck, there is a kind of closure.

"I wuh-wi-will not," I say gently. I kiss the scar and hold Pip close, willing the worry out of my limbs so that I don't crush my wife. "Never again. I *sh-shall* not."

"God, you're more scared than I am," Pip says softly, voice a waft of breath against my ear and filled with worried awe. "You're shaking."

"Pip—I'm s-sorry. I'm just so *confused*. It is no excuse, but I cannot... I cannot bear not understanding."

"Where the books have gone?"

I nod, miserable, and she sits back to study my face.

"You mean it," she says, reaching up to cup my cheek in her palm. I lean against her, nuzzling. "You really do think that books are disappearing."

I nod again, not trusting my tripping tongue with such a grave pronouncement.

"Are *you* fading?" Pip asks, voice tremulous. "Is it

you? Are you just... phasing out of existence?" She grabs my face in both hands now, and hers are shaking just as much as mine when I lay my hands over hers. Tears pool at the bottom of her eyes, thick but not falling. "Oh my god. Forsyth. What if you can't live in this realm? What if your mind is going first, like Alzheimer's? Is that why you're getting weird and violent?"

This is a possibility that I have not yet entertained, and it fills me with an even greater flood of terror than the revelation that books are vanishing.

What if it is as my wife says? What if it is I who is sick, who is wrong, who is broken? But no, no! Alis remembers the books. Unless Alis is in just as much danger as I?

A quick glance at my daughter, clutching Library and grumbling, eyes red-rimmed and posture miserable, curled in on herself, assures me that she still breathes. That she is still here. Pip follows my line of sight and freezes, her whole body going tense. She launches herself at Alis, flopping down beside the baby and cuddling her close.

Her motherly instincts must be screeching at her, but there is nothing to fight here. There is nothing to defend her child against. Nothing tangible, at least.

Either one of two things is happening.

The first: that I cannot exist outside of my book, and that I am breaking down, slowly, bit by bit, rotting away or fading like mist under a strong sun. And Alis might be equally in danger of the same.

Or the second, and more terrifying possibility: I am not going mad. Books really are vanishing, and Alis and I are the only ones who can remember them because we are not of this realm.

And if that is the case, what happens if *The Tales of Kintyre Turn* are next?

I ponder on this, silent while Pip attends to Alis in an effort to calm herself. Eventually, I return to my office to double check my list and ruminate further. To make plans.

In the end, the most cool-headed, logical thing to do turns out to be, unfortunately, the thing I want to do the least. But I pride myself in my cool-headed logic; I would be too much like my brother if I relied on instinct and attacking first. And, as Pip has pointed out, my patience has been much too thin as of late.

So the cool-headed, logical thing prevails.

I therefore barricade myself in my office and make a phone call that I never, in the whole of my life, would have expected to make.

"Hello?" says the hated voice on the other end when he picks up.

For a moment, the words stick in my throat, and I am ashamed of my own cowardice. But finally, I force myself to speak. For I am the Shadow Hand of Hain, am I not? I am Lordling of Lysse. It is my duty to act with courage, to act in defense of my kingdom, my king, my Chipping, and my family.

"Mr. Reed. I..." I swallow hard, begging my tongue to stay limber. Through the phone, I hear him gasp, no doubt recognizing my peculiar accent. "I need your help."

FURNISHINGS

olinde licks Words of Finding out of the mouth of a traveler on the road, a young man with a cow to sell at market, sent out by his mother. Solinde has no use for a dried up heifer and seduces the boy instead, lays down with him in the thorns, and laughs when he begs for her name and proposes marriage in the same breath.

She was trapped once by giving up her name to a young farmer with stars in his eyes; she won't do it a second time.

Words don't last long on Deal-Maker lips, so Solinde casts the spell over a map she plucked from the boy's pocket as soon as he and his milky white waste of grain have vanished behind the bend of the road. The spell indicates that she must cross the water to the north, and so she sings a great turtle up from the depths of the channel and compels it to ferry her across on its wide back.

On the sandy beach, she considers killing the turtle, eating the meat and keeping the shell for potions-work, and then decides that it would be too impractical. She is mortal no longer; she does not need to eat. She is a Deal-Maker; she no longer needs to craft weak potions out of herbs like a common hedge-witch. She sends the turtle away, never knowing how close it came to its own demise.

On the beach, she uses up the last of the boy's Words

of Finding, and follows the pull of the spell up into Nairn. It is a sleepy seaside village on the southern coast of Gadot, filled with small cottages and treasure shops crusted with antique bottles of sea glass and knickknacks made from painted shells. The Words lead her to a shop at the top of the street filled with antique furniture. It is all sturdy and plain, made in an age when functional was more important to mortals than beautiful, and the great chores of farming and manufacture took twice as much time because no human had yet discovered the Words that made life easier.

As with the shoes, Solinde cannot decipher which particular item amid the jumble of dust-grayed furniture shoved in a pile of tripping hazards in the back corner is the totem for which she came. It is either the listing wardrobe, or a wide chair made entirely of iron ore, or an old lamp post with a shattered glass pane. Magic wafts from the pile like a rotten odor, but she cannot pinpoint its origin.

The proprietor asks if something has caught her eye and offers to help her unearth whatever it is she wants. Frustrated, Solinde calls down the lightning instead. The proprietor screams and flees. The shop is filled with such wonderfully old, dry wood that it goes up around her like a bonfire on Solsticetide.

Outside, and above, a handful more stars wink out.

FOUR

By the time Elgar Reed has driven to Victoria, *The Chronicles of Narnia* and all the attendant dramatic adaptations and audio books have dissolved. Even the copy of *The Lion, The Witch, and The Wardrobe*, which I had left on Alis's shelf, has vanished. I photographed it with my cell phone, along with the covers of every other book Pip and I own, and it is now gone from the digital album. The photo is just black.

Reed and I have coordinated his arrival so that Pip is at the school when he rings the doorbell. I have worried her enough with my behavior; to invite over a man I had professed just three weeks prior was my enemy and who would never be welcome in my house would be enough shock to have Pip seriously questioning my mental health. And she is already concerned as it is, worried that I am falling apart in this world I was not Written to inhabit.

As am I.

I fear that perhaps I am losing more than the books. Or that the world is destabilizing around me, and that is why I am imagining stories that Pip and the rest of the denizens of this world have never known, stories that I have been telling to Alis. So that is why I have called upon my creator. If anyone will know that I am *wrong*, it must be the man who invented me, yes? My wife knows me as I am now—Syth Piper—but Elgar Reed knows Forsyth Turn.

Or, at least I hope he does. I have no illusions about the fact that I was written to be a secondary character, with fewer than twenty spoken lines in the whole of the eight-book epic that follows my brother, my greatest passions convenient throwaway lines to him. As much as it galls, it is something I must labor to come to terms with. My Writer may have invented me as a supporting character in Kintyre's life and world, but I am a person, whole and entire unto myself, and that is what keeps me shielded from any sort of philosophical existential trauma. I am a man. I am complete.

When the doorbell rings, Alis pops her head up and cranes around to look down the stairs. "Ma ma ma?" she asks from her jumper seat in the doorway of my office.

"Not even remotely, sweeting," I say, brushing by her and dropping a kiss on her head as I go. She is safe enough in the jumper seat for now, and I will be bringing my guest back up to the office right away. "But a very good guess based on sound deductive reasoning. I applaud you."

Alis swivels in her chair to watch as I head downstairs, chanting "Dah da dah da daaa!" as if she is a cheerleader waving pompoms instead of a slightly soggy Library. I appreciate her support, for my heart is in my throat and I can feel my hand starting to shake as I reach for the door knob.

"Thank you for calling me," Elgar Reed says when I pull open the door. Neither of us extends a hand to shake. There is a small case by his feet, for Victoria is not so close to Seattle that he'll be able to easily travel back at the end of this evening. I have offered my Writer the guest room while he is here, as a good lordling ought. It is bad manners to ask for someone's help and then make them lodge in an inn. Though, to be truthful, the length of his visit depends on Pip's reaction when she gets home.

Not trusting my tripping tongue, I gesture for Reed to enter, and then offer to take his coat. True to Pip's prediction, the snow outside is nearly knee-high where I have shoveled it off the walk. And she threatens that it will only get deeper, in a rare and unusual amount of precipitation for the usually temperate island.

Silent, probably nervous, and clearly unsure of his actual welcome—his eyes dart to my hands to assure himself that they are indeed free of Smoke, I can only assume—Reed follows me to the kitchen. I have the tea set already laid out. We stand there in awkward and stilted silence as the electric tea kettle does its job. Upstairs, Alis chatters to herself.

When we both have our mugs prepared to our liking, I show him upstairs. As I feared, instead of coming directly into the office, Reed stops and bends down to shove his jowly face into Alis's line of sight. For a moment, my daughter regards him with wide eyes and skepticism of an amount that I would call entirely healthy.

"Hello, my lady..."

"A-Alis," I supply, grudgingly. Pip and I had been trying to keep our daughter as much a secret from Reed as possible. Sharing her with my creator is one of the prices, unfortunately, of trying to get to the bottom of all this. I couldn't have invited him over on the sly had I asked Martin and Mei Fan to take Alis today; Pip would have wanted to know why.

"Alis Turn," Reed says, reaching out to, I assume, pinch her cheek.

"Alis P-Pie-Piper," I correct, and then smile as Alis intercepts Reed's unwelcome and uninvited touch by smashing the hard button-eyes of Library on his arm.

Reed makes a face at the drool-damp fabric and straightens, and I hold Alis's jumper to the side to allow him to pass into my office. He is less openly hostile toward its contents this time around, though he trundles straight to the wall where Smoke is hanging and stares hard at the hilt of my blade.

"This is beautiful," he breathes, and I'm not certain if he means to praise me, the elves who forged it, or his own imagination for thinking it up. I bite back my snort all the same, because—and I must remind myself of this—I am the one who invited him here.

"And sha-arp," I say instead, as a warning. His free hand, which had been inching upward, drops to curl around his mug instead. He turns to face me.

"Where did we go wrong?" he asks, voice low and, for the first time, not filled with conceited self-importance. He sounds small. Sad. "We started off fine. Didn't we?"

I have no answer for him. I very much want to say: "*We did not,*" or "*You are too much like Algar Turn,*" or "*It terrifies me down to the smallest atom to be in the presence of my creator,*" or even "*You are an arrogant elfcock and I wish very much that you would go throw yourself into the jaws of a kraken,*" or, lastly, "*You embody everything that is abhorrent about my brother.*" But I cannot say that to him. Not after I have asked for his help.

Instead I take the coward's way and gesture to the list of books I have taped to the wall. "What is your opinion of this?" I have had to write several more titles in red during the seventeen hours between my calling Reed and his arrival.

Reed sets down his tea on my desk—beside the coaster, not on it! He is just as boorish as Kintyre!—and steps closer, eyes narrowed. When he steps back, his eyes widen in shock, and I am glad that the tea is no longer in his hands, because he surely would have dropped it.

"These are..." he begins, and then seems to lose his words. "I thought—"

His reaction is both a relief, for it means it is not just me, and impossibly infuriating. Because if it is not just me, then *what is happening?*

"You are not the only one who has noticed," I say softly, reassuringly. For a strange, sideways moment, I feel almost paternalistic, worrying that he is taking this news badly and is about to take a turn. Reed flaps his mouth shut and gropes his way to my chair. He sits blindly, eyes stuck on the papers, and manages to both find and bring his tea to his mouth without looking or spilling, which is a point I must count in his favor. "Perhaps... have you spoken to other authors?"

Reed shakes his head, then nods, then shakes his head again. His white hair flies around his ears in small clouds of wisps. I wait for him to elaborate, and instead, he just takes another scalding drink. Finally, red-faced and coughing, he says:

"No one else remembered. I was at a convention last week, and I just... casually mentioned *Cinderella*—"

"No one understood the r-reference, I ta-take it?"

"Not one."

"Shoes, rings... magic lands," I say, pointing at the red titles with my own free hand.

"Fantasy." Reed gulps.

"This is both satisfying and terrifying to hear," I admit. "I had asked you here to evaluate my mind, to decipher if I was..." The words stop up in my throat, suddenly clumping together in a sticky mass. "Be-beginning to dis-disintegrate."

Reed swings his gaze up to me, eyes wide with shock and concern. I had thought that if I made my confession casually, the fear would not... would not... Ah, but it has, and I will not give in to the childish urge to punch the wall.

"But perhaps we have stumbled upon another answer," I say, turning away from the damnable *fear* I see in Reed's eyes. Not for me; surely not for me. He doesn't even know me.

An answer, I tell myself. Focus on this other answer. Though what it may be, I cannot even guess yet. Only I, my creator, and my daughter remain unaffected. So what could the connection be, beyond the obvious? If it even is something beyond the obvious.

With no data, I feel as if I am thinking myself into helpless, irritating circles.

Eventually, Reed's shock dissolves enough for him to say: "You... disintegrate? *What?*"

I set down my tea and cross my arms over my chest. It is a defensive gesture, but I cannot help it. His genuine surprise unsettles me. I do not know how to handle it. I did not expect Reed to... genuinely *care* as much as he apparently does. Which, in itself, is an idiotic assumption, because why else has he been pestering but *because* he cares?

I do not like being made to feel an idiot, and my defensiveness deepens.

"I noticed the stories starting to disappear shortly after Solsticetide," I say brusquely, hiding my annoyance behind my mug. "Thus far, I have not been able to account for it. They are not on the Internet, nor in libraries or in video rental shops. They are not on Netflix, nor any of the many social media sites. It is like they simply ceased to be. At first, I feared that it was my own mind that harbored the problem..." I have to take another moment to unstick my confession from my throat. "F-for this realm is entirely de-devoid of magic and Words. But then I realized that Alis remembered some of the books too. She asked for *The Wizard of Oz.*"

"Toto," Alis adds, obligingly and with great gravitas. She pets Library's head gently, running her little fingernails through his matted mane. "'Ook."

"Yes, sweeting," I say to her. "The Toto book." I turn back to Reed. "But if it wasn't my memories, and it wasn't this realm, then I decided that I must speak to you."

"But what would I possibly know about this?" Reed asks, voice thready with dawning horror.

"If it was something to do with me, I thought you might know what. If it was to do with this realm, I thought you may be in the position to explain it to me. And if it was something to do with... with my presence here—" I swallow hard against the new clump trying to form. My heart is fluttering against my ribs. "Th-then perhaps you may kn-know of it. Per-perhaps you might have gotten wi-wi-wind of it f-f-first."

"And if it's none of those things?" Reed asks. He has gone still. Not like a predator, waiting for his opportunity to pounce, nor like prey tense and listening, but like all the life in him has utterly stilled; like every cell has paused while he struggles to decipher what could be happening.

"The-then, if I am honestly a threat to this realm," I say, and my voice is cracking, the backs of my eyes burning, the lump in my throat now so large that I can scarce take a breath around it. I long to go over to Alis and scoop her into my arms, bury my face in her neck, banish my creator, and weep. But I must say it. I must speak it out loud: "If the barriers are collapsing, if something is making all the other realms of fantasy literature disintegrate because of the actions I took to cross into this realm, if it is my *fault*, then I thought that you... you could... you w-would be able t-t-to wr-wri-wrii—"

I can't say it.

Forsyth Turn, spymaster and *coward.* I can't say it.

It takes a moment for him to grasp what it is that I mean to communicate, to *request*. But when he does, he gulps and whispers: "Would be able to write you back into Hain?"

Oh, how shameful.

That I could not even beg this boon for myself. Instead, I can only nod miserably.

Of course, I have no desire to leave my wife and return to the world of fiction from whence I was birthed. I have even less desire to leave behind our child—or, more terrible still, be forced to bring her with me, leaving Pip with empty arms and an empty home. But the most terrible of all would be to force Pip to watch me die.

I expected to die here, of course; I am aging. The scar that Bootknife left on my cheek is a thin, white diagonal line. It is pointing, it seems, directly at the first small cluster of white hairs that have started to appear at my temples like Starflowers in a meadow. I am thirty years old now. In my world, I would have been considered very much middle-aged. But here, I've barely scraped past a third of my life expectancy. I'm not certain if the genetics—if I can be said to have genetics—and the nutrition of my former existence will play out in a negative way in this realm, but here, I at least have access to foods and medicines I had never even dreamt of in Turnshire.

So I expected, yes, to die as an old man: wrinkled and loved and surrounded, I had hoped, with grandchildren. Not at thirty years old and crumbling from the inside out, while my wife clutched my hand and sobbed. I would much rather return to my world, never to see her again, than put her through that.

While I am wallowing in my misery, Reed stands. He looks as if he is about to embrace me. And that, perhaps, is one step too far, even for me. Instead of allowing it, I brush past him and scoop up Alis instead. Hugs I want, yes, but not my Writer's.

Reed clears his throat and has the decency, at least, to turn his attention to the list on the wall while I pull myself back together. Alis drops Library and pats my face slowly, clearly affected by my melancholy mood. Her repeated "Daa daa"s are gentle and quiet.

When I am prepared to face my maker again, my breathing is even and my tongue sits still in my mouth, my eyes dry. I set Alis against my hip. Reed clears his throat and gestures to the list, pretending that he is not trying to stare at her from the corner of his eye.

"So, there's three of us, that we know of, who remember what's missing. Clearly we're... connected." He doesn't say *family*, which I appreciate. "And I honestly have no idea if any other authors have ever met their own, ah, characters, or I'd ask them."

"Let us assume that they have not," I say, pleased that the sentence has come out without the terrible stutter that only seems to plague me these days when I am around Reed, or when I am dismayed by upsetting my wife, or when I must use a phone. "So, what else is unique about your world? What sets it apart? What might... have made this a possibility?"

"Everyone's got elves, and dwarves, and fairies..." Reed muses. He scratches his chin through his beard, thinking, eyes flicking as he does his mental comparisons between tomes I cannot see. "Some of the magic, I guess?" he hazards after a moment.

"Words?" I ask.

He brightens, sitting up straighter, eyes alight. "Yeah," he says. "Words. No one else uses Words."

"And Deal-Makers?" I ask. "Is it possible that the magic of the world you created was unique in that it is only there that Deal-Maker Spirits exist. Yes? Unless...?"

Reed puffs up, his belly thrusting out when, I'm sure,

he meant for it to be his chest. "I didn't steal that idea from anyone," he says. Then he deflates a little. "Though, it's sort of based on the idea of the genie."

"Ah, but djinn must grant wishes," I say, the frustrated circles spinning in my brain, the twisted paths of serpentine logic that have refused to shake out suddenly slowing, becoming clear and straight. "And Deal-Makers must make exchanges. There is a very particular set of rules to the exchanges as well, which Pip's thesis says is singular among fantasy books."

Reed scrubs at his eyes, the usual ruddy color of his cheeks draining into a strained, disbelieving pallor. "Wait, wait... are you telling me that I wrote... that I accidentally *invented* a kind of magic that has such perfect and powerful rules that I inadvertently caused it to *exist?*"

I expected ego in the question, and find only stunned fear instead.

"Essentially."

He sits down again. Hard. "I... whooboy," he wheezes. "Okay, I... right. Okay. I can... I can handle that."

He does not, in fact, look as if he can handle that.

When I first met my creator, I felt pity for him. The shock of meeting me certainly leveled him. That night at the convention bar, he had spent the entirety of the hours it took me to relate my tale to him simply staring at my face. For my own part, I was unsettled by how much he looked like my late father, so I had instead stared at my hands, or my then extremely pregnant wife, or at my drink.

But his existential panic had radiated out of him in waves while I spoke. Had he been a ghost, the whole bar would have been filled with spirit lights and chilling fog.

And it was a feeling I knew well. I had suffered my own panic at the state of my existence, what it all meant, the legitimacy of my life on the whole when I learned that I was created by a Writer to serve merely as a human-shaped prop for my elder brother's heroic adventures. I am not so out of touch with my own emotions that I cannot admit that the shock of the revelation pushed me to tears. Something which Reed did not do as he listened to me recount my story. Instead, Reed had seemingly decided to come to terms with our situation by becoming a demanding, arrogant arse whose self-congratulatory narcissism drove me to finally banning him from the lives of my family entirely. But here, again, I see the vulnerable, concerned, confused man I first met at *FantaCon*; a man who is unsure, and scared, and real.

"I really, really think this isn't what I was expecting when I won all those worldbuilding awards," Reed mumbles, and tries to put his head between his knees.

His substantial belly gets in the way, however, and rather than watch him struggle, I say: "There is Winter Sherry downstairs. Or rather, the closest thing I have found to the Pointes' excellent Winter Sherry. I would much rather have Drebbinshire Whiskey, but..." I let the invitation to partake and the change in topic pull Reed away from his panic.

"Drebbinshire Whiskey," Reed says thoughtfully, and when I put out the hand that is not holding my daughter to help him stand, he stares at it for a moment. Then he raises his eyes to mine, verifying that I am really inviting him to touch. When I nod slowly, he takes my offered hand, and together we lever him onto his feet.

He follows me down to the living room, as I knew he would, and plops right back down onto our sofa. I put Alis on her blanket and move to the liquor credenza.

"I will admit to missing Drebbinshire Whiskey," I say, conversationally, as I pour us two cut-crystal glasses of sherry. Small-talk ought to pull us both out of our heads, and fears; small-talk masks all manner of social and emotional turmoil. "It had the unique property of making one's stomach tingle warmly. I theorize it is because the grain was grown in fields fertilized with dragon ash."

"Ah, yes, the Dire Dragon," Reed murmurs, and obligingly taps the rim of his sherry glass against my own when I proffer it. I wonder if I should tell him about the rogue and the dragonet that our little adventuring party met in the Stoat Forest, about the truths the lad had shared, and about his connection with the drakeling. About where dragon-hoards really came from, and how I had paid for our first home with the drakeling's tears.

No, that is a story for another time. If, indeed, this fragile peace between my creator and me lasts, and there is another time. Instead, I say: "I wonder... if the magic that is making the other books vanish is coming from inside, well, yours."

"Mine?" Reed asks, startled, spluttering as he nearly chokes on the sherry. "I wouldn't... I would never... I haven't written a *thing* since I met you."

That confession, in turn, startles *me*. "What? Nothing?"

"Not a word of fiction," Reed says, and it sounds like an oath. A promise. "Honestly, I'm too scared to, now. I keep thinking about Tristan and... and the other characters in the *Shuttleborn* trilogy. My editor has all three books—it's too late now—but if you and Kintyre and Bevel are real, then even just contemplating what I put Tristan and Vana through on Grimrock..."

I want to offer him reassurance, but I have none to give. If, indeed, I have siblings in creation, and if they know that they are creations, then anything I say to Reed now will either distress him further or harm them. And, as Reed has said, it is all written now. It is too late.

"Then the vanishing books are because of nothing you've done," I say softly, when his guilt has smothered the rest of his sentence, and, it seems, the desire to continue.

"But it makes sense if it's coming from *The Tales of Kintyre Turn*," Reed says softly. "That's why only the two of us"—his eyes cut to Alis briefly—"I mean, three of us remember."

"Remember what?" my wife says from behind me, in the direction of the front door. I actually physically jump. Sherry splashes against the back of my hand.

I feel my blood run cold, to the accompaniment of Alis's delighted, "Ma ma ma maaa!"

"Blast and drat," I hiss. I meant to have Elgar Reed out of our house before my wife got back. Send him off on a walk, break the suggestion to Pip, have time to soothe her before Reed returned... it is too late, now.

I turn, feeling an absurd swoop of dread in my gut. My wife is no creature, no gorgon, no monster who will strike me dead, nor turn me to stone with her basilisk glare, and yet I cannot help but fear what I will find in her eyes.

Worse than anger, or confusion, or betrayal, Pip is *blank*. She has shuttered herself off, closed up her gaze in a way that I have not seen her do since she shook off the Viceroy's control. This is the same protective mechanism she used then, to keep her emotional turmoil hidden from me. She is hiding once again.

"Welcome home," I say softly.

Pip blinks at me, slow and empty, and then sheds her boots and coat, leaving them right there on the floor as she crosses immediately over to Alis to scoop her up. Our daughter gives out a few more pleased "Ma ma maaa!"s, but then quiets when she realizes that nobody is tickling her, or cuddling her, or talking to her. Her eyebrows furrow in a miniature version of my own confused scowl.

"Pour me a glass of wine," Pip says, and I know the

order is for me, so I set down my sticky glass of sherry and obey. If nothing else, it gives me time to get over my startlement and formulate an excuse. Or an apology. Though I am not certain if Pip will accept, or desire, either.

Pip sits on the armchair, furthest from Reed, Alis dandled on her knee. She goes through the motions of a game of giddy-up, but Alis is too busy craning her head around, staring at the three silent adults, to be having fun.

I hand Pip her wine, and sit on the loveseat. That leaves Reed alone on the sofa. The three of us are seated around the coffee table, out of touching range, in an awkward triangle.

With one hand around Alis's back to keep her steady, Pip takes three deliberate sips from her wine, and then says, her voice like gravel: "Explain."

Reed looks to me, uncertain how to begin, and so, with a silent sigh, I say: "I feared for myself. I needed to be sure that I was not... disintegrating." Pip winces, but still does not look at me, still does not unfetter her expression. "I had no wish to distress you, so I—"

"Invited over the one person we agreed we never wanted around our daughter, and then failed to tell me?" Pip snaps, and the fire twinkles briefly in her gaze, her cheeks flushing pink before she slams it all shut again. "Decided that the best idea was then to compound this by *hiding* it?"

I have nothing to say to excuse or explain what I have done, so I bow my head slightly in apology and answer to both.

"Lucy... Mrs. Turn—Piper." Reed corrects himself hastily when Pip turns a narrow scowl in his direction. He adopts a paternal, condescending posture that I know will irritate Pip further. "Your husband was only trying to get to the bottom of this."

"With all due respect, Mr. Reed," Pip says back, echoing his condescending tone. "Stay the fuck out of it." Reed splutters, and Pip swings her head to me. "And you. We're supposed to be a *team*. You're supposed to *talk* to me."

"I tried, Pip!" I protest. "I tried, and you told me that what I thought was happening couldn't possibly be true. You dismissed me when I told you that the books are vanishing. And then you told me that my anger when you did not listen was unfounded and misplaced! So what am I to do, but to choose to investigate it with the only other person who may know enough about my... existence... to believe me and discuss it rationally?"

"So you'd rather sneak around with Elgar Reed than try to convince me?" Pip says, and her face is so full of rich disbelief that I feel myself smothering under the blanket of it.

"You cannot speak of this as if I am philandering with him!" I say, aghast.

Pip snorts and shakes her head. "Don't change the topic," she says, stern. "The point is that, instead of trying to talk to me, you did exactly what we, *together*, decided never to do."

"I *tried*, Pip, but you got it into your mind that I could not possibly be right, and by the Writer's left nutsack, this is the bloody Rookery conversation all over again, you *stubborn creature!*"

Reed jumps at the combination of my profanity and my volume, and covers his groin with his hands, eyes round with shock. Pip continues to glare at me, and Alis waves her fists, gurgling angrily, upset that I am yelling at her mother.

"See, this?" Pip says calmly, once the ringing echo of my voice has dissipated from the cathedral ceilings of our living room. "This is exactly what I'm talking about."

I throw my hands up, inviting the eyes beyond the veil of the skies to witness my exasperation. "And so you will focus on my anger instead of my words. It is no wonder that I am frustrated enough about these concerns that I seek assurance elsewhere, Pip!"

"Well, I can't be rational with you when you've got yourself so wrapped up in this... this Turnish anger!"

Alis shakes her fists more vigorously, clearly siding with her mother, the little turncoat.

"Turnish anger?" Reed squawks.

Pip gestures at me with her empty wine glass in demonstration.

"I fear growing into my father," I admit. "I fear desperately that I will grow loud, and boorish, and cruel."

"Forsyth," Reed whispers. "Never. You would... you would *never*. *Kintyre* is the one I wrote to inherit your father's temper. Not you."

"But his cruelty?" I press.

"Would you ever even consider harming your daughter?"

"Never!"

"Then there's your answer. Forsyth, I deliberately wrote you to be kind to animals and children and women. You're—"

"The sissy," I finish for him, spitting the pejorative, and yet still thinking of my foxes in the covey forest.

"Well," he says, shifting uncomfortably, squirming with guilt. "The beta male, I guess."

"With Kintyre as the alpha?" I guess.

"Yes, but..." He rubs his arms as if to chase away goosebumps, and then runs his fat palm across his sparse pate. "You do know that, in real life, the alphas are the jerks?"

"Don't generalize," Pip warns Reed. "Don't make this about how the douchebag dudebros shoved you in a locker when you were a baby geek. The truth of it is that Kintyre is your power-fantasy author-avatar. You're a Nice Guy who always finished last, and you invented Kintyre to make yourself into what it is you think women actually want—the heroic bad boy. That's why women chuck themselves at Kintyre the way they do. Because you've always wanted to be knee-deep in puss."

Reed turns a vibrant, mortified red. "There's nothing wrong with a little fantasizing," he mumbles. Another heavy, damp silence settles over the room. Reed drains his sherry glass. Alis chews her fist, watching us fretfully.

I take a deep breath, willing my frustration into a box behind my ribs and jamming it shut. "Pip," I say, as calmly as I can. "I apologize for breaking our rule about my creator. But I *needed* to see him. I needed confirmation that I was not losing my mind, as you feared. That I was not... vanishing."

Reed nods vigorously, and though I do not need his support in this, it feels satisfying to be justified in it all the same.

"And are you?" Pip whispers. "Vanishing, I mean?"

"I know about the missing books, too," Reed says, sparing me from having to answer. "And Forsyth thinks Alis does as well. She remembers *The Wizard of Oz*."

"Toto," Alis agrees miserably.

Pip sets her wine glass down on the coffee table, and I see for the first time that her hands are shaking. "Okay," she whispers. "Okay." She swallows hard and buries her face in Alis's neck for a moment, breathing in her daughter and a sense of calm. When she raises her head again, the protective shutters are gone, and her deep brown eyes are filled only with worry and determination. "But you're not vanishing?"

"I don't know. I don't *think* so."

Pip's chin starts wobbling, and she sucks in a breath,

blinking rapidly. Her lashes turn into wet spikes, but her cheeks remain dry. I can see her swallowing, clenching her teeth, trying to remain impartial, to be academic, to *think this out.* "So, *books* are vanishing," she mumbles, holding her shocked sorrow in. "*This Wizard of Oz.* Any others?"

"Many," I say, instead of listing them all.

"And we think the reason why can be found in my books," Reed says. "Or, at least, it's coming from in there."

"But is it dangerous?" Pip asks. "So some books are missing, so what?"

"Alexandria," I remind Pip gently, and her eyes grow wetter, though she still doesn't cry. My brave, thoughtful wife.

"And there's the possibility that my books might be the next to go, even if the issue is coming from inside them," Reed says, his voice so low it is almost as if he dreads saying it out loud, lest his own creator hears it and mistakes it for a wish. "And if my books go..." He trails off, looking first at me, then at Alis with meaning.

"Right," Pip croaks, cuddling Alis closer. "Of course. So, how would we find out?" Pip asks. "And how do we stop it?"

"There are no Deal-Maker Spirits on this side of the page," I say. "If there were, I could bargain my return. Then I could track the problem to its source. Perhaps even sic my brother on it."

"Your *visit*," Pip corrects me. "You *would* be coming back."

A lump appears in my throat, searing, and I must do some swallowing and teeth-clenching of my own in the face of Pip's tightly controlled emotional breakdown. "Of course," I swear, my voice a crackle. "Of course I would, *bao bei.* I would never... I would *never...*"

"Maybe I could write—" Reed begins, but he doesn't get any further than that because, suddenly, the air shatters.

There is a flash of horrifyingly familiar light, which condenses into a pulsing sphere, dazzlingly white and oblong, hovering in the air. A breeze begins in my living room, and within seconds, it roars into a gale-force wind, as irresistible as the funnel of a tornado, pulling me toward the portal.

"Forsyth!" I hear Pip holler, and above that I hear Alis's thin, high scream.

"Wait, Lucy, don't—" Reed shouts, but the rest of what he says is lost in the howl of the wind, and the dark that steals up over my consciousness.

DEALS AND SHADOWS

The Call comes in the middle of the night, while Solinde is searching a disreputable tavern for another mortal foolish enough to Deal with her. Drunk though they are, these rogues and bandits are shrewd, and will promise a woman seeking bargains alone nothing, though she offers them everything.

Solinde had not thought that records of the ritual for which to summon her—specifically *her*—still existed in mortal libraries. Her late husband claimed to have been in possession of the only scroll that specified which items were required to bring her forth, but as in all other things, he must have been *lying*. She *feels* them.

The Sigil is there, and yes, there is a Star-stone that Fell from the Sky, the Scale from the Siren's Lover, and the Compass that Never Points Home, all speckled with the Blood of He Who Calls. And all on a Hearth that Warms the Shadow.

The Sigil could have been recorded elsewhere, and Star-stones fall from the sky every day. The great Nerved King sheds his scales every time he crawls up the side of a hull; they fleck the waves near a shipwreck like clouds of pollen. But the Compass that Never Points Home, there is only one of those. And the last Solinde saw of it, she had "accidentally" slipped it into the satchel of a sail-or who had stopped at her husband's farmhouse on his way down to the docks. That sailor's ship was wrecked, last she heard. The Compass that Never Points Home should be at the bottom of the Icedance Sea. So who, now, was using it to summon her?

At first, Solinde resists the Call. She is on a quest, and she won't be put off it. She will have all the totems, until none remain, until all the stars have gone out and there is nowhere left for her sisters to hide he for whom she searches. But then she intuits that if she allows herself to be summoned, she might possibly be able to work this Deal into something that will speed her search.

Delighted at the thought of befuddling her Summoner, Solinde closes her eyes and is *summoned*.

When she opens them again, she finds her tableau in perfect arrangement on the warm gray hearthstone of what is obviously some wealthy merchant or well-off lord's study. Her Sigil has been traced into the ash. The scale is threaded onto an elaborately knotted rope necklace. And, oh, that is a bit clever—there is a compass, but not her compass. It is not the enchanted compass, but a compass all the same, and its needle has been irreparably bent and twisted out of alignment. It will never point home again.

Smart. Cheeky. Definitely a Summoner worth staying for.

And there is a young man with soot on his finger—though it is barely visible against the dark cast of his skin—a small cut on his palm, and a look of surprised horror on his face that is slowly melting into self-congratulatory awe. This could be useful.

Solinde waits for him to peel himself away from where he has stepped back against a wall of books, presumably when she appeared. She turns, putting her back to him, confident in the knowledge that he will not—*cannot*—harm her. There was only one portion of Deal-Maker Blood loose in this world, and she knows this lad does not have it. He can compel her to do nothing, just as he cannot force her to overtax her power, and he cannot hurt her. So she takes her time investigating the room, looking for any clues that might give her an advantage over her Summoner.

The room itself is warm, and cozy, and filled with the detritus of a scholarly life that has since been abandoned. There is no dust collected upon things, so the lord must have enough staff to clean even a room that has been forgotten, but only in the most cursory way. The ink in its well has gone dry, the parchments on the table are curling and turning brittle, and the decanter from a set on the credenza is missing, though the two remaining glasses are clean; it was obviously taken away to be drunk in a room that sees more traffic. The air is stale, and the nearest window's sill is adorned with the fine needlework of a spider, drooping under the weight of the accumulated dust, undisturbed. This window has not been opened in many months. Perhaps even years.

When she turns to face the lad again, he is standing straight, head held high, chin at a defiant angle. He is dressed well, but carelessly: his trousers are wrinkled, his fine linen shirt untucked, his waistcoat and neckcloth missing entirely. He wears no House Color that Solinde can see, only black trousers, black boots, and the white shirt. His equally black eyes are narrowed at her.

Solinde, wishing to have him at ease, wishing to have him malleable, dips a deliberately submissive and low curtsy which, incidentally, gives him the perfect opportunity to gaze into the valley of her cleavage. When she straightens, his eyes remain on her chest, and she allows herself a little smirk. Human men. Even the pups barely into their maturity are easy to befuddle.

And a befuddled Summoner means a better Deal for Solinde.

"I am summoned," Solinde says, in as sweet and formal a tone as she can muster. She wills a blush to bloom on her cheeks.

"Uh," the lad says, clearly uncertain if there is a ritual way for him to greet her. There is not, of course, but she will not tell him that. He clears his throat, shifts his weight from foot to foot, and scratches the back of his head. "Uh, to be honest, I didn't actually think this would work."

Solinde bites down hard on the impatient incredulity that presses against her tongue at his confession. Little fool. Playing with magic he does not understand. But then Solinde allows a joy to rise. This may be easier than she thought.

"It has," she says. "Do you know what it is you wish to Deal for?"

The lad grunts, and shifts, and scratches again. "I think so," he says at length. "But I'm not sure how to say it."

Solinde gives him an elegant shrug. "Say it however you wish. We Deal-Makers are bound to speak only the truth." *Though, not bound to clarity*, she thinks smugly. There are some things the mortals need not know, especially young men who cannot keep their eyes on her own. The lad hesitates still, so Solinde decides the calculated risk is worth it, and adds: "My name is Solinde. Will you give me yours?" She asks it sweetly, head tilted coquettishly.

The lad—he cannot be more than sixteen, or perhaps a runty seventeen—clears his throat. "Wy—" he begins, and then immediately snaps his mouth shut, eyes narrowing. "No," he finishes instead.

Solinde shrugs. "Ah, well," she says, keeping her voice

musical. "Tell me, then: what Deal can I make with you today, Master Summoner?"

"I want... I want my father back," the lad says.

"Is he dead?" Solinde asks. She must know into which realm she will have to stretch her powers.

"No, he... he's *boring*," the lad complains. "He used to go out on adventures and things, but now he's stuck being the stupid Lord of the Chipping, and he makes me study with tutors, and I *hate* it. He used to travel all over the place and fight monsters, and rut with wenches, and now all he does is ride some silly gelding around the Chipping and talk to farmers about the *harvest*. He invites the sheriff over for tea, and it is so *boring*. I *hate* it."

Solinde knows better than to try to talk her quarry out of his foolish wish, but her own loss stings her quickly, unexpectedly, and before she can hold back her tongue, she says: "But surely it is better to have your father here, now, than gone from your life?"

"I want to go out *with* him," the lad whines. "Mother said that when I was a man, I would have to leave her ship, that I would go to land and live with my father, and that I would get to go on his *adventures*. I grew up on the stories! It's all I wanted! But now I get here, and he's a boring old fart. All he does is hold parties and write letters. He doesn't even wench around anymore. He just makes stupid gross eyes at his stupid old trothed. He tries to get me to call the twat my *uncle*, and I *hate* it."

Solinde takes a moment to try to unravel the request behind the complaints. "So, you wish for your father to once more take up a life of roaming and adventure, and for you to be his squire?"

"Yes! That!" the lad says, pointing at her, imperious. "Do that!"

Solinde could manipulate the father's heart, that was easily enough done. She could plant a seed of desire to abandon his duties as a Chipping lord and return to this vagabond, migrant life the lad described. But if the man's lover is persistent, and his sense of duty too great, it might not be as permanent as the lad clearly desires. And she must provide what he desires. She must.

Solinde needs to ensure that the lad is grateful to her, is convinced that she has done her utmost for him, so that he can then be manipulated into giving up a great boon in return. And she has *just* the very great boon she wants from him in mind.

"And if your father abandons the seat of his Chipping," Solinde says softly, being certain to sound as if she is merely thinking out loud. "Who is next in line to inherit it? You, I should think. That would thwart your plans to go adventuring."

"I don't care!" the lad says, folding his arms and curving his shoulders miserably. "I'll run away with him anyway!"

"I'm not suggesting you will not," Solinde says. "But to prevent your father's trothed from retrieving you both, or the monarch from ordering him back, perhaps you ought to wish instead for someone to *replace* your father, rather than for your father to abandon his post?"

The lad looks up at her through his thick black eyelashes. There are spots on his forehead, and Solinde thinks that he could do with attending to his own hygiene a little more stringently; he is obviously of an age where wenches and the attendant activities that come with them are on his mind. He will have to pay a pretty coin for one to lay with him when he reeks of unwashed socks.

The lad's black eyes dart over her face, clearly searching for any sort of trickery, trying to decipher if he is being led into a trap.

He is, of course, but it has nothing to do with Solinde's suggestion that he summon a replacement.

"Who oversaw the Chipping while your father traveled?" she presses him.

"My uncle. My *real* uncle, that is."

"And where is your uncle now?"

The lad makes a face. "He went to another kingdom and married a scholar's daughter. At least, that's what my father says."

"And if he is brought back here, will he take up the mantle of lordling, do you think?"

The lad considers. "Father says that he was very duty-bound. He probably would."

"Well then," Solinde says gently. "That is easily done. I shall summon this uncle, your father's brother, for you."

"Might as well bring his wife, too," the lad mutters. "Or he'll probably just go away again to look for her. They're in *love*, Father says."

"And you feel love is abhorrent?"

The lad shrugs with a studied nonchalance. His face is easy to read, however, and the pain that swims across it tells a clear tale. He has loved in the past, deeply, and it has hurt him. Solinde recalls that he said his mother had abandoned him to the care of his father, and wonders how any mother could do such a horrid thing.

She has not been asked to do it, but if she ever learns this mother's name, she might choose to seek the woman out and concoct a Deal that will see her shredded, just as she has shredded her son's affection.

"I will do this," Solinde says. "But now, we must agree to our terms."

The lad looks up, straightens again, and frowns. "Well, what do you want?"

Solinde laughs, her flirtatious tinkly-bell laugh, and the lad blinks, momentarily dazed. Good. "My dear sweeting, I cannot demand. The rules say you must offer something of equal value. I may only say yes, or no."

"Equal value?" the lad muses.

"I am bringing two people into this house. That is no small feat of magic," Solinde whispers.

"Two lives..." the lad says. "Oh, got it! Will you take away my father's trothed?" His eyes glimmer with a sudden blood thirst, and the corner of his lip curls. "Could you kill him?"

"I cannot kill for a Deal," Solinde says with complete honesty. If Deal-Maker Spirits could kill as a component of a Deal, she would have been free of her mortal husband decades ago, and he whom she seeks would never have been sent away to begin with. Worse still, her husband had made it part of her bound condition to safeguard his life. She'd been forced to nurse him when he'd gouged his leg with a scythe and the wound had turned putrid. Oh, how she wished to break the laws of the Deal-Makers then.

"Bugger," the lad swears. "Then, um... two lives, huh..." He scratches his head again. "I don't really... um, is there someone *you* want?"

Solinde feels a thrill tremble up her spine. "Yes," she says, her voice rumbling full of honesty and desire.

"And... um, are they within my power to give to you?" the lad asks, his own excitement making him eager to please.

"You have the power to send me where he is, yes."

The lad thrusts out his hand. "Then that's my deal. You bring my uncle and his wife here, and I'll wish for you to go to him? Is that fair? Two for one, I mean?"

"If you will do me this, I will call it fair," Solinde says, raising her hand for the shake.

"But it isn't, really," the lad says, recoiling. "Hold on, will that backfire on me?"

Solinde grits her teeth and tries to maintain her smile. She wishes to give him no answer, but the lad presses.

"Will it?"

Between clenched teeth, she says, "I promise that he will bring no harm upon you."

The lad's eyes widen. "But, wait, he might harm others?"

"No one you care for, I swear to it. Now—take my hand!"

The lad clearly wants his life of adventure with his father badly enough that he is willing to trust her. Fool. He reaches out and, before he can change his mind any further, Solinde snatches his hand. Their flesh tingles and sparks where it touches, the heat of the Deal-Magic pouring down her spine like warm honey.

"Oh, yes!" she cries, the pleasure of the magic running in orgasmic rivers under her skin. Around her, the previously stale air begins to churn. The parchment on the desk flutters to the floor, though the breeze is not strong enough to wipe out her Sigil in the hearth ash. "I reach out and summon to you the brother of your father and his wife!"

Solinde closes her eyes, watches behind the lids as the tendrils of Deal-Magic begin to churn and writhe, reaching out, across Hain, across Urland and Brystal and Gadot, out over the seas, out into the skies and... touches nothing. Nothing!

"Another kingdom!" Solinde spits, eyes snapping open. "You little liar! They are in another *realm*. They are beyond the veil of the skies!"

"They are?" the lad cries, and tries to tug his hand away. "I didn't know. I didn't know! Let me go!"

"Though it will weaken me near unto death, I will do it!" Solinde shouts over his pleas. "For he whom I want resides in another realm as well. It will be equal. All you must do is say his name."

"I will!" the lad says. "I will. Just let me go! It burns!"

"Say that you gift to me Varnet, son of Edvane, first high priest of Kingskeep!"

"I gift to you Varn—hey, no! Wait a minute!" the lad yelps. "I know who that is!"

"Say it!"

"No!" the boy says. "No, I won't!"

"Say it!" Solinde screeches, squeezing his hand so hard that the lad's knees go out from under him, and he is dangling from her grasp. "We have a Deal! *Bring him to me!*"

"No!"

"Then you forfeit!" Solinde shrieks. "You are a liar, and I will take my prize!"

"What?" the lad sobs. "No, no, let me go!"

"You have shaken hands with a Deal-Maker, boy!" Solinde bows low over him, pinching the side of his mouth in a taloned grip. "I will keep my side of the Deal, as I am bound to do, but you have perjured yourself to me."

"I didn't know!"

"And in recompense for your lies, in exchange for the promise you will not keep, I shall have your tongue. You will tell no more falsehoods. And I shall consume every Word you know. I shall possess your *magic!*"

The lad struggles and squirms, but he is only mortal. Solinde's kiss is harsh, and bloody, and deep. She scrapes the flesh from his tongue with her teeth, and scrapes with it every word and Word he kept there. She swallows his blood, his voice, his speech, his lies.

As the wind around them begins to calm, a pounding comes from the other side of the door.

"Wyndam!" a voice bellows on the other side. "Unlock this door! What is all that ruckus? Wyndam!"

Solinde's lips spread into a bloody smile. "You shall have what you wanted, *Wyndam*, but know that you will never be favored above your father's trothed now. Not incomplete. Not as a *mute.*"

Then she tosses the lad away from her. He falls back against the hearth, and even as he reaches up to verify that he still has his tongue, his other arm sprawls back into the ash, severing Solinde's Sigil.

What happens next does so nearly simultaneously.

Deep behind her breastbone, Solinde feels the Call rupture.

The lad scrambles to his feet and pockets the broken compass, every line of his body filled with terror. He reaches around, knocks a book out of its place, and then pulls on a hidden ring on the wall that was behind it. A door opens, and the lad slips through like an eel.

Behind her, a man whom Solinde assumes is Wyndam's father smashes open the main door.

Solinde, quickly losing solidity, turns. She has only enough time to see his gray-streaked queue of blond hair, the straight white teeth, the cleft jaw and powerful build. She has only enough time to realize that she has been summoned by the son of the one mortal she would happily, *happily,* for the sake of her family, break the rules of the Deal-Maker Spirits and murder.

"No!" she screeches, infuriated, as the lad's accidental dismissal turns her to mist, sends her hurtling out of the room, back to far-away Gadot and away from *Kintyre Turn.*

In a heartbeat, she is across the world from the wretch.

Fury fills Solinde, and in turn, the skies above the hundred isles and canals of the water-surrounded Ertse scream. Solinde walks on waterspouts across the Skipping Lakes. It is a reckless waste of the last of her strength, but she is too angry to care. She is fatigued, drained, half-dead. Her power is stretched thin, as dry as dust from the sheer magnitude of the task, from pulling two adult humans through the realms of the skies and into Hain. She thinks that were she not sent back to an island nation when the Call was broken, she might have perished immediately. As it is, Luck decided to roll up a decent score on her dice, instead.

She drinks in the seawater around her, gluts herself on the replenishing power of it, punishing all around her for her lost opportunity to snuff out Kintyre Turn forever.

The blood on her tongue tells the tale of the lad's upbringing. He had all the kinds of Words the son of a sailor ought—Words of Navigation, Words of Finding, Words of Direction. Words to keep vermin out of supplies, and Words to keep a blade sharp. Words of Persuasion, and Words of Cunning. Words enough for the son of that despicable, hateful man who dared call himself *hero*.

Words that belong to Solinde now; Words that will not melt away after their use, for she named them as her forfeit. And to steal the magic of another creature, to wield that which her kind was not born to wield, is more than recompense enough for two worthless, short-lived humans.

She uses the Words that are hers now. In Ertse, she finds the totem in the errant shadow that will not stay attached to its mortal, and blows it out like a candle.

It is daylight when she does so. When night comes and the survivors of Ertse regard the sky from their rafts of splintered timbers, whole constellations have been snuffed out of existence.

FIVE

The first thing that returns to me is the unbearable sensation of vertigo and nausea. Voluntarily stepping from my world into Pip's was significantly less hard on my stomach and head than being yanked into this one, whichever and wherever it is. I hope, as I lay on the ground, praying that the swirling and heaving of the land will quickly settle. That I have come alone.

Beside me, Alis's sharp, startled whimper dashes all hopes of my being solitary. "Daaaa!" she screams once she has her breath back, hiccupping when she's used it all up, sucking desperately to refill her lungs around her shock. I curl onto my side, and my daughter, sprawled out on the ground and stiff with terror, *shrieks*.

I grope out, missing her little hand on the first go because of the heaving, but get my fingers around her wrist on the second. With my arm as a tether, she crawls up onto my chest and buries into my neck within seconds. "Daaaa—" she wails, and I weave my fingers into her hair, my breath soft on her ear as I make soothing noises, low and gentle. She gulps and gasps, and there is no misery, none at all, so sharp as that of your child being unable to *breathe*.

"Da's here," I whisper against her downy, auburn-black curls, rubbing her back. "Deep breaths, now. You're well, my sweeting. You're well."

"Dah-Daaaa..." she moans, and then goes limp against my chest, miserable and exhausted from her tantrum.

"Forsyth?" comes another groan, and Pip finds the bundle of our bodies before I can turn my head to seek her out. She collapses against my other shoulder, and I feel crushed to the floor by the blanket of my family. It is a welcome and grounding weight, for it means that while I do not know where we are, I do know that we are together, and whole.

"And Reed?" I ask, unable to lift my head to check. The edges of my vision are still dim and blurry. I clench my eyes shut again.

Pip shakes her own head against my chest. Well, that is a blessing at least. The last person I want here is that be-damned Writer of ours. Only the heavens know what he would do if he were to visit his own world—and only the heavens know what this world might do to him in return.

I would wager a large sum on the possibility that there would be more people like the Viceroy, who, upon learning of Reed's identity, would blame him for all their misfortunes and sorrows. And, in the most esoteric sense, they would not be incorrect. For all that we have a tentative ceasefire, my creator and I, I have no desire to spend the entirety of our time here—however long that may be (oh, Writer, are we stuck here now, *forever*? Is there any going back at all?)—protecting that fat, self-important lout from the products of his own shallow, misogynistic imagination.

And Pip would *make* me protect him, despite their enmity.

If, of course, it is into his world that we even *have* been pulled. With books vanishing as they have been, it is entirely possible that we have been catapulted into another realm entirely. Perhaps my realm has vanished, which is why we are here. Perhaps *Pip's* realm is the one that dissolved, and we were shunted sideways into another.

When my dizziness has passed enough for me to open my eyes without the fear of vomiting, I do so.

"Oh," I say, focusing on the rich, wooden ceiling above me—and the concerned face that sticks itself into my eyeline. "Well then. No need to fear. I know *exactly* where we are."

"I should hope so, brother," Kintyre says from above me. He then reaches down a hand to help me up off the rug in my old study.

Attaining an upright position is more of a challenge than I care to admit. Kintyre levers me upward, and I lean back against the desk, cradling Alis against my hip. Bevel, who came into the room just as I was standing, helps Pip. He pats her arm gently and says, "Well come, Lucy Piper. Or is it Turn, now?"

Pip grimaces. "Hereabouts? Better make it Turn."

Kintyre thuds one big, meaty palm square against my back, jolting me a little, and laughs at my sideways glare. "Congratulations are in order then, little brother!"

"Thank you," I say, deciding that if his roughhousing hasn't decreased, at least his manners have improved in the two years I have been absent.

"And who is this wee lass?" Bevel asks, peering at Alis, looking both enchanted and besotted. Bevel always did adore children. He longs, I think, for at least one of his own. The object of his study promptly reaches out and grabs his nose; my daughter has never been shy of strangers. Bevel laughs and detaches her gently, then places kisses in each of her palms.

Alis grunts, startled, and then holds her hands up to me as if to show me what Bevel has done, and to ask why.

"Kisses, sweeting," I say, "From your Uncle Bevel."

"'Isses, Da," Alis says gravely.

Bevel straightens, and his cheeks take on a pleased flush at the honorific. "Oh, well then. Aye, thank you."

"My niece?" Kintyre asks, a little stupidly, I think, for what other babe in arms would I have brought to Lysse? And then pointedly told that his Paired is her uncle?

"Alis Mei Piper Turn," Pip says.

"Alis," Kintyre echoes, and swallows hard. He blinks a few times, and then reaches out, slowly, gently, to run the back of his knuckles over Alis's cheek. "Mother would have been very pleased."

"Aye," I say. "That she would."

"'Isses!" Alis demands imperiously, holding out her hands to her other uncle, and Kintyre obliges with a roguish smile and a courtly bow.

As Kintyre and Bevel fuss over my daughter, I take a quick moment to take in the room. It looks virtually untouched, except for the smashed handle on the door and the way one of the panels is hanging askew in its jamb. On the hearth is a pile of ash and soot—most probably knocked onto the stone by an errant animal attempting to climb down the chimney—and the decanter of Drebbinshire Whiskey I'd kept on the credenza has vanished.

Otherwise, my study is still my study, untouched and unused by my brother. And so it is that there, at that moment, in my study - while still uncertain on my feet, my wife plastered to my side, her own head undoubtedly swimming - that I am introduced to the other new member of House Turn.

The soft click of a boot-step on the wooden floor beyond the study doors attracts my attention, and I look up from where Bevel is making ridiculous hedgehoggy faces at Alis. A young lad's head pokes around the door, and for a moment, I think perhaps he might be a new scullery boy my brother has hired, for there is a smudge on his cheek, as if he has been blacking the kitchen stove.

But when he straightens and stands fully in the doorway, I can see that his clothing is of too fine a make for him to be hired help. He is doing up a hastily donned jacquard waistcoat of Turn-russet, his shirt tails are untucked, and his neckcloth still hangs limp across his shoulders. Lazy. Beneath his shirt is a braided-hemp necklace, from which dangles a large scale that must have come from a kraken or mer-drake.

"Wyndam!" Kintyre says, following my eyeline to the door. "I thought you were in the study."

The lad shakes his head, sullen, and comes in when Kintyre waves him forward. He fiddles a bit with his neckcloth, but never makes an actual attempt to tie it. There is a spot of blood on his palm, and more soot on his fingertips, and I wonder if he's been sitting against a hearth, playing in the ashes as if they were finger paints, the way Kintyre used to do. The lad seems too old for that sort of childish distraction, however.

I would have chastised him for his slovenly appearance before guests were I lordling, but I see that neither Kintyre nor Bevel are wearing their own neckcloths. Instead, both wear well-tailored day trousers, house slippers, and shirts. Neither have waistcoats. Bevel wears a short house-robe of Dom-amethy, dewy and bright, unlike the dusty, ratty travel short-robe he used to wear, with Turn-russet embroidery along the hems that puts me in mind of autumn leaves. And my brother is wearing a Turn-russet slashed doublet, left open, like the ridiculously out of fashion and romantic hero he clearly still sees himself as embodying.

I feel instantly underdressed in my own chinos and purple-gingham cotton button-down. Pip is attired for school, at least, though her pencil skirt is perilously form-fitting and short, according to Hainish fashion. Of the six of us, only Alis is properly dressed, wearing a flouncy dress that covers her toes.

The lad winces when Kintyre manhandles him to stand before him, his large hands on the lad's narrow, slumped shoulders. Kintyre grins, but the lad's eyes are red-rimmed, and his puff of black hair is askew. I wonder what he could have been doing before our noisy arrival that has him looking so furtive. Then I remember what it was like to be a lad of his age, with the hormones, the desperation for time alone, and the things one may do to one's self while undressed, and decide not to wonder any further.

And, because it is characteristic of my brother to always attempt to outdo my accomplishments, it is then that Pip and I meet our nephew: "This is Wyndam Turn," Kintyre says proudly, chin jutting out, chest puffed. "My son."

The lad squirms, and Bevel says, out the side of his mouth: "Bow, Wyndam." Wyndam shoots a glare filled with poison at Bevel. Bevel holds his hands up, as if begging a mercy, and says, "Right, yes, I know. I'm not your father, and I can't tell you what to do. But it's polite, Wyn."

Wyndam rolls his eyes and dips what has to be the single most sarcastic bow ever offered to another human being.

Instead of bowing back, as would have been proper, I offer my free hand to shake. "Forsyth Turn," I say.

Wyndam goggles up at me, and I wonder if my brother has ever spoken of me to the lad. Or maybe his shock comes from the way I am according him the respect of a fellow adult. He wipes his sooty, bloodied hand on his trouser leg.

From what Bevel said, and how he said it, I am already painting a picture in my mind of a young man, newly in the charge of my brother and his Paired, resentful of being treated like a child by two adults who cannot remember that at the lad's age, we all thought ourselves mature, and worldly, and no longer children.

Wyndam takes my hand and shakes it slowly, his grip calculatingly perfect—not too hard, not too limp. He is determined to be taken seriously. He opens his mouth to say something, but then clearly thinks better of it and closes it again. I wonder if his voice is breaking and if he is embarrassed.

I take the length of the hand-shake to study him. The lad must be no older than fifteen, and sullen and silent in a way that reminds me terribly of Kintyre at that age. He has a much darker complexion than any simple tan could afford, which speaks of Gadot ancestry and many long days in the sun. His hair is so black that it shines blue in the sunlight streaming through my study windows—and dancing with dust motes, I notice—and is of a full, wiry, curly texture that no Turn before him has ever sported. His eyes are darker than Kintyre's as well, a jet color that glitters with curiosity.

But despite this coloring, my nephew is a spitting image of my brother in his youth— the jaw, the mouth, even the furrow between his eyebrows when he glowers, though his nose is a bit wider. I have seen people in Pip's world of mixed African and white descent, but never have I seen a young man for whom the mix has been such a distinct advantage. Wyndam has an open, pleasant sort of look to his face, and the kind of abstract beauty that comes of two very classically attractive parents.

In the end, though, it is the scale necklace that solidifies my deduction.

The lad could only be the by-blow of Kintyre Turn and Isobin, pirate royalty and captain of *The Salty Queen*. I do a quick mental calculation and decide that, yes, he must have been the result of an assignation that took place during the adventure Bevel titled *The Siren of the Sunsong Sea.*

As a Shadow Hand who liked to keep eyes on the known troublemakers, I had long learned that Isobin had been gifted with a child. I had, at the time, thought that knowing the identity of the lad's sire was unimportant. His parentage only mattered on the maternal side, as he was aboard ship. Now, I regret not pursuing the matter, for it appears as if Isobin has left him here upon his maturity, as female pirates are wont to do with boy children.

If I had still been Lordling Turn, would I have learned of my brother's offspring—the heir to the Turn seat—sooner? Lineages are hard to tell in a round-faced babe, and the pirate queen makes a point of never stepping on land, except for the gravest of events. Had I not sought the information as Shadow Hand, it is possible I would have been ignorant of the lad's existence until the moment Isobin banged on my door and thrust him at me.

Wyndam turns to Pip and bows again, a little more gracious and honest this time, and Pip sticks out her hand to shake as well. "Lucy Turn," Pip says, and it's a thrill to hear her present herself as such. A delicious little shiver crawls up my spine, and I hide my predatory grin behind Alis as I shift her around to face outward.

Bevel, who was always the keeper of my brother's manners, looks thoroughly scandalized by Pip's lack of a curtsy. But Wyndam grins, reaches out, takes her hand, and kisses the back of it.

"Yup," Pip says, looking up at Kintyre once Wyndam has given her hand back. "Definitely your son."

Kintyre guffaws, slapping Wyndam on the back, and the lad looks up at him, clearly pleased and basking in his father's affection.

"And this is our daughter Alis, your first cousin." I finish the introductions, and Alis, sensing all eyes on her, demands, "'Isses, 'isses!"

Wyndam looks at her as if she is about to projectile vomit on him at any moment— which, to be fair, would have been a probable and logical worry six months ago— so I do not force her on the lad.

"Well, now," Bevel says. "How about we let the staff into the study, Kin, and we take Forssy's family into the nook?"

"The nook?" Pip asks. Bevel offers her his arm; she pretends she doesn't see it and walks herself out.

"The nook" turns out to be my little breakfasting room, which I had carved out of a strange architectural pocket between the kitchen and the dining room that had once been used as a staging area for servers during big feasts. As I had held no feasts, and very few balls, it was unused during my tenure. I'd eaten here often, when I felt too lonely to eat in the large banquet room, or too humble to demand my servants fetch trays and drink up and down the many stairs of Turn Hall. When Pip came to me, a second chair had been added to the table, and it looks now as if a third has been fetched from the banquet hall. Two more appear when Bevel pokes his head into the kitchen proper—one carried by Cook, the other by my former butler, Velshi.

Cook immediately drops her chair, then swoops in and pulls Alis out of my startled hands, bouncing and cooing. Her eyes sparkle as Alis's startled gasp turns into giggles of delight, and Cook's apple-cheeks flush with joy. "Oh, Master Turn!" she exclaims, turning Alis in circles. "Oh, how lovely! I always knew it would be you," she says, pointing slyly at Pip.

My wife isn't certain how to take that, but seems to be enjoying Cook's happiness all the same. She claims the abandoned chair and tucks up to the table.

Velshi sets down his own chair and offers me a

solemn bow and a steady handshake. Velshi has always been the epitome of the serious, professional butler, so I am put slightly off-kilter when his mouth—which, to the best of my knowledge, has never produced a smile in the entirety of his life—stretches and curves into a genuine representation of good cheer. I fancy I can hear the sound of ice cracking.

"My very hearty congratulations, sir. And well come. You've been missed, sir."

"Th-thank you, V-velshi," I stammer, stunned.

Cook drops Alis into Pip's arms, and bustles over to pinch my cheeks, poke at my stomach, and croon, "Too thin, too thin, Master! Don't you worry, I'll get a rabbit pie made up quick as a maenad with a satyr on her hem." And then she is gone, back to the kitchen like she has been shot from a crossbow, doing, I assume, as she promised, and striving to be nurturing in a way I adored all through my sweets-laden childhood, and which I now understand is a very shallow bit of characterization on my Writer's part indeed. As if all married women of a "certain age" want only to coddle babies, spoil children, and feed up men.

Velshi follows after her, and I cannot help but smirk at the dumbfounded look of betrayal on Kintyre's face.

"They've never behaved like that with *me*," he says, and it's dangerously close to a whine. "And what does that mean, Forsyth has been *missed*? Bev!" he says, turning stricken, nail-blue eyes to his lover. "Am I a bad master?"

Bevel only laughs and pats Kintyre on the forearm. "It's only that you're not Forssy," he says. "They knew him his whole life."

"I grew up here, too!" Kintyre pouts.

"You left at eighteen and didn't come back to stay until two years ago," Bevel says lightly, clearly too wise in the ways of my brother's tempers to take the bait, neatly sidestepping the volley of barbed sniping that Kintyre is trying to initiate. Instead, Bevel just sits in what used to be my chair.

There is a credenza in nearly every room used by the family in Turn Hall, which is always kept stocked with water, cups, and the other necessities of life—ink bottles, parchment, quills, small purses for paying messengers, bells to summon servants, extra candles, and the like. The nook's credenza now also comes stocked with Bevel's pipe and orange blossom hash, apparently, for he sets about packing a pipe.

"Not around the baby, please," Pip says, stopping him before Bevel can strike his match.

He looks up at her, startled.

"Seriously," she says.

With a sigh, he taps the hash back into its pouch, but does not put his smoking box away. Instead, he turns his pipe over and over in his hands, as if debating whether to stay or go into the kitchen for his smoke.

In the time that takes, I find my own chair. I am happy to sink down, my head not entirely clear just yet. Though, I wonder if perhaps my blinking vertigo is less from being sucked back into the realm of my birth and more because I have suddenly been presented with a nephew.

I had always assumed that Alis would be the only child of her generation, the true heir of the Turn seat, the Lady of Turnshire. Of course, she would have had to marry to gain power in this realm (in this way, the nobility of Pip's realm is enviably more fair), but knowing my daughter and the two people who will be raising her, she would have found a husband with whom it was worth sharing the power and responsibility of caring for the people of Lysse.

Lewko Pointe the younger, I had secretly thought,

would make an excellent match for my daughter. The boy had been four when last I saw him, and possessed of a sweet and patient temperament which had led into a habit of bringing hurt animals to his nanny to doctor. The familiar melancholic wave of missing my only friend flares fierce, followed by the sudden and literally breathtaking realization that I am *here*. I am back. I can see Sheriff Pointe. I can shake his hand and embrace him. I can kiss his wife's cheek, and dandle his son on my knee. I can share my own joys with him.

A surge of longing so fierce rises up within me that I actually catch myself angling my body toward Law Manor. The estate borders Turn Hall—I could call for a horse and be there within the half hour. Pip catches my sudden change of posture, the direction in which I am facing, and runs her palm across my arm, soothing.

"Later," she whispers. "Eat first. He'll still be there."

"Who?" Kintyre asks, as he finishes fussing with the chairs and sits as well.

"Sheriff Pointe," I say. "He is still at Law Manor, I hope?" I hope; I *pray*. "He has not been promoted away, or...?" I can't even contemplate a tragic alternative. I cannot even blink as I seek out my brother's gaze, desperate to know.

"He's there," Kintyre says, careless in his reassurance, but my relief is so profound it is nearly palpable. "He's fine. That boy of his is a mad hellion, though."

"Lewko?" I ask, sinking back in my seat and chuckling. "I cannot fathom it."

"Fathom it," Kintyre says darkly.

"He is not," Bevel tuts at Kintyre. "You just don't like that his riding seat is so fine at six, when Wyndam can barely keep on his at seventeen." He turns to us apologetically, with a shrug. "Wyn never got the chance to ride at sea. His mother is—"

"Queen Isobin. Yes, I figured that," I say, suddenly impatient. I turn to face the lad, but find only an empty chair.

"Where...?"

Bevel groans and pinches the bridge of his nose, a gesture I have often seen him perform when my brother exasperates him. It seems now that he has two Turns to make this gesture over. "I swear, Kin, your kid has worse manners than you."

"Where do you think—"

"How am I supposed to know?" Bevel snipes back. "As he's very fond of pointing out, Kin, I'm not actually his father. Go find him."

"Wyndam!" Kintyre bellows instead. "Wyndam! Get back down here!"

He sounds so very much like our own father for a moment that I am actually struck speechless. Without my say-so, I feel my shoulders curling down, my head dipping submissively, my tongue fluttering in my mouth, my heart leaping up to flap against my larynx.

Pip stares at me, wide-eyed at the transformation, and I fight against the instinct to hide from that voice. I straighten myself out and put on my Shadow Hand persona like a shield, slow and deliberate. Armed.

"Da da dahhh?" Alis whines, and puts her hands over her ears.

"Q-qu-quite right, sweeting," I say to her. "Kintyre, please. Don't roar like a wounded bull. Use your feet to find him."

"Well, that didn't take long!" Kintyre snarls at me, and it's clear his annoyance at his son's disappearance has been transferred squarely onto me. "Been back an hour, and you're already telling me what to do! I assume by the end of the second hour, you'll be telling me that you'll be having back the Chipping, as well?"

"Kintyre!" Bevel yelps.

Normally, this is where I would back down, but I have grown a spine since I met Pip, and instead, I volley back: "I may have to if this is how you treat those in your care. For goodness' sake, Kintyre Turn, no person should be called to heel like a dog! Have some sense, you blistering great ogre."

Kintyre stares at me in stunned shock, surprised that I have growled back, and he blinks like a dazed cat. Then he lets out a great guffaw of laughter. "Aye, well then," he says jovially, slapping me on the shoulder in what I am sure is meant to be brotherly camaraderie, but instead just feels like forming bruises. "There's the Shadow Hand, back again."

He stares at me for a moment, and I wonder if I have gotten something on my face. Then he leans forward and wraps his arms around my shoulders, drawing me against his broad chest in a firm hug. I turn my head to the side just quickly enough to avoid suffocating against his ridiculous musculature.

"I've missed you, little brother," he says.

"Blast it, Kintyre," I say softly. "And I you."

I cling back for a long moment. Kintyre is too warm, the air stifling, and the back of my eyes are burning, but I am happy. I feel safe, and welcome.

I am *home.*

Kintyre clears his throat and pulls away, dashes at his eyes before anyone can tell if he's actually been crying, and cranes his head around.

"By the Writer's left nutsack, that boy is never where he should be," he swears, and Pip and I can't help the tandem giggle that escapes from us both when we lock eyes. As Pip would say, today has been an emotional rollercoaster, and I think we are both feeling a little punchy.

"What's so funny about the Writer's nutsack?" Bevel

asks, all seriousness, and Pip doubles over, howling with laughter.

I had once made a vow to myself that I would wed Pip and make her smile every day, and that together, we would laugh away every shadow with which my father had stained Turn Hall. I had given up that dream when I crossed into her world, fully expecting never to return to this one.

Now that we are here, though, I decide that right now, in this nook, is the perfect place to renew it. Alis, however, looks genuinely concerned for her mother, and I transfer our daughter back over to my lap.

"Adadadahhh," she says, with a very serious frown.

"I know, sweeting. Your mother has gone mad; it's a very deep tragedy."

"Oh, fuck off." Pip chuckles with affection, lifting her head from the table.

Kintyre and Bevel exchange a confused glance. Bevel mouths the word "fuck" at my brother, and Pip is sent off into another fit of giggles.

Cook interrupts then with the full, everyday tea service—remarkably intact after two years of being used to serve the Great Hero of Hain, which I will count in my brother's favor— and the promised rabbit pie. Bevel serves, and Wyndam appears like a wraith as soon as the last slice is set down at his empty seat.

"Ah," Bevel says. "You'll ignore when your father calls, but set out a meal, and it's like Words of Summoning have been Spoken." His tone is a little more snide than I am used to hearing from Bevel. Wyndam scowls mulishly in response, and digs in without so much as a "by your leave, milord." At first, I am disappointed in Bevel, especially knowing how fond he is of his twin nephews, but then he pushes the remaining pie toward Wyndam as unobtrusively as possible in apology. If

Wyndam notices, he doesn't look up. He just scoops up the pie-plate and eats straight from the dish, his first piece still hoarded before him on his plate.

Bevel catches me watching, and he raises his eyebrow. It's not a challenge so much as an acknowledgment that yes, he is exasperated, but how can one not love a child, no matter how infuriating they may be? I am reminded in this moment that I left the Shadow's Mask to him, and he now possesses all the knowledge I had ever accumulated. In short, he knows all that I know about him. There is a kinship between us now, stronger than friendship, stronger even than brothers, I think. His look reminds me that he knows what I think of him, and that he doesn't mind.

Not certain if I should be disconcerted or not, I dig into my own pie, groaning at the first savory, flaky, buttery bite. Oh. Oh, how I have missed Cook's pies. There are a hundred thousand foods and flavors in Pip's realm, wonders that I had never tasted before, but this... this tastes of home. Heat surges against the back of my eyes again, my vision starting to swim with the tears of joy that threaten to spill over my lashes. I blink rapidly to keep from having an emotional breakdown over pie, and fish a bit of carrot out of the rich gravy. I blow on it to cool it, and present it to Alis.

She is getting to be of the age where she prefers to transfer food into her mouth on her own, so instead of simply opening her lips, she takes the carrot from my hand, and then shoves it in her mouth.

Our little group is silent as we polish off Cook's offering, save for Alis, who seems to be narrating her adventure in pie-eating to Library. I had not thought the little plushie had come along for the ride, but Pip had pulled it from her pocket as soon as Alis had started to fuss.

Tea and pie consumed, Wyndam makes to slink off,

but Kintyre puts a hand on his shoulder and holds him in place.

"We are about to have a very serious conversation, Wyndam, and you're old enough to hear this, I think," Kintyre says. He raises his eyes to Bevel, who nods. Wyndam looks eager and pleased, and sits up, attentive. "Except, I'm not sure where to start."

"Well," Bevel says, shifting. "Uh. Well. You know about the Writer, and Readers, of course, Wyn."

The lad nods, confusion curling over his brows. He doesn't see where this is leading, but I do. Pip and I also nod at each other, agreeing that we don't mind if Wyndam knows the truth of our realm's existence, so long as it won't be disturbing to him. Wyndam is seventeen, Bevel said. And he was considered mature enough to be ejected from *The Salty Queen*. Kintyre seems to have taken that as a token that he can be present for what is going to be, most probably, a very long, very detailed, and potentially disturbing discussion.

"Your Aunt Lucy here is..." Bevel swallows hard and seems to struggle with the truth of it for a moment. He has had two years to come to terms with the idea that our genesis myths are all true. But he does not know that Kintyre is the main character of the novels, for Pip and I felt that no one needed to have that knowledge. Nor, we decided, was it fair to tell anyone and risk them feeling secondary or lesser.

Pitying Bevel, I decide to take the burden of revelation from him and say: "She is a Reader."

Wyndam's eyes and mouth drop wide, and he snaps his head around to stare in wonder at my wife.

"I know we said that your Uncle Forsyth had gone far away to marry a scholar's daughter," Kintyre says. "And that is, more or less, true. Just, the far away he went to was into the Writer's realm, beyond the veil of the skies."

Wyndam's look of awe-filled incredulity falls on me. It is... discomfiting. The lad looks as if he wishes to ask a question, but again changes his mind at the last moment, snapping his mouth closed. I wonder if I will ever hear my nephew's voice. He looks to Bevel, clearly eager for Bevel to continue.

"Well, now they're back, because..." Bevel says, lamely, returning to storyteller mode. He stops and clears his throat, because he doesn't actually *know* the reason. "I... I don't know why."

Wyndam's posture sinks, and he hides his face behind his hair again, so that I cannot parse the sudden mercurial shift in his expression. Is he disappointed?

"At first, I thought it was due to bad luck," I say, stepping in to take up our side of the story. "I turned away a guest on the Night of Light."

"It's bad luck?" Pip asks, perking up. "You could have said. I didn't want him there either, but—"

"No," I say, forestalling her. "No, it was the correct thing to do at the time. But part of the reason I invited him over today... yesterday? Today. It was... an attempt to rectify that. As well as the... erm, other reasons."

I don't particularly want to have the argument about abandoning my wife and child again, especially not in front of my brother and his own small family.

"But then, there are the books," Pip says, and it is with a sort of forgiveness, an apology for not having believed me before, and an honest willingness to do so now.

"Books?" Bevel asks. He taps his pipe against the tabletop thoughtfully, clearly longing for his tobacco now that tea is finished.

Pip nods. "Stories are disappearing from my world, but apparently, Forsyth, Alis, and... uh... your Writer remember."

"You *converse* with the Writer?" Kintyre asks, agog.

"Unfortunately," is my rebuttal, and I cannot hold back a grimace. "He is too much like our father for my liking."

Kintyre makes a face, like he has eaten something foul, and it is so childish and ridiculous that I cannot help but chuckle. Wyndam looks intrigued, but I shake my head at him, guessing what he is thinking.

"Algar Turn was neither a man to emulate, nor one to grant infamy," I tell the lad. "He will get exactly what he deserves if we simply do not speak of the drunken, bitter, mean old bastard at all."

Wyndam's hope melts into mulishness, but he does as I request and does not ask. For all that he is sullen and stubborn, he seems to be the sort reared to follow orders. Again, I am reminded that he grew up on the greatest pirate ship in Isobin's water-borne kingdom—as a Prince of Pirates most likely. He will be used to following orders.

I wonder how much different his life has become, and if my brother has had any care to help him adjust. The fall from prince to backwater country lord's son is, I assume, a steep one.

"Back to the books," Pip says. "I feel like this all has to connect."

"I agree," I say. "I would like to do an inventory of my study's contents, to see if there are things there that have disappeared."

"I should help," Pip says. "You told me about tons of books when I was here. You read to me from most of the ones you have. If I don't remember missing books in my realm, you might not remember missing books in yours. But *I* might."

"An unsettling thought," I say, "but a good idea. Very well." We both stand.

"If you want your hands free, you better give me the babe," Bevel says, standing and putting out his arms for

Alis. I hesitate. Only Martin, Mei Fan, and *wai po* have ever minded my child when neither Pip nor I were available. "Come on," Bevel wheedles. "Give me my niece. I have three of them already. And ten nephews, to boot. I know what I'm doing."

I hand Alis over, and she seems to be fine with the transfer. She pets Bevel's dishwater-blond hair, seeming to be entranced by the gray strands that catch in the sunlight. Well, that is a relief. It is good to know that there will be at least one other adult to help with Alis in this realm. I suppose I am meant to trust Kintyre with her, as well, but I am also aware that he's never had to watch a baby before. Wyndam was never in his charge when he was young, and I know that Kintyre rarely stayed in Bynnbakker with Bevel when the latter went home for family visits.

"But what have the books to do with anything?" Kintyre asks, standing as well. Wyndam stays in his seat, eyeing the empty pie dish forlornly. Ah, to be young and a bottomless pit again.

"I do not know," I confess. "But it is both too great a coincidence to really be one, and a place to start."

"Forsyth, I don't know if you saw, but the light when you arrived, it looked like—" He cuts himself off with a glance toward Wyndam, clearly deciding not to finish his sentence. I nod, understanding that he is referring to the Deal-Maker Spirit, Neris, who called Pip down into this realm, and sent the two of us to hers.

"I have no answer for that," I confess. "But I hope to have it soon."

"Of course, the real question is, why?" Pip says. "However it was that we got here, we're here now. The important part is *what for?*"

THIMBLES AND BUTTONS

The milkmaid that Solinde targets next is lush. She tastes of cream and strawberries, and smells of cow dung and straw. She is passive in a way that Solinde has missed, while wedded to a man. The maid lays back and spreads sweet, and says thank you in a trembling voice even as Solinde pulls the knowledge of the place where she has stored the totem from each kiss.

Solinde leaves the milkmaid flushed, skirts rucked up, likely to be found in the hayloft by her master in such a state, and dismissed. Solinde travels west to Nevand, skirting the great citadel of Crownsnest, capital of Gadot, and its silver and crystal palace. The town is exactly halfway between the Stoat Forest and the green belt of farmland that surrounds the kingdom's shining capital. Nevand has grown at the same rate as the palace, though in comfort and entertainment rather than grandeur. The town is always full of festivals and special markets, filled with play and an immortal youthfulness, entertainments and theatres on every street corner.

Nevand is a city of service—inns and taverns, blacksmiths and wagon repair shops, makers of traveling supplies, road-provisions, and fine clothing all lining the major thoroughfare. The broad way behind it is equally lined with every sort of entertainment establishment that the wholesome or the unwholesome could seek while resting from the road. Nevand is the last stop before the city, and their prices remain just low enough—and their entertainments just sensational enough—to entice caravans to tarry a few nights.

Solinde finds the next totem in a tailor's shop. She picks the thimble out of the old man's pocket, distracting him with a kiss she leaves forever curled, forever unobtainable in the left corner of his mouth.

She takes great delight that night in calling the sky flame into her hand, melting the thimble into a puddle in her palm, letting it simmer and burn until all the liquid has evaporated, and all that is left is a fine powder of fairy-dust ash.

SIX

oft and sweet, my wife opens her eyes and meets mine. Her gaze is still hazy with sleep, and it takes several blinks for her to focus. When she does, her lips curl up in the corners and she croaks a sleep-dry "good morning." I answer in kind, craning my neck to press a small kiss against the tip of her nose. It has been too long since we have had a slow awakening together. The last few days have been full of arguments and tensions that neither of us enjoyed.

But to be here, now, in my mother's old rooms in Turn Hall, in the place where we first spoke, the place I fell first in lust and then in love with my wife, makes all our strife seem easily managed.

Together, we look down the length of the bed to the cradle pressed up against its foot. Alis is still asleep, sprawled on her back with her arms and legs akimbo. She sleeps the sleep of those with no worries, and the complete reassurance that she is utterly loved by everyone around her.

I do not remember the cradle, of course, but Kintyre, seven years my elder, recalled that Father had had it returned to the attic for storage. Father had assumed that Mother would be hale enough to bear him a girl child he could use in a fortuitous marriage bargain, or a third son he could send into the military or priesthood. But instead, his branch of the family tree had withered after only producing the heir and the spare. The healers had said that Mother was not healthy enough for a third child, and shortly after my birth, she had begun a slow decline that ended when she perished of a fever that should have been beatable when I was four. No other woman would have my father after that, miserable old tyrant that he was.

The cradle itself is old, older perhaps than the current incarnation of Turn Hall, which had been built by my great-grandfather, Generonius Turn, to replace the crumbling chalk-stone structure built generations before *him*. The cradle is solid, the wooden rails smoothed by hundreds of babes' fat fingers as they gripped them and wailed for their mothers, the edges worn into shining waves of hand-grooves by the fathers before me who had leaned over and braced themselves to either lift or set down their children. The headboard bears the carved emblem of House Turn—a key lancing a lock—and the simple wooden apparatus that allows the cradle to swing gently on its stand still works.

A content lethargy, sweet, and golden, and sticky as honey steals over me. Pip and I had stayed up quite late the night before, making an inventory of my library. There were no books missing that I could recall, save for my illustrated copy of *The Siren of the Sunsong Sea*, which was found easily enough in Wyndam's chambers. Pip and I had assumed that Alis would be asleep in our bed when we finally retired to our room—Kintyre had ordered my mother's rooms reopened and cleaned upon our arrival, much as I had done when Pip first came to Turn Hall. We also expected that Bevel might be reading—or sifting through the never-ending pile of reports that plague the Shadow's Hand—by the fire.

Instead, we found the cradle here, made up for our daughter, and Bevel asleep at the foot of the bed, one arm stuck between the wooden rails. Clearly, he had been trying to soothe Alis, but in the end, she had outlasted him. He was dead to the world, and Alis was using his fingers as a teething toy. She already had three and was obviously intent upon the advent of a fourth tooth, if the amount of drool drying on Bevel's hand was any indication.

"Da ma da ma madadaa!" she had said when we crept into the room, kicking her feet in an overjoyed dance. "'Ook! 'Ook!"

Bevel had startled awake then, leaving his hand in Alis's possession but rising up and laying his free one on the dagger I knew he kept secreted at the small of his back. When he blinked a few more times and woke enough to realize who we were, he let go of the dagger and my daughter both, and sat up. There was, indeed, a book of children's rhymes squashed into the mattress where Bevel had been lying.

Pip had laughed, and reached out to help Bevel flatten his ferocious bed head. It was very different from the last time they had been in this room together, when he had thrown me up against the wall by the door and tried to throttle me. A warmth settled behind my breastbone and for a moment, I felt that this, right here, was what it meant to be part of a family.

I had learned the previous evening that the valet's antechamber attached to the lord's bedroom had been converted into the office in which the affairs of Lysse were now conducted, and that my former valet, Keriens, now slept in his own bedroom in the servant's quarters. Traditionally, the lord's spouse would have taken my mother's room, which was accessible from the lord's through a door hidden behind a tapestry, but the door had not been used in so long that the lock had rusted shut.

Moreover, Bevel thought it ridiculous to have a whole

other set of rooms to himself, when there was plenty of room to store his clothing in the wide wardrobes in the lord's room, enough room on the chaise before the fire for two, and a bed more than large enough for two grown men. Especially when Bevel planned to sleep every night by my brother's side, anyway - when I had called them Paired, Kintyre had primly corrected me. They were not merely Paired anymore, they were *trothed* now. Bevel Dom was his husband, or at least the closest thing to a husband that Elgar Reed's myopic worldbuilding allowed for.

Bevel had slept beside Kintyre every night on the road. Now that they were a trothed Pair, he had no intention of noble propriety or upper-class customs keeping him a door's width away. Lying now amid Sheil-purple blankets with my wife, our daughter nearby, I can hardly blame him. Family should be kept close.

Loath as I am to admit it, my creator was right—no matter how angry and abusive my father was, I had no real danger of following in his footsteps. My temper has been frayed recently, but I would rather throw myself upon Smoke than harm any of the people under this roof.

Pip inches across the valley of the pillow between us and, morning-stale breath taken into consideration, presses a closed-mouth kiss against my lips. "Hi, you," she says.

"Hi back," I reply.

"Everything okay?"

"Everything is marvelous. You know," I murmur conversationally in my wife's ear, "we never did have sex in this bed. We became intimate on the road."

"Oh?" Pip replies, eyes half-lidded with aroused interest. "That sounds like you take the oversight personally."

"You know, I think I do," I whisper against her mouth. Then I reach out and tickle my wife right above her hip, the spot that I know will make her giggle and squirm.

"Forsyth!" she protests in a hiss.

"Shhh!" I admonish through my own quiet chuckles. "Don't wake the baby."

We tussle and kiss, until I have Pip right where I want her— stripped bare and on her stomach. I spend a few long, wonderful moments kissing my way down the tendrils and branches of ivy that Bootknife carved into her skin, wounds I had helped Mother Mouth to tend right here, in this room. A horrible torture, to be sure, but beautiful in the art of them, and proof of Pip's resilience, her strength, and her morals. They are what brought her to me, and I cannot hate the scars.

With one last glance back at Alis to make certain she still sleeps, Pip rolls over. I settle between Pip's parted thighs, pull the blanket over my head, and set about my morning's task. Pip's moans and jerking gasps are muffled in such a way that I know she has her face buried in her own pillow, biting it to stay silent. Her climax is swift in building and comes upon her like an earthquake.

For all that I had been untested in the ways of love when we first lay together, the following two years have been filled with enough instruction that I am now confident in my skills. When Pip's breathing settles, she takes her revenge by crawling under the covers and setting her mouth upon me. I last no longer than she did, and when she rises from the bed to ring the bell for a servant, she is licking her lips with all the smug satisfaction of a satyr who caught a dryad.

We are both up and properly clad in house robes before the servant arrives, trailed by Keriens. My former valet is carrying a breakfast tray, which he places on the credenza. The youth has grown into a wide-shouldered, handsome young man, and I am very pleased to see him.

"Well now, sir," he says with a smirk, and I am also pleased to note that his cheeky sense of humor has not fled in the wake of a change of masters. "You are a sight for sore eyes." He makes a bow and I insist, instead, that we shake hands. "And begging your pardon, Madam Turn," he says, bowing to Pip, who has a puffy-eyed Alis struggling toward wakefulness on her hip, "but those of us downstairs would like to welcome you to Turn Hall properly, and thank you for the privilege of callin' you our mistress, besides."

Pip, startled by the compliment, flushes. "Um, thanks," she says, at a loss for words and clearly stumped by the protocol of accepting such a congratulations.

Keriens then winks at me. "Seems Sheriff Pointe had it all hashed out correctly. I think there was a bet to it, wasn't there, sir? I assume you'll be collectin' on that this afternoon. He was right; you certainly are more relaxed and carefree with a beautiful woman in your—ahem— arms. Though the babe's eyes aren't green, sir, and— oooh, no, stop it, sir! Ah, abuse! Such abuse!" He laughs as I make a show of swatting his shoulder with the tassel of my dressing robe.

"Hush, you cheeky miscreant!" I order, but there is no anger in me. How could there be? I am too overjoyed. "Be off with you and your wagging tongue, and send up the bath."

"Yes sir, please sir," Keriens says with theatrical cringing, and with one last bow to us, he scuttles away. He is barely out the door before I hear his laughter wafting back up the hallway.

Pip is chuckling when I go to pour us both tea, and fetch an earthenware cup of juice made from the bounty of Turn Hall's apple orchards for Alis.

"He was right, you know. You are more relaxed," Pip says between sips of her tea. "You're more open."

"I do not have the stress of managing the household, the Chipping, and my duties to the king weighing upon my shoulders." I shrug. "As the younger son, I finally have all the pleasures and advantages of position and wealth, but none of the troubles. And the king's concerns are Bevel's now, not mine. I need not be a role model."

Pip makes a bit of a face. "But your language has gotten more formal."

"Ah," I say, pausing to reflect on what I just said. "Yes, I suppose it has. Habit, that. Does it... bother you?"

Pip turns her face up for a kiss I am happy to gift her. "No," she says. "You sound more comfortable, actually. Less like you're rehearsing everything before you open your mouth. I didn't realize before how... hard it was for you, how much you were working to fit in back home."

"Back home," I murmur against her hair, struck by the incongruity of that assertion. My wife calls our house in Victoria our "home." And yet here, in Turn Hall, surrounded by servants who missed me and a brother and brother-in-law who, for the first time, have opened their arms and welcomed me into their hearts as family, and a nephew who is... well, I'm sure affectionate in the way of young lads who resent their parents for simply being their parents... and with my greatest friend just one estate over...

Well, it is here and now that I feel the word "home" resonating for me.

Pip senses my hesitation and leans back to study my face. "What is it?" she asks, but already I can see the warm joy of domesticity and a well-spent morning sliding away.

"It is nothing, truly," I say, but Pip levels her "*I know*

you're not telling me everything" look at me, against
which I am helpless, and I blurt, "Only, to me, this place
is home. I know what you meant—I understand, Pip—
but I..."

"You don't feel the same?" Pip asks, stepping back.
Alis, unhappy that the warm snuggle she was receiving
from both her parents was severed so quickly, whines.
I set my teacup on the mantel to give myself time to
contemplate my answer, and Pip follows suit with Alis's
juice.

Finally, I say: "I don't... I'm not sure." It's not an
answer, not really, but she deserves *something.*

Pip breathes deep, clearly attempting to forestall
another shouting match and to maintain her calm. We
neither of us want another fight. Especially so soon after
the last one.

"It's fine," Pip grits between clenched teeth. "Of
course I understand. I don't *like* it, but I understand.
You've lived here your whole life. Of course you were
homesick."

"But it's more than that, Pip," I say. "This is Alis's
chance to grow up the daughter of a noble family. This
is your chance to see what it means to be a lordling's
wife. Your time in Hain was so filled with pain and peril.
We don't know what has brought us here, nor how, but
when that mystery is solved and the dangers dealt with...
imagine, Pip!"

"Imagine what?" Pip gasps. "Imagine *staying?*"

"Yes!" I say, and then amend it to: "For a while,
at least. Perhaps a few years? Not forever. I am certain I could find a boon large enough to trade with a
Deal-Maker, or a spell from a Warlock to send us back
after that."

"A *few years?*" Pip asks. "I was gone for *six months*
last time, and you saw how much of a hassle it was with

my family, and my landlord after that. What sort of train wreck do you think we'd come home to if we stayed a few *years*? They'd declare us legally dead, Forsyth! They'd auction off the house! There'd be nothing to come home *to*."

"Then we could simply remain here," I say, feeling defensive and stubborn.

"Besides the fact that I could *never* do that to my family, could never let them think I was dead or vanished or run away, I absolutely *refuse* to let my daughter grow up in Elgar Reed's world."

"It's not all bad!" I protest. "Am I not a feminist?"

"You are. Of course you are! But who else is?" Pip challenges. "Pointe, okay, but what about the Lord Turn? Will your brother have any qualms about selling his niece off to the most advantageous ally when she's old enough by his standards?"

A surge of doubt slides oily and cold into my guts. "I... surely we'll have her whole adolescence to change his perspective," I argue, but it is a feeble one, I know, and my words betray my doubt. While my brother has never been actively cruel, he also has never believed women to be equal to men. The fact that the only human being he could have ever thought to hold important enough to love and wed was a fellow man says—I am ashamed to realize—a lot about how highly esteemed women are in Kintyre's eyes. And Elgar Reed's.

"And what about the next kid?" Pip asks. "Because there sure as hell aren't any condoms or pills or vasectomies here, Forsyth. And my IUD is probably only gonna last another year. Maybe two, if we're lucky. Could you live without sex for the rest of our lives? 'Cause I don't want to, but I also don't want to have to go into labor here, I can tell you."

"Oh," I admit. "I hadn't thought of that."

"I can't stand corsets. I love my culture's food. And, Forsyth, I *like* teaching."

"There is the free school in Turnshire—"

"You *know* what I mean."

"I do, Pip. I promise I do," I say, desperate, and hurting because she is so summarily rejecting everything that I loved here. "I'm not requesting that we remain forever. Just for a little while. Just to *experience* life here. Alis deserves to know that side of her heritage, too."

"I'm not sure I want her to!" Pip snaps.

I jerk back, stung. The back of my eyes burn, and my heart presses hard against my throat. "Is it s-s-so te-ter-terrible?" I whisper, unable to make my voice louder, unable to shout or weep, too hurt to even breathe. "Is-s th-the l-l-land of my b-buh-birth so hate-*hateful*?"

Pip sighs and sets Alis down in her cradle. Alis shoves her fist in her mouth, wide eyes wet and worried. Then Pip reaches out and draws me against her breast, cradling me as if I were the child. I am not ashamed to admit that I wrap my arms around her waist and hold on, shaking.

"Oh, Forsyth," Pip says softly, petting through my hair. It feels safe, good, and this feels like home, too. I am torn. Oh, I am torn. I thought I had worked through this pain already. That I had moved on.

But now I am here, I am back, and it is no longer a far-away wish, but a reality, and I cannot express how much it tears at me to have two homes, and to be strung between both like a man on the rack.

"I just... I just thought you might be pleased," I say softly.

"And on what planet do you think I'd be fucking *pleased*?" Pip says. The words are abrasive, but her tone is soothing. She is trying; she is making the attempt to remain calm, to understand, and for that, I am grateful.

I straighten and fold her hands between my own,

bringing them to my lips for a kiss, pressing my cheeks against her palms, desperate for her caress and understanding. "I tho-thought you would-d l-li-like it, the chance to be sim-simply a moth-mother! You s-say s-s-so often how fruh-frustrated teaching makes you, how muh-much you miss Alis when you are away working! How for-for-fortuitous, I th-thought! Pip m-may be the mo-mother she wishes, will be accorded all the advantages of being a ladyling! And my da-daughter will be raised with all the r-respect, and w-we-wealth, and p-pr-privilege she deserves! That was my only thought, Pip, I s-s-swear."

Pip cups her hands around my chin, forces my face up so that she may meet my gaze. Her eyes swim with a love that I feel blessed to call my own each time I witness it.

"Oh, *bao bei*," she says, and kisses me. Her kiss is sweet, and slow, and sad, and I cling to her lips with my own, for it has been too long since she has called me that, her precious one. Too long.

When we separate, she resumes petting my sparse, gingerish hair, and I reach up to fold my hands behind her neck, to circle the puff of ivy-leaf shaped scar-tissue on her nape with my thumb.

"I'm sorry," she says. "I'm sorry for not understanding what this means to you."

"Pip—" I begin, but don't know what it is that I mean to say.

"I see now, okay? I get it," she reassures. "This isn't you hating my world. This is you wanting to provide for your family, wanting us to live the kind of good life that you want us to."

"We could have that, here."

"But we have that there, too, don't we?" Pip asks softly. "We both have good jobs we enjoy. Alis is never alone, or made to feel unloved. We have a nice house. We live comfortably, don't we?"

"Yes," I admit.

"Are you really worried about me being a stay-at-home mom?"

"If you would rather work out of the house, then it is your prerogative." I shake my head. "I am certain; I am very happy and very privileged to be a stay-at-home father. I adore my days with Alis. I find hacking fascinating, and engaging. And I know that the university makes you happy, despite how often you call down curses on your students over the dinner table." I risk a smirk, and she echoes it. "I know that."

"But you feel torn."

"And wouldn't you, Pip? What if you'd had to stay here, and now we were in your world, among your comforts and what was familiar to you? The clothing and the cuisine, the friends and family that you had missed?"

"I get it," Pip says. "Honestly, I get it. I'm sorry."

"Me, as well."

Another kiss, another long and quiet moment, listening to each other breathe and feeling the tension, the disappointment, the anger dissipate.

"Look," Pip says at length. "We've got time here. It's not like there's Google. I'm sure there's going to be days of research to figure out what happened and how we ended up back in Hain, and, knowing the way that Reed builds plots, there will probably be another quest. We'll get the chance to get out, see your world, experience it. And we'll have plenty of time at home, here, too," she says, emphasizing the word with a deliberate warmth. "And at the end of it, we'll find a way to go back, just like you said. And I—" Her voice hitches, broken for a moment, and alarmingly damp-sounding. "I hope you'll want to go back with me. Bu-but if you don't, then I... we can *talk* about it, and..."

"Oh, no, no, Pip. Never," I promise, kissing it into the skin of her neck, her forehead, over her eyes, against the tears rolling down her cheeks. "Where you go, so will I go."

"But you were going to ask Reed to write you back," she sobs.

Ah. And *here* is the real kernel of Pip's distress.

"Only as an alternative to forcing you to watch me fade away and die," I reassure her, feeling the tears building in my own eyes spill over in a slow trickle. "Only if it came down to that."

Pip sniffles and nods miserably, wiping her nose on the cuff of her robe. "Okay. Okay. I'm sorry."

We hold one another for a long, long moment, each of us unwilling to be the first to let go. In the end, it is Alis's sobbing "Adadadamamamaaaaa" that has us separating. I fetch Alis, and Pip picks up our tea cups. We sit in the wingback chairs that bracket the cold fireplace, and sip. Alis is soothed by my rubbing her back, but still looks worried.

A knock at the door announces the return of Keriens, and with him comes servants enough to carry and fill the copper tub, Velshi with wardrobe selections for all three of us, and a serving girl with a basket of soaps, hair potions, and cosmetics for Pip. The girl looks eager to work with Pip, and I guess that she has a wish to be elevated into the position of a ladies' maid. Judging by her hands, she is the scullery, and hasn't had any opportunity to practice in this household of men.

I feel instantly sorry for her, for beyond a bold slash of wing-tip liquid eyeliner and a plump gloss-slicked vibrant lipstick when there is an occasion requiring it, Pip wears no makeup and does not dress her hair elaborately. Perhaps I can talk Pip into indulging the young woman for the sake of her practice, call upon Pip's sense of duty to the Chipping to allow it. Pip is, I have learned, as generous to students of all stripes as she can be.

The tub is set up quickly, and we are left to our ablutions. The tub is not large enough for two grown adults, alas, so we take turns holding Alis and scrubbing ourselves, and her, clean. When we are dry, I summon my valet and the serving girl back.

Soon enough, I am attired again as befits my station: brown leather riding boots, buckskin breeches, a waistcoat of fine Turn-russet brocade patterned with rows of keys, a proper lawn shirt with my favorite tanzanite cufflinks, and a Turn-russet riding coat to finish it off.

Pip wears one of my mother's day dresses. The kirtle is a rich indigo—the darkest shade that could still safely be called Sheil-purple—under which she has chosen to wear a shift of dark teal silk that stands out brilliantly between the slashed sleeves and in the split of the skirt. She is wearing no corset, of course, because she refused, and only a low belt with a long tail around her hips, in Turn-russet. Alis is wearing the uniform of all infants in this world—a cloth diaper, knitted socks that she is even now attempting to rid herself of, and a billowing tunic that ends at the knee so as not to impede little ones by tripping up their early attempts at locomotion, with tie-on sleeves of a white that I know will not last unstained.

Having changed my daughter's clothing as often as three or four times daily, I do not envy the laundress who will need to boil Alis's tunic to get it clean. Perhaps I should suggest to someone that all of the baby clothes currently in storage at Turn Hall be dyed black to avoid showing the stains, save us all the headaches of the work.

But I cannot deny how proud I am, how happy I feel, when I see my family attired thus. Pip and Alis wear matching purple ribbons wrapped around their heads, though it is obvious that Alis is already plotting against hers, and will be rid of it as soon as she has succeeded with the socks.

Library has also been given a purple ribbon by the serving girl, tied in a neat bow directly under the little feathery puff of fur at the end of his limp tail.

"Well then, how fine we look," I say. "I wish I had a camera."

"Camera, sir?" Velshi says, raising a butlery eyebrow.

"Never mind." I wave the comment away and wonder if this is how Pip felt when she tried to speak about items that were commonplace in her world and completely un-heard of in mine. It feels a bit like if I were a clockwork toy and someone were winding my springs too tightly. I produce a smile that is probably too wide, and too much of an attempt at earnestness, and say: "Well, what do you think, Pip? Shall we save our research for the afternoon, and spend this morning a-visiting?"

"Yah yah yah yah!" Alis opines, and Pip and I both blink at her.

"That's a new word," Pip says.

"Yes," I agree. "And *that*, I think, is Bevel's provincial accent I hear behind it. Well, my sweeting, we'll have you trained out of that soon enough, won't we?" I ask Alis, kissing her nose, and then nuzzling it with my own. "Yes? Yes, yes, yes?"

"Yah!" Alis insists, and I can see that I have my work cut out for me in raising my daughter as a noble lady.

LAMPS

In Araii, it is a tarnished oil lamp. Solinde has traveled far to the north, to the places where the ice barely melts, even in high summer, and the Dark Elves rule the sparse Winter Woods that grow, twisted and harsh, among the tundras of white.

There is a Queen of Elves, Cassiopith, who is human, and it is in her chambers that the oil lamp resides. It is in the back of a cupboard accessed only by the magical maidservants who refill the lamps during the long winter nights. Cassiopith's husband, the Night King, Bearer of the Iridium Crown, keeps the palace locked down tight. Even so many years after Kintyre Turn came to fetch Cassiopith back to her father—and in the end, came to an accord with her father to let her stay as Cassiopith had learned to love her captor—the Night King fears that someone else will take issue with their cross-species marriage and do his wife harm.

Dark Elves are practically immortal. Human women are not.

Thus Solinde chooses to wreak no havoc. Dark Elves are also wickedly keen with their ice daggers. And Deal-Makers can be killed, if someone is persistent enough. She merely slips in and out in the livery of a serving maid. When the lamp is in hand, she flees across the tundra. Under the dancing, rippling lights of the

Emerald Sky Fire, she summons down her lightning and melts the totem, resident djinn and all.

SEVEN

The morning sees Kintyre's letter to Law Manor requesting a luncheon visit replied to in the affirmative, and so the six of us dress for the walk—and perhaps an afternoon's ride—and set out for the neighboring estate. I had asked Kintyre to pen the request because I wanted to surprise Rupin Pointe, and he knows my handwriting too well. It will be nice to see my friend again, and I am anticipating quite the laugh when he realizes who exactly has come to call.

Bevel Dom and I walk at the head of the party, with Pip and Alis just behind us. Alis is desperate to squirm down out of her mother's arms every time Pip fails to allow Alis to investigate something she's pointed out. It seems that Alis is determined to finally walk on her own. Not for the pride of it, but so that she can steer her mother back around to look at flowers, and little stones, and the frog that is sitting on the piled-slate boundary wall between the fields and the road, croaking, "*Ka-iss meh, ka-iss meh!*"

"'Isses, 'isses!" Alis says, reaching for the creature.

Pip shoots me a concerned look, and I double back to hoist Alis onto the wall beside the frog. It is about the same size as my hand, and it sits still as she pats its dry skin gently between its bulbous eyes.

"*Ka-iss meh, ka-iss meh,*" the frog pleads, blinking

wetly at my daughter, and she chants, "'isses, 'isses," in time with its croaking.

"Can she?" Pip asks. "I mean, is it safe?"

"Yes," I say to my wife, and then to my daughter: "Now, my sweeting," I tease. "Don't be disappointed. Those frogs don't actually turn into princes."

The frog shoots me a dirty look and croaks in reproach for ruining its fun. All the same, Pip scoops up the frog and holds it up to Alis.

"Gently now," Pip cautions, and Alis puckers and brushes her lips very carefully against the frog's back.

"Muah!" Alis says.

The frog sags, disappointed, then pecks Alis's cheek in return and hops off Pip's hands and away, back toward the ditch.

"What was that all about?" Pip asks, wiping her palms on her dress and using her cuff to clean Alis's face.

"We know the Kissing Frogs never turn into princes," Bevel says, coming to join us. "But they don't. They all secretly hope, yeah?"

"That's... actually kind of sad," Pip admits.

"Yah, yah, yah," Alis says.

Bevel hops over the low stone barrier into the field and takes one of Alis's hands. With her other wrapped tight around two of my fingers, Alis deigns to wobble along the wall, dancing in delight to have the sun on her face and the attention of three adults.

The sun. I take a moment to close my eyes, turn my face up, and smile. Behind my lids, the sunlight is pink, and I can feel the shadows of the trees that grow along the road passing cool and green over my skin. My freckles will be horrendously prominent after this promenade, but I don't mind. I have learned to love freckles; Pip's are my favorite, and mine are hers. We both hope that Alis has some, as well, and seeing as our daughter inherited my eye color, and her skin is lighter than her mother's, it seems likely.

Oh, how I have missed a good, mild Lysse spring after suffering the deep Canadian winter. With my eyes closed, a stone in the road—though it is hardly a road by Victoria standards, more like a hiking path—snags against my boots and I stumble. Luckily, the wall is there to catch me, and I don't topple Alis down with me.

"Whoops!" Pip laughs, a few paces behind us. She is now walking on the wall as well, skirts rucked up to her knees in a very unladylike (but very Pip-like) manner, the excess fabric crammed behind her belt. "Watch where you're walking, *bao bei*."

"Yeah, watch it, Forssy," Bevel sneers. "Reading too much has obviously made you clum—" He stops, snapping his mouth shut on the automatic insult, his sapphire eyes widening in mild horror. "Sorry," he says immediately. "That was... wow, that was incredibly rude of me. I'm ashamed by how instinctual that was."

He shoots a look over his shoulder, mortified, but Kintyre, who is about twenty paces behind us with Wyndam, hasn't heard him. Though I cannot hear them, in return, I can see the pedantic way my brother is moving his arms, and I can only guess that the lad is getting the sort of self-important lecture that I used to have to suffer when we were younger, and Kintyre thought himself the cleverer of the two of us. My poor nephew.

Though, unlike me, it seems as if the lad is soaking in this fatherly attention, like a lizard on a sunny rock.

Perhaps, though I sense that I am more scholarly inclined than Wyndam, I ought to have a conversation with the lad about looking up to heroes and living in shadows. I very much wish some caring relative had been around to pull *me* aside and tell me that I did not, actually, have to be exactly like the great Hero of Hain, despite being his little brother.

"That you stopped and corrected yourself is apology enough," I say to Bevel, bringing my attention back to his chagrin.

"Still, all the same..." Bevel says, scuffling his feet like a guilty boy. "Authorial Intent is strong, but I like to think we all have the ability to change our characters."

"That we do," I agree, thinking of my transformation from background character in my own life, to being the hero of it instead. "And, speaking of changes, how goes the business of the Shadow Hand?"

"Well enough," he replies, deliberately cagey, knowing that his non-answer would needle me. He smiles slyly.

I do not regret leaving the Mask, and its knowledge, and the duties attendant therewith, to Bevel Dom. But I do very much dislike being out of the loop, as Pip would put it. And he very much likes riling me up.

Since he became my brother's squire, Bevel has been an irritation to me. First, because he usurped what I had thought was my deserved position as the great Kintyre Turn's sidekick and chronicler. Then, as he earned his own knighthood and wealth, he became the brother to Kintyre that I should have been.

And he rubbed it in viciously when we were still at odds. Now that he is my brother's trothed (a position that I do not, I can admit wryly, covet in the least), and the closest thing to an in-law our world allows for, our animosity seems to have cooled into gentle teasing. I would like to be a friend to Sir Bevel Dom, seventh son of a seventh son, the Bulldog of Bynnebakker, and perhaps I am. His manners have always been good, his mind sharp, and his wits quick. But his tongue is also silver, and he is a teller of tall tales; he likes too much to take his humor out of the tempers of others. And I had quite the temper whenever Kintyre and Bevel showed up at Turn Hall, ate my provisions, took what they wished, did *nothing* that befitted my brother as the eldest, and left.

But I have learned patience of a sort in Pip's world that I did not think I could ever possess. Kintyre often accused me of being high-handed, officious, stuffy, and bossy. Living in a world where I had to accept that I was not the cleverest, that there was much to learn and absorb, where things were awkward, and new, and strange, and frustrating, has taught me humility.

So instead of rising to Bevel's bait, I snort at him. Bevel grins and stoops a little to pluck up a stalk of wheat from the field on the other side of the piled-stone wall. It is knee-high and fresh green, and looks ridiculous as he clamps the stem between his teeth and grins at me, daring me to make another comment.

I oblige. "You know, I still remember everything," I say. "You are perhaps the first Shadow Hand in the history of the service to have a predecessor who still lives. I can hack into your work very easily, Bevel Dom, and if I am unsatisfied by your performance, I may just take the Mask back."

"I should like to see you try, Forsyth Turn," he says back with a smirk. "Though you'll have to tell me what you mean by 'hack.'"

"Oh," I say, feeling my cheeks flush with embarrassment. "It's a... ahem. It's a term from the Writer's realm. It means to... well, to access information by rifling through files, but doing so in a sneaky, through-the-back-door manner that is... usually less than legal." Bevel nods along, not at all judgmental of my slip, and so, puffing a little with pride, I add: "It is now my profession."

"You collect information illegally for money?" Bevel asks, and this time, he's frowning. Of all the people he knows who would voluntarily work contrary to the law, I am probably the last person he'd expect. "That... surprises me."

"Not *technically* illegally," I say. "I am in service to my government there, as I was to my king here."

Though that is not entirely true. Frankly, I am not at all a fan of the way Ottawa goes about its business. More than once, I was tempted to bypass firewalls and "accidentally" infect some of the Prime Minister's more hateful bills into unreadability. I am an admirer of democracy, for I have seen the ills of dictatorship in other realms. But I will be the first to admit that I sometimes miss the, well, not "pliancy" of King Carvel Tarvers, but more his willingness to be *counseled*, to weigh his options, to *listen*. As a country lordling, I had a perspective that the noblemen of Kingskeep did not. And as his Shadow Hand, it was my duty to advise. In that, I was able to subtly steer the course of Hain toward what I felt was a more fair and ethical path.

In Canada, I am but one voice among thousands, one vote among millions. And while that is a fair method of governing, it is, I determine, not enough. Not for me, at least. Not for the way I was written.

"So you 'hack' for this new king of yours," Bevel says, trying to understand, and generously allowing Alis to pull the wheat stalk from his lips, which she waves about like a parade banner. "How did you offer your services to him?"

"I found a hole amid their security and sent them a letter through it," I say, which is, at its most basic, true. I had toyed with the idea of simply using a GIF of a gentleman removing his hat and bowing, but that seemed... teasing. And unnecessarily smug. Not at all classy. The email I'd sent instead read formal, and stuffy, according to Pip, but I would much rather be too polite than taunt them into going after me.

"Oh, I remember it word for word!" Pip offers with a

laugh, and before I can protest, recites:

> *"Dear Sirs,*
> *I do humbly beg your excuse, but I couldn't*
> *help but notice, during my wanderings through your*
> *mainframe, that there is an excessively, startlingly large*
> *gap in your firewall protocols at this IP address. Quite*
> *large enough to fit through, I might add, though you*
> *must be reassured that my respect for the brave intel-*
> *ligence officers and spymasters of the Dominion of*
> *Canada is such that I refrained from the temptation*
> *of doing so.*
> *If you require any further information or aid*
> *from me, I would be pleased to offer it.*
> *Yours in Trust, F."*

Bevel howls with laughter. "That's classical Forsyth, yeah? Hired you on the spot, did he? Did your new king send you a purse at once?"

"Ah, that is harder to explain," I say, truthfully. "But in essence, yes."

In reality, in return for my good deeds, I take one cent from each Canadian federal government bank account I can track down, once per pay period, and I transfer it into either my own shadow bank account, or into an equally obfuscated trust for my daughter's future education and needs. The withdrawal is programmed not to appear on bank statements as such. It is not a great wealth, but it is a modest beginning, and in Pip's world, there is such a thing as compound interest. And if it is less than entirely legal, well, I have looked true evil in the face and know that what I do helps to prevent it in my new adopted home. I simply cannot do it with no income. My own morals stretch enough for my conscience to remain appeased.

"How noble of you," Bevel says. "I'm not certain I

would choose to remain a hero had I the option. Being Shadow Hand is almost like being on holiday compared to what Kin and I used to get up to, but even then, there's something appealing about the dream of heading down to Brystal and buying one of those funny skinny houses they build up on the cliffs. I could sit on a terrace facing a sea that is blood-warm, and do *nothing* but drink wine and listen to music for the rest of my life."

"You'd get bored," Pip says. "I know you too well. Forsyth's the same. All of you would get wall-climbingly bored. That's the way you were written."

Bevel cringes at the way Pip so casually mentions our creator, but does not comment.

"Yes," Bevel muses as we reach the gate to Law Manor's grounds. "No matter where you are, or what your occupation is, you have to remain true to yourself. That is something I do understand."

~~~

What had appeared to be a great prank and great fun to me is, I realize as soon as Sheriff Pointe arrives to welcome his guests, horrifyingly shocking to him. He pulls open the door, a smile on his lips, and immediately freezes. Pointe's face goes as gray as his house-robe, and he actually wobbles, grabbing at the door handle with a white-knuckled intensity that frightens me. He makes a few inarticulate, garbling noises, and then sucks in a deep breath, his eyes going wide as tea-saucers as his chest puffs up.

"Forsyth!" he croaks, when he finally has his breath. "Writer's balls! Are you a ghost?"

"Oh, oh dear," I say softly. I take a step up onto the manse's front gable. Pointe visibly flinches. "My dear friend, no. No, I am not."

"You live," he says, and reaches out a hand to me. I
~~~

take it, press it between my own, and let him feel how warm and pliant my skin is.

"I live," I say, and before anything else can be said, he draws me into the tightest, most desperate embrace I have ever known. His fingers dig into my shoulders through my clothing, his arms tight enough to squeeze the breath from me, his face jammed against my neck.

"My Lord Bevel said you had gone away, to a faraway land," he hisses against my skin, sucking in deep gulps of air and trying, I believe, not to weep. "I thought he had just been trying to be kind. But no, it's true. You live."

"I live," I say gently, reaching up to steady him. "And I am come back."

"I missed you, my friend. Fiercely."

"And I you. I missed you very, very much."

"Thank the Writer," Pointe gulps.

"Actually," I say with a grin, drawing back to wink at my friend. "About that. You recall telling me that you did not believe in Readers, in the Final Chapter, in a Writer who scribes the Books of our lives and sets them on the Shelf when they are done? All that?"

"Yes," Pointe says, red-rimmed eyes narrowing at me in reluctant confusion. "We made a bet."

"Indeed we did," I say with a smirk. "And now, you must pay up. For I have taken drink with him."

Pointe stares at me as if I have lost my head entirely and replaced it with that of a Sphinx. Then, for the first time, he seems to notice my family ranged behind me along Law Manor's entry courtyard. His silver eyes snag on Pip and Alis.

"You better come in, you sly old bastard," he sighs. "And *explain*."

≈≈≈

Dorthi Pointe lets out a breathy shout of delight

when I lead our little party into her afternoon tea room, and folds me into an affectionate hug no less desperate and tight than her husband's. Lewko, who has grown into a fine young boy in my absence, clings warily to his father's leg. His memories of me must be vague, at best.

Dorthi runs her thumb over the scar on my cheekbone, the signature of Bootknife's titular blade, then pinches my cheek and calls me handsome. She has always called me handsome, though for many years I did not believe her, and it puts a lump in my throat to hear her say so again.

"Ah, my wife says the scar makes me look roguish," I say. "Though my figure is no longer so trim. I admit I eat perhaps too many of the delicacies of her kingdom."

"Wife?" Dorthi asks, and peers around me. "Oh, Miss Piper!" she crows, and sends a look of triumph toward her husband even as she is bustling toward Pip. "Or is it Ladyling Turn?"

Pip smiles and accepts the kiss on the cheek, and doesn't speak to confirm or deny the name change. Instead, she holds up our daughter. "This is Alis Mei Piper Turn," she says, dropping her into Dorthi's hands. Dorthi is instantly smitten, and too distracted to pepper Pip with any more invasive questions. My wife has learned well the distracting value of a baby.

"Oh, you beautiful wee lady!" she says. "You come sit with me, and we will pour you some milky tea."

"Ma!" Lewko says, following his mother to the table, aghast at her intense adoration.

"You too, my wee manny," she says to her son. Lewko is old enough now to get himself seated and pour milk from the glass jug into his own earthenware cup, then the second cup that Dorthi fetches from the sideboard. Dorthi then sits beside him with Alis on her lap. The Pointes have servants, which was something I was careful to ensure their estate could afford when I entailed Law Manor to the local sheriffdom, but Dorthi prefers to do as much as she is able on her own.

"Yah, yah!" Alis opines as Dorthi settles her.

Pointe, looking proud as a peacock, ushers us all into our own seats, and the servants appear to pour tea, distribute tasties, and see to our needs. Kintyre asks for whiskey, and Bevel kicks him under the table. I am happy to see that the potential for our father's alcoholism to transfer to my brother is being thwarted by his trothed. Wyndam seems to find the whole affair tedious and says nothing, even when asked a direct question, slurping at his tea with alarmingly bad manners as he stares out the window.

I must remind myself more than once that Wyndam is not *my* son, and it is not my place to correct him. Besides, perhaps his behavior is considered perfectly acceptable among pirates, and he is only behaving as a Prince of the Seas ought and sees no fault in his own conduct. I dare not reprimand him in front of others unless I am certain. I would not wish to mortify the lad publicly.

Pip and I spend the meal dodging what questions we can, and making up mild fibs for the rest. Kintyre and Bevel catch on easily enough that we do not wish to tell Dorthi and Lewko about the Writer and his realm.

When the meal is over, Lewko's shyness has evaporated. He is enchanted with Alis and, with Pip and Dorthi's permission, takes her hand and leads her in a stumbling walk toward the back-courtyard door, babbling excitedly about introducing her to their cat.

"Oh!" Pointe says, jumping to his feet when he realizes where they are going. "I should... they shouldn't go alone."

"Nonsense," I say. "Lewko seems very responsible. What harm could a cat do?"

Pointe only shakes his head and says, "You'd better come, Forsyth."

Curious, and happy for the excuse to speak to my friend alone, I follow him to the back. Before we reach the doorway, I can hear Alis' shrilling, in overjoyed tones, "Toto, Toto, Toto!" I wonder if it is a black cat the Pointes have adopted.

It is, in fact, *not* a black cat.

Instead, Alis and Lewko are on the ground, pinned by soft paws the size of their bodies, and *giggling*. A pink tongue about the length of a man laves their faces and hair, flicking out from between fangs the size of my arm. The face is lionish, with bear-ears and a sand-stone colored ruff that is not quite long enough to be a full mane. The creature's chin, should it be standing, would come just about even with my own shoulder, and its tail, complete with a shaggy, golden poof of fur, is wagging so quickly that small clouds of dust are rising from the courtyard stone.

"Hey!" Pip says, for the rest of our party has followed behind us. "It's the Library Lion!"

The creature looks up from its delighted quarry and spots us. For a moment, I wonder if the Library Lion will remember its erstwhile rescuers, but I needn't have been concerned. The Lion bounds to its feet, careful to avoid squashing the children, and lets out the deepest rum-bling purr I have ever heard. It thrums into the marrow of my bones, and when the creature comes to butt its head against my body, nearly throwing me into the wall, I reach to scratch behind one of those soft round ears and murmur, "Yes, hello to you, too. Are you named yet, my friend? Perhaps we should call you Aslan."

"Toto!" Alis cries happily as Lewko helps her up. She tugs at its tail, and the Lion gamely ignores her in favor of lavishing the same attention on Pip.

"Yes, sweeting," I say softly, picking up my daughter to keep her from being accidentally kicked over and stepped on. "He does look just like the Cowardly Lion."

"Cowardly Lion?" Pip asks, her fingers buried in the Lion's ruff. "Aslan? Are they characters from... you know?"

And as quickly as that, all the joy of being back in Pointe's presence evaporates.

"Forsyth?" Pointe asks, hand on my elbow, clearly worried by the way my expression has fallen.

"Do you have a spare practice sword?" I say, pulling my daughter off the Library Lion's tail and handing her off to her mother. "I would like to discuss something with you, and I think I could do with a good spar."

Pointe grins. "Absolutely."

⁓⁓⁓

Law Manor's sparring room is situated in the estate's old hound kennels. Pointe has no love for fox hunting, and no time for the pursuit, really, so he had the shed converted. It is a sensible use of the space.

I take stock of the changes in my friend as he removes his house-robe and good jacket. Clearly, he has dressed up to host his lord. When I was in Turn Hall, he only ever wore his more serviceable gray leather doublet, but that was because I never required him to dress to his station as one of the Landed Gentry if it was just the two of us. Pointe looks good in a neckcloth and waistcoat of worsted cloth-of-silver, but he would never believe me if I told him. He thinks they make him look stuffy.

His shoulders are still broad, his posture still the indolent slouch that hides his true strength and speed, his teeth still white and straight, his eyes still crinkling with merriment. His hair is a little longer, his lantern jaw a little more jowly. But beyond that, he is still remarkably attractive and fit for a man in his late forties.

The lines around his mouth are deeper, though, the bags under his eyes puffier, and his skin more sallow. His hair, once a striking mix of salt and pepper, is now entirely silver.

"Is my brother such a handful?" I ask, stripping to my shirtsleeves as well and accepting the practice sword that Pointe offers me. It is lighter than Smoke, and buttoned, so I give it a few test swings to gauge it. "You've gone completely gray. And you look like you haven't slept in a week."

"Actually," Pointe says, stretching his shoulders, "having your brother back in Lysse has been useful. Petty theft and vandalism have all but vanished. Nobody wants to get caught by Kintyre Turn. Or Bevel Dom."

"Then why...?" I prompt as I choose where to make my first stand on the stone floor.

Pointe shrugs, nonchalant, but I can see the weariness behind it.

"I left marriage too late."

I'm not certain what he means by this, so I salute him and wait for his reply instead. "But you married for love, rather than by necessity. That is admirable," I say as his sword replies.

"My son is too young," Pointe says, stepping back into his stance. "It's a young man's racket, this, Forsyth. And I had hoped to have a protégé by now, someone to do the legwork." He raises his own sword and salutes me.

I concentrate on the first few lunges and parries, fumbling a riposte that I would have aced before. Pointe has only buttoned me once, though, and while I may be two years out of practice sparring, I will do my best to keep him from breaking that record. When both of us have broken apart, taking a few steps out of range to circle and assess one another, I ask:

"And you do not?"

"I had one for a bit, but it just wasn't in him, really. The lad fell in love and went off with one of our kitchen maids. They have a croft down by the border with Chell. Nice pear orchard. She's expecting."

"You have plenty of time to train another," I reassure him, taking the opportunity to try to catch him while his feet are positioned incorrectly. Though, that is hardly a fair assessment, as Pointe's footwork is *always* lazy.

"I don't know," Pointe says, dancing back and raising his sword to block my wide swing. "I feel like I've forgotten half of what I learned from my own father. I had another option in mind, but—"

"But?"

"Wyndam turned me down," he says, managing to back me into a corner tidily. I duck under his sword and whirl around behind him, buttoning his shoulder. He groans, grins at me, and we reset in the center of the shed.

"Kintyre's Wyndam?" I ask, wanting to be certain.

"He seems a bright lad," Pointe says. "Has a good sense of justice. Good fighter. He's much different with a sword than you, says he learned from his mother. I know he can't be sheriff and lord both, but I thought that he could take over from me while Kintyre was lord, while Wyndam is still the lordling, and then, when Lewko was old enough to take my place, Wyndam could take over for Kintyre."

"Hmmm," I say, dropping my sword as I mull this over. "And do you suppose the lad would be pleased to be nothing but a stop-gap?"

"Well, I... never thought of it like that," Pointe admits. He scratches the back of his neck with the pommel of his sword, sheepish.

"And yet, you are the second person in as many days

to tell me of your plans for the lad. And the Pirate Queen abandoned him on land on his fifteenth birthday, so there is yet another choice taken from him. In all of this, I have yet to hear *Wyndam's* opinion of his own future."

"One day, he'll be Lord of Lysse and Turnshire," Pointe says. "What could possibly be better than that?"

"What indeed," I wonder, and then must concentrate as Pointe tries to take cheeky advantage of my distraction.

CAPS

In Sherwilde, to the south, it is a woodsman's cap of Carvel-green. The Chipping is right at the doorstep of Kingskeep, the capital of Hain, and consists mainly of forest. Men earn their way here by maintaining the herds of deer living among the trees. Most of them are destined for the tables of the nobility, but there is no rule saying that the Shepherds of the Herd cannot take a deer for their own use as well. They maintain a careful balance, culling only as many as the herds can spare, and generally the sick and old. Besides that, they are also great traders in rabbit and fox fur. There are no wolves in these woods, for they long ago fled the greater predator that is human men.

Amid the trees live also a colony of Sylvan Elves, and scores of fauns and dryads, who play chase under the canopy-green shadows during the day and make love to whomever will consent to lay with them at night. There are very few of the human population here who can claim to be of pure blood.

The hat belongs to a hunter's son, and he is easy enough to seduce away from his day's work in the tannery. Solinde is frustrated that her search is taking as much time as it is, and she takes it out on him, behaving like a wild thing as she lets him flip up her skirts and take her rough against a tree. She leaves fingernail divots in the bark, which makes the dryad who calls the tree home shriek.

Solinde runs from her wrath like a fleet-footed deer, amused by this lesser creature's pain and anger, the green cap trailing from her hand like a banner. She laughs, and laughs, and laughs as she tosses it into another huntsman's fire.

EIGHT

By the time we have finished our spar, have had a quick splash to whisk away the sweat, and I have borrowed a clean shirt, it is nigh on dinner time. Pointe's butler informs us that Dorthi's invitation to stay for dinner has been accepted by the rest of my party, but I want to confer with their cook about Alis's meal all the same. Pointe steps away to inquire after a carriage for us later tonight, and I make my own way toward the kitchen. When I am nearly there, the sound of Bevel's voice floating out of one of the smaller salons catches my ears and my attention.

"I don't understand why you won't accept!" he is saying, clearly irate. With all the stealth of a former Shadow Hand, I creep toward the door and eavesdrop. Silence meets Bevel's demand. "What, and now you won't speak to me either, is that it? Wyndam Turn, you will put down that book, look me in the eye, and *answer* me."

"Bevel," I hear Kintyre say. "Leave the lad alone."

"Well, *you* make him answer then," Bevel snarls. "As he is so fond of saying, I am not his father, and I cannot order him to do anything. So *you* do it."

"Awww, Bev," Kintyre wheedles. "You know that he—"

"I know nothing of the sort. He's been nothing but resentful and churlish to me since the moment he was dumped on our doorstep!"

"Well, maybe if you didn't yell at him all the time, he wouldn't be!"

"Well, maybe if he just did as he was asked, I wouldn't have to yell!" Bevel lobs back. "And I think Wyndam is perfectly capable of answering for himself! So tell me, lad, a posting with the Sword of Turnshire isn't impressive enough for you? Is it not *grand* enough for a Prince of Pirates? Or is it switching sides to enforce the law that is beneath you?"

Still no answer, though Bevel waits for it.

"Lay off the lad," Kintyre rumbles. "Besides, Pointe is boring."

"Just because you aren't entertained for every moment you're with him doesn't mean you can excuse bad behavior, Kin. The Pointes are Forssy's friends. Besides that, they're our nearest neighbors, and when Wyndam inherits the seat of Lysse Chipping, either Rupin Pointe, or his son, will be the Chipping Sheriff, yeah? Standing in until Lewko is old enough is the smart thing to do—Wyndam will be well versed in the laws that will be his duty to help the Sheriff enforce. Wyndam can't *afford* to have a bad relationship with them, and neither can you, Kin!"

"Oh, Bevel, you need to calm down—"

"I do not! You, Kintyre Turn, must at least try to learn the graces of local politics! I cannot always be here to smooth the way for the both of you, and we both know that there will be a time when I *won't* be."

"Bevel, don't say things like that," Kintyre pleads, softly, gently, a little bit broken. I can hear Bevel's frustrated, resigned sigh, hear the shift of cloth and the soft *tamp* of skin on skin, the gentle wet suck of a kiss. Eugh. "It breaks my heart."

"And it breaks *my* heart to see that neither of you will lift a finger toward your own betterment, for your own sake. Kin, I *worry*."

"Don't." Another kiss, this one longer. I hear a second door on the far side of the room open and close.

"I wouldn't if you *made an effort*. Please."

A kiss. "Very well," Kintyre says, resigned. "Did you hear that, Wyndam? We'll have to promise to... Wyndam? Drat and blast, where has that boy got to *now*?"

"I can't imagine that standing there watching his father make love was comfortable," Bevel chortles. He always was more mellow after an argument with Kintyre has been won in his favor.

"We were *not* 'making love,'" Kintyre wheedles. "We were just kissing."

"Just?" Bevel asks, his tone arch. "With what you were doing with your tongue?"

"Oh, liked that, did you? Shall I do it again?"

"Mmmm," Bevel agrees, and it is at this point that I decide it best to withdraw. Like my nephew, I have no desire to listen to my brother "make love." I make for the kitchens instead.

The sun has set by the time I have been to see the cook about Alis' dinner. I use the kitchen servants' door to go fetch Pointe from the stables for dinner. Requesting a carriage should not have taken so long. I wonder if he also heard Bevel and Kintyre fighting through the salon window and decided to dawdle. But when I find Pointe, he is discussing tack with a groom, and apologizes for having lost track of time. Pointe sends the boy to his own supper when I come to escort him to his.

The sunset is always early in spring, and I soak in the final watercolor smudges of rose, and gold, and violet hovering over the green wheat on the horizon as we walk. I realize that the blooming starlight isn't as intense as I remember it being. Wondering if it was just the haze of nostalgia that had painted them so, I look up.

And then I stop.

Pointe stops beside me, staring up as well, trying to follow my line of sight. "Forsyth? What is it?"

"It's wrong," I gasp, startled by what I am seeing. Or rather, what I am not seeing. I point upward to the great dark swatches of sky. "What has happened to the stars?"

"The stars?" He follows my finger and blinks, realization dawning as he answers: "I... huh. I don't know."

"The constellation of the Thoughtful Faun is gone. Look, so too has the Maiden's Slipper. And the Wizard's Ring."

Fauns. Shoes. Rings.

A thrill of discovery and understanding, of sudden and orgasmic *knowledge*, rushes up my spine and out into my limbs, making my toes and fingers and lips tingle with the excitement of it. I do not have the whole pattern, not yet. But I have finally gotten my grip around a piece of it.

Now to decipher the size and scope of the rest of the puzzle.

~~~

The desire to discuss my revelation with my wife settles in my extremities like a buzzing vibration. I must hold my tongue throughout the meal, however. I need to discuss my discovery with her, first, in private, before I alarm those around me with the news. Moreover, Pip's origins are still meant to be a secret from Lewko and Dorthi. Pip keeps shooting me concerned looks. The double joy of understanding and being amid the crush of friends and family again has probably left me with a manic smile. After dinner, we return to Turn Hall, filled with the warm cheer of good company, good food, and good wine. Velshi is waiting for Kintyre, and pulls him aside to attend to some Chipping business before we have even made it through the foyer.
~~~

We are also informed, by Keriens, who is there to take our coats, that one of my—one of *Bevel's*—Shadow's Men is waiting for him in his private study. Bevel bids us goodnight, sending a look of regret toward Alis. He spent much of the dinner seated beside Lewko, and I am seeing, I think, for the first time, just how much my brother's trothed desires children. That may, I reason, be the explanation for the rift between Wyndam and himself. Does Bevel feel cheated of the boy's childhood?

The remaining group moves upstairs. Wyndam loses no time in shutting himself up in his own chambers, a look of relief clear upon his face. He does not even bid us goodnight. I might almost be offended, if I didn't remember how much I'd looked forward to the end of the day when I was his age. It was a time to escape my brother and my father and read, alone, unbothered. And by seventeen, it was also a way to work on the secret tutelage that Lewko Pointe the Elder had begun with me the years previous, so as to hone my skills as a spy before I inherited the Mask.

Thus, Pip, Alis, and I are left in the hall outside our rooms, a look of bemusement on our faces and the few hours in which I had hoped to speak to Bevel about the missing constellations suddenly empty of distractions.

"Well, *bao bei*," I say, opening the door. "What do you say to putting the young Ladyling of Lysse to bed, opening a bottle of wine, and sharing all the gossip we have accumulated today?"

"Gossip?" Pip asks, but her tone is dryly arch and there is a smile playing around the corners of her lips. I chase it with my own mouth, tasting the cream gravy from tonight's supper. "I never gossip," she protests when I pull back to bestow a peck on Alis's forehead.

"But you listen to it," I point out, and Pip's grin blossoms into full growth.

"That's true," she agrees.

Cook has left milk on the credenza, and it is still cool in its earthenware cup. She must have come up as soon as she heard us return. There is a small bowl of pottage, with a little child-sized spoon, and a tray of pastry sweets, cheese, and stone fruits. There is also a bottle of my favorite wine—a rich, jammy vintage from Brystal, where the warm sea and the high mountains make for difficult cultivation, but gorgeous grapes. (I had crates and crates of this wine in the cellar, which I understand that Bevel has now claimed for himself, as, in this, we share tastes.) It seems that although my staff are not technically mine any longer, they still recall their former lordling's preferences and are happy to accommodate them.

I take charge of Alis's little feeding and subsequent wipe-down as Pip changes into her sleeping shift and goes about the business of pouring out the wine. Alis protests with lusty sobs when we put her in the crib, clutching Library and generally making it known that we are the most miserable, villainous human beings on the planet for making her go to bed, even if we are still in the same room as her. Her direct line of sight is compromised, however, when I draw the changing screen out of the corner of the room to block her view of the fire and its light, shrouding her half of the room in flickering, soothing shadow. The darkness usually works as a balm to her.

It takes Alis no more than five more minutes of sobs, and then she is flat on her back and dead asleep. Pip and I aren't even through our first glasses of wine by the time silence falls. But in that time, I've changed into my own sleeping shift—I am not used to so much fabric and air around my privates anymore, and I can't be certain if I miss my sleeping pants or not—and Pip and I are curled around one another, sitting on the plush lambskin rug in front of the hearth.

Pip fills me in on the goings on of the Pointe household—Dorthi is worried that her newest kitchen girl is going to run off with one of the mermaids she met while on a seaside holiday with her family, the Free School I funded for the children of Turnshire has an open day in a fortnight to allow parents to come see the children's play and recitals, Lewko is falling behind in his literature studies, and Kintyre has funded the opening of second school. It will be located in Faversquare, a smaller market on the other side of Lysse, and will be for those children for whom Turnshire is too far a walk. The last bit of news pleases me greatly, and I share that pleasure with my wife in the form of more chasing kisses.

I missed Pip terribly while we were at odds, and I am determined to show her just how much. Mindful of the baby on the other side of the privacy screen, we seal our noises behind each other's lips and keep it quick. Hands are marvelous, and there is something illicitly thrilling about reaching under each other's clothes like inexperienced youths. As Pip's fingers are the stickier when we are done, it falls to me to fetch the wash basin and cloth, and then the wine bottle and tray of tasties.

Then it is my turn to share the gossip I learned— Rupin's concerns about a protégé, the difficulties that Kintyre and Bevel are having with Wyndam, and lastly, the constellations.

Pip, languorous and soft in the afterglow and the influence of good wine, rouses herself at this last bit of news and fetches a piece of parchment, a quill, and an ink pot from the credenza. The staff also know me well enough that they left stationary for me. Pip struggles with the quill, and for a moment, I am consumed with a bizarre and fierce homesickness for ball-point pens. Once I realize what she is doing, I take the quill from her, lay the parchment flat on the wooden floor next to the rug, and complete the graph. Within an hour, we have an Excel Sheet composed of all the lost books whose names I can recall on one axis, and the names and stars of the vanished constellations on another. It takes me several trips to the window, and one down to my library for a tome on astronomy charts, to complete it, and it is closer to morning than either of us cares to admit when we sit back and take a look at the picture the Excel reveals.

We can only conclude that the vanished books and missing stars are, indeed, related. Too many of the stories for both feature similar props.

Fauns, shoes, rings, I write below the chart. And then, studying the list of constellations, I add, *swords, caps* or *feathers, thimbles (sewing supplies), shadows, thrones.*

Quizzing Pip, I learn that the magic of the vanished books reaches her even here. Gone, for her, is *Robin Hood; Peter Pan; Tom Thumb; American Gods; Earthsea; The Lion, the Witch, and the Wardrobe;* and the whole of the books and episodes of *Game of Thrones.* And many more, most likely, but those are the stories that I can recall best. I am thankful that I am a voracious reader, and that my time as a library assistant seems to be paying dividends.

Unsettled, the amorous mood lost, we fold up this new Excel and hide it amid our Victoria clothing in the chest at the bottom of the wardrobe. Then we crawl into bed, stony-faced and silent, and hold each other tight. It is dawn before the whirring fear in my mind quiets enough to let me sleep.

~~~

A hushed discussion with Bevel over breakfast leads to Kintyre, Bevel, Pip, and I adjourning to my library with the Excel spread out before us on my desk. The
~~~

doors have been repaired, and Wyndam seems extremely put out to be tasked with watching Alis while the adults confer. He says nothing, but makes a grunt of displeasure and stomps away to the kitchen with a still muzzy-eyed Alis on his hip.

"It looks like we've got shared purposes, Forssy," Bevel says, handing me a sheaf of letters from the Shadow's Men, some even from King Carvel, detailing the concerns and research the Shadow Hand has undergone in regards to the matter of the dying stars.

"Shared purposes," I muse. "Yes, perhaps that is why we're here?"

"But what has that kind of power?" Pip asked. "Last time, it took a Deal-Maker Spirit, and a vial of Deal-Maker's blood, to send us through the portal. I'm under the impression it takes a pretty big bargain to get a Deal like that without the blood. You'd have to be willing to give up a lot. Like, giving-up-all-of-your-own-magic a lot."

"And if you did, why use it to bring back Forssy?" Kintyre asks, and claps a hand on my shoulder when I shoot him a disgusted look. "Not meaning to be offensive, brother, but there are greater things to spend a Deal on than bringing back the former Shadow Hand. If someone wanted what you knew, they could have used the Deal to take Bevel, or the Mask."

"Unless they knew that I still carried the information with me," I say, tapping my own forehead. "But how could they? Everyone who knew the former Shadow Hand must presume he died when his—please forgive me, Bevel—shorter successor took over."

"Yeah, that gave Carvel a shock, I'll tell you," Bevel says. "Went to let him know, used your tapestry trick, and I thought he would swallow his teeth, I did. He was happy to hear you weren't dead, though. I told him that you'd just gone back to Pip's kingdom to live happily ever after, yeah? He sends his congratulations."

"And is that what you told everyone else about Forsyth Turn's disappearance?" I ask.

Kintyre nods. "And everyone was pleased for you, as well. They missed you, of course. Especially at first, when, ah, I proved to be better at adventuring than counting grain tithes from your tenants. Took a few tries to get that right. And, uh, helping to plant the next harvest to make up for it." He looks vaguely ashamed, scratching the back of his neck awkwardly. I am filled with the warmth of filial affection. The poor oaf.

I stand back from the desk and rub my hands over my face. I am desperate for a coffee, but all Lysse offers is tea, and it just tastes *wrong* to me now. I sip the cup I brought into my study with me all the same. Caffeine is caffeine. "Then I don't see any reason why anyone could have desired my return strongly enough to make the kind of Deal that would be required."

"So, we're clueless?" Kintyre snarls, and I can see his hand flexing in the empty space where Foesmiter would have hung were he armed for a quest. My brother always did prefer to bash his way through problems, rather than think them through instead.

"I miss the Internet," Pip says softly.

"Why?" I ask, ignoring the confused looks from the others.

"If this has happened before, then there's got to be a record of it, right? It'd be convenient to be able to Google this. Maybe even figure out why it's happening."

I shake my head. "The books were gone from the Internet as well. If this has happened before, I doubt there are any public records of it digitally available. Oh, hm," I add, as an idea flutters into existence.

"Hm?" Pip echoes me, optimistically.

"There *could* be records," I say. "If it has happened

before. However, they must be old ones, for I have read nothing of this in the King's Library, nor were there any memories of it occurring in the days of the Shadow Hands previously stored within the Mask."

"But maybe there's some in the Lost Library?" Bevel jumps in, proving him more capable of thinking forward than I had thought. Ah, but Bevel always was a savvy little hedgehog, even before the information of a hundred Shadow Hands was dumped into his mind.

"Is it accessible?" Pip asks.

Kintyre huffs. "Nearly. There are scholars there now. But it's not open to the common people, not yet."

"Who has taken stewardship?" I ask, curious. The Library was located in Miliway Chipping in our Kingdom of Hain, but contained the combined knowledge of all of the peoples of the world. Technically, it would be up to Lord Micha to run the Library, but the contents thereof would be too valuable to mishandle, especially since the Library had been lost for so many centuries.

"There is an accord, but the scholars of Gadot are being unreasonably tardy about the whole affair, of course," Kintyre complains. "But that's no surprise. It always seems that we are waiting on Gadot."

For the first time in my life, I find myself choking on a laugh because my brother has inadvertently said some-thing that he cannot understand is reflected in Pip's—in *my*—world. A flood of memories of Pip making the very same noise, most likely for the very same reason, washes across my mind. Pip and I share an amused glance, but I wave the question away when Bevel inquires as to the source of our amusement.

"Can we gain access to the Library?" I ask, instead of explaining a play from the Writer's realm that nearly defies explanation in and of itself. "If we go?"

Bevel shrugs. "Sure."

Pip and I exchange a glance. She nods. "Very well, then," I say. "Pip and I will travel there tomorrow. I think it best if Alis remains—"

"No," Bevel says. "As Shadow Hand, I should go with you."

Another glance and another nod, and it seems Pip and I are of an accord on that point, at least. "Yes, agreed," I begin, but then it is my brother cutting me off.

"Not without me, Bev!" he says.

"Kin, we've talked about this," Bevel says, low and urgent, turning to face Kintyre. "I'm Shadow Hand now. That means there's adventures that I have to go on without you. You're Lord Turn."

"Pointe is perfectly capable of—"

"But you shouldn't ask it of him! He has his own duties to see to. You can't assume he'll be able to do both—"

"Well, if Wyndam would just step up, as he's been asked to—"

"This isn't the place for this argument, Kin!"

"Well, if not here, when?" my brother snarls. "I won't have you go without me!"

"There's no danger," I say, trying to placate.

"How do you know that?" Kintyre says. There is a desperation in his expression that I have never seen before, a deep, affectionate worry. He takes his trothed's hands in his, and the gesture is startlingly romantic and honest. "This sounds an awful lot like the beginning of a quest, and I won't leave you out there alone, Bevel."

"If you haven't noticed, I survived all our other quests just fine, Kin! You don't have to make me sound like some maiden that needs—"

"Of course not, Bev! I just…"

"Have been treating me like you can't trust me to keep myself alive ever since I accepted the Mask."

Kintyre turns away, crossing his arms and lowering his chin. His hair is not in its usual club, and falls across his face, obscuring what I assume must be an epic pout.

"Do you resent that I can come and go, while you are tied to Turnshire?" Bevel asks softly, and Pip and I withdraw to the far side of the study when Bevel lays a hand on Kintyre's arm, using the other to cup my brother's chin and force their eyes to meet.

Kintyre nods.

"Wow, drama," Pip whispers. Our own recent fights are still fresh on her mind, apparently, for she curls herself against me and wraps her arms around my waist. I return the embrace and lay my scarred cheek against the crown of her head.

"Change has never come easy to Kintyre," I whisper to my wife, then lean down to press a kiss against the little leaf at her nape. "And I can well imagine that he feels left out of Bevel's excursions."

Pip shakes her head and steps free of me.

"Boys!" she shouts, clapping her hands to get their attention. Both men turn to her with bewildered expressions. "It's just a trip to the Library, right? Knowing this world as I do, it's probably the first step in a Seven Station Quest, but step one is always safely gathering information. I don't see why we all can't go."

"Pointe—" Bevel starts again, exasperated.

"It does us no good to assume he'll say no when we haven't even asked him," Kintyre says. "And it will give him an opportunity to, perhaps, interview other young men"—Pip elbows him—"and women for his apprentice, if he is out in the Chipping on his lord's business."

Bevel grunts, but nods. Kintyre beams, triumphant.

"I was thinking," Pip adds. "It's not fair to leave Wyndam behind, not when he hasn't seen much of Hain, so why don't we make it a road trip?"

"Road trip?" Bevel echoes.

I can't help but chuckle at my wife. "What, you mean load all the kids into the camper-van and go?"

Pip's grin in the face of Bevel and Kintyre's incomprehension is like a sunrise. "Exactly!"

The caravan that leaves Turnshire three days later must be quite a sight, for the farmers whose homesteads we pass all whistle and laugh as we go by, waving their hats and tools, calling "halloos" to their lords and lordlings. I do not blame them, nor the children who follow after our party laughing and begging for sweets as we skirt their farms. Pip has brought a good deal of butter toffee with us, as Alis has discovered a liking for them, and the supply dwindles rapidly.

The Library Lion, whom Lewko primly informed me has been named Capplederry, is hitched to a covered cart. The farms around Turnshire couldn't afford to lend us an ox for our journey, not at this stage of the planting season, and none of the horses housed at Turn Hall have ever been broken to the yoke. Kintyre does not keep a carriage—he says it makes him feel infirm and old—so Father's old trap is moldering in the hay barn under a canvas tarp.

It was Wyndam, in his usual wordless way, who suggested the Library Lion on our second visit to Law Manor to discuss the issue of governing Lysse while we were away. As he often does, Kintyre won that argument, and I was convinced to ask Pointe to stand in while we are on the road. Pointe, the traitor, was happy to do it.

Capplederry is larger than an ox and stronger, it seems, as well. The harness and cart do not seem to be any sort of noticeable burden to the creature. It pulls us along contentedly, pausing only every now and again to groom itself. When we make our relief breaks, we unhitch the creature from the yoke, leaving on the harness, and it chases butterflies through the verge, or naps in a convenient puddle of sunshine. We have no fear of nighttime predators with Capplederry prowling the outskirts of our camps.

Wyndam and Capplederry seem to have formed a fast friendship. Whenever Capplederry is unhitched, Wyndam teases and taunts the cat with switches of grass or a willow branch, eyes alight with pleasure when Capplederry rolls and meows and pounces, an emotion that I have rarely seen in my nephew's gaze otherwise. After a few days of roadside inns and bedding down in the cart when there is no inn to be had, Wyndam takes to sleeping with Capplederry. No matter where the rest of us sleep, the lad is instead curled on the cat's forepaws and gamely suffering its massive tongue grooming him. I cannot hear what he says to the great cat, but whatever it is, it keeps his face buried in the creature's ruff, and Capplederry purring loud as a motorcycle.

Wyndam has equipped himself with a short, curved sword the likes of which I have never seen outside the sketches in the reports of the Shadow's Men. It is the preferred weapon of pirates, for it has great power in the swing and cut of it without having too great a reach for the close confines of a ship. Pip calls it a scimitar, and grumbles a bit about the fetishization of the exotic and orientalism on the part of Elgar Reed. Wyndam practices with it every evening, and when Kintyre joins him for a few practice bouts, the lad's face glows with affection and pride.

Kintyre's is a powerful, bashing, solid technique. He runs and ducks, but otherwise remains planted, hacking and cutting like a castle wall come to life, letting the power of his swing and the weight of his sword take off limbs and sever heads when in battle. This is very different from the courtly form of dueling in which I have been trained. Smoke is a basket-handled rapier, as is the blade I have borrowed from Pointe to carry now. They are thin and swift and deadly sharp, made for slipping silently between ribs and bones, incapacitating quickly and efficiently. My footwork is quick, tripping, rather more like ballet than fighting, designed to flee or chase swiftly. Wyndam's style is different again, a tumbling, curling, rounded dance that is part acrobatics, part whirling dervish. His fights are those of a thousand cuts, scoring his opponent—or, rather, whatever tree he is attacking for practice—with small nicks and slices that would have a human bleeding and sliding about in the gore pooling on a ship's decking.

I would very much like to test my blade against Wyndam's, but the lad is only interested in sparring with his father. Wyndam is only interested in his father, full stop, it seems. The rest of us he treats like little annoyances.

Lucky, then, that the rest of my family is here to occupy my attention.

Our cart is covered, and supplied with two Wisp-lanterns. Pip and Alis ride amid pillows and our supplies, mostly. Though, every now and again, Pip and Kintyre swap out, and she takes her turn riding in the vanguard on Karlurban. He was Pip's horse during her first tour of Hain, and now serves the Lord Turn. Dauntless, my horse, remains in the service of the Shadow Hand, but was very pleased to see me. He remembers who I am, which is heartwarming.

When Pip is riding, Kintyre, in the back of the cart, occupies his hands by weaving large, conical eel-traps out of the roadside ditch-reeds. These prove useful when we make camp by cool streams with shaded banks. Bevel's grilled eel is something to behold.

Bevel drives the cart when Dauntless and I ride the head, and Bevel and I swap when he becomes bored or anxious. Eventually, Wyndam gives up riding in the cart at all, and simply sits astride Capplederry's harness. He doesn't seem to be any extra burden to the great cat, so we leave him to it.

Amid our sleep rolls, road rations, and cooking gear, as well as the prodigious amount of supplies and toys required to travel with a babe quickly approaching the toddler stage, is space for Pip's writing supplies and my old travel desk. The new Excel is spread upon her lap when she isn't entertaining Alis, and she slowly teaches herself to read our script with the children's primers I brought along. In retrospect, never teaching my wife to read the runes of Hain before this was a mistake, but neither of us thought we would ever be in need of them again.

On day four, when Alis is thoroughly bored of sitting in the cart, playing with Library and the other stuffies Cook had sewn for her, she starts to fuss. She is old enough and well-coordinated enough now to sit upright on her own, and so Bevel creates a sort of child-harness out of a spare scarf and lashes her onto his lap on the cart-driver's bench. He even goes so far as to let her hold the reins. Capplederry needs no controlling and seems to take no issue with Alis tugging and waving the leads, and my daughter takes great delight in learning the phrases "Walk on!" and "Whoa now!"

That night, Alis sticks close to her Uncle Bevel, staring up at him with worshipful adoration as he lets her stir the pot of travel stew and make balls of the last of the bread dough. Bevel keeps her safely away from the fire-warmed stone he spreads the dough balls over, and I am struck again by how fond Bevel is of Alis. I know that he has six older brothers, and that each of them have children. It occurs to me that in tying himself to Kintyre,

Bevel has lost forever the chance to have children of his own.

Unless he and Kintyre agree to allow Bevel to sire a child on some woman willing to then give up all ties to it, there is very little in the way of medical or magical alternatives in this realm for two men. My suspicions that Bevel wishes he and Kintyre had known about Wyndam earlier are further enforced whenever I see the wistful way Bevel's gaze cuts between my daughter and Kintyre's son.

Not content with coming in second-best in the hierarchy of affection, Kintyre has Alis lashed to his chest by the time we are all ready to ride the next morning, the carrier wrapping so tight that Alis can only wriggle her arms and legs. She beats the back of her head against Kintyre's chest in joy, feet dancing on the pommel of his saddle, babbling a sweet stream of nonsense that Kintyre listens to with grave attention. As we stop for our noon break, reveling in the bright, high sky and the way the humidity has crept up on us the further south we have traveled, Kintyre unwraps Alis and hefts her over his shoulder like a sack of flour. He carries her over to the blanket Pip has spread out on the side of the road, pretending to ignore her wiggly shrieks of delight.

"See, Kin?" Bevel says as he watches all this. "You didn't squash her at all."

"I was still afraid I might," my brother says, and it's clearly an old and well-gnawed bone between them.

We are right at the boundary of Miliway Chipping. The road is smooth and wide from thousands of farmers trading their grains to other Chippings, and the verge is verdant and spotted with blackberries. Kintyre crouches to show Alis how to pick the ripe ones, and then yelps.

"Ow! I think your daughter just touched my brains!" When I look up, Kintyre is staring at Alis with horror, and my daughter is standing beside him, grinning, berry-blacked fingers filled with squashed fruit. "Those baby fingers are small. It fit right inside!"

"Now, now, sweeting," I say, scooping her up to suck kisses on her cheeks. "We do not shove blackberries into our uncle's ears."

After lunch, Kintyre offers Alis to Wyndam, but the boy only looks away, clearly uninterested, and a one-sided row erupts when Kintyre chastises him for his sullen silence. Wyndam's posture takes on a slumped curve of misery that I remember all too well from when I was the lad's age and Kintyre laid into me. I remind my brother in a tone far too innocent that Kintyre himself did not speak for a full two months while his voice was changing out of sheer embarrassment. Kintyre goes red and cuts his tirade short. Wyndam regards me with a kind of small, private appreciation, and spends the rest of the afternoon shooting thoughtful, considering looks in my direction.

Alis rides instead with me, that afternoon. And when a shrill screech rings out from the wheat field to our left, I am grateful that Alis is with me on Dauntless, and not impeding Kintyre and Bevel's ability to draw their swords.

MIRRORS

Solinde comes south again, into Miliway, in search of the next totem. She is strong enough now, her powers replenished enough, that she can summon not only storms, but also fogs and clouds upon which to ride. In Miliway, a colony of gnomes have overtaken a rabbit warren. Solinde stands above a small horde of them, hidden from view by the wheat that, here, in the most fertile region of Hain, is already as high as the crown of her head. Solinde feels the totem pulling at her blood, her power rushing downward into the ground. She summons a breeze and invades the mouth of the warren, slipping past and around the foul little creatures lurking inside. The air fills with the back draft and the scent of old blood and dusty rot.

When her magic has closed around the thing, she tears it upward, through the soil. A great screaming shriek goes up, the whole colony protesting and startled and swearing revenge in a single voice. It is bloodthirsty and bitter, and Solinde flees on the wind, howling with laughter, a filthy, enchanted looking glass clutched to her breast

Below her, she spots a young woman riding a deer on the Field Road. The maid is beautiful in all the ways that Solinde was never allowed to be when *she* was mortal. She hates the lass immediately, with everything that she is. Petty and vengeful, Solinde throws the mirror down.

It shatters against the deer's antlers, breaking its magic forever.

The maiden screams. The deer rears and throws her off, shaking the shards of glass out of its fur. The gnomes descend upon them like a savage wave. Solinde calls up a cloud and hides within the dense moisture to watch the sport the gnomes make of the maiden. The girl scrambles to her feet, her slippers flying off as she flees through the dirt and between the wheat stalks. Iron pikes—this breed of gnome's preferred weapon—fly.

"Irtax!" the girl shrieks when the deer is felled. The beast's eyes roll white, blood foam frothing on its muzzle as it struggles to breathe with punctured lungs. Its delicate hooves kick and flail, braining several of the least intelligent of its murderers.

The gnomes are short enough for the girl to leap over them when they surround her, but they stab at her dress. Solinde hopes they are also stabbing the maiden's finely formed legs, feeling a great and vengeful need to see the lass's perfection forever destroyed, but the sharp pike-heads only shred the maiden's overgown. Disgusted, Solinde changes the direction of the wind, so that the rest of the gnome colony will scent the fresh blood and descend upon the girl.

But something else, it seems, smells it as well.

The full-throated roar rips through the air, and a blur the color of sandstone leaps over the bushes that mark the delineation between the road and the field. The thing is across the expanse of field like a crossbow bolt. The gnomes scatter and regroup as some human boy clad all in black slides down the creature's mane and yanks the maiden free. Together, hand in hand, the humans run back toward the verge, dodging iron pikes and jumping gnomes. The great creature follows in their wake, batting aside the swarming colony, but never truly managing to break free of them. There are simply too many.

The swarm of red-hatted creatures cling to the cat's fur, scurry at its tail, biting and scratching like aggressive barbs, and Solinde *laughs*. The humans are cornered. Together, they try to scramble up the beast's back. The lad expertly climbs the rigging of the cat's harness, but the girl is less sure-footed, her feet slick with blood and dirt, and the gnomes grab hold of her skirts and drag her back down. She shrieks again, and the cat slashes claws through the gnomes that try to descend upon her, giving the maiden time to scramble to her feet and dash for the hedge.

Another roar of fury goes up from the gnomes as their prey begins to outpace them, and then, abruptly, there is another player on the scene. It is a man on a nut-brown gelding, his blond-gray hair waving like a war banner in his wake as his mount races toward the melee. A sword flashes out of its sheath and into the man's hand as if by magic, the pommel golden and twisted in the shape of great Urlish forge-hammers. The man is broad of shoulder, trim of waist despite his advancing years, and blood-freezingly familiar.

Kintyre Turn! It is like the truth of his identity has become sentient and flown up into the air, clutching her around the throat. *And the lad in black is the idiot boy I Dealt with!*

The unexpected appearance of he whom she hates more than any mortal in this world—save her late husband, and he is no longer in this world—shocks Solinde into inaction. She hesitates just a moment too long, and by then, the maiden who was the target of her ire has escaped, and the Turns and their mounts are cutting through and crushing the straggling remains of the gnome colony on their way back to the main road.

Destroy him! The command rings in her head in the

voice of he whom she seeks. It is not really him, no, but her memory of him, as she last saw him. When he had been young and shrill and impetuous, impotent in his ability to fight back against the wizard his father had sold him to as apprentice, and wrathful in the realization of it.

She summons up a wind, not strong enough yet to be a twister, but building toward it fast. The wind pushes what few gnomes survive away from the verge and toward Kintyre Turn, surrounding him with a tumbling, outraged, crashing wave of iron pikes and sharp teeth. They cut and cling to both his legs and the horses' as they pass. She teases and vexes the gnomes until they are mad with anger, lashing out at each other as much as her target.

She is so intent on her prey that she nearly does not hear the iron pike sailing toward her in time. But hear it she does, and Solinde ducks. Her concentration broken, the whirlwind immediately dies down, and beneath her feet, the cloud shifts and threatens to dump her into the sky. Wrath and ruin on her mind, Solinde whips around to smite whatever gnome dared aim at her. Instead, she meets the determined, grim, jet gaze of Wyndam Turn.

The lad hefts a second iron pike, aiming, Solinde now sees, not at her specifically, but at the lone cloud in the sky, the obvious place from which to assume a weather witch is controlling her vortex. Solinde had heard that Kintyre Turn was in great supply of muscle, but little of brains. Clearly, his son differs.

The second pike sails, shredding through Solinde's cloud, and she drops.

She does not scream, for she has enough power to make the air dense beneath her, to slide into a cold, wet cradle. But she is weakening. She is waning. She has spent too much of herself and her power on this petty pursuit of the maiden, and it has left her with little to expend on her revenge. She realizes, with a bitter lump at the back of her throat, that she must use what she has left to flee. *Flee*, like a beaten hound, like a subservient *wife* banished into a corner by a raging, drunken husband. But it is either flee, or drop onto the ground where the gnomes will swarm her in the fury she whipped up in them, where Wyndam Turn will finish the job he began with the first two iron pikes, or where Kintyre will prove himself the merciless murderer she has always heard he is.

She must *run*. Hating, *hating* that this is her only rational choice, Solinde screams. It breaks across the sky like thunder. Desperate, she reaches out with her power and touches the boy, Wyndam, searches out and grasps the golden thread of connection that their Deal has woven between them. There. She cannot lose him now. Even though she must run, retreat, escape, she can now come *back*. He broke her Sigil and sent her away before she could tie the string of connection to his finger, but the Writer has somehow seen fit to give her the opportunity to do so now. He will not slip her vengeance a second time. And then, task complete, she speeds away across the sky.

NINE

The scream is high and unearthly, a hundred voices being squeezed out of a hundred throats at once, atonal and desperate and harsh. It sounds like *murder*.

Capplederry yowls, a rusty-hinge sound of challenge. With quick thinking that I can only commend, Wyndam reaches down and immediately unhooks the great cat from the yoke. The cart lurches to a halt and Capplederry springs forward, Wyndam clinging to his harness and grinning like a lunatic. No, like his *mother*.

His sword is already bared, as are his teeth, and when Capplederry leaps over the verge and into the field, he rides the wave of the creature's arc like the Prince of the Seas he used to be.

Wishing for Smoke now more than ever, I instead wheel Dauntless back to the cart and quickly pass Alis to Pip, who tucks her into the corner, shushing her even as Pip unsheathes the dagger she's been carrying at her waist all week. It is no match, of course, for Kintyre's Foesmiter, but is quick enough in its own way. Kintyre brings Karl around to protect the cart as well, and Bevel is already standing on the seat, an arrow nocked and ready to fly. I spare a moment to be grateful that Pip is wearing leather leggings for this trip instead of a dress, so that if she must flee with Alis, she won't trip on the skirts.

The shriek dies away. Silence fills the air, thick with

expectation. The wind rattles the wheat, and even Alis is holding her breath, it seems, gasping little hiccoughs quietly. My arm begins to shake from the weight of holding my sword aloft and prepared to strike—I silently curse myself for my two years of laziness in Victoria.

Breath burns in my chest, but I dare not exhale for fear of alerting whatever it is that screamed—or was making some poor other creature scream—to our location. Kintyre and Bevel are still, but Dauntless and Karl toss their heads and paw the road, ready to spring into battle if need be.

A cicada chirrups nearby, as unnerved by the silence as we are, and Pip and I both flinch. Karl knickers, bobbing his head, nostrils flared. The warriors remain still as statuary, watching. Waiting.

A sudden, piercing shriek rends the still air, and in a heartbeat, Bevel looses his arrow. It lands with a meaty *thock*, and there is an angry, vicious burble of fury on the other side of the verge.

"What is it?" Pip hisses, but no one has the time to answer, for on the other side, Capplederry rears up in the sea of wheat, roaring with fury, and hung all over with small red-and-black blurs as tall as my knee.

"Wyndam!" Kintyre shouts, and then he and Karl are over the verge before I have time to wonder whether the horse is even trained to jump.

Atop Capplederry, Wyndam has wound one free hand in the Library Lion's mane and is slashing at the hangers-on with his sword. They fall easily, cut away like ticks and burrs, screaming their fury as they fall.

"Red Caps!" Bevel shouts. "Stay on this side of the bushes!"

I have no intention of throwing myself into a field of horrible, murderous, gnomes, and instead busy myself with sweeping the bushes and cutting down any of the wee monsters attempting to escape the fangs and blades of our compatriots. They are a veritable flock, and I can taste my heart on the back of my tongue, fear that they will swarm over the cart and dip their caps in the blood of my family becoming a rich, burning bile in my throat.

No, I decide, defying my fear. *No, that will not happen! I will not allow it!* Alis, terrified by the noise of battle and struggling against her mother's hand pinning her to the floor of the cart, starts screaming.

It is so heartbreaking that all I want to do is throw myself over her and protect them both, and is so loud that I nearly miss the third shriek. It is closer now, and, I realize, human. It rings in my ears, and I whip my gaze around, trying to locate the source amid the writhing bodies of the Red Caps, the flash of steel and claw, and the tall wheat.

"There!" Pip shouts, pointing. "Forsyth!"

I follow her finger to a scrap of yellow against the green leaves, the billow of corn silk—no, it is *hair*. A hand, pale and delicate, flails toward the open air, and I put my spurs to Dauntless. We trample Red Caps as he speeds toward the struggling human. I seize her wrist and yank her out of the bushes. I have enough leverage to swing my elbow under her armpits and wrench her free, lifting her up onto the saddle. She lands awkwardly across the pommel, thigh digging into my lap. Two Red Caps drop off the skirts of her dress, but another has its pike raised to strike. The woman screams and kicks, and the nasty creature clings. My arms are both filled with reins and woman, and I cannot cut it away.

"No!" I shout, terror gripping my spine, paralyzing me with the gruesome realization that I am about to watch a person be gutted while on my own lap.

A sudden swish by my ear makes me glad that I froze. An arrow appears, as if by magic, sprouting from between the Red Cap's eyes. May the Writer bless Bevel and his aim. Dead, the Red Cap falls away. I wheel Dauntless and our shared burden back toward the safety of the cart. The woman winds her fingers around my forearm, shaking, and tries, at first, to cling to me when I make to lever her in.

"It's okay!" Pip says, sheathing her dagger to haul the woman and her voluminous skirts up amid the pillows and books. "Get up, get up!"

A crack of thunder rips across the air, and though there is one dense thunderhead above the field, the rest of the sky looks clear. But the wind is already scudding the cloud out of sight, and whatever threatening rain the cloud contains will not fall on us here, or now.

The combined rage of the thunder and Pip's voice seem to shake the woman out of her terror, and she scrambles into the cart. She immediately falls sideways onto the floor, startling Alis into another wail. The woman cuts one look toward my daughter, and then scrambles over into the corner to cover her with her own body. She is shaking, bleeding, trailing blood like a sinister snail trail along the boards of the cart, but here is the motherly instinct that Elgar Reed has forced onto every woman he writes, and for once, I am glad of it. Alis hushes under the hands of the woman, leaving Pip and I free to turn our attention to the ambush.

What follows is swift and ugly. I am uncertain what sort of survival instinct Red Caps are possessed of, but it cannot be too great. The remaining gnomes are halting their assault on us to rend the flesh from the corpses of their fallen comrades, dipping their caps in the gruesome muddy mire that their blood has made of the dirt road, tearing away chunks of meat with their iron pikes and vanishing back through the verge with them.

Bevel puts as many arrows into the horrible creatures

as he is able, but soon, they have all fled back into the field, and presumably down into whatever underground cavern they originally bubbled up from. Above the tops of the wheat, I see Capplederry—Wyndam aboard—rising and pouncing on those Red Caps the creature can single out.

Kintyre and Karl come around a gap in the foliage a little behind us, both splashed to their knees in blood. Pip retches, face going a worrying yellowy-pale far too swiftly, but she manages to hold down her breakfast.

"Wyndam!" Kintyre bellows over the verge. "Come on, boy! Bring Capplederry back. We need to move on!"

The lad's head snaps around, and he grimaces.

"Don't make faces!" Bevel bellows. "Do as you're asked!" He mutters something under his breath. "Stubborn lad. Doesn't he know staying will encourage the Red Caps to return?" Then he sets aside his bow and crouches down to touch the shoulder of the woman I rescued.

She flinches hard, and peeks out from under her hair.

"You're safe now," Bevel says, helping her to sit up.

Pip swoops in to scoop up Alis as soon as our daughter is revealed, slumping on the floor and burying her face in Alis's neck. Alis is still unsure whether or not she wants to continue crying, her eyes red and swollen, her chest jerking with panic. I pull Dauntless up beside the cart, leaning over the side to wrap both my girls in my arms. Tucked between her parents, Alis seems to finally understand that she is safe, and the sniffling subsides. Dauntless whickers and lips at Pip's hair, concerned.

Capplederry leaps over the verge then, and the woman yelps, burying her face in Bevel's chest, her trembling increasing.

"No, it's safe." Bevel soothes her, petting down her

long, corn-silk colored hair. It is lucky that he has no blood on his hands, for I fear it would stain. "He won't hurt us."

Capplederry slinks close, sniffing at the woman and purring questioningly, proving his tameness, and the woman finally looks up. I quickly revise my assumptions about her, for she is no woman—she is a lass, and could not be more than fifteen. Her eyes are red-rimmed with her fearful sobs, but are a vivid violet color. Her salt-stained cheeks are flushed a delicate pink, and every movement of her slim, graceful limbs reminds me of the calculated but deceptively effortless movements of a ballerina. Her dress, once pearl-white, is stained pink and red in a spread of handprints that, if I were seeing it from further away, I might mistake for the deliberate pattern of cherry blossoms.

Oh, dear.

Let it never be said that my Writer does not like his women ornamental, especially when they are hurt or scared. If this is how beautiful the women who suffer for the sake of my brother's adventures are, it is no wonder Kintyre Turn and Bevel Dom slept a swath through Hain. It is, instead, more a wonder that Wyndam is an only child.

"By the Writer," I can't help but mutter. "Honestly? This is what is happening now?"

"What?" Pip asks, looking up to watch Kintyre approach.

"A damsel in distress," I scoff. "And just *look* at my brother."

Kintyre has his chest puffed out, his seduction-face on, his best grin sparkling in the sunlight. The lass cranes her head around to watch him approach and gasps, her ample and perky bosom bouncing with each fear-induced pant in her obnoxiously tight corset. Her overdress hangs in artful, shimmering strips off her shoulders and waist, her chemise equally torn, leaving her under-garments on full and scandalous display.

"Never mind your brother," Pip says softly. "Look at your *nephew*."

Wyndam, unlike Kintyre, looks completely *poleaxed*. I have no trouble at all imagining that this is the first young woman he has seen in such a state of undress since he left *The Salty Queen*, and probably the first he wasn't related to or grew up with. And, in the manner of fantasy tropes, none of the women of Turnshire or Turn Hall are beautiful in the way this woman is. They are dowdy, or motherly, or sweetly freckled. Wives and mothers are not *beautiful* here. (Though of course, I disagree and think my wife is very beautiful indeed.)

But it takes an adventure to cross paths with a truly gorgeous woman.

I am, once again, disgusted by my creator and his narrow, sexist view of feminine beauty.

Above the lass's head, Bevel also catches sight of Kintyre's preening approach, and his expression stiffens, his sapphire eyes narrowing into dark pools of jealous anger. Perhaps it is instinct by now, but it is very bad form for my brother to be preening at a damsel in dis-tress *at all*, let alone in front of his Paired.

But when Kintyre draws up to the front of the cart, it is not the young woman toward whom he swoops, but to his trothed. His eyes, his smile, his puffing chest all point toward his Pair, and Bevel's posture slumps with relief when Kintyre bends low and presses a fervent, passionate kiss to Bevel's mouth.

Even after two years and a Pairing ceremony, it seems that Bevel Dom holds on to his secret fears that my brother's affections might not run as deeply as his own. Kintyre is a great lover of female flesh, that is certainly no secret, but it seems that his love of Bevel has outbalanced even that. And it seems that Bevel sometimes requires a reminder.

"Well then," Pip says, clearing her throat. "That's certainly... pornographic."

Dauntless paws the ground, nostrils flaring, clearly ready to get away from the mud that reeks of blood, and loosed bowels, and the faintest sweet taint of flesh just starting to rot in the spring sunshine. But Kintyre's adoration must be catching, for I kiss my wife with more restraint but no less love than my brother is using to devour his trothed. Relief is relief. Then I dismount to nudge Capplederry away from the maiden's side and toward the yoke when it's clear that Wyndam has not the brainpower to hitch the cat back up to the cart.

Wyndam practically dislocates his head to keep his eyes on the maid, and eventually, simply turns all the way around on Capplederry's back. The great cat sits and begins to wash the Red Cap blood off its muzzle with its paws and tongue, ignoring me as I hook it back up. The maiden's eyes flow away from Kintyre and Bevel's display. They land on Wyndam and get stuck there, and I must bite my tongue to keep back a snort. I am suddenly and amusingly reminded of the tale of young lovers from the Writer's world named *Romeo and Juliet*.

I clear my throat, hoping to gain either Kintyre or Wyndam's attention, and only succeed in drawing Pip's. She grins at me, taking in both sets of twitterpated Turns, and jerks her head toward the road. Filled with the same impish glee as my wife, I stealthily remount Dauntless and cluck him forward. Capplederry, never liking to be left behind, immediately follows in his wake.

The cart lurches, and Bevel and Kintyre are broken apart. Bevel topples sideways on the driver's seat, and Kintyre has to grab at Karl's pommel to keep from being tugged out of the saddle and into the bloody mud. Wyndam lurches and grabs the back strap of Capplederry's harness, mouthing an invective at me, but not speaking it aloud, probably for fear of Bevel tanning him over it.

The maiden blinks, and then seems to realize where she is and what she is not wearing. She clutches a bloody pillow to her front to preserve her modesty.

"Come along, lovebirds," I say, to no one in particular, clucking Dauntless into a faster trot.

"Piss off, Forssy," Bevel says, scrambling to right himself on the bench.

"I'm not staying here a moment longer," I reply. "Not even to allow you to further acquaint yourself with the back of my brother's teeth."

The maiden giggles and flushes, hiding her face in the pillow, clearly mortified by my lack of gallantry. Wyndam puffs himself up, looking like a miniature version of his father, and resumes staring at her like she is a warm oasis in an arctic tundra. He must have jammed his smallest finger on the hilt of his curved sword, for he rubs it absentmindedly, as if working out a kink.

"We gotta get everyone cleaned up and patched," Pip agrees, wetting the cuff of her shirt with her tongue and using it to scrub at some of the blood the maiden had gotten on Alis's cheek while she was shushing the babe. "And we are not camping out by the side of the road around here to do it."

"No, agreed. Absolutely not. What's nearby?" Kintyre asks, getting himself back up onto the saddle with some undignified wriggling. He snatches another one of the ruined pillows off the cart and wipes the blood from Foesmiter.

Bevel stands cautiously, in case Capplederry lurches the cart again, and looks around, clearly attempting to slot the landscape into a mental map. "Ah!" he says, face lighting up. "I think we're just north of Gwillfifeshire."

"Oh," Kintyre says, his own expression blossoming into a matching grin. "The *Pern*!"

"That was an excellent meat pie," Bevel says. "Maybe this time I can get the Goodwoman to share the recipe?"

"And it will be good to look in on Thoma and Mandikin."

I assume they are referring to one of the smaller adventures that Bevel did not write down—there were many—for I do not know what they are talking about. And wherever this Gwillfifeshire is, it must be a very sleepy, well-behaved sort of town, for it never came to my attention while I was Shadow Hand.

"Ah," Bevel says, grinning, his thumbs hooked into his belt. "It'll be just the place to stay for the night! The *Pern* has lovely beds."

A collective groan of relief goes up. I had forgotten the quiet, aching pains of being so long on the road, of rocking for so many hours each day in a saddle, and of sleeping on hard ground.

That settled, and with Bevel feeling back in control now that he has our destination mapped out, Kintyre pulls Karl up beside the bench so he and Bevel can chat. The way Kintyre's head swivels, his eyes never leaving the field beside the road, nor his hand Foesmiter's hilt, he has clearly designated himself our watch.

He snaps once at Wyndam to keep his eyes on the other side of the road, and Wyndam mulishly obeys for about seven paces before they drift back toward the still huddling maiden. Realizing that someone must keep their eyes on Kintyre's blind spot, I set myself to the task instead, leaving only Pip to talk to the young woman.

My wife is clever and sees what needs doing. She leaves me to my watch duty, and seems to appoint herself the one to calm and coddle the maiden. After a moment,

I hear her say, "Here, hold Alis for me, will you?" *Ah, the never-ending advantages of babies as distractions!* "I'm going to look at your legs. Thanks. Oh, that's good, none of this looks too deep."

"They ran through my skirts more than my skin," the maiden says shakily. Her voice is sweet, and high, just this side of annoying or squeaky. In contrast with Pip's huskier, womanly voice and Canadian accent, the difference is stark.

"That's one advantage to dresses in this setting, then," Pip acknowledges. "What's your name?"

"La-Lanaea," the young woman says, and her name is like a clear bell on a spring evening.

Oh *dear.* It is a very good thing that Kintyre seems so sunk in Bevel, because I know *exactly* where this would be heading otherwise. Though, knowing now that Wyndam is very much his father's son when it comes to a pretty face, I wonder if Kintyre's confidence with women has passed on to the latest generation. The fact that Wyndam is still perched atop Capplederry and gawping instead of beside the maiden and soothing her hurts himself tells me it might not have.

"And where are you from, Lanaea?" Pip asks.

"Sherwilde," she says. "Ouch! That stings!"

"Yeah, sorry, hold on, I have the numbing ointment in... ah, here's the pouch."

There is the sound of Pip applying Mother Mouth's salve, and then, tentatively, Alis saying, "Ma ma maaa?"

"Hi, baby," Pip says.

"Ma ma!" Alis yowls. "No, no, no, no!"

"Oh!" Lanaea says. "She's fussy."

"She's still scared. Forsyth, can you...?"

I fall back and accept Alis and her scarf-wrap when Pip hands her over. "Da da daaaa da daaa!" Alis complains.

"It's all over now, sweeting," I say. "I promise."

"'Issess, 'issess," Alis begs, and as soon as I have her secure and have urged Dauntless back to the head of the line, I obligingly kiss the palms of her hands and the top of her head, over and over again, until Alis is laughing at the tickling sensation of my four-day stubble, all fear forgotten.

By now, Bevel must be listening in, for he adds, "Why are you so far south, Mistress Lanaea? Sherwilde is near Kingskeep. Do you have an escort, or...?"

There is an awkward silence as we all wait for Lanaea's answer.

"My father sent me away," Lanaea says. "I have family in Miliway, you see, and father was worried about... *her*."

"He sent you alone?" Bevel presses.

"I... yes. I am proficient with a bow, and Irtax is a deer. She is fleet... was fleet—" she sobs, and Pip makes soothing sounds.

"I've never heard of Red Caps in Miliway," Kintyre says. "Bevel, aren't they usually—"

"*Significantly* further south, yeah," Bevel agrees. "They usually stay around the foothills of the Cinch."

"What did you mean, your father was worried about *her*?" Pip asks, which is very good, for I was wondering the same.

"Do you mean you haven't heard?" Lanaea asks, incredulous. "There is a witch roaming Hain! Roaming the *world*, they say. She leaves bodies in her wake, and can summon the storm to her very hands! She is a magpie thief, and nobody knows what she will value, only that when she finds it, she will *take* it and leave ruin in her wake. She came to Sherwilde, and... she forced herself on a... and the *dryad* will be scarred for life..." She sobs again, and does not finish her sentence.

"A witch?" Pip asks, flatly, and for once I realize that

Pip has no clue how dangerous such a powerful, angry creature can be. She has not grown up fearing the tales of witches, for no such things exist in her realm. There, those who call themselves witches are merely humans, with no magic but a goodly religious respect for nature and living creatures. Whereas I know of witches, *real* witches. I have feared them. But Kintyre and Bevel have actually battled one. And according to Bevel's scrolls, it was no easy task.

I turn to gauge the reactions of everyone behind me and catch a flash of fear and guilt passing over Wyndam's features as swiftly as a cloud over the moon.

Hm. Interesting.

The lad knows something of this witch, I would stake money on it.

Though Pip asks Lanaea a few more questions, the maiden seems reluctant to explain further, too shaken by her ordeal and too fearful of the witch to speak of her louder than a whisper. Pip helps the maiden out of her ragged, torn dress and into one of the two I had per-suaded Pip to pack for our journey. Then Lanaea gorges herself on some of our cold rations and falls into a fitful sleep. Pip, I notice when I tear my eyes off the road, is scribbling on the Excel, muttering something about a witch driving out Red Caps, and stars going out.

Kintyre's vigil remains steady, but he and Bevel re-sume their conversation in hushed tones.

"We should find someone in Gwillfifeshire with sol-dier's training to take her to her family here in Miliway," Kintyre says softly. "She can't go on her own."

"You know, there was a time you would have offered to take her with us, or escort her home yourself, or... you know..." Bevel says, voice low, but not so low that I couldn't catch what he was saying. The rest of what Kintyre might have offered Lanaea remains unspoken, but not unknown.

"I'm too old for that nonsense," Kintyre says softly. "Besides, I have all that I want here, don't I?"

Another wet sound, and I turn my attention back to the fields, duly punished for eavesdropping by having to listen to my brother kissing Bevel some more. I can now well believe that the tales of their post-battle bedsport romps are not as much an exaggeration as I first thought when reading Bevel's scrolls. Kintyre seems to be quite amorous when his blood is up.

And while my brother is preoccupied, I ponder on the question of why, not once, not even in the heat of battle, I have never heard my nephew's voice.

SWORDS

Her rage and wrath carry her far, and Solinde drifts over the mountains, lost in thought. Her cloud dissipates as her strength wanes, and Solinde must descend and rest. Deal-Makers do not need to eat, but they are liquid in more ways than they are solid, and Solinde is parched.

A small town beckons from the foothills of the Cinch Mountains, and she climbs toward it. She learns it is called Cinchside, and she accepts water from one of the goat drovers standing by the well in the center of the town square to refresh both herself and her magic.

In her heart, she feels the storm. On her finger, she feels the tug of the golden thread. Connected.

I will rest, and then I will find you, she vows. As her rage cools, her heart settles. Her mind clears, and she decides that being flung away from the battle was a fortuitous turn of fate.

Follow them, she decides. *Stay close. Decipher their plans.* And then, when the defeat would be at its most mortifying, most embarrassing, and at the most inopportune moment for him, ensure it. *Strip Kintyre Turn of his life, yes, but also of his legacy. Make him suffer. Make the people of this world, those who worship him, hate him instead. Do as he has done to Varnet and set all against him.*

Another sensation pulls at Solinde, and for a moment,

she doesn't recognize it. Then she remembers. Totems. Her quest.

She toys with the golden thread, tugging just to feel the lad's discomfort on the other end of the string. She considers as she amuses herself, catting with the lad's attention. She has Kintyre Turn within her grasp. No more than a night's worth of rest would be needed, and then she could follow the thread back to its source and trick the boy into murdering his father for her. Or maybe someone else in their party—there must be someone among his family or friends that resents him. It may take days. It may take dozens of visits. It will be a slow game. The kind he whom she seeks preferred.

And until then, she will heed the call of the totems as she comes across them. She is clever. She can do both. Perhaps, if she is lucky, she will find the totem that will vaporize the prison-realm next, and he will be here, at her side, as he is meant to be, when she finally pulls enough puppet strings to make Kintyre Turn throttle amid the tangles.

Decided, Solinde uses her indefatigable fount of Words to locate her next target. The totem is not in the town proper, but several leagues above it, in the side of a mountain. Solinde tarries by the well, drinking her fill and making inquiries. The locals tell of a creature that moved into the area two summers before, and while few have seen it, they hypothesize that it has the ability to become man-shaped and walks Cinchside in the clothing of a rogue.

Solinde disregards the warnings—for no creature could be more powerful than her, even the ones who can shift form—and climbs the difficult path up the mountain. With Kintyre Turn so close to being hers, she will not spend herself and her power so unwisely. She will stay hydrated.

Halfway up the mountainside, she finds a sword of great power amidst a dragon's hoard. The dragon itself is not at home. It has probably gone to hunt amid the mountain goats, and riddling ravens, and goblins that plague the mountains, if the pile of bones just to the side of the cave's entrance are any indication.

The hoard is small yet, so Solinde guesses that the dragon is still quite close to a hatchling. Solinde cannot help but feel the pang of sympathy for the drakeling's clear status as an orphan—there is no indication of a second or third dragon anywhere nearby, nor another pile of gold upon which to sleep. There is, strangely, a cot set up against one of the walls, and several changes of clothing hanging from the outcroppings as if from pegs. Here, too, is an oil lamp, a pile of half-used candles, a small tower of tattered books, and eating utensils.

Perhaps the stories of the dragon taking man-form are true. But then, if they were, wouldn't...

Ah, Solinde has hesitated too long. The cave's inhabitant has returned.

The sword is sheathed and jammed point-first into a crevasse in the stone wall to keep it from falling over. Solinde has only enough time to yank it free of the stone and unsheathe it, baring the blade. She doubts she'll need the sword to defend herself—her magic ought to be enough—but she finds herself strangely reluctant to harm the dragon.

The creature that lands at the wide mouth of the cave cannot be more than several decades old, the size of a draft horse and red as a bruising kiss. And the lad who slides off the crude leather saddle harnessed about its chest looks to be the rogue the townspeople described. It is not a dragon who becomes a boy, but a dragon *and* a boy.

"Dearest!" the dragon says, alarmed, when the lad

advances. He wears the black leather of a highway thief, and the wary look of one who's had his friendship with a dragon questioned too many times.

"I have come only for this," Solinde says, brandishing the sword. "Out of my way, and I will let you live."

The lad and the dragonet exchange a glance, and then simultaneously step to the side to allow her to pass. Once Solinde is in the open air again, she hears the dragonet snort in disgust.

"Hush now, dearest," the rogue says. "It's only a sword. We can buy another. It doesn't matter. We've learned better than to fight and seek revenge, haven't we?"

"Yes," the dragonet says sulkily, and that is the last Solinde overhears.

She calls up the wind as she descends the mountain, and dreams, for a moment, of keeping the sword as it is, so that she may have the satisfaction of plunging it into the heart of he who bears one of its nine sister-blades. But Kintyre Turn is out of her reach for now, and she will not risk this totem being the one that will open the gateways between her and him whom she loves.

The caldera of the volcano that long ago erupted and formed the Eyrie still bubbles and burns, and Solinde rides the wind to its lip. She takes great pleasure in watching the sword twist and melt, fancies she can hear the enchantment upon it *screaming*.

As night falls, the constellation of the Boy King fails to rise.

And still *he* does not return to her.

TEN

Gwillfifeshire is small, just a way station for the surrounding agricultural land's bounty, really. There is only
one town square, at the center of which is a crumbling
old well inhabited by a ghost. I know this because Bevel tells me as much as we approach. Pip is alarmed, but
Kintyre launches into the story of the night they stayed
in Gwillfifeshire, their last small adventure before the one
that sent Pip and I into the Writer's realm, and how the
ghost is actually quite sweet and loves minding the local
children when their parents are kept late in the fields.

The buildings are close, and cramped, made of a gray
stone that looks slightly dreary, even in the bright afternoon sunshine. The roads between them are just wide
enough for our cart-and-cat to pass, and we are forced
to skirt the edge of the square to reach our destination.
A market is in full and fine fluster, with women selling
pickling supplies and men bartering livestock before the
breeding season begins. There are butcher's stalls, and
baked goods, fabric and spell-workings, and baubles.
Spring begins a month earlier in Miliway than it does in
Lysse, so there are already strawberries and leeks on display, alongside wagons of the first-crop hay.

Suffice it to say, we make quite a display of our own
for the market-goers: two men on horseback, one of
which is splashed up to the animal's fetlocks with blood,

two women and a babe in a cart pulled by a massive cat-creature, a grim-faced cart driver clutching a bow, and a lad splattered with yet more blood atop the cat. Murmuring follows us where the crowds part, and just before we reach the edge of the square, a large man with an even larger moustache pushes his way forward and exclaims, "Why, Master Turn! Master Dom!"

"Lord Gallvig," Bevel says cordially, with a bow from his place on the driver's bench. I cannot recall if Bevel had an excellent memory before becoming Shadow Hand, or if it is the Mask who remembers the man's name. I had the Mask so long that I honestly could not tell you if my head for faces came from it or from me. Or just from the way Reed wrote me.

"Well now, what's all this?" He gestures at the blood.

"Red Caps," Kintyre grunts. "Or there used to be. In the wheat field just north of town?"

Gallvig nods. "They've been getting bolder," he says. "The Prepars lost three cattle to the little monsters. Thank the Writer that no human has been hurt yet."

Bevel sighs. "They have, actually. This is Lanaea," he says, gesturing to the maiden in the cart, and raises his voice a little to add: "Lanaea of Sherwilde? She says she has family here."

"Ain't you Jakko's daughter?" someone calls from near the well, and Lanaea raises herself up as best she can on shaking legs, Pip helping her stay upright.

"I am!" she says. "Do you know where his sister may be found?"

"She's Anne Farthing, now," the man calls. "Down at the *Pern.*"

"I know it," Bevel says, after Lanaea calls her thanks.

Bevel bows to the lord again, then urges Capplederry back into motion.

Capplederry's movement makes Wyndam grimace,

grit his teeth, and hunch lower on the creature's back. I seem to be the only one who's noticed. Bevel has his eyes on the path, and Pip is occupied with keeping the wounded maiden comfortable. Wyndam puts a hand to his side, curling his arm across his ribs. The lad wears black, but for a moment, sunlight glints off a patch of slick red on the back of his fingers.

Foolish, proud boy. I wonder if, in attempting to look macho for Lanaea, he has done himself harm. How much blood has he lost? How long has infection been given to take root?

Why hasn't he said anything? I think back to all the times Wyndam has been the center of my brother's attention, and another piece of the puzzle that is my nephew slots into place. He idolizes Kintyre. He would be shamed if Kintyre knew he had been harmed in his first battle alongside his father.

Little does Wyndam realize that Kintyre will be all the more proud of him if he knew that Wyndam was harmed and yet fought on. And he would care greatly that Wyndam was being foolish enough to hide it. The one thing Kintyre Turn has never done is hide his injuries from Bevel. As foolish as Kintyre could be about some things, playing with his own life was not one of them. Perhaps because he loves himself so well, but his narcissism has saved his life more than once.

But Wyndam's reluctance also offers me an opportunity. Here is my chance for that heart-to-heart I've been wanting with my nephew.

Kintyre pulls Karl back when the horse attempts to follow us, and dallies a moment longer with the lord.

"There's precious few of the Red Caps left, I'd wager," Kintyre says. "They'll scavenge their own dead for a few days, so you shouldn't be hassled. After that, they sleep, so tomorrow afternoon would be the ideal time for you to mount a party to drive out the remainder of the infestation."

"They burrow," Gallvig points out.

"Black powder," Kintyre suggests back. "Just don't be standing on the tunnels when they collapse. You'll lose part of the field's yield, but that's better than letting them carry off a child."

Gallvig nods, shakes Kintyre's hand, and thanks him. Then he turns and heads straight to what appears to be the black smith's shop. By the time I've turned my attention back to Wyndam, he is sitting up straight, but with the forced stillness of those who are trying their best not to be jolted. His dark face has gone yellow-gray.

We arrive at the *Pern* tavern shortly afterward, and Wyndam is all awkwardness as he slides down from Capplederry. He puts his hand out to help Lanaea descend from the cart, but then switches it at the last moment when he realizes the one he'd originally offered is covered with blood. This fumble makes Lanaea lurch against his shoulder, and she frowns at him, obviously not impressed.

She leans instead on Bevel, and I dismount and hand Dauntless off to a boy whom Bevel greets warmly as Thoma.

Wyndam clenches his fists, annoyed at himself, and turns on his heel, scuffing away to slouch against the wall. Pip sighs and runs a hand through her hair, clearly debating whether or not to say something to him about it. As I begin the process of unbuckling Capplederry's rig, Pip approaches Wyndam and thrusts Alis into his arms.

"Watch her," she says, "and I'll help them unpack."

Wyndam moves to protest, but Pip holds up her hand, firm.

"Also," she says softly, leaning forward to put her body between Wyndam and Lanaea, laying a motherly hand on Wyndam's arm. "Stop staring at her like she's a piece of meat or a hydra. No girl likes to be gawked at and objectified. Go over and just be kind; don't try any cheesy lines or anything. There's no need for any weird chivalric gestures. Just be... normal. Just go be you. She's just a girl. You know lots of girls. You grew up surrounded by them. Nothing scary about that."

Wyndam shoots her a look over Alis's head that would be comical in its disbelief if it weren't for the genuine surprise and fear it conveyed.

"Look, I know," Pip says. "Liking someone, and wanting them to like you back, that's some scary shit right there. I get it. My advice? Stop thinking about her as a girl, and think of her as a *person*. I know you want to get your dick wet, but be her friend first." Pip makes a face at her own advice. "But also let her know that you're interested? None of that friend-zone crap."

Wyndam gapes at her helplessly, and Pip shrugs. "Actually, I don't know why I'm giving you advice. I've always been utter shit at this flirting thing. Maybe talk to Bevel? I don't even know."

With one last arm-pat, she turns to unlatch the tailgate of the cart. Wyndam, Alis held limply in his arms, looks even more poleaxed than before. My daughter, annoyed with being passed around and held like unwelcome furniture, wriggles to be let down. I am pleased to see that Wyndam has enough sense to keep a grip on her, even as her movement jostles his injury. There are too many wheels and legs for me to be comfortable with her trying out her newfound skills in walking in this forecourt.

The front door of the tavern is opened by someone who can only be the Goodwoman. She is fertile looking in a way that I am certain Reed would dismiss, but beautiful in her bounty. Her cheeks are roses, her hair autumn wheat, her figure round with a well-fed and well-loved life. In short, she reminds me very strongly of my own mother, the lost Alis Sheil Turn.

She takes stock of our party, wipes her hands on her apron, and says, "Thoma, when you're done stabling these... interesting beasts... and taking a care with the cart, run to the Prentice and fetch him back; the horse has need of his healer's skills, if not this knucklehead." She swats Kintyre affectionately on the shoulder, and then plucks at the Turn-russet jerkin he is wearing. She reaches out to repeat the gesture with Bevel's. "Good to see you two great ninnies have got yourselves sorted at last. Now, inside, inside, and we'll set you up the tub."

"And those meat pies, Goodwoman Farthing?" Kintyre asks hopefully.

"Aye," she says, and shoos him along. She then turns to Pip. "Three rooms, Madam?"

"Four," Pip says, taking Alis back from Wyndam and cutting a look between Lanaea and the lad. "Thanks."

"Aye, well come, then," the Goodwoman says, and reaches out to help take some of Lanaea's hobbling weight onto her own shoulders. "And you are, lass?"

"I... I do believe I am your niece, Madam," Lanaea says quietly. The Goodwoman startles, and leans back a little to stare at her face. "Well, I'll be. You look just like Jakko."

The lass beams at her.

"Come, inside with you, my dear. And you too, boys," she says to Wyndam and I, standing slightly uselessly on the cobbled forecourt.

I am startled into motion, and reach into the cart to retrieve our sacks. Wyndam moves to do the same, and then jerks when he lifts his arm, grimacing and hissing and curling back around his injured side.

"I'll get the bags," I tell him in a whisper as the others disappear into the tavern's taproom. "You just get up-stairs. I'll follow and tend to your wound when everyone else is settled."

Wyndam shoots me a startled glance, eyes cutting between me and where Kintyre is visible through the taproom window.

"Oh, Wyndam, tut tut," I say with a sly, teasing grin. "You did not honestly think that your brains came from Kintyre, did you?"

A tentative smile curls against the side of his mouth, almost reluctantly. He shakes his head once.

"Smart lad. Inside you go," I say softly. "And we shall keep this between us."

Thank you, he mouths at me.

I remove all the bags we need and pile them at the door for a servant to take up to our rooms, taking care to tuck the traveling healer's kit into my belt. Wyndam grabs his own bag and slings it over his shoulder with deliberate care before he goes inside.

Thoma is enraptured with Capplederry, and the cat is very pleased to have the boy scratching its muzzle. I suppose all that dried blood must be dreadfully itchy.

"Help me with the yoke, please, my young fellow," I bid him. "When your healer is fetched, you may play with the kitty as long as you like. Capplederry likes to be brushed."

The boy's brown eyes widen with glee, and he is quick about his business, though he rushes nothing. He is well versed in the duties of a groom. When he is off, I bypass the taproom, where I can see that our party is tucked into a large booth in a sunny corner. The rest of the tavern patrons are pretending to ignore them while peering around their own noses. Though it has been years since Kintyre was last in Gwillfifeshire, it is clear he has not been forgotten.

Mounting the stairs to the tavern's rooms, I slide on my Shadow Hand persona. I will need my wits about me, for, as I insinuated to Wyndam, I suspect that my nephew is very, very clever.

When I reach the top of the stairs, I see that the inn portion of this tavern is comprised of six rooms. It does not appear as if the Goodwoman and her son live in one of them, so I guess that there must be a separate set of apartments off the back of the taproom. Perhaps they even share the kitchen.

Wyndam has obviously chosen one of the rooms at the very end of the hall. It is the only closed door.

I enter without knocking, and my nephew doesn't look startled when he turns to face me. He was rummaging in his bag, which he'd propped up on the foot of the rope cot, one hand leaning hard on the foot-bar as he tries to stay upright, so he must have heard my approach. I wonder if his time aboard ships attuned him to the creak and groan of floorboards, or if my skills at walking stealthily have simply atrophied.

"How bad is the bleeding?" I ask softly, closing the door behind me. It is better to start with sympathy, I decide, and see if a gentle conversation with his caring uncle will shift the boy toward truth. If it doesn't, then perhaps I will have to resort to Words of Persuasion. They are Words known only among those of us who dig out secrets for a living, and I do not like to use them against sentient creatures, but I am beginning to feel a sort of slow dread creep upon me, and I need to know if my fear that Wyndam's lack of voice and trust has ought to do with the rest of our troubles.

I hope very much that it does not, that there is a simpler explanation, but I also know how it is that my Writer chooses to structure his narratives. Very little in the way of bad news is coincidental.

The lad remains silent and only shrugs. The motion causes him to wince, and I cannot help the paternal eye roll, nor the way that I tut at him and push him back toward his bed, simultaneously tugging at his buttons so I can relieve him of his shirt and get a better sense of the severity of the wound. Wyndam bats me off, not wanting to be coddled, and pulls his shirt off over his head, which stretches his wound terribly and makes him gasp in pain. Foolish, stubborn boy. Better to have let me at his buttons.

"Wyndam, my lad, whyever didn't you *say* something?" I admonish gently, leaving him an opening to reply as I crouch to study the smear of blood on his stomach. There is a gash in his abdomen—deep enough to bleed, but not so deep that it has torn muscle. I do not think it needs stitches, though the edges are crusted with drying blood and whatever filth was on the iron pike wielded by the Red Cap that delivered the blow.

Wyndam grunts, looking away, and my temper rises, getting the better of me. I have been gracious and generous with his uncooperative nature until now, more so than perhaps I might have been before Pip chastised me for the shortness of my fuse since Alis's birth, but that is at an end.

Time for the Shadow Hand to try to get through to the lad.

I stand and smack Wyndam on the ear. He reels back, affronted and gaping, holding the side of his head.

"Are you paying attention to me now, Wyndam Turn?" I snarl.

The lad nods.

"Good. Then, if you shall not speak, you must *listen*. I despise having to resort to abuse to gain your attention, so it will benefit us both if you mark my words now, so as to avoid having to do this again."

He nods once more, his hand slipping downward and folding with its pair in his lap. He drops his eyes down as well, chastened.

"No, look at me," I command, and he obeys, his jet eyes flashing wide. "That's better. Wyndam Turn, I am your uncle and your blood, and I do not know what you think of me or why you will not speak to me, but I will have you know that *I care about you.*"

The lad's mouth drops open, shock playing around his features.

"We have never had a conversation, true, and I had not known of your existence a fortnight ago, but that does not mean you are nothing to me. You are my brother's son."

Wyndam scoffs, and crosses his arms defiantly. Then he winces as the motion pulls on his gash. I step toward him, slowly, hands loose at my sides to prove my peaceful intent, and the lad does not flinch. I push his own arms down, gently, and out of the way so I can get a better look at his stomach.

"You misunderstand, Wyndam," I say, going over to the room's sideboard. The Goodwoman has left water and cloths in this room, probably accustomed to the demands of road-weary and dust-caked guests, and I re-trieve a cloth and bring it back to the bedside table with a bowl and the pitcher. Alongside these, I lay out the pouch of poultices and salves that Bevel had acquired from Mother Mouth before we left Turnshire. "I do not love you simply because you are my brother's heir."

The lad's posture relaxes a little, and I can see him watching me out the side of his eye. Slowly, he leans back, giving me full access to the wound. He is giving me his trust, tentative though it is, and I let some of the Shad-ow Hand slide away, let a little more of concerned Uncle Forsyth come to the fore.

"Wyndam, I know very well how it feels to live in the shadow of Kintyre Turn," I say gently, soaking a cloth, wringing it out, and beginning to dab at the most filthy-looking part of the wound. The room smells of fresh straw, the ghosts of a thousand beeswax candles, and dried ale. I lean close to the wound, and above the ambient scents of the room detect only the scent of the sweat Wyndam worked up in the battle, and tang of fresh blood. Nothing smells festering or rotted yet. Good. "By the Writer's calluses, I know that he talks over others, and I know that he has very set ideas of how one should be and what one should pursue. That I was not keen on the adventurous sort of pursuits he craved was a great disappointment to him, and he never ceased to attempt to bully me for failing to be as robust and inclined toward action as he."

Wyndam jerks and hisses as I dig a shard of iron out of the lip of the gash, doing his best not to wriggle or jump away. He fists his hands so hard in the canvas covering of the straw mattress that his knuckles go white.

"To be fair," I chuckle, doing my best to minimize Wyndam's pain by distracting him as I clean more grit. "I angered him in return by calling him a fool, and a blockhead, and making it very clear that I thought he was a ridiculous buffoon with more muscles than brains."

I risk a glance upward, and see that Wyndam is watching me carefully, listening even though his jaw is tight, the muscles leaping as he grinds his teeth. It occurs to me right then that I have done some of my most important bonding with others while I am tending to their wounds, and I wonder what that says about both me and Elgar Reed.

"The fact of it is, Wyndam, my regard for you has very little to do with who your father is, and everything to do with the sort of young man that you are," I say, when the wound is as clean as I can make it, and I have wiped all the blood off his skin. "Lay back now, so I can flush the wound."

The lad obeys, and I tuck a dry towel against his side to catch the runoff before tipping a tot of Drebbinshire Whiskey out of the flask I retrieve from my pocket. It seems a shame to waste dragon whiskey on a wound, but it is all I have, and it is in sacrifice to my nephew's health. I also don't want to alert Kintyre to Wyndam's predicament by summoning up Thoma for a glass of alcohol from the *Pern*'s taproom. Wyndam had gone to great lengths to keep his injury a secret. I know I would be gaining no favors or trust from my nephew by advertising it.

Wyndam jerks and writhes, but does not shove me away. The muscles of his abdomen jump and crunch as he fights his own instinct to flee the source of pain. He breathes harshly between his teeth, chest jerking with his gasps, and still the lad *makes no sound.*

I pat the excess liquid away, and then daub Mother Mouth's healing salve over the gash. The scent of lemon and menthol drift up, tickling my brain and summoning up memories of performing these same actions on Pip's back while the wounds she suffered under Bootknife's attention healed. They are interwoven with other memories of when Bevel saw to the cut that same villain left on my cheek. Both healed cleanly and scarred well——I have no doubt that Wyndam's wound will do the same, and that the mark it will leave behind will be very handsome and rakish indeed.

"I think you are an admirable young man," I repeat as I help Wyndam into a fresh shirt from his pack. He moves carefully, and winces every time his abdomen flexes. "Though you clearly dislike it, you have been invaluable to Pip and I in caring for Alis, and I appreciate your willingness to put aside your distaste and aid us. Capplederry adores you, and I know the creature tolerates only those with great heart, and great integrity. Capplederry has the capacity for great loyalty, but only toward those who are worthy of it. And your willingness to leap straight into a skirmish with Red Caps is commendable. Perhaps a little foolhardy," I say, grinning at him so that he knows I am making light, "but commendable. In that way, you are very much like your father. He acts before thinking, true, but always with the greatest of intentions and in defense of those who cannot defend themselves."

Set back to rights, the lad perches uncomfortably on the edge of the bed and squirms, clearly discomfited by my praise. And still he says *nothing*. I stand and lay my hands on his shoulders gently, in as paternal a manner as I can, trying to exude safety, and concern, and protection.

"Now, I am uncertain if you dislike me because of who I am, or something you've heard that I've done, or simply because your relationship with your father and his trothed is strained. But I want you to know that I am not Kintyre Turn, nor am I Bevel Dom. I am Forsyth, and I am your uncle, and that means that no matter who you are, or what you do, I am obligated by both my admiration and my kinship to listen to you, and respect you, and aid you where I may. And to love you also, if you will allow me to do so."

The lad looks embarrassed by my frank talk of affection. But this is exactly the sort of toxic masculinity that Reed upholds and which I abhor. Forcing oneself to be unemotional, to never speak of the softer feelings, is extremely damaging, and causes all sorts of issues with misplaced anger and entitlement. So instead of dismissing it, I move one of the chairs bracketing the room's hearth directly before Wyndam and make a show of sitting. I lean forward, elbows perched on my knees, fingers woven in a nonthreatening, thoughtful pose under my chin.

"And all I wish in return, Wyndam Turn, is that you

would come to me if you need me, and for you to *speak* with me. I shall not judge you for what you say."

Shame floods the lad's face, and he drops his head into his hands and moans. He makes a complicated shrugging, hand-wringing, toss-away gesture that I cannot interpret, and moans again. It ends with him tugging on his pinkie finger, a gesture I have not noticed him engage in before today. My first thought, that it was due to an injury he sustained in the field today, returns —but his finger is not swollen, or bruised.

The last time someone I cared about suddenly adopted a new and strange gesture, with no explanation, I nearly lost Pip to Bootknife. Thus, I will not assume that Wyndam's finger-tugging is unconnected to whatever is happening until it is proven to be so. It is possible that I am merely being paranoid, but, as the saying goes in the Writer's realm, it is not paranoia if they really are out to get you. And as the family of the main character of *this* realm, they usually *are* out to get us.

Wyndam catches me watching and drops his hands, and his head, defeated. He sighs, a long, weary thing filled with regret and exhaustion.

"Go on, lad," I urge him. "I am listening."

Wyndam raises his eyes to me and then, very carefully, very clearly, he mouths the words: *I can't.*

"Can't what?" I ask, and then pause.

Wyndam squirms, rubs his pinkie, flexes his fists, and stalls. He stares at me, begging me to understand with his eyes.

Ah.

Well, then. That is not what I expected.

Flustered by this soundless revelation, I need a moment to compile my thoughts and decide what to say next. After reassuring Wyndam that I would be back in very short order, I poke my head into the rooms down the hall until I find the one where my own bags have been stowed. I retrieve writing supplies, then head down to the taproom for wine for both Wyndam and I. I have a feeling that this is going to be a long and potentially frustrating evening, and a little social lubrication never harmed the process.

Our party is still in the corner booth, empty tureens and dirty forks pushed to one side. Bevel is playing with his pipe, flipping it bowl over stem across his fingers. He is alternately speaking or chewing on his bottom lip, clearly wishing he could smoke. But Pip has Alis on her lap, and Bevel is thoughtful enough to remember her request about smoking around the baby. Kintyre has a whittling knife in hand, turning what appears to be an illustration of the tumbled monument we saw on the knoll at the edge of town into a wood-stamp.

Pip and Bevel are engaged in a lively discussion about storytelling, and Kintyre nods along while Alis is making some sort of finger-painting on a spare piece of parchment with pie-gravy and bits of parsley. At one time, I might have felt a pang of hurt at realizing that everyone had eaten without me, but now I understand that they simply must have been too hungry to wait.

"*Bao bei*," Pip greets me when I bend to gift each of my girls a kiss. Pip's on the lips, Alis's on her nose.

"How was the famous pie?" I ask.

"Fantastic," Pip says. "Another thing we need to get Bevel to write down for us."

"If Mistress *Pern* condescends to give it to *me*," Bevel snorts. "Where have you been, Forssy?"

"Upstairs with Wyndam."

Kintyre looks up from his pile of shavings. "Talking?"

"More or less," I hedge. "I have only come to fetch us some dinner."

"I'll send up a tray," says the Goodwoman, who has

wandered out from behind the bar. "And *not* the recipe, mind you, Master Dom."

Bevel groans theatrically.

I give her a short nod. "Thank you. Wine as well, please. Ah, and how is Miss Lanaea?"

"Getting clean," Goodwoman Farthing says. "The boys gave her first crack at the tub."

"How gallant," I say, arching a teasing eyebrow at Bevel. "And both of you here, and not there?"

"*Bao bei!*" Pip scolds, but she is grinning.

"Well, Wyndam was missing, and I thought he must be—ouch!" Kintyre yelps, jerking. "Bevel, don't kick me!"

Pip muffles her laughter against Alis's shoulder, peering out between the strands of her own hair at Kintyre, her brown eyes glittering with mirth. "God, I can't believe I'm sitting right next to you, having this conversation. This is so crack fic."

Kintyre raises an eyebrow, but Pip just muffles another chuckle against Alis. Our daughter seems to think this is completely unacceptable and reaches out to Bevel with a sharp, "Beh beh! No, mamma!"

Bevel sets aside his pipe and rescues his niece, pulling her across the table and brushing the wood curls off her feet before settling her in his lap.

"Well then," I say. "If I'm to be so thoroughly overlooked by my own family, I will return upstairs."

I say it with a smile, but in truth, the dart of Alis preferring her uncle's company over her father's does sting. I know it doesn't actually mean anything, that Alis isn't really choosing Bevel over me, but I am used to being the one my daughter reaches for. True, the only other adults in her life are *wai po*, Mei, and Martin, and Alis does, in her way, always prefer novelty... but still...

Ah, well. I shake myself, amused by my own lingering melancholy, and follow the Goodwoman up the stairs.

She has a tray of dinner for Wyndam and I, and I have work to do.

Wyndam stands from the bed, and then falls with very little ceremony upon the meat pie as soon as the Goodwoman is out the door. A day spent on the road, and then in battle, has left me no less hungry, and we are silent for some long moments as we eat. When we have finished, when the tureens are set aside and the wine poured, I put my travel desk on Wyndam's bed, along with parchment, a quill, and the bottle of ink.

He stares at all of the paraphernalia with trepidation. I have seen Kintyre look at dragons that way, and the utter fear and helplessness with which my nephew regards the quill unnerves me. Something is very, very wrong here.

"Wyndam," I say gently, reaching out to put a comforting hand on his shoulder. He startles so badly that some of the wine he's holding sloshes out onto his cuff. He raises his hand to lick away the wine, and turns his face away, shrugging off my touch.

"Wyndam," I try again, the question stopping up in my throat before I can fully articulate it. The sadness of needing to ask it almost makes it unbearable to ask at all. Knowing that there will be greater melancholy still if he answers in the affirmative is worse. But ask I must. "You can write, can't you?"

Wyndam's shoulders slump. Oh, no. My poor nephew.

How awful, to not only be missing out on such an essential skill—and all the pleasure it brings—but to also know that he is probably one of the few, one of the only people in Turnshire who is illiterate must have been horrifically grating to him. To know that the scullery maid could write and he could not...

"Can you *read*, at least?" I ask, voice shaking.

Wyndam shakes his head again. Oh, what a tragedy. I

feel the pain of it as a hot pang in my breast, and a small anger in my gut. Had my nephew been raised on land, amid his father's people, he would have lacked for nothing, *least* of all instruction in this. It is terrible, but worse, it is cruel. Everyone deserves the chance to improve themselves, to read about their rights and to communicate on their own behalf through writing. Everyone has the right to all the advantages that being literate provides. And more than that, no one should ever be deprived of books. Of stories. Of... magic. *No one.*

And yet, it does not surprise me that he had very little formal education on board his mother's ship. I expect that his mother is also illiterate, keeping no log books. I recall now that Wyndam had Bevel's scrolls in his rooms, and I wonder now if it was to look at the woodcut illustrations, or if it was because he was trying to practice reading out of view of Bevel and Kintyre.

"You are constantly surrounding yourself with books you cannot read," I say softly. "It must be *torturous*, especially knowing your great admiration for your father."

Wyndam scowls at me, but I think he is too disappointed in himself to protest my assumption.

Kintyre and I, of course, as the sons of Turnshire's lord, had very fine educations— though I paid closer attention and retained more than my brother did. Bevel had been illiterate, as many of the working class were, when he met Kintyre, but my brother had taught him to read on the road. What had initially begun as an opportunity to practice his writing eventually combined with Bevel's natural talent as a storyteller to create the story-scrolls that comprise *The Tales of Kintyre Turn*, and had earned him his fame. Neither man, I am certain, would have teased Wyndam for his lack of skill in this.

With irritation pulling down his brows, crinkling the skin beside his eyes, Wyndam seizes up the quill and starts to block out a few shaky letters. He must know something of writing and reading, then, but his skills are extremely rudimentary. And even so, his handwriting is cramped, difficult to read, and he keeps stopping to shake out his hand, gripping his wrist as if his fingers were moving contrary to his desire. The pinkie finger of his left hand, his dominant hand, keeps jerking as if being tugged upon by an outside force.

Wyndam attempts to for a few frustrating moments, and then he throws down the quill with a silent, resentful snarl. There is a blotch on the page that might have been an attempt at a drawing, but I cannot be sure.

"Whatever it is that has stolen your voice, you cannot write it down, either," I say. "You cannot even *sketch* it."

Wyndam nods, face crumpling in guilty misery.

"Did you do this to yourself?"

He nods, then shakes his head, then nods again. He rubs his left pinkie finger and scowls. And then, suddenly, Wyndam's eyes go round. His right hand shoots out, grasps mine hard, and he pumps it once, twice, *meaningfully*. He looks me in the eye and keeps shaking my hand.

"Oh, Writer's calluses," I hiss, realization flooding over me, making my knees wobble. Wyndam, grim, just nods. He waits, and watches, as the puzzle pieces come together, slotting like Tetris bricks as each clue, each observation I've made over the past week come together to form a whole picture. I grope for the nearest chair to flop down into.

Wyndam curls in on himself, ashamed.

"Oh, Wyndam Turn, you p-poor, fo-foolish boy," I whisper, face in my hands. "What have you *done*?"

WATER

Solinde returns to Cinchside for more water and rest. When she has taken her fill from the well, she tucks herself into a shaded corner of the public garden. It is a peaceful place, filled with the scent of green, growing things, and blooms reaching for the skies.

Birdsong weaves a lullaby that, combined with the dappled sunlight, fills Solinde with a warm sort of lethargy. It reminds her of the days when her son was small, before his magic had begun to manifest, and her husband was away at market. Those days, Solinde would bundle her son into a patchwork blanket she had made of work-torn clothes, and in the shade of the barn, whisper the secrets of her sisters into her boy's ear.

She cannot afford the loss of moisture that weeping will inflict, but all the same, she cannot hold back her bitter sobs. It is *cruel*, unaccountably cruel that the Writer would bless that egotistical, violent Kintyre Turn with family and progeny while her own son is reviled and shunned and now, missing. *Taken.*

A jerk against her pinkie finger pulls Solinde out of her miserable contemplation, and in her mind, she follows the golden thread of her power. She cannot *see* or *hear* anything happening around Wyndam Turn, but she knows, without a doubt, that he is at that very moment attempting to circumvent the conditions of their Deal. She took his words and his Words, and she will not allow the boy to communicate it any other way. Solinde will allow him no leeway.

She tugs on the thread, pulling the little brat off balance, deliberately interfering with whatever attempt he is making.

Wyndam Turn alone is no threat. But working with his father, and that annoyance Bevel Dom, he could swiftly become one.

And that would not do. Not at all.

ELEVEN

When Pip comes to bed later, she is just on the sensible side of drunk.

"Okay, Bevel Dom?" she slurs, voice a pleasant, buzzing blur. "*Amazing* storyteller. I finally get all the hype."

I have been abed for a few hours already, wearied by my conversation with Wyndam, and undesiring of returning to the taproom once my nephew made it clear that he wanted to be left alone for the rest of the night. I have been *thinking*, which my wife will say I have always done to excess. The fact that I have not yet fallen asleep perhaps proves it.

I war with my desire to tell her everything I have learned, and the unerring sense that Wyndam would not like his follies shared. On top of the blanket, I turn the compass that Wyndam gave me, over and over. Its needle is broken, deliberately bent, and I know that this is one of the items he used to summon the Deal-Maker Spirit who took his voice in return for...

Me.

When I had asked him what he bargained for, he had simply and straightforwardly reached out and poked my chest. When I asked why, Wyndam had grimaced and turned away. He could not, or would not, explain.

When I had asked him to draw the Deal-Maker Spirit's sigil, the quill had juddered and jumped again, and it had turned out an unintelligible splotch. Wyndam had raged then, silent and heartbreaking, and thrown the ruined papers into his fire. He had slumped to his knees, sobbing with horrible, ugly hiccupping sounds, and I had held him for as long as he allowed it.

And then, before I departed, he had given me *this*. A broken compass. Without my library or the sigil, I could not know the particular Spirit he had summoned, nor could I research her preferred tableau and summon her myself to undo his Deal.

I had no answers. Only more questions.

I was left alone to ponder Wyndam's motivations for summoning me. What did he require that I alone could provide for him? What did he *need* that was so great it cost him his voice? And for that matter, how had he convinced a Deal-Maker Spirit to perform such a costly act of magic?

The Viceroy had been in possession of a vial of Deal-Maker Spirit's blood, and that had given him power over Neris. In forcing her to drink her sister's blood, it also would have doubled her magic. And the Viceroy was the only warlock I knew who was powerful enough to compel a Deal-Maker Spirit like that.

What had Wyndam done, or said, or given that could have been *enough* to pull not only me, but Pip and Alis back into this world?

My thoughts are an ever-churning flood of concern, and fear, and facts that are tumbling through my mind like the cascade of a waterfall smashing into the talus of boulders below it.

Pip flops face-first onto the pillow next to mine, reminding me to pull out of my mind and pay attention to the present. Something I am sometimes not very good at. "Where's Alis?" I ask Pip instead, trying to distract myself.

"Kintyre and Bevel were kind enough to babysit," Pip

says, slipping under the covers and pressing in close to my side, flinging an arm over my chest and a leg across my thighs, proving that she is entirely naked.

"Oh?" I ask, and the familiar smell of Pip's skin, the soft, wet feel of her tongue against my neck, manages to still the rapids of my mind enough for me to breathe deeply, set aside the compass, and turn to wrap my wife in my arms.

This will solve none of my current problems, but it certainly will make me feel better. And perhaps allow me to relax enough to fall asleep. As my wife has pointed out many times, the brain works on problems while one sleeps—defrags as a computer does—and every problem that seemed impossible to overcome, or every concern that was unfathomable the night before, always seems easier to circumvent or solve in the light of morning.

"Oh," Pip agrees, and then her wonderfully warm mouth is on mine. She tastes of the scrumpy she likes so much, and I lick the taste of apples from around her teeth.

Pip doesn't let up on the kissing enough to allow me to properly shuck off my sleeping clothes, and I find that I don't mind. She curls on top of me under the covers, pulling them up over our heads. Everything feels sensitive, hushed, and serious, and I want this to be right, want to burn off everything extraneous, burn every worry that I carry in the furnace of heat in Pip's mouth, the fire of her touches, the humid, close air under the blankets. The bone-melting burn of desire in my veins leaves me trembling under my wife's hands, desperate for connection.

Pip, however, seems intent on taking her time, pressing her lips to the sensitive underside of my chin before dragging her nose down to the hollow of my throat. Pip probes the dips and planes of my neck and shoulders, tugging aside the collar of my night shirt, mapping my skin with her tongue as I sigh and moan and arch beneath her.

Ah, ah! My lovely, pushy, bossy, beautiful wife.

Pip's legs wind around my waist, an instinctive move as natural as breathing, and my cock is hot, pulsing against my stomach, trapped beneath my sleep shirt but unmistakably present. The aching heat of it is making its demands known in the lift of my hips.

"Patience," Pip says, and though I cannot see it, I can hear her smirk.

The first touch of Pip's tongue leaves me moaning, too wrapped up in pleasure to be in the least embarrassed by the sounds I'm making and desperately pleased that our daughter is visiting her uncles tonight. I'm barely aware of my own impending orgasm before it's ready to crash over me like a wave.

"Up, up," I beg, stymieing my climax, tugging at her wrists, her elbows, one hand winding soft and sweet into the mop of her hair. "Please."

Pip hums and obliges, pushing my sleep shirt out of the way, writhing up and then, oh. Yes. *That.*

It should look ridiculous, the way the blanket tents over her head like a Halloween costume, the way that the firelight seeps in around the edges. Instead, it paints her nude body in orange and black stripes, guilds the soft edges and curves of her.

"*Bao bei,*" I moan.

"I know," she pants. "Me, too."

And then we are falling together, so perfectly it leaves me reeling. A sob startles me, unexpected and choked sounding, and I realize that it came from me. In the wake of such a spectacular climax, my defenses are blown, and every anxiety, every worry, every secret I've been holding on to, every fear that has been plaguing me since we arrived here surges up and out of my throat. My weeping is raw and harsh.

"Oh, *bao bei.* Forsyth," Pip says, sliding off and alongside me. Sweat slicks her way, and she clings to me, wrapping her limbs around my torso as if she could fend off the sadness with her own flesh. She pets my hair back off my forehead, running the tip of one finger over my scar, worried.

And I cannot do it. I cannot carry this secret, this fear, alone anymore.

"Wyndam has done something foolish," I sob. "And I am terrified by what it means."

And then, in the cathedral of our bed, I confess.

≈≈≈

As this Station of the quest ought to be relatively peaceful, Goodwoman Farthing grants Lanaea permission to travel with us to the Lost Library, and to stay a few days while we retrieve what we need. The Goodwoman waves us off from the front step of the tavern. Capplederry licks Thoma's hair up into a ridiculous coif in farewell, and I cannot help the involuntary gesture I make, smoothing down my own now-clean hair in remembrance of all the times the Library Lion has done the same to me.

"Of course," Pip sighs, as Lanaea climbs into the cart with us. "The damsel in distress who shouldn't, but somehow does, become part of the party. I should have known."

"Known what?" Lanaea asks, clearly having only caught the second half of what Pip said.

Pip just shakes her head, grinning, and when Lanaea holds her hands out for Alis, Pip happily hands our child over. Pip has spent the last week being Alis's climbing frame, entertainment device, and feeder. I can well imagine she is restless, and ready to focus on her Excel or studies. Maybe even ride Karl later.

I very gently, under my breath, suggest to Wyndam that if he were to ride in the cart with Lanaea and Pip, he could accomplish the dual goal of spending time with the maiden he is so obviously smitten with and study reading. The lad promptly joins the ladies. Like Wyndam, Lanaea has had little formal education, and so Pip is happy to practice her own letters by showing them to the two young people, even though she thinks she is only teaching the one.

The children's primer is bound like a book, and Alis is thrilled to see one of those. "'Ook, 'ook, 'ook!" she chants from Lanaea's lap, clapping her hands as Pip runs through the runes. "Yah, yah!"

The Lost Library is only a day's ride away from Gwill-fifeshire, and Capplederry seems to know exactly where we are going, for the creature moves at a faster pace than I have seen it go since we set out from Law Manor.

We encounter no trouble on the road this day, though Kintyre and Bevel are both sharp-eyed and vigilant, even as they engage in their normal teasing banter from horse-back. This leaves me to steer the cart, though it is hardly necessary to do so, and gives me time to mentally review the question of the constellations, the missing books, and now, the added complication of Wyndam's Deal. What had the lad meant to do? And had it happened as he had hoped, or was my presence a misfire?

And more than that, how are we to reverse it?

We reach the Lost Library at dusk, and though, from afar, it looks the same, I see when we get closer that the once wild vines protecting the outer walls have been tamed, and the front gates are now flung wide and wel-coming.

I direct Capplederry to the side of the fountain, near-ly exactly on the spot where Pip and I camped out during our first trip to the Lost Library. The great cat is eager to be free of its yoke, pawing at the straps and grumbling. Wyndam jumps down, and I wince just thinking about the way it must have jolted his gash, and obliges the lion. Capplederry yowls in joy and bounds around the court-yard, paws spread wide and head tossing, tail lashing. The cat rubs itself along the green wall, leaving behind tufts of road-dusty fur, and the vines rustle in welcome.

There is another set of travelers in the courtyard, though they are in the far corner, and the tents they have erected are the thick, oiled-canvas kind that generals and princes use on the battlefield. These must be the quarters of the scholars and wizards who have been summoned to help restore the Lost Library. The number of chairs and portable desks scattered in the sunlight—and the way large, long pieces of fabric scrawled over with notes and maps are pinned to the side of the tents—reinforce that guess.

Kintyre swings down off Karl, and Bevel hands him Dauntless's reins once he has dismounted. My brother leads the horses over to the fountain basin for a drink, and then sets about the tasks of currying, brushing, walking, de-saddling, and all the processes of making a horse comfortable that we all know, but prefer to leave to him. For Kintyre it is, I think, a ritual, a way to relax after a long ride. He murmurs to the horses in the evenings, re-braids their manes into the tight buds that keep them clean and free of debris, and generally pampers them. In return, Dauntless and Karl seem happier, more energetic, and more inclined to behave.

Wyndam returns to the cart to hand down Lanaea, who hobbles over to the fountain's side with him to refresh herself. Wyndam is still nervous—and unfortu-nately, still silent—but at least he is no longer gawking at the lass. I have hopes that even if things do not work out romantically, he takes this opportunity to become more confident in himself and his romantic prowess, while still respecting Lanaea and her own personal individuality. Will he find happiness and perhaps a wife in the first young maiden he has ever met that he is not related to? Probably not. But I shan't stand in his way if he wants to date her.

Date. I chuckle at myself, and the strange way Pip's world's vocabulary has leaked into even my own inner dialogue.

The flap of one of the side tents opens, and a young man approaches us without haste across the flagstone of the courtyard. As he is in no hurry, I take the time to observe the Library and note the changes. The flagstones have been swept, the weeds pulled, and the fountain has been cleaned. The walls of the Library have been scrubbed of their mold and moss, and shine sandy-golden once more. In short, the Library has been returned to its years of glory.

Even the large circular stained glass window at the top of the portico has been restored. The last time I was here, it was so dusty and overgrown with weeds and dirt that I had barely even registered it as a window. Now, it sparkles in the spring sunshine, filaments of thin silver and flecks of gold melted into the glass to give it extra shine. The work is very fine, the lead between the individual panes so thin as to be nearly invisible from the gates, and the jewel-toned colors of the glass are rich and luxuriously deep.

The scene depicted is, of course, that of the Writer at His Desk. In the bottom third of the pane, Elgar Reed sits with a quill in his hand and a pensive look on his face, a great tome laid out before him. Of course, this is not the Elgar Reed I know; this is the Writer. He is berobed in swirling silver cloth, his beard long and white, his eyes sparkling diamonds of depth and knowledge. Above his head, dynamic, glittering lines of lavender and turquoise glass—which represent the Magic of Imagination—shade into richer, plummier shades and transform into the recognizable shapes of trees, lakes, mountains, a land-scape dotted with fish and fauna, seasons and spirits, flora and fairies. In the top third of the window, all the colors shade toward the saturated, and are limned in gold. Here, it depicts the Great Races: the centaurs, goblins, dwarves, elves, merfolk, and of course, humanity.

"Well, that's not even remotely unsettling," Pip says, following my line of sight. "It's a Jesus-Elgar. Pffft, he'd love that."

Bevel, winding the reins and generally settling things around the cart to his liking, startles and blinks at her. "I forget, sometimes," he says. "That you... know him. That you're a..." He trails off, reluctant to say it out loud when we are in public. Which we both appreciate.

Instead, he jumps down and begins unloading the things we'll need for camping overnight. Before Bevel or any other family member can snatch her away, I lift Alis into my arms, settling her on my hip.

"Hello, sweeting," I say. "I've missed you."

"Dah da," Alis agrees, sighing and tucking her head under my chin, resting on my clavicle. "'Ook, yah, mama, 'itty, 'ook, Beh," she continues, obviously trying out every new word she's acquired lately. "'Isses?"

"Kisses," I agree, and put one on each of her cheeks. "*Kah*-isses."

"Kah-isses," she parrots readily.

"Kah-itty," I say, pointing to Capplederry.

"Kah-itty."

"Beh-v."

"Behv bev bev."

"Bah-ook."

"'Ooks!" she says stubbornly, gesturing at the books

piled in the cart and favoring me with a look that clearly says she fears too much time on a horse has scrambled my brains.

In truth, I have missed my daughter very much. In Victoria, we spent hours of every day in each other's company, and now, I must share her with others. I do not resent my family their extended time with Alis, but I regret that it comes at the loss of my own. Judging by the way she curls her fists into the placket of my traveling robe, Alis agrees with me.

"Halloo, and well come!" the man approaching us says. He stops a few paces away and bows at the waist. "I am Saetesh! Of House Kell." When he stands straight, I can see the obvious marks of mixed elvish ancestry—the slim build, the curtain of straight white-blond hair, the high cheekbones and narrow nose. But the rest of the man is pure House Kell. He is only slightly shorter than Kintyre, with bronzed skin and cutting cheekbones. He wears a robe of Kell-azure layered over the scholar's uniform of dark trousers and boots, a rumpled azure waistcoat with a dangling neckcloth, and a lawn shirt that he probably hasn't changed since yesterday. For all that he is elvish in appearance, the man looks like he fell asleep atop his desk—rumpled and lined, and spotted with ink.

It is a bit like looking in a mirror. If the mirror could make me more handsome at the same time. I like him immediately.

I bow to him as much as I am able, and say, "I am Forsyth Turn, Lordling—humph. Well now." I am lordling of nothing, I remember suddenly. I am no longer the heir-presumptive to the family seat. My title has passed to my nephew, and the only one I hold now is my scholarly one. "Apologies, *that* is Sir Kintyre Turn, Lord of Lysse Chipping and Turnshire, his trothed, Sir Bevel Dom, and his son, the Lordling Wyndam Turn. I am Master Forsyth

Turn, and this is my wife, Madam Lucy, and our daughter, Mistress Alis Mei. And that is Miss Lanaea of Sherwilde."

Saetesh makes a leg at each of us in turn, saving a beaming grin for Lanaea and Alis. Elves live so long and reproduce so rarely that children are sacred and wondrous to them. They would consider a lapful of babes an exuberant bounty; I have known elves to attend human parties and fall to their knees, weeping with joy when a brace of toddlers have tried to climb their hair. Saetesh of House Kell identifies himself with his human parentage, but behaves toward children as an elf, and I cannot tell therefore where he has been raised. What a delicious mystery.

But my mind is already twisted with mysteries enough, so I regretfully set this one aside.

"And did you arrive safely?" Saetesh asks. "There is a witch on the roads, they say. A weather witch, no less, and she's out for your treasures," he warns. "So you must be careful when you leave here, aye?"

"Oh, aye," Bevel agrees, looking back over his shoulder at Lanaea. He says nothing further about it, but he is clearly recalling the thunderhead that hovered above the field where Lanaea was attacked, for I am recalling the same thing.

This is the second time we've been warned of this wandering witch.

A third warning, and I might grow concerned enough to suggest we try to intercept her. Things that happen in threes in this world *mean* something.

"And have you come to tour the Lost Library?" Saetesh asks, scholarly exuberance palatable as he turns back to face me, the obvious spokesperson of our party.

Behind him, I can see Kintyre rolling his eyes and elbowing Bevel, mouthing, "*bookmouse!*" It is an insult he's used frequently enough with me that I do not appreciate him teasing someone else; especially someone who may prove to help us. I send a disapproving glare at my brother, who immediately looks contrite.

"We've come to do research, actually," I say to our welcome party.

"Oh!" Saetesh breathes, clearly excited. "We've not had any researchers in before. Please, please, be very well come. My colleagues are in the geology section today, cleaning up, so I shall have to be your guide."

"Cleaning up what?" Pip asks.

Saetesh grins and leans toward her as if confiding a secret, but he answers loudly enough for all of us to hear: "It appears as if some of the samples were sleeping golems—they get a bit cranky when woken. They smashed the display cabinets."

"Do you need us to slay them?" Kintyre asks, hand already on Foesmiter's pommel.

"Slay them?" Saetesh asks, alarmed. "Writer, no! They were perfectly content with a bit of a mineral oil washdown and a bedtime story. Went right back to sleep, the poor wee things."

Bevel and Kintyre exchange an incredulous glance.

"You... convinced golems to just go back to sleep?" Bevel asks.

"They were very small," Saetesh says, holding out a fist in demonstration. "And most of them were crystal. They yawn very adorably, for rocks. They're very happy to remain a part of the educational display so long as they're treated respectfully. It's a warm, safe place to sleep where they won't accidentally be trod on."

"But golems get huge!" Kintyre protests.

"Yes, after several hundred centuries," Saetesh says, smiling and wagging a finger at my brother. "And when they outgrow the cabinets, they'll probably go sleep in the rock garden out the back of the Library." He claps his hands and returns his attention to me: "Now, research?" His eyes stray to Kintyre behind me. "Will you... *all* be coming inside?"

"Yes," my brother grunts.

Saetesh's eyes drop to Kintyre's hand on his sword. Kintyre lets it go. Saetesh's smile gets a bit tighter. Kintyre is a great admirer of the arts, and the deep well of his affection for anything creative always raises froth and waves when something beautiful is destroyed—more so if it was vandalized, or dismantled so long ago that there's no way to even know what the original sculpture looked like. He clearly resents Saetesh's wordless implication that he is a know-nothing buffoon with no appreciation for the architectural wonders of the Library. Especially since, with all his travels, Kintyre has come to appreciate architecture quite profoundly.

"Very well. But please be aware that the books in this Library are very, very old, and though they've been under a spell of stasis for several centuries, they were old even *before* then."

"You're warning me, but you're not worried about the baby?" Kintyre asks, offended.

Saetesh turns back to tap Alis's nose. "Absolutely not," he says. "I can tell a book lover when I see one."

"'Ook, 'ook!" Alis agrees.

"Exactly! Well done, small one!" Saetesh says to her. For us, he adds: "Now, if you'll all follow me, please."

Wyndam helps Lanaea to her feet, and Bevel says, "You can stay out here, if you would prefer," to the two young people.

"I want to see it," Lanaea says. "My legs aren't that bad."

And where Lanaea goes, Wyndam is sure to follow. The lad lays a hand over the gash in his abdomen, but nods his assent. He would do much better here, resting, but he is my brother's son in this, and so I save my breath to blow away pixies.

Capplederry bounces along beside us, and squeezes in the front door immediately after Wyndam, purring like a revving engine.

"I don't think..." Saetesh begins, but then goes quiet when Capplederry bounds up the aisle that splits the main floor of the Library in half and heads straight for the massive mosaic that fills the back wall under the balcony at the far end. The main part of the Lost Library is a wide, circular dome, with two levels of shelves. Under the dome's central skylight, upon the balcony, there is the podium where stands the Parchment that Never Fills.

"Looks good there," Kintyre says, pointing at the podium.

"Ah, yes, it..." Saetesh stops, scratches the top of his head, and sheepishly asks: "Now, you'll forgive me, but... did you say your name is *Kintyre Turn*?"

"Aye," my brother says, his grin spreading.

"*Ah*," Saetesh says. "Well. Apologies, then. I was... excited about visitors and wasn't fully listening. And, yes, thank you for returning the Parchment."

"Of course," Kintyre chuckles.

When I turn to ask Pip her opinion of the Lost Library now that it is restored, I find her standing in a puddle of multi-colored sunlight in the middle of the aisle. The massive shelves spread out behind her, like the wings of a creature from her world. With her head tipped back and her eyes closed, arms down at her sides but fingers stretched toward the books as if she could read them all simply by touching them, yearning to do so, she looks divine.

"Look, sweeting," I whisper to Alis. "There are more creatures in the Library than Master Kell thinks. Mama's an angel."

Pip, who manages to hear me, snorts and puts her hands on her hips, leveling a smirk at us. "Kinda the furthest thing from, *bao bei*," she corrects, walking past us to join Capplederry in perusing the mosaic and winking saucily at me as she does.

"There are many creatures in the Library, to be sure," Saetesh says. "The baby golems in the geology display, pixies in the rafters, spiders the size of your fist out in the reading garden— honestly. Just last week, we found a fairy nest between the pages of the Royal Peerage. And of course..." He gestures to Capplederry.

"But Capplederry is a part of the Library. Here," Pip says, running her hands along the mosaic. Saetesh looks like he is about to have a fit, but he dares not correct the Madam Turn on her poor artifact-handling etiquette. "See?"

She is pointing at a curiously blank spot on the wall, shaped almost precisely as if a large lion standing rampant should be occupying it.

"The old mage who sealed this place must have pulled Capplederry from the wall to guard the Parchment that Never Fills," I say, understanding it myself only as I'm saying it aloud. "That is why his coat matches the stone walls."

Capplederry comes to wind around and between Saetesh and I, exactly as house cats wind between the legs of the human they prefer, scent-marking us and purring. By now, I am quite used to Capplederry's affection and weight, but Saetesh is knocked off balance and down onto the rug. Capplederry follows, curling around him and nuzzling at his face, begging for scratches.

"Amazing," Saetesh breathes. He is hesitant at first, but when Capplederry makes no move to harm him, he digs his hands into the great cat's ruff. "Truly incredible."

"Indeed," I agree.

"It's so affectionate," he observes.

"Capplederry was very alone for a very long time," Pip says, reaching down to push the hair on one of the cat's forepaws up, exposing the scar the manacle left on its flesh. "The old wizard chained him up to protect the Parchment."

"That's not very fair," Lanaea says, and I am struck by the offense she seems to take at this injustice. "That's horrible!"

"That's why we freed him," Pip says.

"And that's why he followed us home," Kintyre adds.

"I have studied in every great library in Hain," Saetesh says, voice filled with tremulous awe. "And I have never seen anything like this. Not even in the Viceroy's Ivory Tower."

"Ivory Tower?" Pip blurts, surprised. "What, as in...?"

"As in, the tower is the whole of his castle, which is made up of ivory," Bevel says. "With the Viceroy defeated, we were able to purge it of the evil spells protecting it and open it up for Spell Scholars."

"Yeah, but," Pip says, looking slightly queasy, "an *ivory tower?*"

"Yes. And?" Bevel asks, head cocked to the side, his sapphire eyes squinting in hedgehoggy confusion. "It's polished dragon teeth mostly, I think, but also the ribcages of some sea creatures and the claws of monsters."

"Clumsy metaphor," Pip murmurs, almost to herself, and ah, yes, that is where I have heard that phrase before. She leans in closer to me and whispers into my ear with her lips shielded: "I didn't realize Reed had such a hate-on for the academics who critiqued his work."

"Do you suppose that was the intended correlation?" I whisper back.

Pip blinks owlishly. "And you don't?"

"It seems a bit obvious," I offer. Pip *looks* at me, and

I sigh. "Yes, of course, our creator is anything but subtle. You are right."

We break apart, and Saetesh, who had obviously been straining to eavesdrop, does not look away. He has a thoughtful look on his face.

"Well now, Master Kell," I hedge, deliberately changing the topic. He seems to know it, as well. Ah, scholars. They are always so quick to find an inconsistency. And, I've found, able to identify troublemakers around their precious books. So, in keeping confidences, Pip and I have just, I fear, branded ourselves as such. "Where would you keep the astronomy texts?"

"Astronomy?" Saetesh repeats, the color draining from his bronzed face as he does so. He pushes away Capplederry and comes to stand directly before me. "Master Turn, *who are you?*"

"Just an interested scholar," I lie.

"But one who travels with a hero, a babe, and a creature so fantastic I've never seen its like before. What scholar needs this much protection, and yet, at the same time, what scholar would bring their family along while they seek answers?"

"One with, I hope, the other half of the puzzle pieces," I confide in him.

"And what part of the puzzle does the Lost Library hide?" he asks, stepping close.

I raise my free hand and point up. "Hopefully, if we are lucky, the stars."

Saetesh looks baffled.

"Surely you've noticed," I say.

Saetesh looks up as if he could see them now, in broad daylight and through the dome. "I... I haven't. I've been focused on books. But... you're right. I did not see the constellation of the Rabbit-in-the-Hedge last night. I thought about it when I looked up, but then I forgot..."

"There's this weird blind spot," Pip says, gesturing at her temple. "I mean, until it's pointed out, it's like we're the only ones who're noticing."

That is as much as she says, though I know we are both thinking that it is because we are from outside this realm.

Shoes, rings, and wizards, I think. Swords and chairs, shadows and thimbles and stars. A lad who made a Deal and cannot tell anyone what it was. A family pulled into fiction, or back home again. Bookshelves slowly going bare. A sky going black. And now a weather witch stalking Hain, stealing trinkets and treasures alike. But how does it all connect?

SILVER AND SOIL

he next two totems, Solinde manages brusquely and efficiently. They are nearby, if she travels swiftly, and drinks deeply, and she wishes to make these attempts before facing the Turns.

Just downriver of the Salt Crystal Caverns, under a tree topped with foliage that shines white during the day and silver at night, she finds and destroys a circular totem that looks like nothing so much as a belt buckle with a stylized "M" across the center. The silver tree rustles and tinkles as she approaches, the leaves chiming musically, and shrieks while she departs.

In Carapath, under a temple in a village perched on one of the many cruel and barren mountain foothills that reach their dry fingers into North Urland, it is a crate of soil, old and crumbled with white mold.

She hopes with all that she is, with every drop of her being, that these totems are what will free her son, and rages with all the power of the storm when each proves unfruitful.

Ah, but the Turns are on the move; she feels the tug of the golden thread against her finger. She must shift her attention to the idiot boy. He is nearby, just on the other side of the Cinch. Solinde drinks her fill from a freshet, and then rides a thunderhead over the peaks, the fog of her determination boiling down into a grassy plain broken only with a low, grassy knoll and the occasional stone, and the naked relics of a long-felled castle, bared to the world like bone through a wound.

Solinde is powerful, and resourceful, and she is ready.

Twice, Solinde has faced the most hated enemy of her beloved Varnet.

Twice, she has failed to end him.

Kintyre Turn will not escape her wrath a third time.

TWELVE

The astronomy reference tomes are shelved in a Gadotian-style building at the back of the main dome, complete with a watchtower and a rudimentary telescope of its own. When we make our way there, Kintyre and Bevel peel off to go explore the reading gardens, which are dotted with benches and overgrown flowers of every species imaginable, according to Saetesh.

Wyndam tags along with us, but immediately pulls Lanaea over to a display of navigational instruments. There is a case of cross backs and astrolabes, sextants and a kamal, which consists of a small board with a knotted piece of twine through the center. Wyndam holds one of the knots under his chin in demonstration, and extends the board away so that the edges make a constant angle with his eyes. Clever lad. Lanaea seems impressed.

In my arms, Alis's attention is drawn to the ceiling. It is painted black, and is flecked with gemstones that mimic those lights that have gone missing from our sky. It seems that once, different colors of ribbon used to connect the diamond-stars into their constellations, but they have long ago fallen to tatters and rot, and are hanging in dusty strips.

"I can't say where you ought to begin," Saetesh says, gesturing in a helpless shrug. "This is not my area of expertise. But I can fetch Robsfarn. They should be able to help."

"Thanks," Pip says. When Saetesh departs, he throws one last suspicious look over his shoulder. "What do you think has him so paranoid?" she asks me, reaching up to tug at one of the ribbons. It crumbles in her hand.

"I think perhaps we have been imprudent in how openly we've been discussing your, ah, *origins*," I suggest.

Pip frowns and pinches the bridge of her nose. "Perfect. Well, not much we can do if he's got a bug up his nose about it. Let's read some books."

"This way," I say. "If this Library is set up like the others I've known in Hain, then the historical records should be along that wall."

And along "that wall" they are. The books here are thick with dust, and I Speak Words of Preservation and Repair as I skim my fingers along the leather-bound spines, taking pleasure in the way the subtle ridges of the gilt lettering can be distinguished with my fingertips. Pip's eyes take on a glazed look as I Speak, and I realize that she can Hear Words no better now than she could the last time she was in my realm. For her, a Reader of Legend, the magic does not work. It slides off her mind like oil across the surface of water. It does not cling to her, does not seep and settle in her as it does the humans of this realm.

I look down at Alis to assess her reaction, and my daughter is staring up at me with parted lips and a rapt expression. Does she Hear me? Or do the Words sound, to her, the way ink bleeds across paper, as Pip once described it?

Words do not work in the Writer's realm, just as any of the spells I have memorized never did. I tried to make them function, but it was like something *essential* was missing from the air in Pip's world. As if the vital breath of *life* needed to activate the magic was completely absent, and the spells could not take their first, necessary inhalations after being birthed from my mouth. They strangled, stillborn on my lips.

Here, they breathe again, and so do Words. And I wonder—oh, how I wonder—if Alis could make them *work*. Pip remains stubbornly unmagical, like lead that refuses to transmute despite the number of alchemical potions splashed over it. But Alis is a mix of my gold and Pip's lead, and I do not know what that makes her. No such alloy exists, to my knowledge.

Pip and I have just begun to read through the titles, saying them out loud and deciding whether this book or that might hold the information we might need, when a man's scream rings out.

Startled, I nearly crush Alis. She wails unhappily, and pulls at my hair as I pass her off to Pip. My wife, who had been wearing the scarf we use to wrap Alis against our bodies, does so now, and quickly. Pip then draws her dagger. I draw my sword, straining to hear.

The scream comes again.

"Saetesh!" Pip breathes, and then we are rushing toward the outer door.

Wyndam and Lanaea have beaten us to it. They are standing in the threshold, attention directed upward. Wyndam has his clever curved sword drawn, and Lanaea clutches a tarnished flagpole in her hand. The tattered remains of an old naval flag hangs off it, flapping in the wind of whatever it is before them, blowing dust and cloth fragments back into the room toward us.

I am determined to be the one between my family and danger, and Lanaea allows me to push her behind me. I step out into the daylight and notice, as she steps back, that her hands are shaking around the pole. But her grip is firm.

Several lengths above the courtyard, just high enough that if he were to fall he would certainly come to harm, Saetesh dangles in the air. However, broken limbs will likely be the least of his concerns. For wrapped around his head is a creature of nearly indescribable horror.

Saetesh is flailing, legs and arms wheeling, tucking, and kicking. He pulls at the thing on him. It is purple, and squirming, and many-limbed. Gelatinous and partially translucent, it squishes and sinks wherever Saetesh strikes it. But it does not seem to feel the blows, and re-inflates as soon as his fists are gone. It looks like nothing so much as an octopus, or one of those tentacle-monsters Pip showed me in an animated pornographic film.

I have seen sketches of such monsters, but I do not know their name, nor their origin. They are certainly not native to Hain.

Saetesh screams again, but his voice is weaker, muffled. His jerking blows are growing less energetic. I fear that the creature is obstructing his airway, or has its dripping, leaking limbs curled around his throat.

"Oh my god," Pip says from over my shoulder. "I think that's one of those D&D brain-sucker monsters. I didn't even know you *had* those here."

I wish, suddenly, that I had Bevel's bow and arrow. In the absence of such, I push Lanaea toward a side entrance of the astronomy building, hoping that there is only one of these horrifying blob creatures outside, and say, urgently: "Quickly, fetch Kintyre!"

Pip cannot go, not with Alis encumbering her ability to run and Alis's safety to worry over. Wyndam and I have the weapons, so we must stay. That leaves only Lanaea. The lass nods once, her lips white and her eyes wide, but clearly willing to do what is necessary despite her fear. It is jerky, but her resolve is firm. I believe she too worries that there are more of the things outside, but understands, as I do, that someone must tell my brother and his partner. She clings to the pole and runs. I applaud her sense in remaining armed—without actually applauding, of course.

And then I turn back to the sky. I debate rushing out and jumping up and snatching at Saetesh's ankle, but I fear I cannot jump that high. Perhaps Wyndam can, but he is also wounded. Otherwise, there does not seem to be anything keeping Saetesh aloft, unless it's by the power of the creature, and without the ability to reach him, we are helpless to render any kind of aid.

Wyndam makes a gasping noise of surprise and points. From behind the dome of the main library, a cloud begins to coalesce. It quickly grows steel-gray and thunderous.

And upon the thunderhead stands a woman, her hand extended as if to shake. Wyndam tugs my arm once, hard, and points with his sword.

"It's her," I say, and it isn't a question. My nephew just nods.

"Will you trade me for him?" she shouts over the growing din of her thunderhead, and there is a malicious humor in it.

The Deal-Maker Spirit has black hair, which blows and dances in the wind above her head like an inky hurricane. She wears an expression of grim glee. Saetesh has stopped struggling, and I fear he may be dead. Fury at my own impotence chokes me, and for a moment, I am as wordless as Wyndam.

"No Deal?" The Spirit laughs, and her voice is the wind in the sails of a ship tossed at sea. "Well, then, as I'm not therefore permitted to kill you..."

I see what she intends to do a fraction of a moment before it happens, and I sprint out into the courtyard in time to catch Saetesh's limp body around the chest before it hits the flagstones. A loud crack rings out, and I realize that, being shorter than Saetesh, I was not able to keep his legs from hitting the ground. His left leg is hanging at a painful angle, and I am thankful for the tall boots that are stabilizing it and keeping it from flopping in a way that might make it worse.

The purple *thing* remains midair, writhing and rippling.

I crumple under Saetesh's weight, and the jolt of us both hitting the ground shocks him hard enough that his eyes fly open and he sucks in a great lungful of air. Oh, thank goodness, he is *alive*. He turns his head weakly, struggling to sit up, clutching at his broken leg. I shush him and lay him out on the stone, bid him be still and catch his breath. He cannot, of course; the pain is too great to allow him to be still, and his injury is too severe for him to be able to run or crawl away. Yet I cannot abandon him. I stand over him, all my attention and all my ire aimed upward.

On her thunderhead, the Deal-Maker Spirit is watching us intently. "You are not Kintyre Turn," she says to me, as if this disappoints her. "You must be the stuttering, useless younger brother."

"No," I say, for while I still stutter on occasion, I am not useless, nor have I ever been. "But you may come down and test your assumption if you like."

"Oh, what a delightfully silver tongue," the Deal-Maker hisses. "So sharp."

I raise my sword point in her direction. "My steel is sharp, as well. Do you care to taste it?"

The Deal-Maker Spirit laughs. "And if I decline? Are you offering to allow me to taste something—augh!"

The arrow that Bevel loosed slides right by the Spirit's head, parting her hair and grazing her ear. On the ground, Bevel cusses and nocks another. "Should have kept her more distracted, Forssy," he says, drawing back the string.

"I am afraid I am not very experienced with witty banter," I apologize. "I did my best." For I had seen them coming, and had been trading barbs with the Deal-Maker to keep her attention on me.

Kintyre snorts, Foesmiter unsheathed and a grin playing around his mouth. "I've missed this," he says softly.

"What, the danger?" Bevel teases.

"Yes," Kintyre says, and the bedroom eyes he levels at his trothed are deep enough to drown in. Which is what I wish they would do, because, *uhg*, my brother's seduction face will never cease to repel me.

On her cloud, the Deal-Maker shrieks, "Kintyre Turn!" and raises her hands, clawing at the sky. A frigid wind blows down into the courtyard, shivering the leaves of the vines around the outer wall and filling the temperate air with the bite of deep winter. "I will claw out your heart!"

"And how do you propose to do that?" I shout over the gusting gale, my breath hanging in front of my face for a brief second before it is whipped away.

"How?" the Deal-Maker roars.

"You have no Deal. You can kill none of us!"

Behind me, Wyndam hunches over, shivering. I can see that Kintyre and Bevel are also cold, though they dare not move from their defensive positions, and below me, Saetesh huddles up into a shaking ball, protecting his leg and chattering in the arctic gale.

But I have weathered two winters in Pip's realm, and while cold compared to Hain, this chill is nothing on the frigid air that numbs all sensation in your face. All the same, my hair whips against my cheeks and forehead, stinging, and the icicle fingers reach down under my collar to scratch down my spine. My fingers go immediately stiff around the grip of my sword; I fear one strong blow will knock it from my grip.

"I may not," the Spirit concedes. "But he can!" She gestures to the gelatinous blob, and it shivers and shakes with squealing pleasure.

I have half a moment to wonder what Deal the blob made that this is what she asked of it in return. Then I have time to ponder no more as it curls all its limbs in tight and rockets straight at my brother.

Foesmiter is swift, however, and Kintyre cleaves the creature in twain midair. Bevel looses his second arrow, but a bolt of unexpected lightning bats it from the sky.

"Is that all?" Kintyre challenges, and from behind me, Pip groans.

"God, don't say *that!*" she yells. "It's just inviting something to... there, see what I mean?"

And we all do, for the two segments of the blob have begun to shudder and sprout limbs, and before any of us have the opportunity to do more than shift our stances, the two smaller creatures are launching themselves at Bevel and Kintyre. The Deal-Maker cackles, and behind me, Wyndam makes a choking noise.

"Have you fought these before?" I ask the lad, and he shakes his head. "Pip?"

"If they're like hydras, then cutting them up will only make more of them!"

"And how does one kill a hydra?"

"Fire!" Saetesh chokes from below me.

"Fire," I repeat, scanning the courtyard. My flint is in our travel packs, and I know no Words to make flame. There are spells, of course, but the wind is too strong to allow me to sketch out the runes in the dirt.

While I dither, it is Wyndam who rushes back into the Library and emerges with a wooden staff. He is wrapping a tattered flag around the top, creating a makeshift torch. But where would he...?

Lightning flashes again as the Deal-Maker shrieks in delight, her focus on the battle below.

Ah! Clever boy.

With all of the Deal-Maker's attention on Kintyre and Bevel's attempts to bat the creatures away without chopping them up into smaller foes capable of over-whelming them, Wyndam darts underneath the cloud, staff upraised. Lightning always touches down against the tallest—yes! A crack and a shower of sparks, and Wyndam is sailing forward with all the grace of his life at sea and jamming the crackling torch against the side of the blob trying to latch onto Kintyre's face.

The fire splutters and hisses, the blob boiling instant-ly. It squeals like a tea kettle, heaving and bubbling, its many limbs bloating and popping. Bevel jams one of his arrows against the torch, the wooden shaft catching fire before the evaporating blob can extinguish it, and pierc-es his own blob. This creature too writhes and distends and steams. Before it is fully evaporated though, the creature manages a defense. It coalesces all of its limbs into a single, powerful trunk and strikes Bevel directly in the cheek.

He drops like a sack of rocks.

"Bev!" Kintyre shouts, diving for his trothed, but the remains of the blob wiggle free of the flaming arrow and jam themselves immediately into Kintyre's nose and mouth. He jolts back, arms flailing wildly. Wyndam's blob has disappeared, but so too has his fire, and I don't dare try to cut the thing throttling Kintyre away for fear of doubling our problem or hitting my brother.

Something long and metallic sails over my head, catching my attention, and the Deal-Maker Spirit ducks and snarls. "You have grown bothersome, Wyndam Turn!"

As the thing he threw at her clatters onto the flagstones, I realize that it is Lanaea's flagpole. But if it is here, then she is...

Lanaea gets her hand around the guard of Bevel's dropped bow, rises, and spins to face the Deal-Maker. She grimaces, obviously disturbed by the Spirit's fury, but does not hesitate. Her draw is artless, but her aim is true.

The Deal-Maker Spirit *screams*.

An arrow sprouts from the top of her arm, and the thunderhead booms and lights up with her pain. Wyndam darts forward, reigniting his torch, and then swings around and slams it against his father's head. Kintyre goes down, and Wyndam keeps the torch on the blob as it rides him. Both blob and man howl, but Wyndam does not relent.

The scent of burning hair is brief, and then whipped away by the wind.

"No, *no!*" the Deal-Maker screams, and Lanaea lets another arrow fly. The Spirit tries to bat it away with her good arm, palm splattered with her own blue blood, but the second impacts next to the first, tumbling the Deal-Maker sideways.

Blind with rage and pain, she flings her arm outward and a dozen bolts of lightning collide with the flagstones at once, throwing up a shower of sparks so thick that I must squint. Dirt and shattered stone fragments explode outward in stinging projectiles, and I raise my arm to cover my face. The force of it knocks me onto my back, and I roll over and crawl to Saetesh, coughing and blinking to clear away the grit. I cover his body with my own and shield him from a second volley of lightning strikes. None hit us, but the flagstones closest to us heave and superheat, bursting and flying all around us. All I can do is press my face against his shoulder and cover the vulnerable back of my neck with my free hand.

Thus far, I have proven to be entirely useless in this

fight. The least I can do is protect those who cannot escape it.

Wyndam lurches back suddenly, the torch in his hand spewing greasy black smoke, and flings the thing away, drawing his sword again. Kintyre sits up, swaying, one side of his head covered in soot, and I am terrified that his son has melted his flesh away. But Kintyre scrubs his sleeve over his face, and beneath the soot, his skin is unmarred.

Of course, it would not do to have a disfigured main character. It is almost unfair how the things that would kill another man, or see him maimed, barely affect Kintyre at all. But those are the rules of our world.

I am struck by a sudden inspiration.

Rules of our world! Yes!

Raising my sword, I shout to Lanaea: "A third arrow! Fire again!"

"I cannot—"

"It always works in threes! Trust me! It will work!"

I can see her fear, her trepidation. What if she misses, she is thinking, and she draws the Spirit's ire? What if the arrow is blown off course by the gusting arctic winds and injures one of us instead?

"*Trust me!*" I repeat.

The wind is so strong now that Lanaea's hair is like a veil across her eyes. All the same, she nocks, kisses the fletching, and releases. And, as I knew it would, the arrow strikes true.

The bolt shivers in the junction between the Spirit's shoulder and chest, a mere handspan away from the other arrows. Lanaea must have been aiming for her heart, though the wind pushed the arrow off course.

The Deal-Maker Spirit screams again, jolted so hard she tips over onto her back. Beneath her, the cloud suddenly shreds and turns into pale, tattered flags of fog. There is barely enough for her to stand on when she struggles back to her feet, and she clings to it, blue blood weeping down like rain.

Pip, more attentive than I, bursts out of the building behind me holding a barnacle-encrusted glass bottle, Alis still strapped across her chest. Directly beneath the Spirit's cloud is the *last* place I wish my wife and daughter to be, but there is no power left, no lightning crackling and hiding in its billowy depths. Pip catches a precious few drops of blue blood, and scoops still more off her own face with the lip of the bottle mouth when she misses her mark.

"I shall not let you!" the Deal-Maker snarls when she realizes what Pip has done. But she is listing sideways, unable to raise even one clawed hand to call her punishment down.

All the same, I put myself between them.

"Begone!" I throw at her, sword brandished.

"I will have your death!" she replies. "I will have *all of you!*" She wrenches one of the arrows out of her own arm and flings it at my head. I step to the side, out of its path, letting it whiz harmlessly by.

"Not likely," Kintyre says, staggering to his feet.

And then, suddenly, from under him, a single remaining scrap of blob monster springs to life, crawling up his legs, scuttling up his back like an oozing spider, and launches itself at the Deal-Maker Spirit. It slaps into the side of her head, and her eyes grow round.

"What's it doing?" Pip asks, the bottle of blood clutched in her arms, cradled close to Alis, who has her hands over her ears and is crying at the noise.

"I don't know!" I shout back.

The Deal-Maker gestures wildly with her good arm, and in a heartbeat, she is making her retreat, the remains of her cloud whisking her south and west.

"Impossible!" the Deal-Maker screams, just before the cloud carries her out of sight. Her voice rings out in the suddenly windless courtyard: "Impossible! *Impossible!*"

I turn to congratulate Lanaea on her well-aimed shot, but the words die in my throat.

The lass is sprawled back against the cobbles, hair flung wide like seaweed and Bevel's bow shattered. Blood pools in the dips and hollows of the flagstones behind her head, rich and reeking of copper. It stains her corn-silk hair and pearlescent gown. It blooms like a gunshot from between her breasts.

And sticking straight up from between her ribs, there is an arrow.

It is one of Bevel's, and the shaft bares the perfect blue print of a hand.

It is the arrow I dodged.

I feel my throat close up, the bubbling glow of victory lanced and draining, bile heaving in my guts.

Oh, Writer. What have I done?

I hear a scrape and a clatter on the flagstones behind me, the hollow metallic clang of a sword striking stone, and then Wyndam is beside Lanaea, clutching her shoulders and screaming.

Soundlessly.

VOWS

If her plan to attack the Lost Library has failed, Solinde is satisfied that she at least managed to end the perfect little bitch that evaded her that day in the field. But that is, unfortunately, the only satisfaction she receives.

Retreating is ignoble. But necessary.

The wissenesser shrivels up the moment it touches Solinde's skin, her body too damaged to resist sloughing off the moisture remaining in the creature, and with it, Solinde absorbs what little the wissenesser was able to consume from Kintyre Turn's mind.

Wissenssen live in small tidal pools and mucky bogs, and Solinde had found this one moping beneath a mud bubble in the brackish swamplands around the Urlish coast. The creature was easy enough to Deal with. It wanted into the Lost Library, wanted to feast on the minds of the scholars working there, and in return, it had agreed to share whatever it learned with her. Never knowing, of course, that she knew that Wyndam Turn was heading to the Library, and that she was manipulating just the right strings, saying just the right words, to ensure that this mind-flaying creature would do the deed that Deal-Makers were never allowed—kill Kintyre Turn, and all those he loved.

But now, all thoughts of killing Kintyre Turn have fled.

The Great Hero of Hain has become, in ways that Solinde never expected to have ever fathomed, *unimportant.*

For Solinde is now in possession of the knowledge that there is proof, without a doubt, that the Writer and Readers exist. Actually *exist.*

There is a realm beyond the veil of the skies, a world of Readers whose Eyes watch the lives of everyone in Hain. There is Authorial Intent, and when everyone's Last Chapter is written, there is a Shelf where, after her death, the book of her life will be set. And that means that every ill, every horror, every pain that Solinde has ever had to endure was deliberate.

An anger so black, so unlike any she has felt thus far, an anger that plumbs depths within her soul where even Solinde did not know hate could seat itself, boils up through the cracks and fractures in her sanity.

Did Varnet know? she wonders, and she misses her son so fiercely that she feels as if her bones could melt under the deluge of it. *Is that why he is missing? Is that why he was taken? Is that why I cannot find him?*

Solinde is laying on the highest turret of Swordshearth castle in Urland, and below her the king tups his mistress and makes sounds like a beached whale. His bellows disguise Solinde's own as she pulls the two remaining arrows from her arm. She has no power to summon a storm and quench herself, but the sea-salt spray that drifts upward as the waves crash upon the walls of the castle bailey is enough. She absorbs it greedily, directs the bulk of its restorative power to her wounds, and absolutely *simmers* with rage.

A Reader! she thinks again. *I stood above a Reader, and it looked so... human! So small and petty and worthless. There was a child strapped to its chest, a half-breed whelp. How dare it bestow its attention, its compassion upon a Turn when my Varnet is more powerful, more clever, more worthy? How dare that Reader be here, while my son is... my son...*

Solinde sits up, a revelation crackling through her mind like lightning across the mountains.

The idiot boy's Deal! His forfeit had granted her enough power to pull down a *Reader*, simply because she had not known that this was the person she had grasped with her power.

A *Reader*. Who could, according to legend, speak to the *Writer*.

A Reader. Traveling with Kintyre Turn, mortal enemy of her son. Either of whom surely must know what had happened to Varnet, where he went. If they were not responsible for his vanishing into another realm themselves.

A Reader. Who could lead her back to her own realm, show Solinde how to crawl the cracks in the skies that she can tear but never see through.

A Reader who would help her.

Or else.

Decided, Solinde stands.

The Writer will pay for what he has done to me. To Varnet!

There is only one more totem left.

And when she has destroyed it, her son will be returned to her, and together, they will have their revenge.

Solinde raises her face to the ever darkening veil above her. It is nearly black now. Less than a hundred lights twinkle in the heavens. There are so few constellations left with their attendant stories.

Soon, she will crawl and wriggle her way into the realm of the Writer. Soon, soon she will *end him*. When she is reunited with Varnet, she will have power enough to do it. Together, they will have power enough for anything. And together, they will watch this world, this

Kintyre Turn, this idiot mute boy, and this Reader *drown*.

And she knows just the right leverage to use to make it so.

THIRTEEN

Alis is wailing.

The rest of the world is silent, but my child, my baby, is screaming. I feel like joining her, feel like exorcising every horrible, ugly feeling that is churning and roiling in my guts in a shrill, anguished cry. Instead, so as not to terrify her further, I swallow hard on the taste of my despair. I feel as if I am doing her a disservice in pretending that I do not wish to scream as well. As if I am betraying her, somehow, in lying about what I am feeling.

Pip kisses Alis's forehead over and over, clutching the bottle of blood and our daughter both, whispering soothing nothings as fat, shocked tears roll down her cheeks and soak into Alis's hair. Her hands are trembling, but Alis doesn't seem to notice in her own distress.

The commotion and screaming draws out the rest of Saetesh's colleagues, who were hiding behind the gallery pillars in the reading garden. Silently, they shuffle into the courtyard, hats doffed and held before them, expressions shocked, or pitying, or worried. A wide halfling man that, I think, is part dryad, kneels immediately before Saetesh and scoops him up. Saetesh screams again when his leg is jolted, then turns his face into his colleague's chest and balls his fists in his sleeves.

"If you puke on me, I'll puke right back on you," the halfling warns Saetesh, its voice reedy, its flesh made of crackled bark.

Saetesh makes an incomprehensible moaning sound and shakes his head slowly.

"That's... super gross," Pip says, trying not to look directly at his leg.

"There are healer's supplies in our camp," the dryad-born creature says to me. "Come to us when you're..." He does not finish his sentence, only swallows hard, then turns and goes. The rest of his colleagues, six others in all, trail after him, leaving us alone with... what is left of Lanaea.

Wyndam has let Bevel pull him away from her. But when Bevel reaches down to touch her neck, it is clear by the shuttering of his gaze that he finds no pulse. Even to me, the least skilled warrior of the lot of us, it is obvious that all breath has left her body. If the arrow did not kill her, then the amount of blood she lost when she fell back against the flagstones and cracked open her skull did. Ruby rivulets run along the decorative divots in the stonework, an archaic sort of geometry in gore.

Wyndam crawls over to the astronomy building and rests his back against the stone, staring up at the now clear sky. His jet eyes are red-rimmed, and starkly dry, but his cheeks are still flushed and stained with saltwater. His hands are painted with her blood, and he holds his fingers against his lips, smearing the stain against his mouth like a last kiss, mourning.

The despair that has been dragging upon me finally grows too burdensome to sustain. "Th-this is-s-s ah-all muh-my f-f-fault," I blurt, and I am choking on the words, barely able to get them past my tongue, where they scorch to ash on my lips. I crumple down onto the charred flagstones. My head feels too heavy to keep up, and my sword drags in the dust. "I was com-com-plete-letely *useless* j-just now, but I c-c-cou-could have kn-knocked the ar-arrow away-ay in-instead of j-juh-just si-side-step-ping it. F-F-Forsyth Tuh-Turn and his d-damn c-clever footwork-k, aye, Kin-Kintyre? What good is all th-that p-p-posturing, inde-deed."

Bevel, no longer needing to be delicate, yanks out the arrow. Even in death, no one deserves to remain stuck like slaughtered livestock. He chucks it aside, fury bunching his shoulders, and then clenches his fists. "I'm going to have to go back and tell Anne that we got her niece killed. Oh, Writer's balls. I'm going to have to tell *Thoma*. Lanaea's father sent her to Gwillfifeshire for safety, and I should have been a better shot, should have..." He trails off and snarls, punching the stones at his feet. Kintyre grabs his wrist to keep him from doing it a second time and possibly breaking his own hand.

Pip shakes her head and scrubs her hands through her hair. "No. I was the one who said this was the First Station. I was the one who said it was safe for her to come. This is *my fault*. God, I'm such a *fucking idiot*. You realizing that the books were going missing was the First Station! Then, there was showing up here... the attack in the field... and now the Library. This is the *Fourth*. There's always a goddamned attack at the Fourth, and some newly introduced character *always* gets Redshirted, and I just... I just..." My wife's voice cracks, and she crumples as well, shoulders shaking as she slides to the ground beside me and folds herself small against my chest. Alis, cocooned now between her parents, quiets. "She deserved better than to just be *fridged*."

I hold my wife close, rocking her and letting my own tears mingle with hers. My tongue flutters against the roof of my mouth in my shocked despair, and I cannot speak, not now, but I can make soothing noises.

And behind me, Wyndam is still, and silent. Dead, for all that he breathes still. I had wished so fervently for

Lanaea to be Wyndam's Pip. Instead, she was his Melinda. I have known that pain, and I would wish it on *no one*, least of all my nephew. Least of all on Lanaea herself.

"If we have to blame someone, blame the Deal-Maker Spirit," Kintyre says, pulling Bevel shakily to his feet. "She attacked *us*."

And in a flash, Wyndam is on his feet, one finger jammed into his chest and a silent fury boiling across his face. He shouts a whole string of expletives and words that are silent and too fast for me to lip-read. But it is clear who Wyndam blames.

"And what is wrong with *you*?" Kintyre says, at the end of his patience, and his tether. He pushes Wyndam back, out of his space, but the lad is right back in it, swinging a punch that Kintyre shifts to the side to avoid. "Damn you, just *say it*, boy!"

"St-stop it," I say, standing, scrubbing my cheeks with my cuffs. "Both of you, stop! Wyndam, e-e-enough!"

Wyndam ignores me and swings again. Kintyre stops his fist with his palm, and I expect him to wrench the lad's arm around and behind his back, as he's done to me many times in the past when we were roughhousing. I forget, however, that Wyndam was trained by pirates.

The lad drops his center of gravity. Kintyre, having shifted his own in preparation to grapple, is startled into letting go of his arm. Wyndam crouches quick, swings one leg out in a circular sweep, and knocks Kintyre back onto his arse.

I don't have time to relish the look of shock on my brother's face, however. Wyndam is up again in a flash, hands on Kintyre's tented knees, using the momentum to flip over in a midair somersault, landing with his feet on either side of Kintyre's shoulders. He grabs his father's collar and hauls back his other fist, but Bevel is there in an instant, tenacious as a bulldog. He clamps his arms around Wyndam's cocked elbow and wrenches the lad back. This time, momentum and gravity work against Wyndam as Bevel deliberately rolls back onto his rump, rocking back and flipping Wyndam into the wall of the astronomy building with his feet.

But instead of slamming into the stone and going down, Wyndam continues the spin, plants his feet flat against the wall, and springs back, knocking Bevel back down from where he was rolling to a stand.

"This is some serious Kung Fu shit right here," Pip says, from over my shoulder, and I glance at her quickly to see that she has now stood as well. Alis is sniffling, but otherwise occupied with examining the old barnacles pressed against her arm. "We should probably stop them."

My attention is drawn back to the fight when Wyndam lands a punch on Bevel's jaw. Bevel, already woozy from his knock against the flagstones fighting the blob monster, drops for the second time in twenty minutes, and now, I am annoyed. Bad enough that they are brawling instead of talking it out like families ought, but they are doing it mere steps away from Lanaea's remains. Kintyre springs to his feet, meaty paws open to catch Wyndam around the waist, and Pip is right.

"*Enough!*" I bellow in my best Shadow Hand voice, and both Wyndam and Kintyre freeze where they stand. "Kintyre Turn!" I bellow. "Go fetch a blanket and the healer's kit from the cart! Wyndam Turn, you wake Bevel up right now and check his head for injuries."

"But I—" Kintyre begins, at the same moment Wyndam gapes at me and begins gesturing rudely.

"*Now,*" I roar. Kintyre and Wyndam obey so quickly that I can practically see the blur of their motion.

Wyndam gently nudges Bevel awake, helps him sit up and rest back against the wall of the astronomy building.

Pip goes over to check for a concussion—his balance seems fine, but he has trouble keeping his eyes open, and for one long moment, we are all certain that he is going to vomit. Wyndam flutters around Bevel, checking his scalp for cuts and generally looking contrite, and Bevel stills him with a soft, cupped palm on the lad's cheek.

"Heck of a right hook, my lad," Bevel says softly. "Quite impressive."

Wyndam looks torn between pride and confusion at being praised by the man who generally only yells at him for mistakes.

Bevel chuckles, pats his face once, and says, "Now, open your shirt, Wyn. Let's see if you've torn yourself open."

Wyndam looks startled.

"What, you think we didn't know? Poor guardians we'd make, then. And poor warriors to boot."

When Kintyre returns, a blanket thrown over his shoulder and the healer's kit in his hand, along with one of our water flasks, he joins the other two to mother-hen and cluck over their scratches and bruises. Alis squirms and wriggles and protests until she can stand beside Bevel, clinging to his knee and staring very seriously into his face as Kintyre dresses the cut on his forehead. Bevel keeps a loose hand around her ankle, to keep her from wandering off, and does his best to smile through the winces.

Her hands finally free, Pip avails herself of one of the empty phials in the healer's kit and very, very carefully pours the blue Deal-Maker's blood into the easier-to-transport glass container, capping it tightly and slipping it into her bra.

And I?

I take the blanket, lay it out on the flag stones and carefully, respectfully, roll up Lanaea.

≋

The cart is cleared out, and Lanaea's remains are placed reverently in the middle. We relocate the rest of our gear to the open stone beside the fountain, building a makeshift camp of pillows and blankets. Capplederry creeps up to the cart, sniffing and meowing piteously. Wyndam has to push the great cat away to keep it from pawing at Lanaea's body, and eventually, his shoves devolve into clinging to Capplederry's ruff and sobbing piteously into the fur there. Kintyre and Bevel give him the space he needs.

When the lad is all cried out, he joins the rest of us where we sit on the lip of the fountain's basin, washing away the blood. Alis has been stripped entirely, and as the water only comes up to her waist, she is quite enjoying stomping around making big waves, her terror of a few moments ago forgotten. Alis is on her bottom as much as she is on her feet, but the water doesn't go over her head when she is sitting, and her mother has a close eye on her. Pip has her boots and her leather trousers off, her shirttails pulled low, and is dangling her feet in the basin with Alis, kicking gently and splashing when Alis gets close enough. But her face is grim, her complexion wan, and her freckles stand out in sharp contrast, the way they always do when she is shaken.

"My hair," Kintyre moans, clearly attempting to lighten the mood as much as is respectable. He is holding up a few scraggly, singed ends that frame his ear.

"Better than you suffocating to death, you idiot lump," Bevel says, but reaches up to help him try to scrub away the thick, greasy soot and purple slime all the same.

Wyndam's shirt still hangs open, and he splashes and scrubs at his face before he sits directly beside me, gesturing to his stomach.

"It looks better," I say to him, wetting a bit of ragged cloth and dabbing away the crusted, yellowed ointment. "It hasn't reopened."

"That's lucky," Kintyre says, head tipped over and one eye squeezed shut as Bevel, kneeling along the basin with sleeves rolled up, scrubs his hair with soap flakes. It smells of lavender. Kin splutters when Bevel scoops up water in one of the cooking bowls and dumps it over his trothed's head with no warning.

Kintyre shoots him a look, and Bevel grins cheekily. If Lanaea were not laid out a few paces away, I know they would be celebrating in their usual post-battle, pseudo-pornographic manner. As it is, they are affectionate, but subdued. All the same, it seems to physically pain Wyndam. He looks away, eyes on the cart as I dry his wound and reapply the ointment.

I don't know what sort of emotional depth main characters have in other fantasy works, but it seems that Kintyre and Bevel are not feeling this loss as keenly as the rest of us. Or, at least, they are *pretending* not to. I recall Pip's words, her assertion that some "minor" character always perishes during the Fourth Station. I think back on our quest, and... ah, yes. Pip chose to free Capplederry instead of slay him.

But if what my wife says is true, then Kintyre and Bevel have lost a minimum of eight other companions in similar circumstances before. Perhaps they are not being callous so much as simply trying not to let her death wound them too deeply. To carry on carrying on.

They are not hardened to these deaths, only exhausted by them.

I catch them sharing a sad gaze in a tender moment, when they think no one is looking, and turn away. Let them have their privacy, and let them mourn in their own way. We are all devastated.

When Wyndam is patched, and his shirt is closed once more, I take the time to observe the scholar's tent in the distance. Three of Saetesh's colleagues are milling around the door to the tent, and one is hurrying toward them with a large kettle, still steaming from its time over their nearby cook fire. I assume the last two are tending to Saetesh.

I feel obligated to go over, to inquire after his health, but at the same time, the last thing I am feeling is social. I want to curl into my sleep roll, wrap myself around my wife and daughter, and bid Capplederry to knock the ball of the sun lower in the sky. There are hours yet before sunset, and I am weary in a way that I haven't been since Mother's death.

Body, soul, and mind, all I want to do is shut off, shut myself down, and sleep. But no, not yet. For Kintyre rises from the edge of the basin, shaking water from his hair, and sits down beside Wyndam.

"Come now, Wyndam," Kintyre says, his voice firm yet gentle. "Enough is enough now. Speak to me, son."

Wyndam takes a long, slow moment to drag his gaze away from the wrapped bundle on the cart, sliding his eyes along the ground before they land on his father's boots, and then shift upward. The lad takes a deep breath, opens his mouth, then clicks it shut again. He peers over his father's shoulder to raise pleading eyebrows at me. I tilt my head to the side in a question: *Are you sure?*

His answer is a small, shaky nod, and a thinning of his lips as he rolls them inward to bite at them, nervous.

"I'm not gonna like this, am I?" Kintyre rumbles, watching our silent communication.

"No," I say. "But you must hear it all the same, Kintyre. *And*," I add hastily as Kintyre bites his own lips in a manner identical to his son's, "you must keep your temper."

"Aye," he grunts.

"Do you swear?"

"I swear!" he snaps, impatient and belying his promise immediately. I hold up a scolding finger, and he contritely says, "Apologies. I'll try."

"Very good," I say, and then take a deep breath. "Now, where to begin? Wyndam has lost all ability to speak."

"What do you mean, you can't speak anymore?" Kintyre shouts, startled, and swings back around to goggle. "Explain!"

"Kin..." Bevel sighs. "*Temper.*"

"Sorry!" Kin snarls. "But... how long has this been going on? Why didn't you, I don't know, write it down? Writer's calluses, Wyndam, I am your *father!* Did you think I would turn you away when you came to me for help?"

Wyndam looks at me helplessly, desperate.

"Kintyre," I say. "Quiet, please, as you promised. And let me explain."

≈≈≈

We leave the Lost Library empty handed. I had returned to the astronomy building with Robfarn, Saetesh's half-dryad colleague, to search the collection by Wisp-lamp light, but we are unlucky. There are no tomes or tales of disappearing constellations, but, now that I had pieced together what I hoped was more of this mystery, I hadn't really expected it.

In the morning, Saetesh is conscious and watching as we load our saddlebags, packing all of our traveling supplies onto the backs of the horses or onto Cappleder-ry. He is propped up in a chair in the sunshine outside the tent, a travel desk already on his lap and a wan but genuine smile on his face.

Before we make the long, slow walk back to Gwill-fifeshire, I decide to speak quietly with him.

"Well, now," he says, exhibiting the customary elvish good cheer in the face of darkness. "That shall be, I think, my first and *last* adventure. Do you suppose Sir Dom will write about this one? If he does, I hope I come off as heroic."

"You were very brave," I comfort him. "How is your leg?"

"It was a clean break. Olissa says it will heal well, and I have elvish blood on my side. I shall be dancing at Solsticetide."

"I hope so, my friend," I say, and shake his hand. In another life, I might have invited him back to Turn Hall for the duration of his healing, become his patron and given him free reign of my library, perhaps even made a true friend of him. He could have been one of the most profound relationships of my life, held alongside Pointe and Pip. Now, I must say my goodbyes, knowing that if this quest is successful, and Pip, Alis, and I return to Victoria, I will never see him again.

A sort of bittersweet resentment crawls up my throat, but I swallow it back down. I cannot afford to mourn for friendships missed. I have neither the time nor the emotional capacity.

I make my farewells, and go back to our horses, passing Bevel as he comes to make his and Kintyre's farewells too. Behind me, I hear Bevel apologize to Saetesh for his getting caught up in what was clearly a fight between the Deal-Maker Spirit and Kintyre, but Saetesh waves him off and only bids Bevel to depict him handsomely and with a twinkling smile. Bevel laughs, though it is strained, and promises that if he writes up this adventure, he will do as Saetesh asks.

I know, of course, that Bevel will not, cannot write a

scroll about this quest.

Ever.

～

Returning to Gwillfifeshire is as horrible as we all feared it would be.

The streets are less crowded, because it is not market day when we return, but we draw followers all the same. The funeral procession creaks and trundles its way toward the Pern, people gasping and covering their mouths when they realize that there is a body in the back of our cart, and one person missing from our party.

What we had hoped would be a joyous homecoming for us, filled with handfuls of scrolls and stuffed with gaiety and new information, is somber instead. Someone has run ahead, because, when we enter the inn's courtyard, the Goodwoman and her son are already standing on the threshold, clutching one another. Anne and Thoma are subdued. There is no screaming, no hysteria, for Lanaea was virtually unknown to them, but there is a damp misery for the life and niece lost. And such horrified guilt in Kintyre and Bevel.

And in me.

Nothing is said. No one asks for explanations. No one rushes to blurt excuses. We simply look at each other, mute and miserable, united by our grief, yet separated by that gulf of the unfathomable loneliness that contemplating our own mortality always brings.

At length, Anne nods, just once, and then turns away and ushers Thoma inside. Kintyre and Bevel are joined by two other men—strangers from the crowd—and together, they lift Lanea down and carry her into the inn after Anne. Pip and I follow slowly, the marshalls of our grim parade of townspeople.

The women of Gwillfifeshire descend upon the

Pern to cook, and clean, and comfort Anne and Thoma. Someone washes Lanaea's body. Someone else anoints it. Someone styles her hair and dabs cosmetics on her lifeless lips, and someone else lays her out in a side room. Kintyre and Bevel hunch in the corner booth of the taproom, as far away from everyone else as possible, carving wood and smoking pipes, and scratching pencil on parchment. Pip, Alis, and I sit at the bar, where we can take it all in. No one asks us questions. We are not ignored, but we choose not to participate. Food fills the tables, and though no wake is planned, everyone in town, including Lord Gallvig, slowly trickles in.

Music breaks out like a rash of whooping cough: slowly at first, in fits and spurts as a fiddle and a harp are tuned to one another. Someone runs home and returns with a flute, and the music becomes faster, louder, until suddenly, all at once, someone adds a voice, and then another. And then a whole chorus takes up song after song after song.

> *Far beyond the curtains of time and fate,*
> *Beyond the misty vale of the Reader's tears,*
> *The Writer sets down his quill, his intent filled,*
> *The narrative played out, the ink bottle empty.*
>
> *Here the story is finished, here joy abate*
> *Here an end to pain, and an end to fears.*
> *Here is the story told as He has willed.*
> *Here the empty spot on the Shelf left for thee.*
>
> *My heart fills with such a complex weight,*
> *Grief, thick like syrup, in my breast appears,*
> *My own tale, with you missing, I must rebuild.*
> *Until my own The End also folds over me.*

The mournful, chanting tone of the dirge-music drives me out to the front step of the tavern. I do not worry that anyone will tread on me, nor that they will want to pass me, for it appears as if the whole of Gwill-fifeshire is in the blazing hot, candle-bright room behind me. The party reminds me too much of Solsticetide, of the beginning of this adventure, of a time when my family was safe and my life stable. Or so I thought.

Foolish Forsyth.

And so here I am, again, alone on a step, staring up at the sky and wondering, wishing, my mind a tangled skein of facts that I cannot unravel, cannot knit together to form a pattern that makes any sort of sense. I see the pieces. I know there must *be* a pattern. But I do not know what it is. I do not know *why*.

And without the *why*, I cannot *stop* it.

Oh, I am utterly *stupid*.

What use am I? What use is the know-it-all younger brother of the hero, the man who is supposed to find answers in books, when he searches and still yet finds *none*? What good is a scholar on a quest who holds no information?

No good at all, that is what.

Impotent in my stupidity, I clutch the sleeves of my jacket and grind my teeth, forcing myself to breathe deep and steady. To re-evaluate what I know. To take out what little information I have and look it over once more, reorder it, try to assemble it in a new way.

Wyndam called down a Deal-Maker who took his voice. The stars are burning out. Books are vanishing at the same rate as constellations. And there is a weather witch who is not a weather witch, but the Deal-Maker who stole Wyndam's voice and will not allow him to tell us why.

Above me, only one solitary, lonely figure of stars

remains: *The Great Tale.* Together, the stars form the picture of a desk, a figure seated behind it with quill in hand, and another standing alongside, reading over the first's shoulder.

And there is no *reason* for it. None that I can *see.*

The constellation of the Writer is entirely *useless.* It does not move. It does not look down on me, and call me "son," and explain. It does nothing but *twinkle,* and I *hate* it. Isn't this the part of the narrative where the Deus is meant to Ex Machina?

And Reed can't even bloody well do *that* right.

It isn't until the sun is fully set, the sky near-black without the constellations to light it, that Pip finds me seated by the front door, watching the people come in and out, and asks: "Where's Wyndam?"

I had not forgotten the lad, not really, but his misery had been so encompassing that he had refused all food and company and gone directly upstairs.

"I would say his room," I guess. "But you are about to tell me otherwise?"

Pip points a finger-gun at me and fires. "Gotcha. I just went up to put Alis down. He's gone."

"Blast," I curse. "Stay here, I'll... go see if he went for a *walk.*"

I huddle into my jacket, pulling up the collar against a chill in the spring night that has more to do with my state of mind than the temperature. There is no clue as to which direction Wyndam might have gone, if he has gone for a walk at all, so I decide to make for the areas we have already passed through, as they would be the best known to him. It is a good choice, for I find him by the edge of the crumbling old well in the middle of the market square. The well is made of more gray stone, shored up on one side with red clay brick and weather-whitened wooden joists. A cypress tree crowds against the side of the wall, twisting along the mortar paths and splaying like a mourner's umbrella over the open pit of the well. Around its roots, the stones of the square heave and buckle, unable to resist the strength of life and time.

And on this wall sits Wyndam. He has his head between his hands, and he is hunched over. The paving stones between his feet are wet, and I choose not to comment on that. Instead, I walk to his side, making a deliberate and obvious amount of noise so as not to startle the lad, and then sit gingerly beside him. The wall shifts a little under our combined weight, but doesn't collapse. Still, mortar dust rains down into the water far below us, with a few small pebbles that make soft, echoing, plinking noises.

"I would ask if you want to talk about it, my lad, but..." I say softly, and beside me, Wyndam snorts. "The truth of it is this, nephew: you are Kintyre Turn's son. And he is a hero." Wyndam stills, and I turn my face up to the sky, mourning the loss of the stars that were so comforting, so bright in my childhood, and hoping deep within my guts that I will be able to restore them. That other children will have the opportunity to revel in the magic of their glow.

Wyndam grunts. He is listening, but he doesn't like it.

"I have come to understand that you dislike people comparing you to your father," I go on, "or judging you by his merits and achievements, but in this, you must acknowledge your connection. You are the son of a hero, Wyndam Turn, and that means that, simply by virtue of your existence, those with harm and evil in their hearts will hurt those closest to you *simply because* they are closest to you. And that threat is even greater if those people are women. Villains... *Writers* are forever harming women to hurt male heroes. It is lazy writing, but a staple of the genre, which, unfortunately, makes it a fact of life for us."

Wyndam jerks to his feet, face twisted with disgust.

"No," I say, guessing what has him so wroth. "No, I am not excusing it. I am *warning* you, my lad." I sigh, scrubbing my forehead with the heel of my hand, exhaustion and grief pulling on my body. I want to sleep for a week. "This is not what you expected life with Kintyre Turn to be, is it?" I say gently.

Wyndam shakes his head.

"I will tell you a secret, nephew mine," I say, leaning close. "It was nothing like how Bevel's scrolls paint it for me, either. We are, both of us, living in the shadow of a hero who never truly existed. Bevel is a romantic, and his scrolls are a fantasy. The road is a hard, exhausting, boring, filthy place," I say. "It is gruelling. And it is horrible. Bevel writes fairy tales."

He looks as if he'd like to protest. I wish he could.

"I do not say this to disillusion you, Wyndam, but to apprise you of the realities of it. Were you to, say, take up your father's sword and mantle, for example, we would very much wish for you to be prepared for what you might find."

Wyndam looks up at me, jet eyes wide and shining, mouth dropped open with slowly dawning understanding. He presses his hand against his chest, expression hopeful.

"I do not see why you couldn't," I say, conspiratorially. "It seems there is already a great tradition of the Lordling Turn leaving home to go on an adventure. First Kintyre, when he was heir to the seat, and then me. If you were to take the title, you would be the third. I would even venture to say that it's practically expected, at this point."

He chews on the corner of his lip for a moment,

tugging at his own sleeves, thoughtful.

"Stay with us for now. Finish this adventure. See how you like it, first."

And if I don't? his gaze challenges.

I shrug. "Then there is a position with the Sword of Turnshire. It is not as exciting as questing, that is true, but there is... there is infinitely less heartbreak, my lad," I say softly. "And you will have the opportunity to prevent the sorts of things that happened to Lanaea."

Her name sets off a bout of furious, tight pacing, and he scrubs angrily at his eyes. When he slows, I stand, sling an arm around his broad shoulders, and guide him back toward the *Pern*.

"Come, my lad," I say softly. "Let us say our good-byes, properly, and then get a drink into you. And tomorrow... tomorrow, we shall leave for tomorrow."

When we return to the inn, we join the rest of our family in the corner booth. Pip is staring, wide-eyed and stiff with surprised horror, at a ghost that is floating in the middle of the room, corralling delighted children.

"That's Mandikin," Bevel says, when I shoot him a questioning glance. "She's Gwillfifeshire's childminder. Pip's never seen a ghost before."

"No," I agree. "I don't believe they have ghosts in the Writer's world."

"Shame," Kintyre says. "They're a good way to gain closure. Look."

And there, behind Mandikin, is a new ghost. She is so freshly dead that there is still color in her cheeks, in her corn-silk hair and pretty pink lips. The hems of her pearlescent dress and sleeves are so barely transparent that, if I didn't know better, I would have assumed that Lanaea was still alive.

STORIES

olinde is a Deal-Maker Spirit who prefers the sea, the shadow's hearth, the cool of night. She loves water and waves, and was imprisoned inland for so long that she grew parched for wonder and water alike. A fury boils in her like thunder, like a gale, like a hurricane, and it has been howling for release since the day she was tricked into Dealing away her own magic and freedom. She has walked the world, leaving ruin and tears in her wake, like a tidal wave of wrath. She has extinguished whole realms with her fury.

And yet. *And yet.*

The fire of the stars still burn, though they are few in number, and her son is still not returned to her. But soon... soon. There is, she feels, but one totem left. And it is nearby.

She leaves Swordshearth and the sea at a crawl. It takes her the remainder of the day to reach the Eyrie by cloud. But there, she seeks a totem unlike any other. It requires a spell that pulls at the very core of her being to find, as it is veiled beneath a layer of enchantment so strong that it feels like trying to claw through granite.

Already wearied from her failure at the Lost Library, it takes the full length of the night to unpick the magic woven over the totem. As the hours pass and the last constellation wheels overhead, Solinde finds herself slumped against the stone desk, her feet skidding in the grooves in the stone floor worn by the thousands upon thousands of pilgrims who have come to worship at the altar of the Great Writer.

When the sun rises, Solinde's head pinches, her fingers are numb and stiff, and her body is a riot of aches she hasn't had to suffer since her mortal life ended. The indignity of it enrages her, though she hasn't the energy to do more than crackle and rumble about it. She sleeps on the granite and gravel floor, head pillowed on her hair, and calls down the rain to wash away the dust that cakes her lips from her hard work.

When she wakes, the totem has fully materialized. With the enchantment in place, one could have stood right at the Desk that Never Rots and never see the totem, never smell it, never *touch* it. But now, it is here. It is a jumbled, mechanical, clacking beast of a thing. The device embosses glyphs of power onto paper, vellum, skin, anything upon which its tiny hammers strike their blows. But these are a Creator's runes, and Solinde cannot read them.

She feels her eyes become slits, her pupils elongate, and her tongue flicks between her teeth, black and long, licking her chops. It matters not that she cannot read the runes. She doesn't need to understand this totem to destroy it.

She laughs, delighted that her quest is nearly at its end. And then she feels disgusted and guilty. How could she laugh when her son is not free, when it is possible that he is rotting away in the ground? How could she have done that? She holds on to her sobs until she has stumbled over to lean against the cavern wall. Then, with the stone supporting her, she sobs like she hasn't done in months, until she is gagging and heaving.

She has no time for this weakness, this *motherliness,*

and yet she must wait for the sensation to pass. She must purge herself of it.

When she has done that, she stands, and calls down *fire*.

The totem is resistant. It fights. It will not melt, or crack apart, no matter how many times she strikes it with lightning. But she will not lose to an inanimate hunk of metal. Raising her arms, head thrown back, power hooking into the deepest anchor of her magic, Solinde calls down a storm the likes of which this part of the world has never seen.

FOURTEEN

There is a thunderstorm over the Cinch Mountains, right around where the Eyrie coves begin. Possibly even directly above the Rookery. It is so large that I can see it all the way from Gwillfifeshire, perched above the wheat plains as I am in the second story bedroom of the *Pern*.

Below me, Lanaea's wake continues, music and laughter ringing long into the night. The relief that her ghost will stay on, that she is not lost before her father can come down from Sherwilde and bid her goodbye, is palatable and heady. Whether she'll remain after that is unknown. Mandikin stays for the love of the children. Lanaea's passions and unfinished business might not be so strong, so ever-existing. There will always be children in Gwillfifeshire. Lanaea's business may last a shorter amount of time.

There are no ghosts in Turnshire, as far as I am aware, and I wonder idly, watching the storm from the window seat, if that is because I was a good lordling who made his people happy. Or if it was merely a convenient plot hole for Reed to exploit.

Behind me, Pip and Alis both sleep soundly. The storm seems to have woken only me. I cannot hear it from this distance, of course, but the lightning is bright enough, and I am wary enough, that it pulled me away from the brink of slumber. That the storm is so concentrated, that it is so large and yet does not drift or ebb, makes it clear that it is not of natural make, and I do not have to wonder if it is the work of our weather witch, the nameless Deal-Maker who has stolen Wyndam's voice.

Thus it is that I am awake and watching the skies when the very last constellation flares, each star burning bright as a sun for a split second, and then bursting like a firework, trailing fairy dust down the solemn black velvet of the sky before fading into nothingness. My stomach lurches, and my whole body goes numb with horror. The hair on the back of my neck pricks up, and a shudder races underneath my skin.

On the other side of the windowpane, darkness—true and complete darkness—falls.

I stay up watching the storm die out, straining my gaze toward the east, back toward Turnshire, hoping, hoping for the first hints of dawn. After many silent, tense hours, my exhausting, strained vigil is rewarded. The sun rises.

I will admit that I had genuinely feared it would not. What is one more star to snuff out, after all?

I have never been one to pray to the Writer. I never really was certain I even believed in such an omnipotent creature, never sure I thought the stories true, never fell into the winding, grasping silks of *belief.* And now that I know him personally, I would still not pray to Elgar Reed.

Yet, in those few seemingly endless hours between the death of the last stars and the rising of the sun, I cannot help the tripping, stuttering, whispered mantra of pleas from tumbling from my lips. They are not prayers, not really. Maybe they are a negotiation, instead, but with whom, I cannot say. Maybe I just hope that if I say it aloud, if I make my wishes known, someone—something—will hear and make them truth.

What I want more than anything is reassurance that

this is not my fault. That my leaving this world did not end it, and is, in all likelihood, not the reason it is crumbling. But during that cold and lonely vigil, the self-doubt comes creeping in. For half a night, I live in terror that the Final Chapter has come, just as the zealots had always predicted, and that it is all due to me. That the world will be Shelved *because of me.* Because of my desire for the love of a clever woman. I fear that because of my desperation for validation and the opportunity to be a hero in my own right, outside of my brother's shadow, the world would suffer.

No, they are not prayers. But with the sunrise, they have been answered all the same.

And when the sky above Gwillfifeshire grows first silver, then indigo, and a sliver of the palest coral-orange leaks into the blue, when it gilds the thatch roofs and chimney stacks with warm spring light, I finally give in to my fatigue, end my vigil, and crawl into bed.

I sleep for several hours, and wake when Alis begins to fuss, kicking my hip in her unhappiness. Pip rolls over and grumbles against the side of my head, reaching out to rub Alis's belly in a move that is automatic at this point. Alis only wails louder, and the faint tang of urine in the air tells me why. I am about to heave myself out of bed when Pip springs up and scoops our daughter off the bed, jostling her away for a fresh nappy and a wipe-down.

I sit up, trying to pull my wretched hair back into some semblance of order, and watch, silent. Something is not right. Perhaps it is that I am more tired than I think, after staying up as I did, but no... Pip is behaving strangely. She is being short with Alis, her movements jerky, her temper abrupt.

I wonder for a moment if she too had too little sleep, but then I catch her expression from behind the curtain of her hair: her mouth is a thin knife-slice, her eyes tight, her jaw clenched. She is *angry.*

"Pip?" I ask, sliding out of the bed. I was too tired to put on a nightshirt, so I am dressed in nothing but my Victoria-bought underwear. They are much preferable to the drawers I wore under my fencing trousers before leaving this world, and definitely more comfortable. But now, they make me feel uncovered and scrawny in the face of my wife's bad mood. "Are you feeling—"

"I'm fine," she bites off, securing Alis's new nappy and sending our daughter off to toddle toward me. Alis, fresh and happy—and apparently oblivious to the tension in the room— careens into my knees, arms outstretched and fingers wiggling.

"Dahdah da! Hi!" she says joyfully, wishing me a good morning with another new word I didn't realize she had absorbed. "'Isses, 'isses!" I kiss her hands, palms first, and then knuckles. Content with this greeting, Alis decides to explore the room, and I let her get on with it.

"You are not fine," I say to Pip, careful to modulate my tone so that it is not accusatory. I watch Alis explore under the sideboard. The worst she will probably find under there is a dust bunny—the Goodwoman is an excellent innkeeper.

"Leave it," Pip growls, pushing to her feet and beginning her own morning ablutions.

"And if I do not wish to?" I ask, rising to join her at the washstand.

Pip throws a wet cloth at my face, and it splats against my cheek with a comical noise loud enough to startle Alis. For a moment, I stare at Pip, shocked at this affront. Alis tumbles over and grabs Pip's nightdress, a concerned litany of "ma ma ma ma no, no, ma no," falling from her lips.

The tension between Pip and I crackles and snaps, a live electrical wire of disbelief and smug anger. I feel a bubble of *something* in my throat, and it could be a shout, or cruel words, or an exclamation of hurt, but instead, it comes out as a crooked, giggling guffaw. Pip's pissiness also cracks. A giggle escapes out of the corner of her mouth, and before I know it, we are both doubled over, laughing like naughty children pulling a prank on their nanny.

"Sorry, sorry," Pip says, picking up the washcloth from where it has fallen to the floor and dropping it back into the basin. "I'm an asshole, sorry." She hefts Alis onto her hip, reassuring our daughter that we are not truly angry.

I wring out the cloth and finish the job she began of washing my face.

"Whew," Pip says, still chuckling. "I think I needed that." And she does indeed look as if she had needed the laugh—her shoulders are no longer hunched, her expression no longer pinched. She leans up on her tiptoes and kisses the damp scar on my cheek. "Sorry."

"Happy to oblige," I say with wry humor. "Now, would you like to talk about it?"

Pip sighs, offering me a crooked twist of her lips that isn't really a smile. "If I say no?"

"Pip..."

"Fine." She gusts out a sigh, hands off Alis, and takes her shirt and trousers down from the peg on the wall where she had hung them to air out overnight. For obvious reasons, the Goodwoman had not made her scullery do the guests' laundry the evening before. Pip keeps her eyes on her clothing—an obvious avoidance tactic— and I accept it, as she is still talking as she does so. "I'm feeling... cranky," she says. "No, not cranky. I'm... I don't know what to call it."

"Unhappy?" I venture.

"That," she says. "Yeah, and angry. And grieving. I'm

upset with myself for getting the Stations wrong. And I'm sad for Anne and Thoma, and Lanaea, and her father Jakko, who probably doesn't even fucking *know* that his daughter is dead yet, and it's just not fucking *fair*. She is *dead* because of us. Because of *me*."

"Pip," I say gently, deciding that now is as good a time as any to wrestle Alis into her own leather-bottomed baby socks and canvas frock. "You must be fair to yourself. It is because of this world. Lanaea would have died amid the Red Caps if we had not found her."

"So, what, you're saying it was her fate?" Pip snaps, jerking her belt closed with force enough to make her wince.

"Perhaps. Not so bluntly, but—"

"It's *my fault*, Forsyth," Pip says, and wrenches on the laces of her doublet hard enough that I anticipate she will have a time of it unpicking the knot again this evening. "I am *supposed* to be the *clever one*. And what have I done?" she says, throwing up her hands. "What good have I been? I've steered us wrong, I've screwed up the quest-order, I've ruined everything. We're stalling. The narrative is building sideways instead of upward. We are spinning our wheels in the mud and wasting our time at— at—at Libraries! And funerals! We are doing *nothing*."

"Pip, peace. We don't have all the answers. We barely know the questions."

"Exactly!" Pip says, swinging around to shake a finger in my face. "That's what I mean! Exactly that!" She spreads her arms, fingers splayed, gesturing to the room. "Who is the villain here? What are we trying to achieve? What is our goal, our overarching want? Who is impeding our ability to get that? Where the fuck on the plot mountain are we? What part of the Hero's Journey are we in the middle of? What are we questing for? Never mind knowing how to save the day, we don't even goddamn know what's going wrong or why! I *don't fucking know*, Forsyth. I don't *know*. And it's driving me *mental*."

"*Bao bei*," I say gently, setting Alis back on her feet and going over to wrap my wife in my naked arms. The feel of her leather doublet and trousers against my bare chest and thighs is a unique and slightly arousing sensation, but I push that back in favor of comfort. "*Bao bei*."

"I'm frustrated," Pip admits, tucking her face against my neck. I kiss my favorite leaf scar, sweet and soft. "I feel... useless."

"Oh?"

"Last time, when it was just you and me, I was... I don't know, engaged? Useful? I feel like you and Kintyre make all the choices this time, and Bevel and Wyndam are doing all the fighting, and I am just... hauling around a baby. I'm *useless*."

"*Bao bei...*"

"I am!" she protests. "I'm a liability even, because you're all distracted with protecting us. And there isn't even a trade-off. What good is a useless party member who offers nothing? God, I can't even, I don't know... I can't even *cook* or anything."

"Bevel would take it as a personal offense if you did," I point out.

"And I suck at it."

"That too," I allow, seeing as she said it first.

Pip pinches my arse, hard, in punishment for agreeing with her. I jerk and yelp a little. She apologizes for the pinch with a kiss on my neck.

"The whole thing has just been, 'here, stand in the back with the baby.' And I just..." She trails off, pressing her forehead against my clavicle, annoyed with herself. "I'm more than just a glorified baby carrier. It's just not *me*. Not at home. And I hate it. I had purpose there. Here, I'm just... uhg!" She snarls, leaning back and burying her fingers in her hair, clenching. "I *hate* how useless I'm being!"

"Perhaps it is because your role here in Hain has changed. Last time, you were the Damsel in Distress. And now, you are the Wife. The Mother. Possibly, the Mother to the New Hero."

"*No,*" Pip says emphatically. "My daughter will *not* be the new Kintyre Turn. If this has to be a Family Legacy style series, then Wyndam can be the next hero."

This was the very thing I had discussed with him, the very thing I'd warned him against. "And so you will wish the sorrows of the main character on my nephew instead?"

Pip looks up and glowers. "Forsyth, that's not what I meant, and you *know* it."

I sigh, giving a small nod, and she curls back into me. Behind me, I can hear Alis rifling through my pack, pulling out clothes and throwing them over her head, dragging them along the floor.

"'S funny," Pip says, and her voice is small, contemplative. "Here we are, parents, and both of us are desperately fighting what that means in Elgar Reed's world."

"Yes. We neither of us wish to be *my* parents," I say, soothing. "And I chafe at what it means to be a father in this realm as much as you despise the way that Elgar wrote mothers. We wish simply to be ourselves, and this world does not allow for it."

"Even Kintyre and Bevel hate it," Pip says. "They told me last night. Kintyre's so damn disappointed that Wyndam chose to go to a Deal-Maker Spirit instead of talking to him. And Bevel's working so hard to get Wyndam to see that he only wants what's best for him. But they catch themselves shouting orders all the time, instead of treating Wyndam like the adult he thinks he is. We're all turning into the rigid, opinionated assholes the hero flees at the start of the book."

"Kintyre and Bevel have not had the fortune to be as self-aware as I have," I agree. "Nor have they had the benefit of being outside this world. I would dearly wish for my brother to meet *your* parents, *bao bei*. I rather think they would have good advice for him."

Pip chokes on another guffaw of laughter, chuckling and spluttering.

"Yeah, no," she says. "That's... no."

"Then perhaps we can impress upon them to try to follow Rupin and Dorthi's example. Lewko seems well adjusted."

"That's because he's not the main character's kid. The Writer doesn't *need* him to have a miserable home life, or to hurt a woman he loves to give him enough man-pain to become a hero. Lewko's home life will stay just peachy."

"And you think Wyndam is being groomed to be a hero?"

Pip pulls back to meet my eyes, her own wary and wet. "I don't know. Do you honestly think Elgar will write more, knowing us, now?"

"I cannot answer that," I say. "Part of me says no, for he knows what pain he inflicts. But part of me says yes, for he also knows he can mine us for plot ideas. And *The Tales of Kintyre Turn* is a bestselling series. Perhaps the last bestselling fantasy series in existence, in your world."

Pip sniffles. "That's a terrifying thought."

"Pip," I whisper in her ear, squeezing her close again. "Pip, last night, the last of the stars went out. I watched them. There's nothing left."

"And you think that means there are no more books in my world?"

"I fear so, yes."

"We're the last ones," she whispers, terror crawling into her voice. "What if—"

"I don't know," I say. "The sun still shines, though. As does the moon. Perhaps there is time, yet, to save this realm."

"How?" Pip asks.

"The weather witch, the Deal-Maker, she is destroying treasures and precious items. And the stars are going out. Which is making the books vanish. I feel sure that they are connected."

"But *why?*" Pip asks, and her voice crackles on the question. "*That* I do not know, *bao bei.*"

"I *should,*" she says, tears splashing against my bare shoulder. "*I* should. That's my role, and I don't know, Forsyth. I'm so scared. What if we all snuff out of existence, and it's all my fault? Because I wasn't clever enough?"

"Shhh, shush, darling," I say softly, rocking her gently, petting her hair. "We'll figure it out. We will."

"I hate it here," she whispers, voice hitching with the sobs she is trying to suppress. "I tried, Forsyth, I did. For you. You were so happy to be home, but I can't... I *can't.* I *hate* it here. I want to go home. Where it's safe."

Disappointment comes swift, my stomach dropping and my spine heavy, but it is not surprising, not really. As much as Pip had promised to give my world a fair chance, I knew she could never find peace and joy here. Not after so much evil had been done to her within my home realm. Not with the prospect of even more pain.

Not knowing that this world was always and forever one infinite cycle of the Hero's Journey, over, and over, and over again. Unending. Not knowing that there is never any *peace.*

<p style="text-align:center">~~~</p>

Despite my offer to watch Alis for the day, Pip tells me that if her only role in this adventure is to care for our daughter, then she will play it to the hilt. There is no little bitterness in this proclamation, but she is also resolved. She takes Alis along with her when she joins some of the women from town in a morning of sowing summer wheat. We have agreed to remain in Gwillfifeshire to rest and attend Lanaea's internment this evening, and the relocation of her ghost to join Mandikin's in the town well.

Kintyre has left to aid Lord Gallvig in planning the rousting of the remaining Red Caps from the north field. Wyndam had been delighted to be invited along, his worship of his father having been restored back to full strength. Capplederry follows after him, licking its chops and flexing its claws, so it is obvious that the creature knows they intend to hunt, which leaves only Bevel and I to linger over our breakfast.

Several messenger hawks catch up with Bevel while we dawdle. It is good that we have stayed, as I wouldn't have wanted to contend with all these letters on the road, were I he.

The hawks all bear the seal of the Shadow's Men. Feeling the strain, Bevel welcomes my help in reading through the missives, his head still throbbing from the concussion whenever he tries to read.

The notes paint a picture of a world harassed and terrorized by this Deal-Maker, and we compile a list of all that she has destroyed, but it brings us no closer to understanding who she is or what she hopes to achieve from it.

Lunch returns Pip and Alis to us. Pip slides into the booth, eager, and Alis is very pleased to be able to sit between "Da Da" and "Bev," crumpling scrap parchment in her fists and saying "'Ook, 'ook!" as she destroys it.

"Forsyth, I've been thinking," Pip says, the glitter of academic interest back in her eyes, and the flush of high emotion and glee at her own cleverness back on her cheeks, which makes me incalculably pleased to see.

"Should I be afraid?" I tease, enjoying her high mood.

She swats my shoulder from across the table, grinning. "Shaddup. I've been *thinking*."

"About?" Bevel asks, tidying our work into piles and gesturing for the barmaid who has replaced the Goodwoman today to bring us ales and lunches.

"*Deal-Maker blood*," Pip says, leaning in, her voice low and confidential. "Neris said that the Viceroy had another Deal-Maker's blood, and that was how he was able to compel her into calling down a Reader. Otherwise, the spell wouldn't have been powerful enough."

"Yes. And?"

"And so, how did someone have enough power to call down the *three* of us? What was bargained away? What could possibly be enough? And how could they have boosted the power?"

"What are you suggesting?"

"Forsyth, you know how Elgar writes!" Pip said excitedly. "He's lazy. He connects everything! We have a Deal-Maker Spirit who is ravishing the countryside destroying things, we have vanishing stars and vanishing books, and *what else?*" she asks, excitedly professorial. "Who else has had contact with that Deal-Maker?"

"*Wyndam*," Bevel breathes. "Wyndam did."

"And what did he Deal for?"

"Me. But we don't know why," I say. "But he traded his voice for it."

"Did he?" Pip asks shrewdly. "Are we sure that was what he offered up? Or was it a result of being tricked? You know that people get fooled by Deal-Makers all the time. Why would it work out perfectly this time?"

"You think it didn't?" I ask.

And then, behind me, I hear a footstep. It is Wyndam and Kintyre, back from their meeting, and Wyndam is shaking his head frantically.

"It did not go as planned?" I ask, and he nods. Then he grimaces and clutches his head, his pinky finger twitching.

"Wyn?" Kintyre asks, grasping his shoulders.

"He cannot communicate about the Deal," I tell Kintyre, rising to lay a hand on his shoulder to soothe his worry. "The Deal-Maker is preventing it."

Wyndam scrubs his hands through his hair and nods again, wincing and flinching at the pain it is causing. He holds his affected hand tight against his chest.

"Then stop!" Kintyre orders him, and Wyndam shakes his head again. He meets his father's eyes, mulish and stubborn.

"We're on a roll," Pip says, also standing in her excitement. "Aren't we, Wyndam? We're on the right track?"

He nods, and his knees buckle. Only Kintyre's grip on him keeps him upright. My brother hustles his son into a chair.

"Are you sure you want to keep going?" Bevel asks, and Wyndam nods, his face draining of color.

"Okay, okay," Pip says, pacing in our private corner of the taproom. "Right, let's think this through. Wyndam made a Deal. He called us down. On purpose?"

Wyndam nods.

"And did you offer your voice?"

He shakes his head. Then he gulps on air, looking as if he might vomit. Bevel hastily hands his ale to Kintyre, who presses it to Wyndam's mouth. The boy swallows, and I hope the alcohol will help ease his pain.

"So she took it without you knowing she would." Wyndam doesn't bother to nod this time, saving himself the agony.

"Does us being here have anything to do with the things she's destroying to make the stars go out?"

Wyndam looks up, stricken, mouth agape in horror.

He shakes his head frantically.

"Then the Deal was something you wanted for yourself, then?" I ask.

He nods and sways in his seat. Kintyre pushes him back, snaps his fingers at the barmaid to get her attention, and demands a bowl of cool water and a cloth.

"What for?" I muse as Kintyre bathes Wyndam's forehead and face, wiping away his pain-induced sweat and staring at his son's face with genuine parental love and fear.

"My poor son," Kintyre murmurs. "My poor beloved boy."

Wyndam cracks an eye and stares up at his father, reaches up with his good hand and wraps it into the placket of Kintyre's shirt, right above his heart. His eyes are filled with regret and apology.

"What good am I?" I ask Bevel. "What reason would Wyndam have for wanting me here?"

"I wish we had the Cup that Never Empties and a mirror right about now," Pip says with an ironic snort. "We could use a good scry. And to think I lambasted you for using it to spy on me."

"We could go," Bevel ventures. "I mean, the Salt Crystal Caverns aren't that far away from here."

"I don't think we'll need it," I murmur, watching the way Wyndam's eyes never leave Kintyre's face, the small curl to his lips when he is the center of my brother's attention.

I crouch at my nephew's side, so we are eye to eye, and put my hands on his knees, forcing myself into his line of vision. "Wyndam," I say gently, my Shadow Hand voice low but present all the same. Insistent. "Wyndam, my lad, you brought me back here on purpose, didn't you? Because you were unhappy."

"Unhappy!" Bevel squawks behind me, even as

Wyndam turns his eyes away from mine, ashamed that I have guessed correctly. "What could he possibly have to be unhappy about? He went from being a water rat to the respected Lordling of Lysse! He has books, clothes, a fine horse, hot meals! And a position with the Sword of Turnshire if he wanted to get off his lazy arse and take it! What's to be unhappy over?"

Wyndam's gaze snaps back around, filled with fire, and he jerks his chin in Bevel's direction.

"Because those are things you want for him, Bevel Dom," I say. "Not what he wants. Am I right, my lad?"

Wyndam nods again, jaw and fists clenched.

"I don't understand," Kintyre says slowly. I manfully refrain from making my usual jab about him understanding *anything*, for now is not the time for petty jibes or filial teasing. "You were unhappy in Turnshire? But what could bringing Forsyth back do about that?"

Wyndam, obviously, cannot answer, so I propose this to my brother instead: "What would you do, brother, if you did not need to be Lord of Lysse? If I was there to step into your place once more? What benefit does my return bring to you? To the Chipping?"

"We could... return to the road?" Kintyre says, but he sounds unsure.

"No," Bevel cuts him off almost immediately. "I will not be giving up feather mattresses and fresh-baked bread ever again."

"But this is not about you, nor your desires, Bevel," I point out. "This is about Kintyre's. Would you go, brother?"

"Well," Kintyre says, shifting. "Not without Bevel, obviously."

"But you would need someone to mind Turnshire in your stead?"

Another nod.

"Then this is what you asked for," I say to Wyndam, and the lad nods, miserable. "You wanted to go on adventures with your father. But to do that, I had to be here. You knew Kintyre wouldn't leave without the Chipping being cared for."

Kintyre splutters. "But I wouldn't—I'm *retired*. I *like* sleeping late!"

I sigh, shaking my head. "And *this* isn't about you, Kintyre. It's about what Wyndam wants."

Kintyre blinks at me, then swings his gaze down to his son. "Well, why didn't you just ask? Wyndam? Why didn't you just *tell* me you want to... I don't know, go sow some wild oats?"

Wyndam just shrugs, the non-answer of teenagers of *every* realm who desperately do not want to discuss their transgressions.

As Kintyre struggles to understand, I muse: "This has *nothing* to do with the vanishing books, the missing stars. All this time, I was searching for a connection, but there isn't one. There is a Deal-Maker Spirit who, in the form of a weather witch, is roaming the world and destroying trinkets and treasures. And at the same time, stars are going out. And at *the same time*, stories are vanishing from the Realm of the Writer. *Those* are connected, yes, but *not me*, not my presence here in Hain," I say, rising slowly, confident that I have guessed correctly when Wyndam jerks his startled gaze back to me.

It is a relief, a greater one than I thought, for I feel a weight I had not realized I was carrying lift from my chest. I feel like I can breathe for the first time in weeks. This, all of this, is not my fault. It is not because I escaped *The Tales of Kintyre Turn*. It is not because I know my creator and turned him away on Solsticetide. It is not because I am a character where I should not be, nor that the book of my life is shelved in the wrong realm.

It is because a Deal-Maker Spirit is tearing apart the world, and because a selfish lad desperately sought his father's attention and approval.

But it is not *because of me*.

"You and Wyndam would have been free to live the kind of adventure his mother no doubt told him Kintyre Turn lives, correct?" I hazard, and Wyndam nods. "Bevel, Wyndam had your scrolls in his chambers. He was teaching himself to read with your adventures. He was envious of them. And so, he decided to do something about it. Am I right, my lad?"

Wyndam, slumped miserably, nods again.

"We are mistaken. The Deal-Maker you called down was no weather witch. She is a sea spirit—her magic is in water. She is the preferred call of the pirates, am I right? You've had her tableau memorized for years."

Wyndam nods again, the minutest of movements.

"And so, I am here, but it is not as you thought it would be, this adventuring." Wyndam does not move, but it is clear he agrees all the same. "You offered her something in return for us, and it must have been great to make the Deal equal. But it was not equal enough, and so she took your voice along with it."

Wyndam looks up and shakes his head. He opens his mouth, tries to mime the words, but is overtaken again by the pain and must sit back, wincing.

"So, whatever it is that the Deal-Maker wanted, she didn't get it?" Pip asks, pushing forward, intrigued. Wyndam rocks his head back and forth on the back of the chair, panting and pale.

"But taking your voice was ancillary..." I muse, and Pip snaps her fingers.

"Got it! It wasn't your voice, it was your *Words*!" she crows. "Deal-Makers can't use human magic, so she must have needed it to... to, I don't know, use Words of Finding for the items that snuff out the stars, or something! It's *just* the kind of smarter-than-you double-speak bullshit that Reed likes to write! He would *totally* do that!"

Wyndam groans, curling in on his hand, forehead beading with sweat.

"We shouldn't ask him any more questions," Kintyre says, concerned. He flutters around Wyndam with the damp cloth like an agitated hen. "He may pass out soon."

Wyndam glowers at him stubbornly and struggles back upright.

Pip reaches into her bra and retrieves our phial of Deal-Maker blood. She shakes the phial slightly, watching the viscous blue liquid slosh and ooze against the side of the glass. It is the color of cornflowers, and it swirls with sapphire and silver glitter, a galaxy in glass. It looks like it should be a tonic for making hair shinier, or helping a child sleep. It does not look like the most powerful potion ingredient in existence.

I know literally dozens of wizards, witches, and warlocks who would gleefully commit homicide to possess Deal-Maker blood. And it is rare, terribly rare, for Deal-Makers do not live in this plane and are rarely injured.

In fact...

A thought occurs to me, and I turn to face Pip. "How did the Viceroy obtain a phial of Deal-Maker's blood?" I ask.

"Huh?" Pip asks, sidetracked from her own contemplation.

"It was the one thing we never questioned: Neris said that she was compelled to grant the Viceroy the Deal that brought you to Hain because he had in his possession a phial of Deal-Maker's blood. But it is *rare*, and more than that, it is difficult to collect. So where and how did he *obtain* it?"

"He was the villain," Pip ventures after pondering for a moment. "It's possible that he just... *had* it."

"No," I say. "No. Elgar Reed thinks himself cleverer than that. If the Viceroy had such a powerful magical item, then there must have been a *reason* for it. There must have been a plan. But what?"

Pip's eyes widen, and then swing around and narrow with laser precision on Wyndam. "She wanted to trade you a person for a person, didn't she?"

Wyndam gulps and nods.

"Who?" Bevel asks.

"Who do you think?" Pip asks, straightening. "This is the sequel. It's got to be the first story's villain. If only for a cameo."

"But he's *dead*," Bevel protests.

"Is he?" Pip asks, challenging, professor-ish. "Did we see a body?"

"Why?" Kintyre growls. "Why should a Deal-Maker want to free the Viceroy? Especially when it is simply another Deal-Maker who has him?"

"And is preferably torturing his ghost for the rest of eternity?" Bevel snarls.

Pip turns to look at Alis, who is still sitting happily at our table, crumpling paper and babbling to herself, then back to Wyndam.

"Don't you think it's a big coincidence that all this happened right after both Forsyth and Kintyre Turn had children?" she asks slowly, teasing the thesis out in her head, pulling at the idea like taffy with her words. "This is a narrative featuring kids, *heirs*, which means it's *about* heirs. Legacies. Inheritance..." She is looking off into the middle distance, fingers curling and uncurling around the phial. Her fingernails tap against the glass, and the rest of us wait, breathless, silent, as she chews on the problem.

Then she gasps.

Her eyes and mouth drop wide, round with under-standing and horror.

"Oh my god," she whispers, and sits down hard, the phial gripped tight in her white-knuckled fist. "Oh my *god.*"

"What?" Bevel asks, gaze jumping between my wife and I.

And I understand it myself the moment Pip breathes it.

"Her son," she hisses, pulling her attention back to us, looking up into my face with such horrified desperation that I must jam my hands into my pockets to keep from scrambling across the table to fold her in my arms like an undignified day laborer. "That's what she's after. She's trying to figure out where he is, what realm he was pulled into. The stars, *bao bei*, the books! The Viceroy had a phi-al of Deal-Maker blood because the son of a bitch was her goddamn son!"

Elgar Reed wrote me to be uncomfortable when I am ignorant or wrong. And when I am right, when something clicks into place, when I *understand*, it is a relief and rev-elation so intense, so sweeping that it feels very much like a full-body, rolling orgasm. I gasp, feeling my face flush-ing, as soon as I understand what Pip means.

"Oh," I breathe, and I am not even remotely ashamed to admit how *sexy* I found her line of reasoning. I feel the hairs on my arms and neck stand upright, my pupils blow wide, my mouth suddenly flood with saliva, and my britches grow uncomfortably tight. By the *Writer*, do I love my wife. "See, *bao bei?*" I ask, sweeping forward to give her a scorching kiss. "You *are* the clever one!"

"And *that* was Station Five," Pip whispers into my mouth.

FAILURE

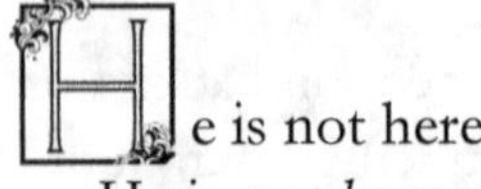

e is not here.

He is *not here*.

There are no more totems to destroy, no *stars* left to snuff. And still her son, her Varnet, is *not here*. A red sunrise lingers on the horizon, as if it fears that she will dowse its light now that all his sisters have fallen under her hand.

Sisters, Solinde thinks grimly. She stands on the Desk that Never Rots and thrusts her clawed fingers upward, ripping a hole in the sky.

She calls upon the others, commands them to come forth, thrusts such a torrent of power into the sky that the rain falling into the Rookery froths and floods up to her ankles.

"Sisters!" she wails. "What have I missed?"

Laughter leaks downward from the tear: a multitude of clangoring, spiteful voices in a pantheon of crystalline, atonal sound.

"*Tell me!*"

"There are no totems. The realms are gone."

"All but the one where Varnet is held! Must I travel to the land of death to retrieve him?"

Jangling laughter flashes across the sky like lightning. "No."

"I will have my vengeance."

"You said that before, sister. Yet all you have accomplished is blackening a sky."

Solinde screams, a long, brutal, shrieking howl of fury and agony. The birds of the Rookery who had taken shelter from the storm burst out into the air to escape her cry, a squid-ink wave of drenched feathers and white, rolling eyes.

"There must be some reason," Solinde pants, curling in on herself, her voice hoarse and crackling, barely above a whisper. "Some reason the totems did not work."

"Give up, sister," the others chant, and jeer. "Fail, fail!"

"I will *not!*" Solinde hurtles back. Lightning rattles the desk beneath her feet as it crashes into the mountainside, sending sparks along the surface of the pool her rage has made of the Rookery. The ivy clinging to the cliffside rips away in the wind, its leaves and sticks swirling in the vortex spinning around Solinde, the witch in its eye, the spirit that is its mind.

Its mind.

Knowledge, Solinde realizes. *The totems are gone. They have not worked! But there is one still who will know. One who understands the world as no others have before. One who will know where he is!*

Solinde closes her fists and clamps up the gash in the sky, gagging the laughter and the cruel jibes, the hissing and snarls of those who were once her bosom family.

Forsyth Turn's bitch, Solinde decides grimly. "The Reader!"

FIFTEEN

yndam is asleep upstairs, having finally accepted Bevel's offer of one of Mother Mouth's poppy milk
potions. Thoma volunteers to take Alis into his room for
her afternoon nap, so there is someone nearby for her if
she wakes and begins to cry. This leaves the four of us
adventurers to make plans.

"So, now what?" Pip asks, her whole body slumped
with weariness.

"We have two choices," I say, making a point of meeting each of the gazes of those crowded around the table.
"We could return to Turn Hall to research this Deal-Maker. Wyndam has given me to understand that he had the
Deal-Maker's tableau memorized, that she is oft called
down by the sea-faring kingdoms. And we know one of
the required items is a broken compass. But the binding
she has upon him is preventing him from being able to
communicate with me as to how I may call her down
again; he cannot even trace her sigil out for me. I know it
is not within the Shadow's Mask, or I would suggest Bevel
don it, and we call her down now. But there, in my study,
it will be written down. And we can make plans for once
she is summoned."

"We'll have to review *all* of the Shadow Hand's notes
on Deal-Makers in the Turn Hall library," Bevel groans,
and I cannot help but grin at his put-upon moaning. For

all that my brother's trothed is an excellent spy, I noted in our review of his missives that he is a reluctant and inconsistent administrator.

"But at least we can call her down, Deal for information and Wyn's voice," Kintyre says, shifting in the booth. With all of us pressed together for privacy, he is bunched in against the window. He extends one of his massive arms along the back of the seat for comfort, hemming Bevel in, who doesn't seem to mind.

Pip shifts closer to me in response to the cuddling going on in the other banquette. "And the other option?"

"We go back to where this whole mess began," I say, wrapping an arm around her shoulders, mirroring my brother's actions. "The Rookery. We go back to the Desk that Never Rots. And then we find a way to talk to Elgar."

"And how would we do that?" Pip asks. "If he hasn't found a way to contact us by now, I don't think he can. And I sure as hell have been racking my brains since day one."

"Then back to Turnshire it is," I decide for all of us. "We venture toward the known solution instead of venturing out on the potentially pointless quest."

"Hey," Kintyre says, offhandedly. "Some of my best adventures and biggest problem-solving moments happened while on pointless side-quests."

"True," Pip says, snapping and aiming finger-guns at him. "But this isn't your story. This adventure is Forsyth's, and his luck doesn't work the way yours does."

"M-mine?" I ask, startled by Pip's insistence.

"Well, you've been the driving force so far, haven't you?" she asks, looking up at me. "You were the one who started compiling information about the missing books, Wyndam called you down into this realm, you sent us to Pointe's, you encouraged us to travel to the Library. You've been the impetus of the narrative action, bao *bei.* Thus, this is your adventure." She turns back to my brother. "And that is why we will *not* be going on any side-quests."

"But I—"

"No," I say firmly. "Kintyre, it is decided."

"Oh, is it?" He bristles. "And when were you appointed our leader? You do so like telling me what to do, Bossy Forssy—"

Bevel pinches the arm laid across the back of the bench hard, twisting the flesh of Kintyre's inner elbow until it turns pink.

"Yow!" Kintyre yelps, and quickly draws his arm back.

"Hush, you," Bevel says with a glare.

"Yes, *brother*, do use your *brains, for once*—youch!" I huff as Pip delivers me a pinch of my own.

"Enough, you two," Pip says.

"She's right," Bevel adds.

"And since when are you and Bevel on the same team?" I ask, startled by the low simmering of jealous resentment that bubbles up when I catch the way they are smirking at one another.

"We're married to Turns," Pip says. "We were automatically a team as soon as we both said 'I do.'"

Kintyre and I both grumble and rub our abused skin, but don't gainsay it.

"The *point* is," Pip says, bringing us back around on topic, "we're in agreement that we need to figure out who this Deal-Maker is and summon her. So, we're headed back to Turnshire?"

"Yes," Bevel agrees, and prods Kintyre in the ribs with his elbow until my brother reluctantly grumbles his assent.

"Then what about this?" Pip asks, pulling the phial of blood from her bra and holding it low so anyone else in the taproom will not see it.

Kintyre shifts uncomfortably, eyes lingering a fraction of a second too long on the gap in her shirt where her breasts are framed, and then clears his throat and turns his eyes to the phial. I suppose some habits are hard to break.

When no one answers, Pip prompts us: "What should we do with it?"

"Leverage," I say. "Save it to use with this Deal-Maker when we summon her."

"How does that even work?" Pip asks, but it's in that self-reflective murmur I have come to learn indicates a question is more for herself, a way to prompt her own thought process into following this new path of consideration. It is not a genuine question for me, and I know that.

Bevel and Kintyre, however, are not familiar with it.

"How does what work?" Kintyre asks.

Pip blinks and jerks her head up to face him, startled by his interruption. "Huh? Oh! Um, I mean, how does the blood work to compel a Deal-Maker. I mean, how does just *having* it give us any control or leverage? It's... uh... well, that's frankly just lazy world-building."

I cannot stifle my giggle at the look of indignant affront on Pip's face, and I do not try to. Bevel and Kintyre shift in their seats, uncomfortable at having to even be cognizant of the shifting tectonic plates of existential meaning beneath their perceived reality.

"I suppose we will find out once we summon her," I say, pushing the conversation forward and giving Kintyre and Bevel a chance to ponder something else.

Pip cuddles back down against me, and it feels nice to have a small moment of respite, to simply enjoy being at peace and close to her. Kintyre and Bevel settle similarly, Bevel's eyes drifting shut as he leans against Kintyre's chest. I am pleased to see how open they are with their affection, knowing how many years Bevel had longed for Kintyre to admit to loving him.

"Hmph," Pip says, reaching up to scratch my chin. In the week we have been adventuring, I have not had the time to shave, and a respectable amount of prickle has been cultivated. "I will admit, *bao bei*, that I do miss my electric razor very much. I prefer a barber's shave, but even the electric would do now."

"Dunno," Kintyre says. "I think it kinda suits you."

"Oh," I say, startled by his forthright praise. "Well. Thank you."

"Shame it's so ginger, though," he adds with a smirk, ruining the moment.

～

I seek out Pip's much-desired barber's shave in the morning, while Bevel and Kintyre are busy restocking our little wagon, and saying their goodbyes around town. Wyndam, still lethargic with pain and a poor night's sleep, is keeping Pip and Alis company in the taproom, clutching the largest tankard of tea I have ever seen.

When I return, feeling more myself but slightly mourning the loss of the fetching scruff, Pip is laying out the new plan for our nephew.

"Of course, if this fails, we could summon the other one. Neris," she tells him. "It would probably take another few weeks to collect up all the items we need to summon her again. But, failing that, we'd have to go all the way back to Turn Hall to find the Shadow Hand's catalog of the others. So, any way you slice it, you'll be voiceless for a month or more, yet. But don't worry, kiddo. We're not giving up on you."

Wyndam grunts his understanding. Then he removes the shell-necklace strung on the knotted hemp rope that he wears about his neck and hands it to her. The scale is about the size of his palm, and is a dappled, shiny blue-green that would camouflage the mer-drake it came from in deep and shallow water alike.

Pip squints at it. "Is this part of—"

Wyndam reaches out and puts his finger on her lips, wincing as his pinky finger trembles.

"Ah, okay," Pip says. "No asking." She puts the necklace on.

Shortly thereafter, Capplederry is hitched to the wagon, our supplies are loaded, and I am pressing an extra purse of coins into the Goodwoman's hands.

"Master Turn," she says slowly. "It is far too much."

"I know," I say, "but please, take it. It cannot replace Lanaea, and I dare not suggest I am attempting to pay for her lost life, but you must take care of yourself in this time of mourning, and your brother when he arrives from Sherwilde. Our living is well off, and you deserve to be able to take a full mourning period with no concerns about finances."

"Gwillfifeshire wouldn't let the *Pern* sink," she says, after a soft, shaking sigh, "but I thank you all the same, Master Turn."

"Good people deserve good things," I say. "*Pern* means so much to so many. I am happy to thank you as I can."

The Goodwoman does not cry, but her eyes do grow wet. She pockets the purse, and then grabs her son by his suspenders to keep Thoma from crawling under the blankets in our cart.

"But, Ma!" he protests. "I want to go on an adventure!"

"But, son!" she says back, trying valiantly to tease in the midst of her sorrow. "Not a chance. There is no way you are going off with Kintyre Turn. Not now. Not ever."

"Ma," he protests again, but does as he's told and

stands beside her skirts.

Kintyre and Bevel offer their farewells, and mount Karl and Dauntless, respectively. I am to drive.

I settle Pip and Alis in the back, and then look around for Wyndam. I expected him to be asleep in the cart already, as worn out as he still is by yesterday's interrogation, but he is nowhere to be seen.

"He's gone to the ghost," Thoma says softly when he sees me looking.

Ah.

For a moment, I consider sending Kintyre to fetch his son, but realize that whatever leave-taking Wyndam is engaged in with Lanaea might be better left unseen by him. I would like to hope that Kintyre is compassionate enough not to tease his son for his lingering heartbreak, but I would wager no money on it.

"I'll be back in a heartbeat," I say, and slip away before anyone else can protest, sliding around the corner of the livery stables and jogging toward the town square.

Wyndam is right where I expect to find him, seated once more on the edge of the crumbling well. This time, Lanaea's ghost sits beside him—or rather, hovers in the general area of the edge of the well. Next to the well, there is a fresh, new paving stone, the only red one in a sea of sandy-white, and it is from here that the edge of her skirt trails. She is cupping Wyndam's face, or trying to, and there are ghostly, transparent tears sparkling around her cheeks like fairy lights.

I back into an alleyway where I have full view of the star-crossed lovers, but where I hope the shadow will hide me, and watch. I don't want to interrupt if I don't have to, and we aren't on so strict a schedule that I cannot give the lad a few more minutes.

"Oh, hells," Bevel whispers from beside me, and I jump, sucking in a gasp. I hadn't heard him following.

He was stealthy before he ever became Shadow Hand, though, and has more practice walking quietly than I. "He's really torn up."

"A lad never forgets his first love," I say, keeping my voice low.

"His first? Do you think? He's only seventeen."

"And the Prince of Pirates."

"That's... that's an advantage, I won't lie."

"Hmm," I say, a non-response that Bevel takes as the indication that I have no desire to delve into our nephew's sex life any further than we already have.

After another few moments, Wyndam rises, sweeps a very courtly bow indeed to Lanaea, and exits the square. Bevel darts away behind me, determined to get back to the cart before Wyndam. I linger just long enough to watch Mandikin rise up out of another faded, pale-pink stone beside Lanaea's red one and wrap ghostly arms around the other spirit.

Dead though they may be, I am glad that they have the support of one another in this time.

〰〰

We stop for the night well out of the fields of Mili-way. It meant that we had to ride for several hours after sundown, but nobody minded, as we were all still warily worried about Red Caps, or other marauders that might have been unhoused by the Deal-Maker's circuit around the world. The forest we drive into is dense, and filled with faint sparkings of light that may be wild Wisps, the kind not bred for lanterns. They may also be the glint of predator eyes off the spark of our campfire, so no one goes to investigate.

Capplederry seems calm enough with our environs, at any rate, and the musk of the great cat seems to go a long way toward securing our camp against any animals that may assume a party of sleeping humans are easy prey.

It is probably close to midnight by the time the feast Bevel has prepared is ready to eat: stone-baked flatbread, cheese, and those lovely leaf-baked rolls of fresh venison wrapped around dried nuts and fruit like a particularly Hainish bit of sushi. By the time we sit down to it, Alis is already asleep, and Wyndam must be roused from his own doze to eat.

We are just unwrapping our dinners when a flash of white in my periphery catches my attention. There is something by the cart, where we have left Alis hemmed in by pillows.

Kintyre and Bevel are on their feet in an instant, swords drawn, but I put up a hand to stay them. No use startling whatever it is. We each set down our dinners, and I creep around the side of the cart slowly. Then I let loose a gusting sigh and straighten.

"Shoo!" I tell the creature creeping closer to the cart. It is unperturbed, however, and just takes another step, head raised and eyes bright, innocently defiant.

"What is it?" Pip asks, and when I glance back, I see that she's also stood and has her hand on her dagger. Wyndam is beside her, looking equally grave.

"Come see, *bao bei*," I say, and the endearment does as I hoped it would and reassures her that nothing is immediately wrong.

When she comes around to the end of the cart, she stops abruptly and gasps, hands flying to cover her mouth, instantly enchanted.

"Is that... is that a...?"

"A unicorn, yes," I say with a grunt, and take another step forward. The beast does the same. "Oh no," I say, shooing the unicorn away from Alis. "Absolutely not. None of that now." The unicorn tosses its head, mane shimmering in the shaft of moonlight that dances through the foliage. It paws the ground for a moment, thoughtfully eyes up Pip, then snorts and dismisses her, focusing its attention on my daughter.

"What's it doing?"

"Oh, for goodness' sake," I say, flapping my hands harder at the beast. "She's an infant still. There's nothing for you to do here, of *course* she's still a virgin. Off with you, off."

The unicorn swings around to look at me and aims its horn at my face. Pip gasps again and grabs my sleeve, ready, I assume, to yank me out of the way should the beast charge.

"You're fooling no one," I tell the unicorn, not even remotely concerned. "And you're not having her. She can't even walk well enough to follow. Be off now."

"What's so wrong with—" Pip begins, but I just shake my head.

"It gets *messy*. Either you must let them take your daughter, or you must take them in, and unicorn shit smells atrocious. Like lilies, ever dying. Overwhelming."

That is when Capplederry stands, stretching and yawning with a deliberate, toothy grin and a short, rusty yowl. The unicorn startles and rears up, and on the other side of the cart, Capplederry does the same. For a long moment, they both stand rampant, framing the nest of pillows where my daughter sleeps, sweetly ignorant of the fuss around her.

The unicorn, stymied, snorts at me one last time, paws the ground, and, rearing again, spins on its delicate hind feet. Just like that, it is off, a silver shadow in the underbrush, its mane, tail, and those nonsensical ankle tufts flapping like a particularly attractive banner. How they never get tangled with burrs, I'll never know. More unicorn magic.

"Wow," Pip says, still clutching my sleeve as the creature vanishes into the gloom. "*Wow.* A unicorn."

I snort myself, and chivvy my wife back toward the fire. The men sit, but Pip keeps glancing back at the cart, where Alis is sleeping.

"She is fine," I say. "I saw her. She slept through it all."

"I know, I just..." Pip sets down her dinner again and rubs the back of her neck. "I don't know, I have the heebie jeebies. Lemme just check. I'm kinda paranoid now."

"Very well, go, go." I gesture with my own dinner, and then take a bite. Ah, just as wonderful as I remembered this dish being!

Pip goes, and I am absorbed with watching Wyndam settle the great cat and brush out its mane, praising it with affectionate smiles and hums for protecting his wee cousin. Capplederry purrs and preens.

We are all feeling the camaraderie of another small disaster averted, and are very pleased with ourselves, smug in the security that Capplederry provides, when I realize Pip has not returned. It's been long enough that her own dinner has grown cold on her trencher, the fat from the venison congealing in dark spots on the bread.

When I begin to look around, wondering perhaps if Pip has gone off into some bush to answer the call of nature, Bevel and Kintyre's heads also snap up. Wyndam remains oblivious at first, but as soon as the rest of us tense, Capplederry is back on its feet, and Wyndam has his curved sword drawn.

And that is when we hear it: a leafy shuffle, a sort of muffled yelp, and then the high, piercing scream of a terrified child.

"Alis!" I cry, but I cannot tell from which direction the sound is coming, so I spin like a helpless top on the spot.

And then, most odd of all, a young man's voice rings

through the forest, laughing. That it is a young man is not the odd part; it is the reaction that the sound of his voice causes in Kintyre and Bevel that I find the most strange.

Both men freeze, faces instantly going white and hands balling into fists. Then they swing their eyes around and look directly at Wyndam. Wyndam's eyes are still on the forest, even as he climbs—with a grace that belies his continued fatigue—onto Capplederry's back.

"What?" I hiss, ears still primed.

"No, no, no!" the young lad's voice calls again, further away now. "Behave yourself, Aunt Pip."

Capplederry is off like a shot, but not so quickly that I don't have the opportunity to catch sight of the look of horror that has blossomed on Wyndam's face before both lad and cat are nothing but a shadowy blur in the underbrush.

"What is wrong?" I ask as I charge after them.

Bevel and Kintyre both quickly and easily pace me, Kintyre drawing ahead.

"Brother!" I entreat, even as I am drawing my sword and crashing after him through a shrub in his wake.

"It's Wyndam!" Kintyre calls back, and I cannot, I cannot afford to stumble now. "That was *Wyndam's* voice!"

READERS

The unicorn was not part of Solinde's plottings, but it was more useful than she could have anticipated. And, like the weather, Solinde can easily turn, changing her plans fluidly. Originally, she'd meant to tempt the men of the camp away by calling out to them in the boy's voice. She had put it on for that purpose, but worried that calling them away would forewarn the Reader, and she would have magic prepared to thwart Solinde when she doubled back to the cart.

Simply waiting for the woman to wander into the darkness alone was much easier.

Getting her to be *silent* was another matter entirely. Even now, backed right up against the Desk that Never Rots with her squalling infant in her arms, both of them drenched from their transportation atop the cloud, the woman is still *shouting*.

"Take me back, right now!" she bellows, one hand curled around the babe, the other wrapped around the hilt of her laughingly small dagger. Solinde, standing in the middle of the Rookery, watching, one hand on her chin, the other on her waist, snorts in amusement.

"Are you finished, Reader? Or shall you continue to demand the same thing over and over, knowing that I shall not give it to you?"

The woman falters, dagger dipping, and the child

screams louder.

"Hush, sweetie," the Reader whispers to it, soothing it as much as she can, her eyes never leaving Solinde. "Hush now. It's over, eh? So we're a little wet; it's okay. Just like bath time, honey. It's okay."

Solinde watches with rapt fascination as the stream of motherly nonsense soothes the child into hiccoughing sniffles.

"She is biddable," Solinde observes. "A very good girl."

"She's not biddable *because* she's a girl!" the woman grits out between clenched teeth.

"Ma ma ma," the child says. "Daaa?"

"Your Da's coming to get us, don't you worry, honey," the reply comes, and though her words are light in her child's ear, it is clear that the promise in the threat is directed at Solinde. "And your uncles, too. Kintyre Turn and Bevel Dom, that is. In case you missed that."

"Oh, I understand perfectly well from whom I've pilfered you," Solinde says airily, entertained that the Reader seems to think that the names of her traveling companions would be a surprise to her. "I've known since I Dealt for the boy's voice. You, though..." she says, pointing now at the woman.

The Reader takes a sharp step back, driving her hip against the unforgiving granite of the Desk and wincing.

"You were a piece I did not expect to find on the chessboard." Solide says this idly, reaching out as the woman shrinks away from her touch. Solinde runs her nails over the edge of the scale the woman wears on a piece of rope around her neck. "And with *this*, no less."

"I won't be your pawn," the woman spits.

"A pawn?" Solinde laughs, startled by the sheer ignorance of her own worth—potentially her own power— that her captive holds. "No, no, my dear. You are a queen.

You must know that you are the most powerful piece on the board. And I..." Solinde says as she leans close, mindful of the loose-held dagger, but enjoying the way the woman's eyes widen, and how she tries to crane away from her looming captor. It's amusing. "I am the other."

The Reader slips to the side, ducking away from Solinde, putting the Desk that Never Rots between them, as if it will be any sort of barrier against whatever magic Solinde would care to wield. As if the Reader needs any kind of barrier beyond that which she herself must be capable of creating. Solinde keeps hold of her necklace, whipping it over the Reader's head as she ducks past, content to let her squirm away for the moment.

"A queen who will not be moved around the board by outside hands ever again." She holds the necklace, the scale, the *thing* that could have her summoned down and bound to a tableau, to a disadvantageous Deal, above her head. Lightning turns it to cinders between her fingers.

The Reader jumps, curling her hand over her daughter's ears, and shouts: "Then why am I here?" the Reader asks. "*Again.*"

"You are the perfect confluence of all that I require," Solinde admits, deciding that explaining a little of her reasoning might entice the Reader to aid her. After all, she is a mother as well, a fellow woman. Surely she must have a mother's feelings, too. "I need my son back, and I need revenge on those who have harmed him."

"Again, I'm not seeing how I can help," the Reader says cautiously, but she has straightened up now, her eyes darting, assessing the distance between her and the stairs that lead up out of the sunken cavern.

"Liar," Solinde says gently. "We are two queens. A Deal-Maker, and a Reader. The two most powerful creatures in this world. You know what you can do for me."

"I don't," the woman insists. "I actually don't."

"I want you to summon the Writer. I want you to force him to tell me where my son is. My Varnet."

"No." The reply is firm, but a tremble has crawled into the Reader's throat. "I won't do that. Actually, I mean, I—honestly—I *can't* do that."

Solinde feels her ire swelling. How could a fellow mother deny her this when she is clutching her own babe so tightly? "You would deny a mother her child?"

"I know that Varnet is the Viceroy," the Reader says softly, as if this is some sort of revelation. Of course, Solinde expected the Reader to know everything about her life, *their* lives. She is a *Reader.* "So even if I could, I wouldn't help you."

"Then you must also know where he is. And how he may be returned to me."

Caught out, the Reader's eyes widen. "That doesn't necessarily follow," she hedges.

"But you do *know!*" Solinde snarls, thunder booming in the distance.

The Reader raises her chin to Solinde, defiant, cupping her own child's head against her neck, and the ire in the Deal-Maker boils and froths. How dare... how *dare*...

"How can you be so unfeeling?" Solinde demands. "How can you stand there, cradling your babe, knowing that mine was stolen from me!"

"St-stolen?" the Reader echoes, surprised.

"Stolen!" Solinde screams. "Got on me by force by a human who tricked me into Dealing to be his wife, and sold away by that same unfeeling wretch to the first scholar who would take a child of magic as his apprentice!"

"I... I didn't know that..." the Reader insists. "That wasn't... it wasn't in *any* of the books."

"And so you mean to say that the Writer did not even see fit to write of my *suffering?*" Solinde howls. "Am I nothing in our creator's eyes? Am I so *little!*"

"*Yes!*" the Reader shouts back, for now a breeze has begun to whistle through the few remaining, straggling ropes of ivy that yet cling to the walls of the Rookery. "I hate to have to admit this, but yes! He really is that kind of a dick! He doesn't care what kind of suffering he's forced on his female characters! He never has!"

"And yet, I would bear any suffering gladly if I could be reunited with my Varnet!"

The Reader steps back again, flummoxed. "I don't understand!" she says. "I don't understand this *obsession* with finding him. With getting him back."

"You are a mother!" Solinde cries, and above her, lightning jumps between the building thunderheads. "Would you not do anything for your child? Would you not snuff out the very *stars themselves* in your destruction of other realms in search of her?"

"So the stars are books?" the Reader asks, shrewdly.

"They were prisons where my son was being held away from me against both our wills. For he lives yet, he *must.* They are realms. He must be in one! And yet, I have snuffed every star, and their destruction has not released him back to me. He should have come *back.*"

"But he's—" the Reader begins, and then snaps her mouth shut, biting down on the revelation she had been about to spill forth.

"*Tell me!*" Solinde demands. "You know! You *know!*"

"I don't!" the Reader says. "I honestly don't know where he is right now! Maybe he's dead, and I'm sorry for you if that's true, but I don't know where he would have been taken if he's not!"

Solinde howls and pulls at her hair. "Then I am nothing! If I am not a mother, then I am *nothing!* And there is no place for me in this, nor any other realm!"

"No!" the Reader insists. "No, that's not true. You are defined by more than just your relationship to the villain!

You are more than a wife and a mother. You can be! We are more than just women who stand at the back and hold the baby!"

"Why would I wish to be anything else *but* the one who cherishes and protects my child?" Solinde wails, baffled by the Reader's insistence that such a glorious purpose is merely secondary, or lesser, or unworthy.

"Oh my god, fucking *listen*," the Reader snarls. "If this is the climax, if we've come back to the same spot as a deliberate echo of what happened in the last book, then you have to listen to me. We don't have to do this all again! You can undo this—bring back the stars, bring back the stories, and I promise you, I will help you find another way to be happy. I will help you find a purpose. Please!"

"Generous, thoughtless fool!" Solinde spits, and the winds have started in earnest now, tugging at her hair, her skirts, billowing them behind her like sails. "How dare you offer me compassion now, when I have lost everything? I cannot. I cannot be happy without him. I am only who I am!"

The Reader has misplaced her caution in the face of trying to convince Solinde. She takes a step closer, around the corner of the Desk. Fool. "But that's what I mean! I am a wife. I am a mother. But that is *not* the alpha and omega of my existence. I am... I am a teacher, and fangirl, and—"

"And this is what you want me to be?" Solinde sneers. "Emotional and complicated, conflicted? To busy myself in other things and *forget him*? No." She brushes the image the Reader paints out of her mind, out of the air around her head, with a flip of her hand. "I am a mother. It was what I was written to be. And I can be nothing else. I shall *not* be anything else."

Almost before making the decision to do so, Solinde

has summoned a water spout into her hand. She is angry. She wants to *attack*, no matter how unwise attacking a Reader may be. If it means her death, then so be it. Better dead than without Varnet!

She throws the water spout directly at the Reader's chest, half expecting it to bounce away harmlessly. What it does instead is throw the Reader back, and hard. Her child is dislodged, and Solinde darts forward and plucks the babe out of the air so quickly the little girl has nearly no time to cry out in her surprise.

The Reader slams back against the gravel bottom of the chasm, gasping and arching in pain, and Solinde commands the water to hold her down. It flows against the Reader's chest, splashing under her chin, keeping her supine and vulnerable. She must crane her head away, painfully, awkwardly, in order to breathe.

Solinde stares in awe at the sight of the most powerful creature in existence being forced to submit to her magic, to her will. Incredible. Unthought of. Shocking.

Perfect.

Solinde pulls the babe against her body, an instinctive, motherly move that nonetheless fills her with the kind of fulfillment she hasn't known in decades. The child *feels* right in her arms, makes Solinde feel complete in a way that she hasn't since Varnet was taken from her. Makes her *satisfied*.

And makes up her mind.

"Hush, hush, honey," Solinde says to the squirming child, mimicking as best she can the cadence and voice of her mother. "Hush, see? Just like a bath."

"Maa! Maaaa!" the babe wails, not a bit fooled. She wriggles and kicks and reaches for her mother.

"Yes," Solinde says. "Yes. Mama. Mama. Worry not, my sweeting. Your Mama is right here." She turns the child, dancing away with her in her arms, keeping her own body between that of the babe and its drowning mother. "Your Mama's here."

SIXTEEN

There is no way to track on foot a creature who travels by cloud. We hasten back to camp, and quickly saddle Capplederry and the horses. We secure our cart and supplies under a lean-to of branches stripped from a nearby fir tree, lashing down our packs and binding them in place with Words of Keeping. If... *when*... we return this way with my wife and child, we will be in want of the food and transportation the cart provides.

Stripped of anything unnecessary, we don what protective gear we own, belt our weapons in place, and mount up. Kintyre rides Karl, while I take Dauntless, with Wyndam and Bevel —the shortest of the four of us— upon Capplederry. Even so, the cat bounds with greater ease through the forest than the horses do, and they make it back to the place where we lost the trail with far more swiftness than my brother and I.

"Where now?" I call out, for Bevel is already on the ground, squinting in the low dawn light at scuffles in the grass.

Bevel makes a frustrated sound, punching the verge in his anger. Behind him, Capplederry paces. Wyndam is still seated, and trying to rein the creature in, but it will not be soothed. It is licking at the air, as if tasting for trails on the breeze, head thrown back, mewing piteously.

Kintyre and Bevel are talking, my brother bent down,

hanging over the side of his saddle, their heads together and voices a rumble as they discuss what to do next. They are hiding their mouths, keeping me from being able to lip-read. Why would they do that?

I am angry, yes, and desperate, but I am not behaving unreasonably in my distress. Do they fear I will lose my temper if they admit they have no trail to follow? I am only clutching my sword so tightly and grinding my teeth thus because I am wild, yes, wild with worry for my family. And if Dauntless is dancing and whickering in echo of my agitation, then it is only because I am so rattled by the thought of my wife and child in the hands of that Deal-Maker, that *weather witch who*—

Wait.

I stop, force my body to relax, pull Dauntless into a stillness, and *listen.*

Another low rumble fills our small, gloomy, dense patch of forest. Not my brother's deep voice, as I had first thought. No.

It is *thunder.*

"Quiet!" I shout abruptly. Kintyre and Bevel both swing their attention to me, and, assessing my posture, turn their own ears to the sky. "Listen!"

Just as I command it, another grumble of thunder, muffled by the trees and unmistakably far to the south, whispers through the air.

"I saw a thunderstorm amid the mountains of the Eyrie," I say, my own voice a hush in the quiet of the forest. "On the night of the wake. It was possibly directly above the Rookery. And it..." I venture, slowly, hoping, *hoping* that I will be right in my guess, and feeling nine kinds of foolish for not making the connection sooner: "It was right before the final star went out."

"So, that was where she was, but will it be where she *is?*" Kintyre asks, his own voice low as we all keep our ears trained for the next clap of thunder.

"She has no reason to leave the area. There are no more stars," Bevel suggests.

Wyndam makes a wide gesture then, waving his hands meaningfully. And yes, his pinky finger is jumping, pointing toward the south, toward the Cinch Mountains and the Rookery.

A knowing look passes between Kintyre and Bevel, one that in any other situation I would have called boyishly gleeful about the chase we are about to give. Bevel swings back aboard Capplederry.

"Lead the way," I tell my nephew, and bend low over Dauntless's neck as my mount turns and gallops with all haste after the bounding cat.

~~~

Dawn shades to daylight. We skirt Gwillfifeshire in favor of the Howling Pass through the Cinch. This brings us to the door of a dwarf queen who owes Kintyre a favor. Traveling the under-roads shaves hours off our journey, but it is still already sunset by the time we emerge from underground. The road has deposited us on the far side of the Valley of the Tombs, and when I express my amazement at how far we have traveled in so short a time, Kintyre makes mention of an enchantment that the dwarves weave that makes the distances shorter.

I wait for Pip to pipe up and call it shoddy world-building instead (albeit, in our urgency, a welcome bit of poor craftsmanship). But Pip is not here, and my throat closes up when nothing but an obvious, echoing silence replies. When I cover my mouth with my gloved hand, blocking the noise threatening to escape, Kintyre looks away to give my grief its privacy.

I do not wish to make camp, but our mounts are exhausted, and I am so saddle-sore that I can barely remain
~~~

upright. The moment I am off Dauntless, I wobble over to where Bevel has begun laying the fire. I lie down, and do not rise again. Wyndam, whom I had, just a few days prior, counseled through his own shattering grief, lays a blanket over me. He fusses at me when it's time to eat, and forces hot broth and warmed wine into my gullet when I would otherwise prefer to sleep, in order to make the daylight come all the sooner. It is wise. I will want all of my strength and to avoid distraction from hunger pangs, but I cannot help but feel resentful and petty toward him for insisting that I remain awake long enough to eat.

In the distance, the storm we've been chasing rages on, unnaturally prolonged, and all I can think of is that my wife is underneath it, electrocuted, *drowning*... and that my daughter must be screaming for a da who is not there. My chest feels hollow and chill. I cannot seem to swallow hard enough to push down the burning nothingness jammed in the notch under my larynx.

My extremities seem to be twitching and tingling, and I cannot seem to stop fidgeting in my panicky anxiety. I am filled with infuriating, impotent frustration at being one step behind.

We are back on the road just as dawn creeps over the foothills of the Cinch. The wine did its work, and I slept, though it barely feels like it. Thank the Writer my rest was dreamless. I do not think I could cope with nightmares in my sleeping hours as well as this waking one.

We skirt the northernmost edge of the Stoat Forest and head instead straight up into the massive ring of the former volcano caldera that forms the Eyrie. As the name suggests, the skies are filled with thousands of birds whose nests our passing jostles, and they scream and swoop at us, angry for our disturbance. A riddling raven pulls at the forelock of my hair, screaming, "Rude! Rude!

Rude man, rude!"

I bat it away, and it rejoins the flock, hurling curses down on our heads.

But the birds dare not follow after us as we ride toward the storm.

The wall of rain is stationary, and disconcerting in how it neither shifts or moves. On one side of the gray curtain, all is dry, save for where the water is rushing down the stony side of the mountain, sweeping away dry soil, debris, and small rocks in a torrent of tiny rivers. On the other side of the curtain, the rain is a continuous stream, fast and fat. And we have no choice but to enter it.

Shoulders hunched nonsensically to keep the water out of our shirts, we are drenched within seconds. The cold of the water cuts straight to the skin, and I must push my hair out of my eyes, slicking it back against my skull.

Eventually, the terrain becomes too treacherous for the horses, and we search for a dry, well-protected outcropping or cave in which to shelter them. Which is how we come to the mouth of what is clearly someone's *home*. Albeit abandoned.

There is a cot against the back wall, stripped of all linen, and a small stool of rough design tucked against a shelf of rock that is just about the correct height for a table. To one side of the bed, I see the unmistakable pile of slivered and shattered gold fragments that make up the nest of a dragon. The hoard is small yet. And there is no adjacent hoard of a greater size, so I assume the dragon is young, possibly even orphaned. Maybe more of the Drebbinshire Dragon's surviving progeny?

The air does not smell of dragon, however. There is no whiff of sulfur or the musk of warm reptile. There is no clothing here, no perishables. Whoever lived here once, no longer does. And it was abandoned recently enough that nothing has begun to rot or mildew. As a shelter, it is perfect.

Capplederry and Wyndam prowl around the entrance—just to make certain we are alone, and that the horses will remain unharmed if we leave them here—while the rest of us guide our mounts inside and drop to the floor with different levels of enthusiasm. I am agitated, incentivized by the peril, but wearied by the pull of the worry. It drags upon me like an excess of gravity, and all I wish to do is bury my face in Dauntless's mane and weep.

No. No.

There is no time for that.

Bevel slips the reins over our horses' heads as soon as we dismount. He and Kintyre begin the process of tightening their sword belts, double-checking that all their weapons are in place. I copy them, anxious at the delay. Already, I feel the tug in my breast to stop dawdling, the intractable panic at the fearful thought that while we are fiddling, my wife and child are being tortured, or are dying... or are dead.

I resist the urge to seek out a towel, for we are just going back out into the deluge as soon as the horses are secured, but I do try to squeeze as much out of my hair as possible. A cold drop gets under my collar, making me squirm and shiver as it slides down my spine. My fingertips are wrinkled, and I feel so saturated with water that my skin is clammy. I am so wet, I wonder if I will ever be dry again. I feel bloated with the storm, a corpse already absorbing water, even as I yet breathe.

If my wife and child die, will I continue to breathe? Am I dying already, because they are already dead?

"I hate being wet!" Kintyre moans, voicing my own displeasure, his voice just loud enough to be carried over the torrent and the howl of wind outside. He is shivering. We are all shivering.

"Kintyre, shush!" I hiss back. "This is meant to be stealthy!"

"Surely the Deal-Maker Spirit must know we are on our way to her by now, so shushing me is stupid," Kintyre volleys back, and between us, Bevel chuckles.

Oh, I see how it is. My brother is going to beat on me, verbally, to relieve his own anxiety. Bevel must be *tickled* that he isn't the only traveling companion for once, and that it isn't all aimed at him.

Fantastic. I am so thrilled.

At the same time, I refuse to be my brother's punching bag on this account. Petty of me, perhaps, but I am too angry to let it go. "And if she does hear us, and our ability to sneak up on her unnoticed is compromised, whose fault will that be, you oaf?"

"Whose fault is any of this!" Kintyre lobs back, and it is a closer hit than I would care to admit.

"Yours, I would think!" I snarl, my temper rising to meet his thrusts swifter than I thought it would. I am fretful. And I am exhausted. I am fueled only by a meager breakfast and adrenaline—along with a dark, gasping hope that we will not be too late. There is no reserve remaining for patience. "You're the hero! Shouldn't you have been watching for danger? I trusted you!"

"She's your wife, not mine!"

"And your niece!" I shout, and what was a stress relieving verbal spar has suddenly become all too painfully real. "You would think that you would care about that, but seeing how you treat your son, I may have to revise my opinion!"

I instantly regret dragging my nephew into this fight, especially since he is not here to defend himself. Especially since he cannot defend himself, not verbally. But it is too late now, for Kintyre yells: "And what would you know about my son? You *haven't been here*!"

"And you're the one who urged me to go!" I riposte. "Brother, I know that you want Wyndam to be your *friend*, but you will never be so to him. You are his *parent*! And you must parent him!"

"I don't—"

"That's right!" I snap, thrusting my finger at his face. "You *don't*. You pal around with Wyndam and leave Bevel to be the bad parent, which has nearly irreparably damaged his own relationship with the lad!"

"Hey, now, leave me out of this—" Bevel begins, but I am too incensed, and talk over him instead:

"Wyndam is your son, brother, not your adventure companion. You must stop treating him like an extension of yourself and start treating him as a character in his own right! Wives, and siblings, and progeny are more than just props for your heroism!"

Kintyre steps back, hands up, placating, startled and a little hurt-looking that what began as playful complaining has turned so serious and heated so quickly. "I'm just trying to—to not be—"

"I know what you are trying to do!" I snarl. "And trust me, I am just as careful, just as concerned with Alis."

"How can you?" Kintyre roars, flinging his hands up and rocking forward again. He will not retreat, his pride will not allow it, and we are practically nose-to-nose now, for all that I must tilt my head back to meet his eyes. Foesmiter rattles against his hip. "You were so young! I was seven when you were born; I lived with him longer. I got it *more*."

"And I got it after you *left*," I point out. "So we can cease this attempt to determine who was damaged most by our father and be honest about our motivations with our own children. Neither of us want to be Algar Turn,

Kintyre, but we must still be fathers!"

"I don't want to!" Kintyre roars, and it is so loud that even the storm seems to pause for a moment, startled by the sound.

And behind me, of course, in the temporary silence, I hear a hitching, breathless, hastily gagged sob. The three of us turn, like naughty children caught begging sweets from Cook, to find Wyndam and Capplederry standing at the mouth of the cave. Capplederry has its foreleg up, tongue out, as if we shocked it in the midst of grooming—which, from appearances, we probably did. Wyndam looks pale and yellowish, his normally full hair flattened against his scalp with the rain, his mouth a trembling line.

He looks *heartbroken.*

"Wyndam..." Kintyre says softly. "I didn't mean—"

"Enough excuses!" I say, already seeing the way my brother's face is twisting in his attempt to find a way to avoid an apology. Angry, and quite ready to deliver the brotherly pounding I would never have dared to administer in the past, I have Kintyre halfway across the cave in a flash, my fingers pinching his ear as he twists and yelps.

"Apologize!" I yell. "Right now!" And I thrust him toward his son.

"Ouch!"

"*Now,* Kin," Bevel adds darkly, arms crossed over his chest, looking dangerously intractable.

"I never wanted to be a father..." Kintyre says moodily as he straightens, rubbing his abused ear.

"How dare you make your son feel worthless!" I shout, and draw my fist back. Before I can let fly, Bevel has my elbow, wrestling me back. "You pathetic, selfish *bastard!*" I say. "Do you have any idea? Any *idea* how it is to be the unwanted one? To be told by the father you adore that you are *nothing?* That you are not good enough? That you are an accident he *regrets? Do you?*"

A rumble of thunder, and an arc of lightning between the clouds outside, punctuates my question, and a humbled, awed silence follows it. Wyndam's expression is slack with amazement, Kintyre looks absolutely ashamed of himself, and Bevel has eyes only for his trothed, big and dark and sad.

"Because I *do*," I whisper, though I doubt any of them heard it.

All the same, Kintyre sucks in a breath and swallows hard.

He will not accept the chastisement though, I can see it already. Kintyre Turn can never do wrong, can never let anything be his fault. This is a posture I am familiar with, that I know all too well, from every fight we've ever had since the day he turned eighteen and slunk out of Turnshire dressed in a Sheil-purple jerkin.

Kintyre will not let me have the last word, because it means he'll have lost. And I am right. And there is nothing that vexes him more than my being *right*.

"Well," he chokes. He swallows, eyes darting around, fists clenching and unclenching, looking for a reply everywhere but in my own face, brushing the golden-blond hair that has gone sandy with rain off of his forehead. "If you weren't such a—"

"I will *not* stand here and play a game of 'whose fault this is' with you, Kintyre!" I snarl. "We are *adults*, now. Our father is *dead*, and there is no longer any use in putting me down to win the affection of a man who had none to give us anyway!" I stomp my foot on the ground to gain his attention, to bring those guiltily wandering eyes back to mine, despite the childishness of the gesture. "We are grown men! It is our responsibility to behave as such!"

And like a strike of lightning, so sharp and so abrupt that I wonder for a moment if I actually *have* been struck, an epiphany occurs. I am shot with the sudden realization that I do have a father figure in my life who *does* adore me, who does see my value, and who *wants* to spend time with me.

Everything I ever wanted in Algar Turn, I have in Elgar Reed.

Perhaps he is crass, and crude, and shallow, but he is still a smart man who can learn things. He still holds great affection for me. And for my wife and daughter by proxy.

And I have done nothing but push him away.

Why?

Because he reminds me, physically, of the father who hated me. I am punishing one because of the other, and that... that is not fair. I have not been *fair* to my creator.

He has made mistakes. Yes. But I have had no patience.

My revelation has no time to settle, however, because Kintyre is not finished: "Responsibility! What do you know about responsibility!"

"Ha!" I laugh. I am so stunned by the ridiculousness of this accusation, that I actually *laugh.* "I am the one who knows nothing of responsibility? I, who shouldered all of yours as well as my own for two decades?"

"While I was saving Hain! While I was *out there,* doing good!" Kintyre gestures broadly, as if the people he has rescued are all congregated at our feet, applauding him.

"You could have done good in Lysse!"

"Not as much good as *you* did as its lordling!"

"You could have!" I say, floored by the backhanded compliment. "You could have. If you had just worked with me! If you had just *listened.* If you had just come back and stepped into your responsibilities!" I accuse.

Kintyre drops his arms, an arc of rain following in their wake. "But I have become lord, haven't I? I returned all your quest items on your promise, and I took up the mantel!"

"And Bevel does half the work!" I throw my own gesture at my brother's trothed and Bevel raises his hands, palm up, warding me off, determined not to participate in our fight.

"As a good spouse ought!"

"Mother *never* did half of Father's work!"

"How would you know? She was *dead* before you were old enough to know what it is that a lord's spouse is responsible for!"

The blow lands heavier than Kintyre swung it, and I feel myself stagger under it. "That didn't stop me from learning it all the same!"

"Bevel—"

"Bevel has his *own* occupation," I sneer. "Or is this another one of those things you have forgotten in your arrogance? Bevel is not always and forever your *squire*, Kintyre. He is not solely your chronicler, nor your walking apology! He is a knight in his own right now, and Shadow Hand on top of that. Need I remind you that it is a great deal of work to be Shadow Hand, and that I was *Shadow Hand and lordling both*, and you *never knew!*"

Kintyre gapes at me. "You sound proud of that!"

"I *am!*" I roar. "I got one over on you! I had a whole life that you knew nothing about, and therefore *could not ruin!*"

"I never!"

"Melinda!" I snarl back. We are somehow back in each other's faces, our anger bringing us nose-to-nose. I have to crane my neck painfully to meet his eye, and the discomfort just fuels my fury.

"You have Pip—"

"And you tried for her first, too, even being able to observe what I felt! Everything you have ever done,

Kintyre Turn, you have done for your own glory, or your own greed, or your own comfort." I scrub my hands through my sopping hair, infuriated and frustrated and unable to find the right way to express it, wanting so much to just hit him. "And now this! You treat your son as you wish to, not as you ought to, and now *my wife and daughter are taken from me*! So I demand, for the last time, that you put aside your childish self-importance and apologize to Wyndam! This world may have been written to be your playground, but *this is not all about you!*"

The last of my words ring like the crash of a gong around the Eyrie.

My traveling companions are silent, agog.

And as the echoes die, a slow and trickling *revelation* creeps into the wake.

"It... *huh?*" Kintyre asks, voice strangled with the kind of existential terror that I think even meeting a Reader had not yet produced in him.

"It is..." I say softly, a whisper in the evaporating echo. "That's it. That is exactly it. This wish, this *Deal* would not have worked if it were connected to anyone but you. It *is* all about you. It's all about *you!*" I shout, pointing at Kintyre, gleeful in the fulfilling and satisfying completion of understanding. That wash of orgasmic bliss splashes over me, tickles my scalp and toes and everything in between and I know, I *know* that I am right.

"What are you—"

"The whole of this tragedy is due to your lack of responsibility, Kintyre." The words are hard, but I cannot manage to wipe the grin from my face as I say them, pleased beyond measure at my own cleverness. "You refuse to grow up, and the whole of the world suffers for it! This is always the way, is it not? My brother, the legendary *hero*, the man for whom the world was created! Throw a tantrum or desire a thing, and the whole damn *realm* accommodates you *because it must!* The way the under-roads work, the fact that Wyndam's Deal should not have been struck with so imbalanced a payment, but was. Even what just happened here—how did we *accidentally* come across the exact sort of cave we needed? Because that is the nature of our reality! *Everything* is always about *you.* Because you, Kintyre Turn, *are the main character!"*

Kintyre goggles at me, all rage suddenly evaporating as he sways on the spot, the high color on his cheeks draining away as he blinks. "I'm the *what?"*

SEVENTEEN

"Wait—" Bevel tries to interrupt, his own face going pale and his eyes dropping wide. I've known neither man to ever swoon, but I wonder now if I will witness it. They grasp each other's arms and gulp in tandem, and it would be funny if I wasn't so angry. "*Kintyre is—*"

"The main character, yes! *The Tales of Kintyre Turn*, by Elgar Reed," I spit. "And how horrifying is that, Bevel Dom? Our whole world, our whole existence, our whole *meaning* is to support *that!*" I cut my hand at Kintyre, and he puffs up with wounded indignation.

"Aye, and why not?" Kintyre snarls. "I'm the only one of the two of us who has ever accomplished anything!"

"Accomplished!" I repeat, aghast. "*Accomplished!* After everything I have read, I am more inclined to believe that it was Foesmiter and Bevel who did all the hard work. You were just *there*, rewarded for simply existing! The ultimate power fantasy—strong, desired by beautiful women, and hated by powerful villains that you nonetheless were able to easily overcome, and how? By simply being *special!* Pah!" I spit. "The rest of us are heroes as well, brother mine! But we have *earned it.*"

"It's simple to be a hero when you've had every advantage handed to you," Bevel says softly.

Kintyre's answer is throttled immediately. He goes silent, and stares at Bevel with wide eyes. The anger and defensiveness in his posture slackens, as if melted away by the rain and our words combined, and he slumps.

Then he turns to Wyndam, places a large hand on his son's shoulder, and says: "I'm an arse. I am a complete arse, and I'm sorry I haven't done better by you."

Wyndam tentatively reaches up and lays his hand over his father's. But his face is still tight, his jaw clenched, the skin around his eyes pinched. He is listening, but he doesn't, I think, trust Kintyre's contrition just yet. My poor nephew. What sort of life has he led on that ship, what sort of hurts has he endured, that he does not trust an earnest apology?

And Kintyre does sound earnest, in a way I've rarely heard from him before.

"We'll get your voice back. I vow it," Kintyre goes on. "And when you have it back, I promise to actually *listen* to you when you use it."

"And if I don't get it back?" Wyndam asks.

But his mouth never moves. The voice is clear and strong though, rising above the wind, and as one, we each duck out of the cave and lift our faces upward.

Above us, standing on a cloud, is the Deal-Maker.

And in her arms is my daughter.

"Alis!" I cry, and she pops her head up from where it had been pillowed on the Spirit's shoulder to peer down at me. She is completely dry, unlike the rest of us, the water simply not falling on her, nor the Deal-Maker.

"Dah!" she cries in complete delight, reaching down toward me, kicking her feet in her little habitual dance of joy. They thump against the Deal-Maker's hip, and the Spirit winces. "Dah dah!"

A relief so profound surges up out of my guts that I actually hiccup out a sob. My daughter is *alive*. Alive and hale, it seems.

"No, sweeting," the Deal-Maker says with Wyndam's

voice, gently pushing Alis's face around, cutting me off from her view. "He is not your da now."

"What?" I shout, part surprise, part demand for an explanation. "You cannot—"

"Oh, but I can," the Spirit sneers, this time in her own voice. "I already *have*. I will rob you both of that which you took from me! I have already taken something from Kintyre's son. And I fully intend to finish the job and destroy the rest."

Kintyre draws Foesmiter and puts himself between Wyndam and the Deal-Maker, teeth bared. He is bristling with protective fury. "You will not!"

The Spirit sniffs at him, as if he were no more concern than an irate squirrel.

"And it is only fair that I take something of yours as well, Forsyth Turn," she says. "I would not want you to feel left out. According to your disagreement just now, that has been a sore part of your childhood. Do not worry; you will have your equal share. Your daughter is now mine, Forsyth Turn. And I shall raise her myself, make of her the strong, powerful woman you men would never allow her to be!"

"Daaaaaaaah!" Alis *screams*, going stiff in the Deal-Maker's arms, her face turning dangerously red as she howls. It is a temper tantrum the likes of which I have never before seen Alis throw, and for an absurd moment, I am proud of her. Then I fear how easy it would be for the Deal-Maker to just change her mind and drop my child.

"Alis, sweeting, stop!" I call up.

"Daaaaa! Daaaaa! *No!*"

"Give her to me!" I beg the Deal-Maker, arms up to catch Alis in case the Spirit takes my plea literally. "Please!"

The Deal-Maker is grimacing at the shrieking going

on right beside her ear, but otherwise seems calm in the face of Alis's kicking, flailing misery. She slings Alis down, carrying her around the waist like nothing so much as a football.

"No," the Deal-Maker says. "The child will be mine, now."

"You cannot—" I sob. "You can't fathom—"

"What, her power? As the half-breed brat of a Reader? I can guess! And I think I can rear her to their glories better than you, you small man."

"No, I—Re-Readers have n-no magic!" I shout, knowing that I am betraying a secret that Pip and I agreed to keep close, in order to preserve the small advantage that fear of her power might cause in our enemies. But I am without any other option. "The legends are false!"

"Are they?" the Deal-Maker asks, smirking at me as if she knows that I am lying. Only I am not.

"She can't pos-possibly be of any ad-advantage. Pl-please!"

"No magic, my girl?" the Deal-Maker asks, holding Alis away from her to inspect her. The arm's reach puts Alis into the rain, and my daughter gasps and stops screaming immediately, curling up into a miserable, snuffling ball, waving at her head to get the water away. Then the Deal-Maker glances down at something behind her. "That explains much, if it is true."

She pulls the soaking Alis back against her side, freeing one hand to make a cutting gesture behind her. The cloud drifts further up the mountain, and half-blinded by rain, I chase after them.

"Forssy, watch out!" Kintyre shouts.

His warning is just in time. I slip and skid to a halt just a few lengths shy of the rim of the Rookery, and its fatal drop. The Deal-Maker's cloud sails unimpeded into the open air above it.

The Deal-Maker moves her hand in an elaborate twisting motion, My stomach plummets at the thought that she has just done something to Pip. Something *final* now that she knows the last secret of the Readers. Below us, over the lip of the precipice, a pained cry floats up through the eye of the storm. A pained cry that means my wife is *alive*.

I want to shout again, to bring the Spirit's attention back to us, off of Pip and the awful things she may be commanding. But as soon as I take a breath, I see Kintyre's head shake, very subtly, in my periphery.

Behind me, through the continual hiss of the rain, I hear Bevel sweep his new bow over his head, pulling it from where he was wearing it across his body. Silently, carefully, he fetches an arrow from his quiver. Wyndam's hands remain empty, and very cautiously, very slowly, he winds his feet into Capplederry's harness straps, ensuring that he will remain in place without his hands to grip.

And then, before I can blink, Bevel's arrow is nocked and loosed. At the same moment, Capplederry has sprung into motion, leaping and darting silently sideways, out of the Deal-Maker's field of vision, but ever closer, making no noise so as not to startle or alert the Deal-Maker to their movement and ruining Bevel's shot.

I expect the Deal-Maker to howl and drop, but instead, without turning her head away, she flings her free hand toward the arrow, and a bolt of lightning incinerates it mid-sky. The Spirit laughs, her attention back on us in an instant. She is gleeful.

"Adorable!" she sneers. "Did you think I would allow myself to be shot agai—augh!"

One of Capplederry's large paws rakes across her back, opening four deep gashes. The momentum of it spins her forward and down, and Alis is flung from her grip.

I think, perhaps, that I am going to faint. I have never done so before, but it seems like a viable alternative to watching as my only child is dashed upon the gray granite of the Rookery's lip.

But Wyndam and Capplederry are there, the great cat leaping upward a second time. Alis slams into her cousin's chest. He folds over her, protecting her from the jolt of Capplederry's landing, and both of them rock dangerously as the great cat bounds back toward us.

"Inside!" I shout to Wyndam. "Back into the cave!"

They are already more than halfway back when the Deal-Maker regains her feet with a screech. Bevel, ready for the opportunity to take another shot, loses three more arrows in quick succession. The Deal-Maker destroys the first, and narrowly dodges the second. The third she ducks, falling to her hands and knees on her cloud.

"Not again!" she snarls. "You shall not best me again!" And then she raises her hands.

At first, nothing happens.

And then, from inside the cavern, Capplederry's roar rolls back toward us over the noise of the storm. The Deal-Maker yanks on something I cannot see, fingers clenched around an invisible string, and Wyndam sails back across the sky, legs flailing against nothing as he is dragged backward by his left pinkie finger. He has Alis tucked close against his chest, protecting her as best as he is able, and when he slams against the rock under the Deal-Maker's cloud, a loud grunt of pain is punched out of him. He mouths a silent shout.

"It is not so easy as that!" the Deal-Maker snarls, and the cloud drops to envelop Wyndam and Alis in its fog.

Kintyre, Foesmiter bared, rushes forward, swinging and chopping at the Deal-Maker, but she is too quick. Before he can land a blow, she is back in the sky and sailing first up, then over the lip of the Rookery's chasm. The rock where Wyndam had landed is bare.

The storm around us sucks toward her, imploding on her vanishing figure. The ever-contracting kernel of cloud dives down into the Rookery.

"Follow!" Bevel shouts to me. "Forsyth, come on!"

But I am frozen. I am still where I stand, horror and fear rooting me to the spot. Kintyre dashes ahead, but Bevel doubles back, grabs my sleeve, and yanks at me.

"Forsyth Turn, now is not the time to suffer a fit of the Soldier's Ailment. Snap out of it! Your daughter needs you!"

"I... I c-can't..." I choke, trying to make him see, trying to make him understand the depth of my despair, the utter terror that if I follow, I will have to watch my child die. And I will be powerless to stop it.

"I don't have the strength to waste on carrying you!" Bevel shouts. He rears back and lays a slap across my face. The pain doesn't register so much as the insult of it, and I blink and goggle at him, profoundly stunned that my brother-in-law has struck me so.

"Yell at me later, idiot!" Bevel snarls. "Move!"

From below us, I hear the sharp, high scream of my daughter, and it is enough to urge my feet into action.

I will not have to watch my baby die if I can *save her.*

Bevel turns to run as fast as we are able, up the mountain. Kintyre and Bevel are nimble as billy goats, and I grind my teeth, draw my sword, keep my head down, and do my best to spring from rock to rock in their wake. After what feels simultaneously like an eon and just a few seconds, we are at the top of the stairs hewn in the rock that lead down to the Rookery. I follow Bevel down the steep stairs as swiftly as I can. We both jump the last five, landing in a skidding run on the rain-slick loose gravel of the Rookery, and speed toward the Desk that Never Rots.

The Deal-Maker Spirit stands upon it, straddling a

largish lump of twisted, blasted metal. Laid out across the rest of the Desk is Wyndam, his legs and throat dangling across the short ends of it, his neck arched and bare like a sacrificial virgin upon an altar. On his stomach, Alis is wriggling and screaming, "Ma ma ma! No ma no!" She is reaching down toward the ground.

And sitting exactly where we had once lashed the Viceroy, Pip is bound, tied identically to the leg of the Desk that Never Rots. She is slumped over, her eyes closed, her skin a dangerously sallow gray. Through the tight coils of the water-logged vines holding her up, I cannot tell if her chest is rising and falling or not. She is gagged with what looks like her own sash.

The Deal-Maker has the flat of Foesmiter between two palms, and Kintyre is struggling to bring the blade down on her chest. His face is covered with sweat, the muscles in his shoulders and biceps rippling with his effort to skewer her, his jaw clenched and jumping.

She is significantly stronger than I had anticipated, for she seems to be holding her own. Bevel skids to a halt and lets fly another arrow, and the Deal-Maker twists to the side, gouging her own palms but ducking in time to avoid being pierced. Kintyre yanks his sword back and out, away from where our children lay, and loses his balance as a consequence, going down hard on Pip's legs.

She gasps and jerks upright, eyes suddenly wide and rolling.

"Enough!" I shout. "Enough fighting! Let us end this a cleaner way!"

The Deal-Maker looks up at me and laughs. Blue blood runs in rivulets down her palms, down every curve of her sodden skirts, and pools around the charred metal.

"Oh, I agree, Forsyth Turn, useless second son and failed Shadow Hand," the Deal-Maker sneers. "Let us end this."

She raises her hands to me, palms out and sparking at the tips with electricity, and I hastily drop my offensive stance and raise my own hands in a placating gesture, my sword dangling from the heel of my thumb. "Now, now!" I say, shrill in my desperation. "Have we all not perpetrated enough violence?"

The Deal-Maker laughs, and the night-black cloud boiling and rolling, filling the whole ceiling of the Rookery, churns with her amusement. It swells and heaves and blocks out the sun. The only source of illumination is the near continual flash of lightning dancing in the cloud's depths. It throws harsh shadows against us all, making faces look stark and extreme, and hard to read.

"Give us our children," I say quickly, "and we may yet come to an understanding."

"There is no understanding we can come to," the Deal-Maker spits. "For you cannot give me my child in return. No! My child was stolen *first!*" The Deal-Maker screams, and a flash of lightning crackles above her head, punctuating her anger.

"The Viceroy needed to be—"

"My son!" she wails. "My son, my Varnet, who has never had the *opportunity* to show the world that of which he is capable! The capacity for power and love that was in his heart!"

"He had *plenty,*" I counter. "Carvel Tarvers forgave him too many transgressions in my opinion! Had I been Shadow Hand instead of my predecessor, I can tell you that Varnet Magicborn would *never* have been given the post of First Vizier."

"He should have been king!" she howls. "He was special. He was *powerful!*"

"He was barking mad!" Bevel shouts back, another arrow prepared and waiting for the right moment. His arm shakes with the effort of keeping it drawn and at the ready, and he scowls, but he does not lessen the pull. He is half lost in the dark and shadow, the cloud that spins around us like ragged cotton floss revealing and obscuring in uneven, unpredictable patches that make it impossible to predict an attack or keep everyone in sight.

The Deal-Maker's eyes roll in her head, white showing all around like a spooked and rabid dog. "And who made him so, Bevel Dom? Hmm? Who thwarted him in every endeavor? Who spoiled *everything* for him?" The Deal-Maker points at him, her bleeding hand contorted like a harpy's talon.

"I hope you're not saying this is our fault, too," Kintyre groans, struggling to his feet. "I've had enough crow to eat today."

The Deal-Maker screams again, unimpressed with his gallows humor and witty banter. She raises her hands above her in claws, lightning crackling between the spires of her fingers. Kintyre dodges to the side, keeping Pip—who is still looking around with wide-eyed confusion, her head dipping and lolling—out of the line of fire.

Then, suddenly, before she can loose the fire in her hands at Kintyre, Wyndam's leg swings up in a tight, powerful circle. His calf lands squarely against her gut, and the Deal-Maker lets out a great "oof!" The lightning splashes against the gravel at her feet when the kick folds her in half and tumbles her right back off the Desk. The rain gentles, but the storm above boils on.

Wyndam—clever, agile, fierce Wyndam—uses the momentum of the motion and rolls back off the desk as well, landing with his feet on either side of the Deal-Maker's shoulders. In a flash, his curved sword is pressed against her neck hard enough to draw a pearl of aquamarine blood. Alis is pressed against his side, tucked in safe with his other arm, looking wind-blown and wide-mouthed with surprise.

And then she giggles. "Yah!" Alis says, wiggling joy-fully.

Well, it seems my daughter is a bit of a thrill-seeker. I have flashes of her climbing too-tall trees at age seven, riding too-fast horses at age twelve, kissing too-wrong people at age sixteen, flying atop too-flaming phoenixes at twenty. Writer, preserve me. And my nerves.

"Wow," Bevel says, coming around the desk cautious-ly, still aiming at the Deal-Maker. "What did Pip call that? Right, that was some seriously impressive Kung Fu shit right there."

Wyndam nods once, not taking his eyes from his captive.

I come up to his other side, lay my sword against the Deal-Maker's throat, and nod. Wyndam backs off, jostling Alis on his hip until she is secured better in his grip. Alis is clearly fed up with being manhandled, and she squirms and shouts, trying to get down. Wyndam puts her on the ground and snags her back by the back of her dress when she tries to move, holding her in place like a package on a string, but giving her space to wriggle to her heart's content.

Bevel stands on one of the Deal-Maker's wrists, and I on the other, watching to see what her next play will be.

Neris liquefied and escaped downward through the loose gravel, but this Deal-Maker seems either genuinely trapped here, or for other reasons either cannot, or is not ready to retreat.

"I am defeated," Solinde spits. Suiting words to ac-tion, she actually turns her head and spits upon my blade. Disgusting.

"And you expect me to use you ill?" I challenge, be-cause I am sorely tempted to do just that. Or kill her. For the crime of harming my child and wife, I would gladly kill her. Even more so for the horrors she has inflicted on the rest of the people of this world. For Lanaea. For the pain that Lanaea's passing causes her father, and Anne, and Thoma. Caused Wyndam.

For all that, I would *gladly* snuff out this monster.

But I am no monster myself, and will not allow myself to become one.

"Run me through!" the Deal-Maker taunts. "Run me through, and release me from my misery."

"What by the Writer's calluses do you have to be *miserable* about?" Bevel shouts, exasperated. "You are an all-powerful, nearly immortal creature literally *dripping* with magic! What could *possibly* be making you miserable?"

"My life is not my own!" Solinde says. She moves to tear at her hair, but I am wary, and will not allow her the opportunity to overpower me through a performance of being distraught. "I may make no Deals for myself! I may make no *choices*! You cannot comprehend the agony of being tugged about by the invisible hand of fate with no *recourse*, no *escape*."

The truth of her agony strikes me like a palm slapped against my sternum with martial force.

"I think you'll f-f-find I very well can," I say, sucking desperately at the air. The Spirit scoffs and chews on her disbelief. "I am n-not patronizing you," I rush to reassure.

"Then what?" the Spirit sneers. "Do you wish to Deal? Will you force upon me a trade? Perhaps the life that I no longer want in exchange for your petty desires?"

Behind me, I can hear Kintyre shift, hear the click of Foesmiter's sheath against his buckles. I turn my head just enough to watch as he plunges his free hand behind the vines and down my wife's shirt.

"Oi!" I shout, but then Kintyre straightens, holding the phial of blood that Pip had been storing in her bra.

"We can with *this*," he says. "We can make you do any

Deal we want, no matter how imbalanced."

The Deal-Maker's confession sparks an idea in me. "But it ne-needn't *be* imba-balanced," I say hastily. "What if you *could* choose?" I ask. "If you c-could m-make a Deal for yourself, what would you ask for?"

The creature on the ground ceases her writhing and stares up at me with black eyes as wide as tea saucers and a mouth that gapes. "You... why would you ask that of me?"

"I want to know," I say, even as behind me, Kintyre and Bevel shout their displeasure at the question.

The Deal-Maker goes quiet, draws into herself in a thoughtful manner that I have seen no other person do outside of my wife.

It is, I realize, that defense mechanism of the traumatized. A cold anger surfaces in me, at the men who have turned these vibrant people into fearful ones, into people stuck forever in the war of their minds, in the battlefield of what was done to them, in the crossfire of the trauma they faced and the world as it really is, not as it is perceived through their fear-hemmed glasses. The creature expects me to harm her, to rescind my interest, perhaps even use the knowledge as a weapon against her. To flay her with her own admission.

"If you tell me, I will do my best to make it a reality," I say, trying hard to modulate my tone into that of someone sincere and trustworthy, for all that I have a blade at her throat. "And with the power of the phial of blood, you may be sure that I have the means to make a big enough Deal. *Provided*," I add, when a thoughtful gleam sparks in her gaze, "that it is a Deal that will harm no others."

"And what do you wish in return, then?" the Deal-Maker sneers at me. "What will you force me to deliver, with my own blood?"

I thought it would be harder to say, really. I thought the struggle would be more profound, that the desire would pull me in two directions. But here, now, in the very place where I first made the same choice once before, with my wife bound to the Desk that Never Rots, and my child screaming in her cousin's arms, with every muscle aching, sweat beading my brow and blood in my eyes, my hand groaning against my shaking sword, it is easy.

So easy.

I feel a calm settle over me like a weighted blanket, reassuring, and safe.

"Send us home."

Behind me, my brother gasps, and Bevel shouts, "*What?*" I hear their feet in the loose stone, scuffling, losing their defensive stances in their surprise. I should feel guilty for startling them, for not telling them before I told this stranger, this *antagonist*, that I have made up my mind, finally.

I love Hain. But I cannot live here. I cannot.

Not with my family's happiness at stake. Not as the brother of the hero. Not when we are *disposable, harmable* for the sake of the plot. I will not raise my child in a place where I will fear, every moment of every day, that someone will try to get to Kintyre through her.

Letting the Deal-Maker up seems a foolish thing to do, but I do so anyway, in a show of good faith. Wyndam unsheathes his knife and moves to free Pip, but the Deal-Maker flings out a hand toward him and says, coldly, "Not yet. You cannot have my leverage until I am satisfied that I will not be double-crossed." The lightning above our heads crackles ominously, warningly.

Wyndam stops and wavers on the spot, unwilling to risk Alis. He scoops her back close, ready to flee if he can. Pip grunts and yanks at her bonds, annoyed.

The Deal-Maker darts forward, and before I am aware of it, she is cupping my chin between her thumb and forefinger, pinching. Her flesh is cold, clammy, like that of a fresh-caught fish left to dry out in the bottom of a boat. But there is a pinch, a pain, a *pull* in her grip that is not physical. It feels like hooks stabbed through the flesh of my lungs, pulling them aside, revealing my heart.

"You are so noble," she hisses, her face inches from my own, and this close, I can see that her teeth are pointed, her tongue black. "You are so *trustworthy*. Why do you think that everyone's heart will be as honest as yours?"

"Because I *have* to believe it," I say, honestly, and it is a very odd feeling, to be speaking with her fingers on my chin. To be staring bleak madness in the face and being calmly truthful. "I have to believe that villains are only villains because their wishes oppose those of the pro-tagonist. And if, and when, their wishes are fulfilled, in a peaceable way, they cease to be villainous."

"And if I am truly nothing but an unfathomable evil?" the Deal-Maker taunts. But her eyes flick across my face, searching for... lies? Duplicity? She licks her lips, suddenly human in her shaking fear and hope. Little tells that betray her nerves. Make her understandable.

I study her eyes, her expression, looking for the lie in her words. Looking for the desperation, the anger. "And a-a-are you?" My voice trembles in my throat.

The Deal-Maker blinks, clearly not expecting to be asked this question. Then she shakes her head and grins wryly. "Perhaps," she admits. "Perhaps not. Perhaps I am just an angry, thwarted woman, as you say. But perhaps I truly wish the ruin of this world. Will you take that chance?"

Around me, my companions, my *family*, raise their

voices in a shout of:

"No, don't do it!"

And, "Are you barking mad? End it!"

And two voiceless grunts.

"I think I am prepared to do so." I straighten my posture, and lower my sword. "I will give you what you want, and you will send Alis, Pip, and I back to where we came from. Back to the Writer's world."

It seems like the whole world pauses and holds its breath.

There is a long, silent moment as the Deal-Maker assesses my honesty, my conviction. And then, slowly, softly, she begins to *laugh*.

"Oh. Oh, but you are a fool," she says, and though she is attempting to make light, I can hear the misery in her voice. "And I am more a fool for believing you. A wish that powerful? Even with that phial of blood, even with the excess magic it will grant me, I cannot do so strong a Deal without the true weight of your *desire* behind it."

She points, with her free hand, at Wyndam. "Taking his Words and his voice required but a paltry amount of magic, and in exchange, I was able to call down three! A Reader, a half-breed, and you. And do you know why it worked?" She laughs again when I attempt to shake my head. "Because Wyndam Turn *wanted* it. More than anything else in the world, he wanted you here so he could go adventuring with his father. He is a selfish, reckless boy, but his desires hold *power*."

"That's not true!" Bevel snarls, defending the lad, the son of his heart, if not his loins. "Maybe once, but Wyndam is not a child, and he is not a *reckless* boy."

Wyndam colors under this praise, startled by Bevel's open pride in him. Kintyre reaches out with the hand that is not still wrapped around Foesmiter and touches

Bevel's arm. It is a soft, tender gesture, speaking of gratitude and love.

"The boy's intention is not the question here," the Deal-Maker says with a scoff and a small shake of my chin to pull my attention back to her. "You offer me a Deal, Forsyth Turn, but what you ask of me is a large thing, and I am unconvinced that you carry enough desperation for the Deal to be well struck, for me to be able to complete it. You lack the *conviction*."

"I want to go home," I repeat, firm, girding myself and throwing every ounce of conviction into my voice that I am able to muster. "I do."

"I do not believe you," the Deal-Maker chides, and fear stabs at my breast. I don't understand it. Why would I fear this Deal-Maker witch scouring my heart of hearts? I have nothing to hide; I have no regrets. I am content, and yet... something small, some kernel of resentment glimmers, unexamined, in the far corner of the treasure chest of my heart, and the Deal-Maker's dark shadow swoops in and grasps it in her maw. "Do you honestly and genuinely wish to return to a world where you are unknown and unappreciated? Where you are maybe even *unwanted*?"

Behind her, Pip shakes her head futilely, mouthing against the gag, pulling at her bonds.

"Here, you were Shadow Hand," the Deal-Maker taunts. "Here, you were *lordling*, and could have, in time, risen above the paltry country seat, earned a city title of your own and a *noble* wife. You could have done your bloodline *proud* for once. Outshone your irresponsible, witless oaf of an elder brother with your reform and politics."

"Those *were* my dreams, I will admit that. But I have achieved them, albeit in another realm. What care I about titles in a world where there are none? There, I have love, and a wife, and a daughter!"

"And no *meaning*," the Deal-Maker hisses.

I do not stagger back at this verbal blow, but it is a near thing.

"Meaning..." I echo, resettling my grip around the hilt of my sword, and, not for the first time, nor probably the last, I wish that I had Smoke with me instead. "Meaning does not come from one's employment, but how one loves. And is loved."

"And yet..." the Deal-Maker sneers.

I try to speak, to rebut, but I find my voice has fled. I have nothing to say, and I feel utterly *gutted*. These fears I barely even understood I possessed, these hurts and worries that I carried and pushed down, crushed and compacted until they had formed this dazzling diamond of hurt, are now *exposed* to glitter and grieve in the daylight.

My mouth flaps. My voice withers. My lungs burn for the next breath, which I cannot seem to take for fear of the words it would be used to form. Over the Deal-Maker's shoulder, Pip's face is white, her freckles standing out in horrified abundance.

"And you," the Deal-Maker says, turning now, putting her back to me, my distress, and my impotent ability to defend myself. Fear fills Pip's eyes now, fear of the creature before her... No. *No.*

Not of the creature. But of her power. Her *truths.*

"And you, Reader... what of the deepest wish in your heart of hearts?" the Spirit asks, voice like silk and sin.

It is not fear of the Deal-Maker I see in my wife's gaze.

It is fear of what the Deal-Maker is about *to say.*

Please, Pip's eyes communicate to me. *Please. I'm so sorry.*

The Deal-Maker grins in impish delight. "You cannot tell me that there is not a part of you that regrets it.

A part of you, however small, that wishes you had never held out your hand and invited the useless younger son of an equally useless lord into your life."

Oh. Writer. Oh, Writer. *No.* No.

Is it true?

It can't be *true.*

Pip is weeping, eyes wide and cheeks red above her gag, tears staining the cloth in blooming gunshots of saltwater.

"Your love was so new, duckie," the Deal-Maker hisses. "You had suffered so much, and you had only really loved one another for one day. And yet, you invited him into your life, accepted care of him, made him your *burden,* and why?" The Deal-Maker reaches out, talons trembling, and digs her fingers into Pip's greasy nest of hair, her fingertips pressing against Pip's skull. The Deal-Maker's eyes flutter shut, and Pip stiffens, her own eyes rolling up in her head, her whole body shaking.

"Stop!" I beg. I plead. "You're hurting her! Stop!"

But the Deal-Maker pays me no heed. She reaches into Pip's mind and *drags.* "Because you felt guilty for leading him on? Because he was nice, and nice guys so often finish last?" the Deal-Maker asks, her voice taking on the cadence of my wife's: "He's a bore, isn't he? You have to teach him so much—the world, the language, how to make dinner and make love? Virgins are such a pain in the ass." She says it with my wife's inflection, her voice taking on more and more of Pip's verbal tics as the Spirit delves deeper into her heart. Pip convulses under her hand.

"That's not..." I begin, but then stop, because these are the truths she has pulled from my wife's heart, and I will not invalidate her fears, not now, not here. Not when the last thing Pip needs to hear is me condescending to her.

"What does it matter to you?" Bevel cuts in, his voice

filled with equal parts bafflement and anger. "So what? So they both have a secret part of them that is terrified of being committed to one another? So *what?* What Pair *doesn't* have fears and concerns? That doesn't make Forssy's desire any less true."

"Yeah," Kintyre adds. "No one's perfect."

It's the strangest thing to hear my brother say, and despite the tension of the situation, I cannot help the single guffaw that crawls out of my chest.

"And *this* is what you believe?" the Deal-Maker sneers, rounding on me again. I am happy to be the center of her attention, so long as Pip and Alis are not. "Can you tell me truly, and honestly, that this is the Deal you wish to make with me? Knowing what you now know?"

"Why are you doing this?" I choke. "Why are you... I was going to Deal with you! I don't understand!"

"You are a *fool*," the Deal-Maker repeats. "And a naive one, at that. You believe a villain will cease to be so if they get what they want? Pah! And what if what I want is at odds with what *you* want. After all, you have always striven for his death!"

"What is the point of all this?" Bevel bellows. "Why do we keep going in circles? We said we'd give you what you want!"

"And you *lie!*" Solinde shouts back. "For what I want, you will never grant! Others, perhaps, but not Kintyre Turn! Not his accomplices, his compatriots, his spawn!"

"You haven't even told us what you want, though!" Kintyre says, and he must shout it, for a great wind has begun to stir. A dread so complete that I cannot even draw breath settles in my guts.

The Deal-Maker is going to call up the storm again. She is going to summon down the cloud churning above us, as she did at the Library, and she is going to *flee*. Pip shouts again, and the Deal-Maker laughs.

"What was that, my dear?" she taunts. "Speak up!" She sweeps down and swiftly cuts the knot at the back of my wife's gag, taking a hank of hair with it.

"You can't. You keep dancing around it because you *can't* ask for it. That's it, isn't it?" Pip shouts over the growing wind. Her hair is flying about her face, slapping her cheeks, stinging her eyes, and she shakes it back, trying to spit it out of her mouth without the use of her hands. "I never understood why you couldn't just go get him yourself, but it's because you can't be specific and you *need* to be. *You don't know what happened!*"

"Then cease to tease me, and tell me!" the Deal-Maker howls. "What don't I know?"

"It was another Deal-Maker!"

The Spirit stops and stares at Pip like she's grown an extra few heads all of a sudden.

"*What did you say?*" the Spirit hisses, and her voice is acid on the air, corrosive and popping, eating away the oxygen so that we must all gasp at the force of her words.

"The Viceroy hasn't been sealed away magically, or taken to another realm, or anything like that. He was traded away in a Deal."

The Deal-Maker clutches at her chest, as if her heart has actually, physically, in that moment, *broken*. "Betrayal," she hisses. Then she throws her head back and shrieks it: "*Betrayal!*"

While the Deal-Maker is busy railing at the sky, Wyndam sidles forward and slices Pip free. He makes a motion for her to follow him silently, but Pip is too angry now for that. She shoves the vines away and hauls herself upright, snarling. "Christ on a crutch! All this because you didn't goddamn know he was right under your nose! *That's* what all of this has been about! Burning out the stars, cutting a swath of terror across the world, hauling Forsyth and I here against our will! And all you had to do was go back to the Deal-Maker's realm? That is some goddamn lazy fucking plotting, Reed!"

Pip herds our nephew back, keeping herself between our daughter and the Deal-Maker Spirit.

"Sisters, why?" the Deal-Maker sobs, ignoring Pip's rant. "Why torment me? Why keep this from me! Oh, sisters!"

"You know where he is now, so go to him," Pip urges. She is wincing, and wobbling. I don't doubt that she is probably suffering the most horrific pins-and-needles from her hours of being half-slumped on the ground.

"Go?" Solinde asks, agog. "*Go?*"

"Find him. Take your son, and leave," Pip urges. "Get out of Hain, get out of this world, leave this realm if you can. Take him away, where both of you will be safe. No more heroes. No more schemes."

"You mean to say, where we cannot harm anyone," Solinde says, and stands with a snarl. She looks rather like what I've always imagined a mother bear would look like when its cubs are threatened. "You mean *leave.*"

"Yes," Pip says, fists and jaw clenched, facing down the Spirit's wrath with naught but her own nerve, and no small amount of stupid courage. I love my wife desperately, love her especially when she is like this, when she is incensed and feels it is her moral obligation to educate and better the world. But I do wish she had the good sense to back down once in a while, when her safety is at stake.

"No," Solinde volleys back. "No. I will not go. I *cannot*. I am cast out."

SONS

Solinde does not understand why the Reader does not use her powers, for she does not believe that a Reader, a *Reader*, may be powerless in this realm. The useless younger brother of Kintyre Turn is a *liar*. How can a creature second only to the Writer himself be *powerless*? Solinde does not understand why she does not bring magic down upon them all and simply end Solinde. She has *begged* for death, and instead, these people—these *heroes*—have chosen to practice mercy.

Mercy, against her will.

At first, she questioned why they were foolish enough to spare her, but now, she is grateful. No, not grateful. She owes them nothing, least of all her continued existence.

Angry as she is, she is also *pleased*, yes, and satisfied with their foolishness, for now... now she has that for which she has snuffed the heavens.

She knows where her son is.

He is not in any of the realms she has destroyed, but in the one realm she cannot access. Her home realm. The land of the Spirits. And they knew it. Her sisters *knew* it. All the time she searched and raged, they knew and laughed behind their sleeves, the ungrateful, traitorous *bitches*.

Well. Once Varnet is safe, back at her side where he

belongs, once his strength is restored, they will destroy one last realm. They will take revenge for their separation, their betrayal. And they will do it together.

The Reader is staring at her, imploring her, her brown eyes filled with pity and anger and... oh. *Oh.* What is that, which glints emerald in the depths of the creature's gaze? It is a spell. A spell that is spiced with a scent as familiar to her as that of her son's hair after a bath; a spell textured with the touch of the babe she had been forced to bear against her will, but loved from the moment he was laid in her arms; a spell that whispers to Solinde with all the sweetness of her child asking for a second bedtime story.

It is a spell that is still active.

A spell that Solinde can *use.*

"This other Deal-Maker, this disloyal whore, what is her name?" Solinde asks, and she is too angry to demand it sweetly, but wise enough to modulate her tone. To seem to be begging. "Please."

The Reader hesitates, cutting a glance to her husband, and yes, ah yes. This is *definitely* something Solinde can use.

"You do know?" Solinde whispers, and curls her shoulders inward. "Please."

"Yeah, I do, but—" the Reader starts, and that is enough for Solinde.

She raises her hand, makes a complicated gesture, and is gratified to see that her guess is not wrong. Yes. There is a spell of compulsion carved onto this woman's *bones,* and it bears the signature of Varnet's workings. Workings that she herself taught him. Workings that she knows *intimately.*

The Reader's eyes flash green, and she stiffens, mouth working like a fish.

"No!" the men cry, each of them sounding like

spoiled children, gasping in horror and pouting at the sudden turn in their luck.

Wyndam Turn, as the closest, lunges at the Reader, but Solinde is too quick for him. In an instant, she compels the Reader to duck under his arm and snatch her child out of his grip. The infant's gown tears, leaving the lad holding a scrap of loose fabric. At Solinde's command, the Reader snatches the lad's slim knife from his belt as he flies by, and raises it to her own daughter's throat.

"Stop!" Forsyth Turn wails. Wyndam stops, hands out, a mere hair's breadth away from Solinde's neck, where he clearly intended to throttle her. "Don't do this," Forsyth whispers, his whole body trembling. "From one parent to another. Ha-have p-pity. Pl-pluh-please."

"Why should I?" Solinde asks. Wyndam retreats, jaw held stubbornly, eyes glittering with hate. The Reader obligingly steps back into the circle of Solinde's grasp. "You never took pity on Varnet. And I like this bargaining position *far* better. In fact, I don't think I need you anymore, Forsyth Turn. Nor any of the rest of you. I will broker no Deal with you. Fare well!"

She summons up her cloud, hauling the Reader and her squirming, squalling babe back onto it with her. And then, to the gratifyingly cacophonous and desperate screams of the family Turn, she takes her captives and flees.

There is only one place she is willing to Deal for her son, one location upon which to stage his triumphant return, one setting for their reunion and their mutual revenge.

His Ivory Tower.

EIGHTEEN

he storm chases the Deal-Maker Spirit across the sky, nipping at her heels. In an instant, sunlight is streaming into the soaked Rookery, and I am left with water on my face and no ability to care if it is rain or tears as I keep my eyes on the cloud that is stealing away everything I love. I am a stupid, imperious man, too certain of my own cleverness to realize that of *course* a sequel book would not, *could not* end in the same place as the previous one. Mimic its narrative pattern it may, but they never conclude in the same place. And I, in my arrogance, believed that I could *force* it to.

And look what it has cost me.

"I don't... her eyes were *green*," I hear Kintyre splutter behind me.

"It was the Viceroy's spell," Bevel snarls. "And that was the Viceroy's mother. We never actually got the spell out of Pip—we just sent her to another realm, thinking she'd be safe. We forgot about it! *Idiots*."

There is an ugly grunting, growling sound, and in the periphery of my vision, I note Wyndam kicking the Desk that Never Rots. Kintyre pulls him away gently, folds his son against his chest and holds him tight as Wyndam continues to grunt and snarl as best he can.

"Shhh, son. Shhh," Kintyre says. "It wasn't your fault. Save your anger for when we've caught up with her."

"And we *will* catch up with her," Bevel says savagely. "Come on."

"Come on *where?*" Kintyre demands. "We have no idea where—"

"The Ivory Tower," I say, and the words fall like cannon balls from my lips, heavy and metallic.

"Forssy's right, she went in the direction of the Mooncall Sea. Where else would she go, but the tower?"

"Bevel, we have no ship, and even if we did—"

"We'll cross the sea when we get to it, Kin. For now, move it." Bevel shakes out his wet hair, and then turns for the stairs. "We have very few advantages right now. Let's not waste this one by dawdling."

Kintyre holds out his hand, uncurls his fist from around the vial of Deal-Maker blood. "She doesn't have this," Kintyre says. "That's something at least, right?"

"Maybe it will even be enough. Kin, move. You too, Wyn. Up the stairs, now." Bevel chivvies them, and once again, must turn back to pluck at my sleeves and urge me into motion. "Come on, Forssy."

"I d-don't..." I begin, but I'm not certain how to end that sentence—if I even can end it—so I let it trail into silence. I am numb. Empty, and numb, and dark.

"Don't make me slap you again, brother," Bevel says, forced gaiety in his voice.

His reminder makes me aware of the sting still in my cheek, and I swivel my head to send him a glare. He chuckles, and tugs on my sleeve again. "Come on."

To reach the stone steps, we must pass the Desk that Never Rots, and now that I finally have the mental capacity to take in the changes in the Rookery, I note that the only difference is the lightning-blasted hunk of metal on the Desk. In the piercing daylight, I can see it clearly for what it used to be.

"Unbelievable," I gasp, jerking to a halt so I can get a

closer look. "It's a *typewriter.*"

"A what?" Bevel asks, and comes to stand beside me.

"This is an Olympia Report De Luxe. In race-car red. It's... I cannot fathom... but this is *Reed's* typewriter. From the Smithsonian Museum."

"What's a typewriter?" Kintyre asks, wrinkling his nose at the scorched metal, which I now realize includes, yes, scraps of melted red plastic.

"It's a machine for writing," I say. "Forget our notions of the Writer composing with a quill and parchment. It was upon a machine exactly like this that the Writer created us. Created *you*, brother."

Kintyre recoils from the machine as if it is about to jump up and bite him. Or, if he were to touch it, that it might absorb him back into the mechanics of its innards and nullify the world.

Perhaps the paradox just may.

"That's... that's creepy," Bevel says, also giving the machine a wide berth. "These are the sorts of machines used in the Writer's world?"

"Sometimes," I say. "But they're old."

"Could you use it to get back?" Kintyre asks tentatively. "When this is all over, I mean," he adds with a defensive shrug when we all turn to look at him.

"Can you hack it?" Bevel asks, in complete seriousness, and I am equal parts surprised that he remembers the term, and impressed that he has thought of it.

"No, but maybe... it's possible I could..." I say. Everyone stiffens when I lift my hand. I let it hover above the typewriter, trying to sense any tingle of magic or ill intent. There is nothing. The metal is not even hot. When I touch the typewriter, a single finger tapping against the useless, twisted "t" key, nothing happens.

We let out a collective sigh of relief.

"No," I say again, running my hands over the mangled typewriter. "There is nothing to hack. It is, unfortunately, not the right sort of equipment. And even if I did have my computer here, I do not see what good its mere presence would achieve. There is not an... ah, accessible archive. My skills in that area are obsolete in such an analog realm."

Wyndam makes an impatient sound, and gestures at the stairs with his sword.

Yes. Of course. He is right. I send one last look toward the twisted, scorched remains of the typewriter, and then sheathe my own sword and begin the exhausting trek upward. I make a mental note to send someone from the Lost Library to retrieve the typewriter and secure it in the Library archives, for I have neither the desire nor the strength to carry it away. And it seems somehow wrong to just... abandon the thing upon which this world was made.

～～～

During our return to the cave for the horses, I realize that, in all the bluster with the Deal-Maker and the storm, I had failed to notice that Capplederry, who has proven itself to be one of Wyndam and Alis's staunchest defenders, was not with us. The reason becomes clear as soon as we approach the cave's entrance. It has been half-collapsed, by what appears to be a lightning strike. The rocks around the mouth of the entrance are ragged and raw, new-torn from the side of the mountain, and blemished with soot and the distinctive searing pattern of electricity. Fulgurite glitters in the wet aftermath of the rain, a beautiful, twisted reminder of the Deal-Maker's wrath.

It takes nearly an hour of sweat-inducing, back-breaking labor, but we manage to clear a tunnel wide enough for the horses to escape—a process that is sped up by Capplederry's anxiousness to be free; the great cat pushes and pounces against the boulders, swiping its paws through the open areas and helping to knock the debris loose. We all crowd inside once there's space, and then quickly huddle out of the way as Capplederry makes its escape. The horses, however, are rested and pleased to see us.

But, as it turns out, they are not *alone*. We are so engaged with making certain that everything is correct—I am sore anxious that we *keep moving* as soon as possible—that only Kintyre hears the scuff of a boot at the newly-narrowed entrance of the cave and turns to face it, drawing Foesmiter.

Capplederry, who had sprung through the gap and into the open air as soon as there was space for it, had been left to roam around the exterior of the cave with Wyndam. The cat now comes bounding down across the mouth, blocking off the person's escape. It yowls a challenge at the figure, but the newcomer doesn't flinch. For a moment, I fear we have stumbled upon the Deal-Maker's hideaway, that she has doubled back on us and we have been caught unaware. I draw my sword; the figure raises its hand and says:

"Whoa, wait, wait. I mean no harm!"

Contrary to this assertion, however, a screaming shriek claps across the now clear skies, holding more rage than I have ever before heard. The sudden sound makes me flinch and cover my ears, but Kintyre and Bevel, far more seasoned warriors than I, hold their positions of readiness.

"Oh, hush!" the figure in the doorway admonishes over Capplederry's shoulder, and as my eyes begin to adjust to the light, a full picture of who is speaking emerges from the sound of their voice and their silhouette against the sky.

"Ah!" I say. "You're the rogue and dragonet from the Stoat Forest!"

Capplederry dodges to one side as the scarlet dragonet in question lands practically on top of the great cat's head. This allows enough of the muddy steel-gray light into the cave to prove me right. For there is the overly complicated leather-and-belt ensemble, the dagged-hem hood. The only difference that two years have wrought in the rogue is a fuller chest, broader shoulders, and thighs corded with muscle probably gained in dragon-riding. His dark hair is cropped now, and it looks as if it's been done with a half-blunt knife, theatrically mannish. It only serves to make his face look softer, however, his skinny neck more womanly.

There is a great deal of raised scales and fur, some hissing and spitting, and posturing in circles, but Wyndam and the rogue get their respective companions in order. The dragonet calms more when we all put away our swords.

"Oh, it's you!" the rogue lad says, and his expression is torn between delight at recognizing us, and wariness. He puts himself between us and the dragonet, who is now, two years later, over ten hands taller at the shoulder than it was before. Where its head used to be the size of a horse's now it is easily the size of an elephant's. "Where's the other one? The lady?"

"My wife?" I say, startled that they remember us so well. "Pip is—"

"The real question is what are *you* doing here?" Kintyre demands, confrontational, and just as eager as I to be on our way down the mountain and across the forest.

"This is where we *live*. The storm was gone, so we thought we might come back," the rogue says.

"And what are you doing here, murderer?" the dragonet spits at Kintyre.

"I don't think I owe you an explanation," Kintyre says.

The dragonet hisses and spits a cloud of sparks. "Of all the things you *owe me*, murderer, an explanation is the very least!"

"Calm!" Bevel bellows. "Everyone, *calm!*" The as-sembled people quiet down—even Capplederry, who had begun its low warning growl. "Thank you. Now. What's your name?" Bevel asks brusquely, pointing at the rogue's chest.

"Caerdac," the rogue lad says, cautious. He does not, however, give his family name, which I think is smart of him. "And this is Bradri, and you can't just—"

"We're on a quest we can—"

"Writer's callouses! Kin, stop arguing with the boy and get on your damned horse, we can't—"

"—do what we like, especially since we've got to ride all the way to the Mooncall sea." Kintyre continues, shouting louder to drown out his trothed's admonish-ments. "And *then* find some sort of boat to—"

"This is my home!" the dragonet spits. "And I'll not have you steal from me *twice —*"

"Peace, dearest! They took nothing that —"

"—cross the damned—"

The sound of rock shattering upon rock halts every tongue. We all look to Wyndam, who threw the stone against the cave wall to gain our attention. The horses side-step and nicker nervously.

Wyndam drops the second rock he had been holding in case his first didn't work. Then he makes a wild gesture that takes me a moment to interpret, gesturing to him-self, then mimicking the toss of a boat upon the waves with his hand, as a child might do in a bathtub. Bevel understands what it is Wyndam is suggesting much more swiftly than I. Though I am only a few beats behind him.

"Listen, Caerdac," Bevel says, moving forward and putting his hands on the rogue's shoulders, like a concerned teacher or mentor might. Silhouetted against the sky, the dragonet mantles and hisses in warning. "Far be it for me to have any right to ask this of you, especially as we are trespassing, but we are going into a situation where we cannot know what lies ahead. I know there is no love between us, but I would be grateful if you would do us a favor."

"What favor?" Kintyre asks, still lost.

"How grateful?" the rogue says at the same time, eyes narrowing, calculated and cunning.

"You cannot want for money," Bevel says, gesturing to the pile of gold shards the dragonet has wept.

Kintyre and Bevel exchange a glance and a frown, communicating in that couples-only language that I was once so jealous of and now have for myself with my wife. Did have. *Still have.*

"Uh," Bevel says when the eyebrow waggling and lip licking is complete. "What do you want?"

"I don't... um," the Rogue begins.

The longer this game plays out, the more impatient I get. "Forget it, then. I have no time for you to make up your mind. Brother, let's go."

"Patience, Forssy, maybe we should—"

"No!" I shout. I am already heading over to Capplederry. The great cat remains still as I climb up the harness behind Wyndam. "Enough dawdling. You two, mount your horses. I will not leave Pip and Alis to the mercy of this creature and the Viceroy a moment longer."

"A rescue mission?" Bradri chirrups.

"We were tracking the... the weather witch," Kintyre says, with only the slightest hitch. Clearly he has decided not to reveal all. For once. It seems my brother the hero has indeed grown wiser.

"She stole my sword," the rogue says sadly.

"And she has stolen my wife and child," I cut in. "So if we could cease this dawdling..."

"A hatchling?" the dragonet hisses, eyes popping wide and eye ridges furrowing in dismay, its mantle flaring in alarm. It raises its head, sniffing the air, as if it could find the trail.

"Dearest," the rogue says in alarm.

"No!" the dragonet says back. "Not that nice lady who told us to talk instead of fight. Not a *hatchling.*"

"We aren't going to—"

"We *are,*" the dragonet insists.

"Just wait!" Bevel says. "We know where she's going; we don't need you to follow. We only need you to fly ahead and secure transportation."

"Would you?" I ask, feeling a pull of desperate hope hook itself in between the bones of my ribs, tugging me toward them. "They went east, we think, to the Ashmar-row Isle, to the Iv—"

"We haven't said yes, yet!" the Rogue lad says, over-whelmed by my vehemence.

"Dearest," the dragonet pouts. "Just think. We promised to find ways to better the world. What is better than this?"

The rogue sighs and pats the dragonet's neck. "Oh, very well, you soft-hearted lout. But if we get killed for this, it's your fault. I'll haunt you." The rogue and the dragonet shoulder their way past Wyndam and Cappleder-ry and step into the open.

"How fast can she fly?" Bevel asks, trailing them with the horses' reins in his fists. I don't ask Bevel how he knows the dragonet is female, and I'll make no assump-tions until the creature tells me one way or another.

"Fast enough," the dragonet says irritably.

"Fast enough to catch up to a weather witch?" Kintyre asks.

"Yes!" the dragonet snarls. "And if we do, we shall—" The dragon stops, cut off as the rogue climbs upon its back. There is no harness, not like Capplederry, but the lad hooks his ankles behind some of the small horns sprouting above the dragonet's shoulders, sitting comfortably in a convenient gap between the ridge of spine-fins.

"Do nothing!" I interrupt.

"But the hatchling," the dragonet protests.

"Please," I say. "Don't let her know you're coming. For the sake of my... my hatchling. I fear she will harm her if the witch feels cornered. Once you have secured transport, you can follow at a distance and tell us where they go. But I would prefer that you return straight to us"

The rogue lad looks torn, but ultimately agrees. "And once we've got the ship?"

"We'll be going by way of the Forest Path through the Stoat," Bevel says.

"We'll look for you there," the rogue answers in return.

Impatience tugging at me, I say: "And if we miss you, we'll meet you in..." I look to Bevel.

"Long Pond Harbor," he supplies. "You know the Shift Berth Dock?" The rogue nods. "Get them to tie up there."

"Right," Caerdac says. "We'll sort payment later," he adds, pointing deliberately at Kintyre.

"Agreed," my brother says.

With one last, lingering look at Wyndam—a calculating, narrow-eyed look that surprises me—the lad and dragon are in the air and speeding toward the easterly horizon. I shout "Thank you!" after them, and can only hope they heard me.

"Fortuitous," Kintyre says, mounting Dauntless and

clucking the horse forward. He raises his hand to his eyebrows, watching the silhouette of boy and dragon fade into the endless blue sky for as long as they are visible.

"You *are* the main character," I remind him. "There is no such thing as fortune for Kintyre Turn." However fortunate finding the exact sort of magical creature we require to chop several hours off scouting the harbor for a ride to Ashmarrow Isle might seem.

Kintyre huffs a laugh, still clearly unnerved by the reality that he is the main character of our world, and then our party is off. Capplederry lurches to its feet, and we begin picking our way down the mountain.

Even with Wyndam right up to the cat's neck, half-buried in its ruff, and me seated behind, clinging to the harness, Capplederry does not seem terribly affected by our weight. Everything smells of wet animal, and I imagine that we cannot be light.

But before I know it, we are bounding along the foothills, and rush into the verdant clasp of the Stoat Forest, leaping brush and fallen trees, chasing the scent of the sea.

DEALS

There is an infestation of academics in Varnet's Tower. Solinde bypasses them for now, and deposits her burden on the circular, flat expanse of the tower roof. It is surrounded on all sides by a shoulder-height wall of leviathan vertebrae, and the ivory beneath their feet is a single, smooth bone, made most probably from a massive kraken skull. There is a door chipped into the bone against one side, and a telescope and astrolabe on a wooden table that has long been neglected. Whatever books and notes the various gleaming paperweights were holding down have long since been carried away by the weather or scavengers.

It saddens Solinde's heart to see her son's research so neglected, his works so wasted. She had heard, through what gossip she could obtain in her cottage-prison, that during his glory-filled days as First Vizier to the King, he had developed many wonderful spells and discovered new Words. And now, it is all lost to time, and neglect, and the caprice of the proud, arrogant, cruel Kintyre Turn.

The Reader stands statuary-still in the middle of the roof, where Solinde left her, the child squalling and screaming and wriggling in her unforgiving grip. Solinde watches, amused, as the child levers herself down, onto her feet, and pulls on the Reader's hand, screaming, "Ma mama ma! No, no! Dada!" The child can almost walk on her own, and Solinde pushes down memories of holding Varnet's hand as he wobbled through the barn, determined to get to a nest of that season's hayloft kittens.

From below, she can already hear the clash and clatter of uncouth mortals, tromping their way upward to investigate the storm that has curled the tower in its spinning arms. She has very little time to get what she wants before they are overrun. And she is tired from maintaining the storm, the ivy-spell, and transporting two mortals across the sky. She needs rest before she can dispose of the scholars.

She has no time to rest, however.

Instead, she scoops up the infant, who grabs hold of her mother's leg, hard, and *screams*, clearly fed up with being manhandled.

"No, no, no!" the child wails. "Bad! No! Ouch, ouch, ouch! No!"

Solinde's patience is running poverty-thin, the grains of sand in her internal hourglass trickling away. She can hear the scholars getting closer.

"The name!" Solinde orders the Reader. "Tell me the name!"

"The name?" the Reader echoes. Her voice is dull and flat, her eyes glowing green, but her teeth are clenched, and her hands curl and uncurl into fists. She is *fighting*. And hard.

"The name of the Deal-Maker who wove Varnet's geis. *Tell me.*"

"I don't..." the Reader says, and chokes on her words. She splutters and coughs, all while standing completely immobile, held fast by the glowing green scars that cover her back. "*No.*"

"Do as I command!"

The Reader gasps like she's been punched in the stomach and blinks hard. She shakes her head, and some of the tension in her posture evaporates. She sways on the spot, arms rising, fingers spread, then drops them again. "You don't... have to..."

Solinde sneers. "Of course I have to know! He is my son. Is there nothing you would not do for your own child?"

"You could be... the main character... in your *own* story," the Reader protests. "Why be... content... with being a... a side-bit in... *his*?"

"Because I am his mother," Solinde snarls. "What else is there for a mother to do?"

"So much," the Reader sobs, and she is crying. Tears stream out of her eyes, faintly green in the glow against her cheeks. "We are so much... *more*."

"*The name!*" Solinde snarls, and wraps a hand around the fussing infant's neck, the threat implicit. "*Now!*"

The Reader whimpers. "Neris!" she yells, but the thunder drowns it out. "Neris!" she screams again. "Her name was Neris!"

Relief washes over Solinde like a tidal wave. Her fury evaporates, and with it, the storm. The wind stops so abruptly that the Reader stumbles, no longer braced against it.

Solinde feels herself go pale, and then flush. She slumps, as if someone has cut her strings. Her hand flops against her thigh, and her knees give way. She sinks downward, slowly, trembling. Her face crumples, inch by inch, papery, and suddenly, she feels so very weary, so very *old*. Her eyelids slide closed, moisture pressing out the bottom, tears rolling in two thin, trembling lines down her cheeks, dropping off the quiver of her chin.

"Yes," she whispers. "Finally, yes."

The child, held loosely in her embrace, reaches up and pats her cheek, concerned. The babe is large-hearted, clearly, and cannot stand to see someone else cry, even as she is stiff and wide-eyed with terror.

"*Neris,*" Solinde croaks.

"You have your name," the Reader says, and every part of her is trembling, reaching, tense and fatigued, pale and grime-smeared. Her expression is begging, grasping, pleading, and desperate, desperate, *desperate.* "Please. Please. Give me... my child. Let us go."

But Solinde pulls the infant closer to her, staring down into her face. Solinde feels her expression softening. The Reader waits, hands still wide, and waits, clearly fearful that any move she makes might be the one that prompts Solinde to harm the child.

"He was like this, once," Solinde says softly. "Such a happy child. So easy. But then the power came. And his father feared him. Feared that I would teach him to harness the magic my blood had granted him." Solinde takes the babe over to the table, makes an enthusiastic cooing sound when the child reaches out to the astrolabe, curious. "He lied, you know. Told the great Wizard of the Bedim Isle that Varnet had a natural talent and affiliation for Words. That he had taught himself great magic, that he was a wizard, too. He did not tell the fool that Varnet was special. He had not learned magic; he was born of it. And as such, he deserved *more.* He deserved better." Solinde turns to the Reader, and her voice is growing hard again. "My son deserved *everything.* He nearly *had* everything, until you... *until your—*"

"Hey now," the Reader says, clearly aiming for a tone that is soothing, but that only annoys Solinde further. "It wasn't... me who stirred up... the Necromancer... caused all that trouble with... Ghost Legion of Urland."

Solinde offers the Reader a glowering look, unimpressed with her attempt to push the responsibility for that failure off of Kintyre Turn and onto her son. "But had he not thwarted him, Varnet would have gained the throne of Hain!" the Deal-Maker snarls. "Carvel was a fool, even then, and heir-less! As First Vizier to the King, Varnet was in line to take the throne!"

The child stops patting the astrolabe and starts to look concerned again. "No, no noooo," she says softly. Solinde looks down at her again.

"And now, here is another child born of magic, and what do you do, Reader? You *deny* her. You *lie* and say she is powerless. Ha! And you say it is I who does my child a disservice? Pah!"

"No... *magic*," the Reader insists.

"My son," Solinde whispers, petting the babe's head to soothe her. "My poor, poor son."

"Please," the Reader sobs.

Solinde grins at her. "No," she says. Then she lifts her free hand and her face to the sky, and calls out, silkily: "Sister! I know who you are now. Neris! I bid you with your name to come. Neris! I compel you with what you owe me to come. Neris! I summon you with your name! Neris!"

Neris is not as dramatic as her sister. In one heartbeat, she is not here; in the next, she is. She stands beside the table, hands folded, mockingly demure. But her smile is a knife-slice.

"Hello, sister," Neris sneers. "If I can even call you that now."

Solinde feels shame and anger boil in her guts. She clenches her fists, and in her arms, the child whimpers and wiggles. Solinde sets her down, for there is nowhere she can go. The child wobbles over to her mother, clinging to the Reader's leg and moaning, "Ma mama, up, up!" But Solinde has not released the Reader from her compulsion, and the child is not obliged.

Below them, the mortals have reached the upper level of the Ivory Tower and are attempting to break the enchantment on the lock keeping them from opening the hatch onto the roof. Solinde fears they will burst in, but when they don't, she reaches out with her power to touch the lock and... ah, yes. Varnet's scent, and touch, and sound, it is in this magic, too. The lock is more than just a hinge and metal workings. The spell is complex. It will take them hours.

Now that Solinde has her son's captor, she has time.

"So, you are one of the ones who would shame me for my own rape?" Solinde spits at Neris, arms spread in false welcome. "Blood of my blood, Sister of my Spirit, you would blame the victim of a Deal gone awry?"

Neris laughs and shrugs. "Rules are rules, sister. You laid with a man. You could not come back."

Though the sky is clear, the sea below the tower cliffs begins to boil and foam. Small waves crash against the tumbled boulders along the steep shore, but they grow larger with every surge. "There are no rules that state you must keep all that I desire from me!"

The babe is screaming now, red-faced, clinging to the Reader and howling. Below their feet, the mortals pound on the door, shouting reassurances to the child, and de-mands to let them through.

Nobody on the roof moves to assist them.

"No, there is no rule, and yet..." Neris spreads her hands, grinning. "Why should I give up that for which I Dealt simply because you ask? Out of sisterly love? No, you are no sister to me any longer."

The Deal-Maker Spirit screams, and the child echoes it, petrified.

"And what is this?" Neris says, peering down at the babe. "More of your horrific half-blood abominations?"

"Don't... touch her!" the Reader commands, and Ner-is turns to toss a curling, wolfish grin at her.

"Oh, is she yours, Mistress Lucy? Yours and... ah,

Master Forsyth Turn, was it? Lovely to see you again. Need your kitchens cleaned? Fancy a pot of tea fetched?"

"You are not amusing, Neris," Solinde growls.

"Oh," Neris says, pouting theatrically. "Will you dock my pay?"

"Enough!" the Deal-Maker snarls. "You have Varnet?"

"Yes," the other Spirit says, drawing upright. "But I don't feel like Dealing for him. I don't want to give him up. He's too entertaining. Did you know, he has the sweetest high-pitched scream?"

"You *will* Deal him to me," Solinde snarls.

"I shall *not*," Neris counters. "He killed one of our sisters and compelled me to call down that Reader with her blood. He deserves his torment."

"He killed none of us! That was *my* blood he possessed!" Solinde says. "In an amulet, yes? It was *my* blood, and I gifted it to him, voluntarily, on the day his father sent him away!"

Neris cuts her eyes to her sister and frowns. "You parted willingly with your... you *fool*. Do you know what he has been using it for? What magic he stole, what actions he wrought? How carefully he rationed it out, drop by drop, and how many Deals he made where he compelled our sisters to trade unfairly, to *suffer*?"

"Yes!" Solinde says, beaming and warm with pride. "Yes, my clever boy! He is your nephew. It is only right that you aided him!"

Neris shakes her head. "I see now where his insanity comes from. You are mad, sister."

"I am *driven* mad, sister!" Solinde spits back. A surge of seawater slams so hard into the cliffside that the Ivory Tower shakes. The mortals below them cry out in fear. The babe loses her footing, falls onto her rump, and wails. "And not one of you came to me to help in all the years I was bound to that man. *Not one!*"

"I'll... help you!" the Reader blurts. Solinde can see it in her glowing eyes; behind her frozen desperation, her mind is spinning, weaving, trying to find an opening, an *opportunity.* "I will... Deal!"

"For what?" Solinde asks, even as Neris howls: "No, unfair!"

"Wyndam's voice... and Words," the Reader says.

And, oh, that is a bit unexpected. "Not for your daughter?" Solinde drawls.

"Would... you... agree not to... take her?"

"No," Solinde dismisses, airily. Neris's own rage is building now. She seethes, and her sandy hair rises and lashes in the air like furious snakes, her clothing fluttering warningly.

"Wyndam," the Reader grinds out. "For... Varnet."

"You cannot!" Neris howls. "He is mine to Deal away, or not!"

"I... Dealt him... first," the Reader says, with a narrow-eyed glare at Neris. "Can... again."

"*No!*" Neris screeches.

"But I like having Words," Solinde says. She flashes the Reader a black-mouthed grin, sly and bloody. "It makes me *powerful.* It makes me better. I will keep it. Ask for something else."

With a wave of her hand, she lessens the compulsion on the Reader, lets her speak freely, though she still cannot move. At her feet, her child has curled up around her ankles, sobbing piteously and jerking with exhaustion.

"Christ!" the Reader snarls. "No. Absolutely not! Unacceptable! You will not leave the only black character in this thing voiceless, especially not a young black teen who has been wrongfully stereotyped as a thug. No way! It's this, or nothing. If you want your son, you give Wyndam his voice."

Solinde watches her sister's distress with amusement as she considers the Reader's offer. "Yes," she says at length. "Very well. I can always Deal for another voice, for more Words, from some other mortal fool. Yes, I accept!" The waves below boom in an echoing crash.

She slices her hand through the air, slicing at nothing the Reader can see, severing the string tying her to the stupid boy.

Solinde makes another gesture with her hand, and one of the Reader's arms rises at Solinde's bidding, her hand out, ready to shake.

"I will not let you—" Neris howls, and lunges.

But Solinde is faster.

She seizes the Reader's hand, pumps it once, and Neris is halted midair, as if she has hit an invisible wall. She writhes and screeches, and drops to the ground, panting in fury. The wind returns as a gale, plastering everyone's clothing against their bodies, flinging Solinde's skirts out behind her in flapping banners. The child's screams are carried away. Solinde tosses her whipping hair behind her shoulders, and *laughs*.

"I'm here, Alis!" The Reader tries to soothe her babe.

Neris scuttles to her feet. "Have your mad child, then!" she says, recoiling, ready to sprint. "I will take that one!"

Neris surges forward, and Solinde steps in to block her. The Reader screams in distress, eyes wide and wild. Solinde is forced to grapple with Neris, wrestling her away from the Reader and her oblivious babe.

"No!" the Reader howls, jerking and straining against the spell's hold.

Storm and gale clash and howl - Solide may be a Spirit of the Sea, but Neris is a Spirit of the Sky, and the tornado and squall are her weapons, the cutting wind her sphere of influence.

And then, suddenly, there is a blade inches from both their noses. Solinde jumps back, ready to slay whomever it is that is attacking them. And Neris, who had been held up by Solinde's grasp, slumps. The pointed end of the astrolabe is protruding from under her breastbone, blue with ichor.

The wind her rage had been generating dies off instantly.

Neris falls to the ground, dead. Her corpse immediately begins to bubble and boil, evaporating away. Deal-Maker Spirits leave no bodies behind. That is why their blood is so precious. Even the astrolabe is clean of blood, but red-hot from the temperature of her death.

A rush of relief, of happiness, of joy and love splashes over Solinde. Her extremities begin to tingle; she feels her smile grow, and is helpless to stop it. Her shoulders drop, her fists relax, and she sighs, her eyelids fluttering. Pleased.

For behind Neris stands Varnet. He is there. Her son. Her child.

Everything she loves; everything she has sought. Everything she has fought so hard for, wept for, bled for.

There.

Within arm's reach.

He is clad in the torn, filthy strips of what had once been his magnificent black-and-gold jacket and trousers. His feet are bare and bloody, his face gaunt with pain and hunger and lack of sleep. His normally impeccable slick of dark hair is a wild and ragged tumble. But his smile, his grin filled with teeth like knives, is the same.

"Hello, Mother," he says.

Solinde smiles back. "Hello, my darkling boy."

She holds out her arms.

And like the good, good boy that he is, he steps into them.

Varnet is taller than her now, can lay his head against the top of hers easily, but he smells the same, *feels* the same, warm and alive. She can hear his heart beating under her own ear, pressed against his thin, gasping chest. He is shivering in relief. His hands dig and clutch at her back.

"*Mother*," he whimpers, and Solinde pets his back, his nape. "I missed you."

"My child, my baby," Solinde says, and her voice is hitching. There are tears on her cheeks, a joy that she cannot contain thrilling in her breast. "I missed you, too. You've done so well. So well, my son. I am so proud of you."

Varnet huffs a sob and curls further around her, holding tight.

The world goes quiet as they cling to one another. The storm pauses. Even the babe has hushed. Even the mortals below have gone silent. The world stills. It holds its breath.

And then Varnet pulls away. He reaches up, cups her face in his filthy hands, and kisses her forehead tenderly, reverently. "How beautiful you are, Mother," he says. "How good you are."

"My boy," Solinde murmurs, drifting in the bliss of his touch, his praise.

"And what is this?" he asks, turning to the Reader and her child.

"A gift, my son," Solinde says. She cannot bear to be out of contact with him, and wraps her arm around his waist. He slides his hand over her shoulder, cupping, thoughtfully careful of his strength. "A wife, I think, if you want her."

Varnet laughs. "Oh, now there's a thought, isn't it? Hello, Miss Piper!" he says. "What a delight! I never expected to see you again."

"Fuck you," the Reader spits.

"And still as crass as ever, how lovely. And what is this, wriggling by your feet? A worm?"

"A halfling Reader," Solinde says. "She will be a valuable servant to us when we have raised her to it."

Varnet wrinkles his nose and sneers. "The other half is Turn, I assume? Eugh. Better to exterminate it, Mother, like the vermin it is. If you want a half-Reader child to keep, I'll get one on the bitch myself."

Solinde frowns at the casual cruelty of the dismissal of the babe, but says nothing. Her son is right; a child that is half-Reader and a quarter Deal-Maker will be more powerful still.

"*Please, no!*" the Reader groans, her voice low with horror. "From one mother to another, please, I beg you."

But Solinde says nothing. Her son has made his choice. She watches as Varnet raises his hand, glowing with green.

NINETEEN

I t takes us the rest of the day to cross the Stoat Forest, and we reach the seaside town of Lymecove at twilight. It is quiet at this hour, the windows in the limestone homes glowing orange and welcoming. But we dare not stop. The harbor is on the other side of town, and we cut through back alleys quickly. My stomach growls when we pass the street of sailors' inns, and the enticing perfume of seared meat and fresh bread permeates the air. Capplederry growls back. We push on, though, determined to reach the ship—assuming Caerdac and Bradri found a ship willing to carry us—before we rest.

The air takes on the sharp scent of salt and fish as we head along the harbor-side road and out to the edge of town. It is cool, with a swift sea-borne breeze, and the damp patches that remain on my clothing, along the seams and around my collar, turn abruptly uncomfortable.

Just as he promised, Caerdac is waiting for us at the top of the Shift Berth, in Long Pond Harbor. He is waving enthusiastically when we pull up, though we could not have missed the scarlet dragonet curled on the ground behind him. Bradri's eyes are closed, her wings tucked against her side, and I realize as I slide off Capplederry that she is asleep. Their searching flight must have been long and exhausting.

"Is that the ship?" Bevel asks, peering down the rickety dock. "What is that? A Caravel? I like those; they're fast. That's good."

I can't make out the coloration or markings of the ship—all its lights are doused, and this dock has no lanterns—but there are indeed three masts with triangular sails barely silhouetted against the star-less sky. In this light, I cannot make out what shade they are, but they look almost mustardy from here. I am struck with a thought that I have seen a sketch of this ship before, during my turn as the Shadow Hand. But then again, I saw many sketches of many unlicensed ships, and if this one is docked at the Shift Berth, then I had undoubtedly been made aware of its existence at one time or another.

Shift Berth is the only unlicensed dock in Lymecove harbor. Ostensibly, it is only meant to be where ships who have not sought prior permission may tie up while they are awaiting official recognition in the city harbor. But because of that, it is also a favorite berth for ships who must make emergency stops for rations or repairs, and for those with shady business to conduct, which requires them to be docked and gone within hours. In short, it is perfect for smugglers, racketeers, pirates, and anyone else who is willing to take on passengers at the last minute for a pile of coins and with no questions asked.

"That's your ship," Caerdac confirms. "They were just around the breakers of the cove. Lucky for us. And oh, how we surprised them." Caerdac grins like a naughty child who has gotten away with a prank. "You should have seen the look on the captain's face when we landed right on the deck!"

"Did they fire at you?" I ask, concerned. I swing down from Capplederry's back, ready to render first aid if necessary. It is now a fatherly instinct to immediately look for blood.

"No," Caerdac says. He pulls a length of white cloth from under his leather vest. "We came in under a white banner."

"Clever," I say, and the thought of what I might offer the rogue lad in return for this favor begins to germinate. I had been worrying the nugget of what Kintyre, Bevel, and I might give, or what he might ask for, the entire ride here. Now, seeing how clever, honest, and genuine he's been, I'm starting to get an idea. "What did the captain say? Is he ready to leave immediately?"

"Yes, but—"

"Let's go, then," Kintyre says. "We'll bring the horses aboard, just in case. If nothing else, they can rest and take feed there. Hup!" He spurs Dauntless forward, and my horse, winded and exhausted, trots as if he knows that water and grain and repose wait for him at the end of the dock. Perhaps he does. He has always been a clever creature.

Bevel and Karl follow in their wake. I wave Capplederry and Wyndam on, and turn to Caerdac.

"Thank you," I say earnestly.

"We saw the witch, too!" Caerdac blurts as Bevel passes him.

"You didn't engage her?" I ask breathlessly, dread strangling my lungs.

"Nope, did as you said, just hung back and followed her. And yes—it was definitely to the Ivory Tower that she went," the lad offers. "And... and I saw her set down your wife and child with my own eyes. We turned back after that."

"Thank you. As for your recompense, I thought we could perhaps discuss—"

"A home," the dragonet blurts, and I jerk back, startled. One golden eye opens and stares at my face. I thought Bradri asleep, but of course she would not sleep through our conversation, especially with how covetous she is of Caerdac's person. Bradri lifts her head, shakes her weariness off her shoulders, and peers down at me from the height of her slender neck. "We talked about it, and we've decided that we want you to give us a home."

"Something nice, and dry, and warm," Caerdac says. "It needn't be large, but you're all lords, ain'tcha? You can grant us land in your Chipping. Or a farm. Something with a bit of garden to work for ourselves, and a roof over our heads?"

I feel my grin spreading, that germinating seed of an idea sprouting, leaves of thought uncurling.

"Forget a mere house on a farm. What do you say to a manor?" I ask, reveling in the amusement in the lad's face.

"A... what?" he asks.

"Forssy! Move it!" Kintyre calls from the gangway.

"I'll explain when we return," I say, his urgency tugging me along the dock. I begin to jog, to where I can see the rest of my party handing their mounts up the gangway and onto the darkened ship. Capplederry waits patiently behind the horses, Wyndam half-hidden in his ruff. I am not surprised to hear the snap of leathery wings in the air.

From above and slightly behind me, Caerdac calls: "Oh no! We've done our part, you tell us now! What do you mean, '*a manor*'?"

I grin back over my shoulder at them. "How do you feel about a career in law enforcement?" I ask. "For I have a friend in dire need of an apprentice, and he has a wonderfully large house with many empty rooms. And the perfect livery to turn into a dragon's horde."

"That's not an explanation!" the lad shouts. Bradri lands on the dock beside the gangway, and Caerdac dismounts just as I reach the others.

"I promise I will explain further," I pant, just as Kintyre steps from the dock and onto the wobbly bridge that is the gangway. "Later."

"Now!" the lad says, moving to block the way forward. Kintyre stumbles back when one wine-colored wing snaps open across his path. I hear snorting laughter echo back from the ship's deck.

"I must—" I gesture at the ship, trying not to let my frustration bleed through.

"Then you can explain on board!" Caerdac says.

"You're not coming with us," I counter.

"We are. We secured the ship; we're coming," Bradri insists, sounding petulant. "Besides, there's still the hatchling. I won't rest until I know she's safe."

"You're just a lad," I say. "Both of you. You're too young. Please, I can't be responsible for—"

"I'm no younger than him!" Caerdac says, pointing to Wyndam. My nephew crosses his arms and shifts his weight onto one leg, smirking and smug.

"You're untried!" I say. "I have seen you with a sword, lad, and I shan't—"

"*We're going,*" Bradri hisses, and her throat glows like she's swallowed coals. "The captain already said we can."

"Let them aboard, brother, for the love of the Writer, and let's go," Kintyre sighs. "We'll argue about whether they'll be climbing the Ivory Tower after."

Kintyre ducks under Bradri's wing and starts to climb.

"Oh, wait!" Caerdac says, suddenly looking nervous.

"Now what?" Bevel asks, hesitating on the steps to the gangway.

"It's just that, when I said the ship was for you, the captain... had a few things to say about that."

"Oh?" Kintyre laughs, nearly to the top. "And who might the captain be?"

"Me," another voice adds from on deck. It is female,

deep, sultry, and tinged with a Gadotian accent. "Hullo, sweetie."

"Oh!" Kintyre gasps, whipping around to face the woman who has stepped up to the top of the gangway. "Um. Issie. Hi."

The Pirate Queen Isobin offers my brother a sharkish grin, growing more pleased, it seems, the redder his face turns. "Kin," she replies with a head dip. Her amusement is too thick to read how she really feels about seeing him again. "It's been all of eight months. You've called a surrender on parenthood so soon?"

"Ah, no," Kintyre mutters, rubbing the back of his neck and blushing.

Bevel, who had mounted the gangway behind Kintyre, makes a noise of disgust and shoves his way around his trothed. He puts himself between the former lovers and *glowers.* Ah, yes, there is the bull-doggish expression I know so well. "We're on a *rescue quest,*" he says. "So, if we could get going?"

"Yes, of course," Isobin says, and her voice is smooth as melted chocolate and gilded with good humor. By the deeply etched lines around her eyes and mouth, I would guess that this is a woman who loves to laugh, and does so often. "Well come, Sir Bevel Dom, and welcome aboard."

"That's Lord Bevel," he corrects her, and it is the first time I've ever heard my brother-in-law insist on the honorific offered to him by his trothing. He must feel spectacularly threatened by Kintyre's former lover indeed.

"Is it now?" Isobin says, stepping aside to allow Bevel to bully his way onto the *Salty Queen.* She glances at Kintyre and raises a questioning eyebrow. Kintyre just ducks his head like a naughty schoolboy and slips past her.

I mount the gangway next, and the length of the walk

affords me the opportunity to get a good look at our erst-while hostess. She shares Wyndam's glittering jet eyes—or rather, I should say that Wyndam shares hers. They both have the wildly curling black hair, as well, though Isobin's is pulled back from the crown of her head in tiny braids that hug her scalp, the ends left to flutter around her shoulders like a storm cloud. Her skin is of course darker than Wyndam's, and her lips more plush.

For all that I see much of Kintyre in Wyndam's biological makeup, coming face to face with his mother reveals to me just how much of her is in him, as well. She stands the same way he often does, all of her weight on one leg, hands on her hips, strong and open. Her head is tilted ever so slightly to one side as she studies me in return, her eyes narrowed in a gaze that I have seen Wyndam level on anything that piques his curiosity. In his mannerisms and body language, Wyndam Turn is very much like his mother.

"Madam Captain," I greet her when I reach the top, and offer a bow.

Isobin bursts into a gale of blowing laughter, hands on her hips as she bends and sways with the joy of it. She is like a willow switch: graceful, supple, and I would lay money on her also holding no small amount of sting.

"Oh, then. I like this one. Well come, Master For-syth."

"Thank you," I say. In the past, I would be hurt with the way she laughed at my manners, but now, I am sure enough of my own self and worth that I allow myself a small grin at her amusement.

Caerdac and Bradri land on the deck, defiant and glaring mulishly at Kintyre and Bevel. Capplederry shoulders on next, bumping me aside in an effort to get at the dragon for a good sniff; the cat is a terribly curious creature. Wyndam steps aboard right behind me. He is not exactly *hiding* behind me, but he does not greet his mother. I can't see his face, but I imagine it too is a mulish glower.

"If we may, Captain, we'd like to be off as soon as possible," I say, when it's clear that Wyndam has no desire to step forward.

"Of course." Isobin nods to a stout woman I assume to be her bo'sun, and a sharp series of whistles split the air. Women sailors, each dressed in trousers and shirts, and high leather boots like male pirates would be, scurry into action. They withdraw the gangway and pull up anchor, untying the ropes from the dock. I do not know much about ships, as this is my first time aboard one, so I watch the process with interest.

Beside me, Kintyre and Bevel are huddling close together, whispering and cutting concerned glances at Wyndam and Isobin. Entertained by my family's sudden cowardice, I step aside, grab Wyndam's shoulders, and thrust him toward Isobin.

"Say hello to your mother, lad," I admonish.

"Hello, Mother," Wyndam says. And this time, his voice comes out of his own throat.

The gasp of surprise is out of my lips before I realize I was even going to make the noise. Wyndam's jaw drops wide, and he grabs his throat in shock. Clearly, he expected no sound to emerge from his mouth either. Kintyre and Bevel are at our sides immediately, pawing at Wyndam and talking all over each other, demanding to know what has changed. Demanding to know how this is possible.

"Is it the sea? Some sort of water magic?" Bevel asks. "Because you're on a ship?"

"Some new development has occurred," I say. "But I cannot conjecture what."

"What's the matter?" Isobin asks, perturbed by our obvious upset.

"Wyndam's voice!" I gasp.

"It's slightly lower than when I last saw him," Isobin says slowly, as if we are all great dummies, one corner of her mouth curled upward in preparation for the joke she thinks is about to come, "but I do hear that this is what happens to boys when they become men."

"No, no," I say. "It is not that it has dropped. It is that it's *back*."

"How? Why?" Kintyre demands of me, before Isobin can ask me to elaborate.

"Either the Deal-Maker is dead," I say gravely, and everyone goes silent in shocked contemplation. "Or Pip has traded her something."

None of us want to voice a suggestion as to what that might be.

"I'm sorry, a *Deal-Maker*?" Isobin asks, and just like that, all of her seductive mirth drops away. Kintyre audibly swallows, and he and his son sport identical looks of scared consternation. "I think you have some explanations to give me, Kintyre Turn," Isobin says, face darkening in thunderous anger. "Just what have you been doing with my *son*?"

～～～

The captain's quarters are spacious enough to allow all of us, save Bradri, to sit around the dinner table and talk. Bradri curls up on the deck and sticks her neck through the doorway, her ruff blocking out any eavesdropping. Capplederry has apparently decided that the dragonet is no longer something to spit at and snarl around, and is curled against Bradri's side outside of the room, purring as the great cat naps.

The horses are tied by leads to the mast to keep them from spooking and taking off overboard. In a terribly stereotypical manner, a few of the women of the crew were instantly besotted with them, and linger by Karl and Dauntless, brushing them out, offering water and grain, and re-braiding their manes. Writer, but Elgar Reed has peculiar ideas of what little girls like.

In the cabin, we shed our damp outer clothes, leaving them to steam near a brazier, and avail ourselves of Isobin's warming tea, a hot meal sent up from below decks, and the opportunity to rest. Wyndam sits close by his mother's side, and she pets the nape of his neck as we eat in silence, possessive and delighted to have him back with her.

We are not offered liquor or wine, and none ask for it. We all must be sharp and alert if we're to succeed in the coming battle. And then, slowly, the tale of how and why we came to require *The Salty Queen* is spun into the expectant and sometimes horrified air of the room. For the benefit of Caerdac, Bradri, and Isobin, however, we maintain the fiction that Pip and I had been living somewhere *away*, and not in the Writer's realm.

Ashmarrow Isle is only a few hours' journey from Lymecove and Long Pond Harbor, and when the tale has been told, Kintyre takes his scolding from Isobin quite a bit more shamefacedly and manfully than I had thought he would. Then we are all offered hammocks in which to take some sleep before we must hasten into battle once again.

Caerdac demurs, citing a preference for sleeping tucked up on Bradri's forearm, and Wyndam declares his intent to do the same with Capplederry. Isobin pulls her son aside for a brief private chat first, which ends in a robust chuckle and a pat on the shoulder before she shoves him good-naturedly out the cabin door. The first of his shipboard family descends upon him before he can make it to his target; the bo'sun pulls him into a fierce and sideways hug, startling the boy. As if by magic, there is suddenly a whole gaggle of women around the lad, pinching his cheeks and rubbing his hair affectionately. Wyndam takes the time to kiss each weather-beaten cheek, and lean into every embrace, and firmly shake each offered hand.

As I watch this homecoming, it occurs to me that Wyndam was forced to leave behind more than just his mother when he was sent away. The remainder of his extended family is clearly pleased to see how much he has matured, and to be in his affections once more. I press the back of my hand to my mouth, barring any noises of distress from exiting.

My daughter.

My wife.

I want *my* family back.

When Wyndam manages to shoo the crew back to their posts, he heads to the nose of the deck, where Bradri and Capplederry have arranged themselves in a large, scaly-fluffy, red-and-gold ball of limbs, wings, and tails. When I turn my attention away from the lads and their creatures, I realize that my brother and brother-in-law have scarpered. Kintyre and Bevel are nowhere in the cabin. They had been engaging in some intense nonverbal discussions around the table, even as we related the history of our quest, and I don't doubt that they have slunk off to engage in other nonverbal methods of reassurance and the reclamation of each other's bodies and affection. I have never seen Bevel so insecure of his place with Kintyre, nor have I seen my brother so anxious to convince him.

This leaves only me. The sway of the sea unnerves me, for this is my first time upon a ship, and I do my best to swallow down the mild nausea it evokes, shutting my ears to the whispering rise and fall of waves against the hull. There is so much I wish to speak of with Isobin, so many questions about Wyndam's childhood, about her decision to abandon him on land, about her reaction to Kintyre and Bevel's trothing, but I am so tired I can barely form a sentence. With the urgency momentarily paused, the adrenaline and excitement that had kept me pressing on has been used up, and I am left a trembling, drained husk of myself.

"Well, if there's only one of you, no need to commandeer a hammock," Isobin says, looking me up and down. There is nothing sexual in her gaze, for which I am grateful. She seems, rather, to be concerned in a motherly way. Ah, yes, there is my creator again—the moment women become mothers, they can be nothing else to a man. "You can borrow my bed, if you like."

She points to a section of the cabin that is separated from the rest of the open, low-ceilinged room by a surprisingly beautiful changing screen. The offer is extremely tempting. I can feel my eyelids sinking, my eyes burning with grit, and I cannot seem to stand upright. I am utterly *exhausted*.

But that bed is, most likely, where my nephew was conceived, and *that* does not appeal to me in the *least*. I must make a face, for Isobin laughs and says, "The daybed then, behind my desk. Go on." She waves me toward the great wall of windows that form the back wall of her cabin.

I remain awake just long enough to remove my boots and sword belt, and to wonder if Isobin intends to double-cross us all, or murder us in our sleep. And then I decide I am too tired, and too heart-sore, too saturated with worry for my family, to care. She can murder me all she likes.

"You may choose not to believe me, Forsyth Turn," Isobin murmurs as she douses the lights in the cabin around me. "But trust me when I say that I know how you feel right now. Being without one's children, even if you have separated yourself voluntarily, is draining. Sleep, now."

PLAY

A Deal-Maker Spirit may not deliberately and purposefully kill.

But there is no rule against using an already be-spelled mortal to hold the sword. The Reader stands between Solinde and the small door in the floor of the tower roof, her mewling child whimpering and clutching to her. The Reader is baring a blade that Solinde bid her pick up and use when the first scholar breached the roof and had been scorched immediately by Varnet's defensive spell.

The Reader is weeping, silent and angry, her jaw clenched, but she has no choice but to do as she's bid. Varnet himself is below, reclaiming his Tower from those who had declawed it. Every few moments, there is a scream, and a flash of vibrantly colored light streams from one of the many windows—the burst of a spell. All of the invaders have gone sailing out of those same windows shortly thereafter, their desiccated, smoking, or blood-slick corpses bursting like overripe fruit against the boulders and jagged rocks below; some are even sent in a spiraling arc into the waves, and bashed against the cliff-side with the next surge of the sea. *Most* are even dead when they are defenestrated. Most. But not all.

And now a halo of dead academics litter the ground around the Ivory Tower. Solinde hopes that when Varnet is done, he will summon carrion birds—for she cannot stand the smell of rotting flesh. And once the bones are stripped, they will be useful in spell-working. Solinde fancies that she'd like a bit of a skeleton personal guard. That would be lovely.

As she waits for her son to finish his extermination, Solinde amuses herself by cooing at the babe and trying to entice it to come to her. As much as Varnet was correct in his suggestion that they eradicate the whole of the Turn lineage, it seems a pity to waste Reader blood and power, no matter what it is diluted with. The motherly part of Solinde quails at the thought of exterminating a child who could be raised to know and think better, think *correctly*. A child who, if taken away from its heathen and savage home and raised properly, taught rightly, could become an integrated and useful member of Solinde and Varnet's family.

If for no other reason than to fold more Reader blood into the resultant great-grandchild, should Varnet and the Reader's union produce a male child and they allow him to get offspring on this babe.

It all seems quite tidy, and for now, Solinde is content to cat about with the mouse-child, basking in the warmth of the new day that is dawning over the wild whip of the Mooncall Sea.

TWENTY

Wyndam shakes me awake at dawn.

"We've gotten as close to the Isle as we can go, Uncle Forsyth," he says, his voice low, as if he fears the Deal-Maker will hear. I blink, marvel at the joy the sound of his voice brings me, and then realize it was the title that put the smile on my face, though it is still nice to hear my nephew speak.

"Say that again," I request as I sit up, scuffing a hand through my unruly hair.

"We've gotten as—"

"No, the last bit. Please."

Wyndam smirks at me. "Uncle Forsyth."

"Hmm," I hum, reaching for my boots. "Dear me. How pleasant a thing to hear. Pass me my belt please, nephew."

Wyndam does so, and I use the opportunity to observe him. He looks *better*. Whether it is that the gash in his abdomen has finally begun to heal, or that the sleep has done him good, or that he is reunited with his mother and back at sea, I cannot pinpoint. Perhaps it is simply because he has regained his voice. Perhaps it is all of it. At any rate, he is holding himself straighter, his shoulders more relaxed, an easy smile lingering around his lips just as it does on Isobin. Even the way he walks looks more natural, more comfortable. I realize suddenly that the slight awkwardness in his gait that I had attributed to puberty or a growth spurt is, in fact, because the lad learned to walk at sea. Here, on the ship, his gait is smooth and rolling, and reminds me very much of the rocking, circular, acrobatic method of his fighting.

I long, suddenly, to watch him at his sword practice while aboard a ship. His technique must *use* the sway of the deck in a way that I, with my rigidly formal court-fencing education, cannot fathom. The moment I stand, I realize *why* we have made anchor where we have. The floor is pitching and rolling so much that I am immediately unbalanced and must clutch at Isobin's desk to remain upright.

Wyndam laughs, the snide little wretch, and waits for me by the door as I stagger my way toward him. Together, we exit onto the deck. I am the last to arrive, I see. Everyone else, even Capplederry, is arrayed along the right side of the rails—is that starboard or port?—staring up at Ashmarrow Isle.

Behind us, the sun crawls above the horizon, painting the soft clouds and thick white mist shrouding the cliffbase a bloody red. Before us, the sky is overcast but not storming, and the waves churn in an unnatural tumble against the broken rock. If I were not sure the Deal-Maker was on that island, I would have proof of it in the perversion of the sea's natural rhythms.

The Ivory Tower is just visible, a shadowy finger thrust accusingly upward, polished-bone white and dry. We cannot make out anything in the windows, or amid the slope of rocky ground around it. The Tower sits on the highest-most wedge of a triangular spit of gray stone, barren of all life save moss, old seaweed, and the odd, wizened bit of scrub brush. At the narrowest edge of the wedge, it dips down under the water into a natural causeway, and continues on down, I assume, to the seabed.

It is to this point that we paddle our slim, tippy little catboat. Wyndam and Isobin navigate, confident, while Kintyre, Bevel, and I crowd in the middle, feet wet as we attempt to stay still to avoid capsizing us. Capplederry must remain behind, and the cat's pitiful mewls followed us all the way to the catboat. It had stuck its head over the rail, sniffed and flattened its ears at us, unhappy that we were going away.

I tried to convince Bradri and Caerdac to remain behind as well, but they refused. Whether it was because they were worried deeply about Alis, or because they naively wanted to experience the "glory" of battle, or perhaps because of the strange new way Caerdac can't seem to keep his eyes off of Wyndam, I am not certain. I did manage, at least, to convince the pair to wait until the second catboat of pirates paddled their way to the isle before they took to the skies to be our backup. They would do well with a dragonet as a lookout, especially since the plan was that they would sail up after we had already made the advance attack, in order to further scramble and divide whatever defences the Deal-Maker may have had the chance to re-enchant.

I was well surprised when a goodly number of the crew volunteered their swords for this rescue mission, and I think much of their willingness came from the way Wyndam spoke of his Aunt Pip and Cousin Alis, the genuine respect he parlayed in his plea for volunteers, the courage he painted Pip as having, and the intelligence. Here was a whole ship of women used to being over-looked and talked-down to simply because of what was between their legs; of course they were incensed at another like them being held captive against her will.

The scrape of the boat's bottom against the rock is loud, screechingly loud, in my ears, and I wince. Bevel winces at the volume of the noise as well, but Kintyre is staring ahead, on the lookout to see if our arrival was noticed. We all hold our breath, waiting... waiting...

"Nothing," Isobin whispers. "Out."

We climb out, carefully. She and Wyndam heft the boat between them, and carry it far enough inland that it won't float away before they set it down again. It is an impressive display of stealth and strength, and Bevel pinches Kintyre's thigh when he catches his trothed admiring Isobin's biceps.

Kintyre offers his love an unashamed eyebrow waggle, and Bevel rolls his eyes and shakes his head once. And then they are both focused once more on the business at hand. I do my very best to ignore the lovebites I can see on their necks.

Together, we begin our slow walk to the tower, doing our best to remain in the mist and the shadow of the rock formations. I strain to hear anything over the crash of waves, and catch, briefly, what might be the leathery snap of a dragon-wing against the air. Good, Bradri and Caerdac are aloft. Our support is on its way. It's time to storm the tower.

Kintyre draws Foesmiter, and even in the red gloom, the enchanted sword seems to glow with a golden, pure light. It is eager, I think, to taste blood again. Bevel has forgone his bow and arrow for his own sword, and the rest of us draw with him. Then, swift and quiet, we race for the door.

It is Wyndam who sees them first. He is fleet of foot, being younger than us, and faster, and it is his sudden, startled leap that makes the rest of us skid to a stop. And I am glad I did, for right before me is the severed, mushy remains of a hand. Possibly human, but it is hard to tell with the flesh blackened and peeled away like the skin of a baked potato.

I gulp back a retch.

We pick our way through the field of scattered corpses, and I am fervently thankful that Saetesh was not among the scholars who were currently studying in the Ivory Tower. And I mourn for the lives lost here, lives that had been dedicated to the pursuits of understanding and wisdom. A horrific shame, this, and a horrific loss.

The front door of the tower is unlocked, and I am not certain if I should take this as a sign of boasting confidence from the Deal-Maker, or thoughtless neglect. Either way, it inspires no confidence in me; she clearly did not think the front door was even worth *checking*. So what horrors and blocks await us, more terrible and difficult to pass than a locked door?

Kintyre goes first, checking around corners and in shadows, followed by Bevel, then me, and Isobin. Wyndam guards our backs. The Ivory Tower is not large. The whole footprint takes up no more space than, perhaps, our home in Victoria. The foyer is bare of any decoration or life, and contains only a single room to one side, and a spiral staircase that leads both upward, and down into the dank dungeon the Shadow's Men had told me contained a summoning chamber and many torture devices. On the second landing, we pass by the room they had found Pip in, a luxurious prison that makes a mockery of comfort. By their reports, each story holds only one room—a library, a spell-work chamber, and what might have been small personal apartments.

Even so, there are too many rooms to search, and I hesitate to suggest that we split up, but with six of us, and seven stories... but then Bevel tugs on Kintyre's sleeve and gestures upward with a jerk of his chin. At first, I think it is because he has a hunch, but then I hear it—the insubstantial, ringing echo of laughter.

"The roof," Kintyre whispers, and Bevel nods.

And then we are racing for the stairs. We move as

quickly as stealth allows, and I fear the ring of our boots on the stone is loud enough to warn the Deal-Maker of our approach. We encounter no monsters, though, no booby traps, no spells, and I am grateful to those dead scholars that our path is clear.

Kintyre hesitates at the top only long enough to poke his head up through the hatch, and then drops back down immediately, face bloodless and lips tight.

"The Viceroy," he hisses.

Bevel scowls and holds up his hand, fingers splayed. We attack in five... four... three... two...

Kintyre roars—a startling, unexpected sound—as he bursts up through the hatch. Above my head, I hear Alis scream in fright. Kintyre leaps up onto the roof, Bevel at his heels. I am too slow, and press back against the wall to allow Isobin and Wyndam to jump into the fray before me. Then I scramble out of the hatch, sword clutched in my hand, and blink rapidly to adjust my eyes to the sudden brightness of daylight above the fog.

The roof is wide, circular, and cupped in a waist-high wall with jagged toothy battlements.

Near the center, Kintyre is already engaged in a hand-to-hand grapple with the Viceroy, and Bevel is nearby, waiting for the perfect moment to either spring in and aid Kintyre or run the villain through. Behind them, Alis is dangling by her arm from the Deal-Maker's grip, writhing and wailing. Isobin has confronted the Spirit, sword bare and waiting.

And beside her, Pip stands frozen, emanating a green glow.

But *alive*.

I feel relief surge in my chest, and I sigh. I am not too late. Not yet. But alive does not mean free. The green glow, the writhing of the scars under her skin, it is all sickeningly familiar. The Viceroy's compulsion spell, written on Pip's bones and impossible to eradicate, has ensnared her once again. And more the fool I, for not realizing that even with the spell buried so far beneath her flesh, she was still vulnerable, still susceptible to it for as long as it exists.

You spectacular idiot, Forsyth, *I scold myself. You should have insisted upon visiting a mage to have it lifted before we ever began this quest!*

The Viceroy struggles away from Kintyre and lurches against the wall of the tower. He throws a spell at the ground below, and the smell of sulfur and rotting flesh bursts through the air. There is a roar from the pirates, the great annoyed screech of a dragon, and someone shouts, "The corpses! They're coming to life! Use fire! Use *fire!*"

Kintyre grabs the Viceroy by the shoulder, sword lifted to run him through, but the monster slides free, the tatters of his clothing ripping in Kintyre's fist, and makes an elaborate gesture at Pip. Pip jerks and snarls, but she cannot fight the compulsion of the vine-spell. She lifts her arm, and I see, just in time, that she holds a sword. I bring my own down on it hard, before it can stab my brother in the back, and it clatters away across the roof.

"Pip!" I implore my wife. "Please! Fight it!"

"She cannot!" Solinde snarls at me.

I reach out to grab Pip, but her hands raise as if to throttle me, and I dance back, horrified. Agony is etched in her expression, agony and sorrow. Tear stains track down her cheeks. How long has she been trapped inside her own unresponsive body? How long has she been screaming, silently? How awful. How *horrific.*

And then I realize why I have not seen Wyndam in the midst of the melee. He springs up over the edge of the wall, nimble as a cat, and comes down hard in a whirl around the Deal-Maker. His aim is to rescue Alis, I can tell, but Pip is compelled to twist around, grab him around the waist, and haul him away. He is reluctant, as I am, to harm her in order to get at the Deal-Maker, and backs off.

"Tut-tut!" the Deal-Marker snarls at him. "How rude!"

"Have pity!" Isobin pleads. "Let the child alone."

"Pity!" the Deal-Maker spits. "And who had pity on my child? Who pitied *me* when he was stolen away?"

"Please, I understand what it's like to be separated from your baby. So do you!" she says. "Don't pass that pain onto another mother."

"And what would you know? You were the one who abandoned your son," the Deal-Maker sneers. Isobin startles. "Oh, yes! I know who you are, Pirate Queen! And I know now who this Turn whelp is. He is your Prince of the Seas! I know now that I was summoned to Deal on sailor's lore, and I know what you did! Turning your son off your ship, stranding him away from life-giving *water*! It is you who is the monster, not I!"

Isobin's face twists, and clearly the accusation has hit closer to the center of her own pain than she expected. "Being a mother means doing what's best for your child, even if it breaks your heart. *Especially* if it breaks your heart!" Isobin snarls, blade flashing, and behind her, I see Wyndam's usually smooth acrobatics hitch. He stumbles, surprised, I think, to hear his mother speak of a broken heart, when, all this time, I am sure he has been questioning whether she has one at all.

Solinde dances away, and cuts another arcane gesture into the air. Pip jerks violently, back arching, eyes and mouth opened wide in a silent scream.

"No!" I cry, hurtling myself at the Deal-Maker. "Not again!" A spell of some sort slams into my chest, and I am tossed through the sky, landing hard on my back at the very edge of the Tower. My stomach is driven against my spine, all the air punching out of my lungs. I do not even have enough to yelp.

When I finally manage to catch my breath and scrabble upright, stars dancing in my vision, it is to find Pip standing between the Deal-Maker and the Viceroy. Green-eyed and stiff, her terrible non-expression is tight with horror. In the Deal-Maker's cruel hands, Alis dangles and kicks, squirming and screaming.

Isobin, Wyndam, Kintyre, and Bevel are arrayed before me, a protective wall. Kintyre adjusts his stance, Foesmiter coming up, the tip pointed at the Spirit's head. My breath catches in my throat, for if Kintyre is forced to defend himself against the Deal-Maker, I do not trust that his usual bashing, hacking swordplay style will spare my child.

"Well now," the Viceroy pants, grinning in sharkish glee. "This is a tidy little conclusion, isn't it? I have my freedom, I have my puppet back, and my mother is finally freed of her geis. And she has the grandchild she's always wanted."

He reaches out and rubs his hand gently, fatherly, through Alis's hair. Alis howls, "Ma, maaaa!" She reaches for the comfort of Pip. She wants to be held close, to be soothed and protected, and Pip cannot do that for her. It is killing both of her parents that neither of us can provide what Alis so obviously and desperately wants.

"*Why?*" Wyndam croaks, overwrought and on edge.

I struggle to my feet, lurching toward my family. Bevel is suddenly in front of me, blocking my path, but it is unnecessary. I am numb with horror, my tongue fluttering in my mouth, trying to find the words, trying to find a way to talk us out of this, to fix it, and I can't, I can't. I have nothing. My mind is empty. There are no solutions. Only dead-end pathways.

We have *lost*.

"Why take Aunt Pip? Why steal Alis?" Wyndam demands again.

The Deal-Maker grins in triumph, pleased with our sorrow. Her black tongue lashes against teeth that grow ever more sharp the more pleased she becomes. Her black eyes flash with glee. "Enough people have taken that which my son deserves! He was stolen from me, but he persevered! He worked hard under the aegis of his master. He rose to a position of great power! But your King Carvel *feared* him, *banished* him, took away all that he had *earned*. And then sent *this monster* to execute him!"

She swings her arm toward Kintyre, and my brother is blown back hard. He crashes into the bone floor, skidding until he slams into the wall, shoulder-first. Kintyre grunts and curls in around his arm, and unlike me, he has the very good sense to stay down.

"This child should have been his!" the Deal-Maker snarls. "A Reader! A *Reader*. So powerful a creature and he did not claim her for his own! He should have." She turns and gazes fondly at the Viceroy—dirty, mostly naked, wan and wild with anger and bloodlust. He hardly resembles the clever, smooth monster I knew from my days as Shadow Hand, or the wildly unpredictable yet charming madman in Bevel's scrolls. But the Deal-Maker clearly only sees her sweet babe. "My dear, impulsive boy," she says fondly, voice dripping with acid and affection. "He lacks the guidance of a mother, but now I have him, and we have you *both*."

She looks up, eyes boring into my own, accusatory, like I, as Alis's father, must therefore stand in for all failed fathers the world over.

"I'm... not a... trophy!" Pip snarls suddenly, every word a fight for her. "You... can't just—"

"But I can!" the Viceroy coos into her ear. He makes a complicated gesture with his left hand and... Writer, *no*.

Pip stiffens with horror, arching her back as if trying to writhe away from her own flesh. She is too clothed for me to see her scars, all save one—the little leaf below her ear, my favorite place to kiss her. It has begun to flutter as if it is a real leaf, dancing in the wind of the Viceroy's growing power, and glowing an ever stronger acidic green.

"Say your fare wells, Lucy Piper," the Viceroy says, mouth right against her ear. I want to vomit. I want to punch the monster in the teeth. Not because he is infringing on what is mine, but because Pip is so very frightened. She has confessed to me, more than once, that she has had nightmares about this very scenario—that we had lost that first time, that the Viceroy had stolen her away, forced her to love him, and... and now, her nightmares are playing out. She has spent countless hours with her therapist on this very thing. My anger is for the terror Pip is experiencing, for the sure knowledge that she would kill herself before she let him steal her mind away from her. "For you will never again see these wretched Turns. I am going to kill them now. One by one."

I cannot breathe. I cannot *breathe*. We have *lost*, we have lost. My daughter will live and grow to be an evil thing, my wife will be a slave, or a corpse by her own hand, and I cannot, I am not good enough. I am not *powerful* enough. I am no hero; I am barely a scholar anymore. I am not the Shadow Hand. I have nothing. I am nothing.

And I cannot save them.

"No," Pip moans. "No, no, no. No, I... am a... Reader! And I... *I decide how this is interpreted!* I have power here. I have... I have..."

The Viceroy laughs. "Power? If you had any power, Lucy Piper, you would have used it against me long ago.

You have nothing." He tucks his hand under her chin and turns her face to his, uncomfortable and intimate.

"No," Pip disagrees, clenching her teeth. Though it is a straining effort, though it makes the tendons in her neck stand out, and sweat bead on her upper lip, she *shakes her head.*

"What?" the Viceroy snarls, taking a step back in his shock, raising his green-laced hand. "Stop."

"No! No, I"—Pip looks at Alis with tears in her eyes, the desperate sorrow in them tearing my heart straight out of my chest, stealing all my breath—"I... am a... Reader! I am a Reader... and that is my power! I love... books. I *love* stories. I am a Reader, and I love passionately, with an open heart, and I know, I know, I *know* that *this is not how they end*!"

She is writhing now, and I resist the urge to shout and cheer my wife on, bite my tongue and watch her fight with hope growing in the hollow of my despair. My fists are clenched, my body straining toward her, thinking, projecting: *Fight, fight, bao bei! Fight!*

"I am—" Pip gasps, gags, twists. "I am... I am the little girl who loved *The Wizard of Oz* so much she painted herself green on the first day of school." Pip sobs, her tears falling in rivers down her cheeks, eyes wide and darting, then latching onto mine, desperate and begging. "I am the child who grew up wanting to travel into other realms, to be the hero like the boys. I am the girl who cries when she thinks of the Library of Alexandria. I... Oh. Oh god... Forsyth!" she chokes. "I... remember! The books, I... I remember... the stories..." She clutches the sides of her head and groans, crumbling to her knees.

"No!" the Viceroy shrieks, hand flailing in that magical pattern that has no hold over Pip any longer. "No, no!"

"I am a hero!" Pip snarls, staring up at him from the

bone floor, eyes brown. "I am the hero, and you are the villain, and *you don't get to win!*"

The spell. The spell is broken. And she did it *of her own will.*

Pip has often said that she needs no prince charming to rescue her, that she can rescue herself. And now she *has.*

She snatches up my dropped sword and hacks at the Viceroy. He dances backward, a split appearing across his chest, an upward slash that immediately begins to bloom red.

"Bitch!" he howls.

Pip lunges again, pushing up off her knees, swinging wildly and screaming like a madwoman. "I am the damsel who *rescues herself!*"

"Varnet!" the Deal-Maker wails, and I see what she means to do a split second before she does it. I am too far away to do anything about it, though I push off and dash toward her as fast as I can.

The Deal-Maker drops Alis.

She tumbles to the ground, lands hard on her bottom, her head snapping against the floor. For a breathless second, I fear she is dead. But Alis immediately jerks and screams, and before she can make it to her feet, I have swooped in and gathered her up, turned on my heel, dashed back, and pressed myself as far back against the opposite wall as I can.

I want to fight.

But I want Alis *away* from the fight more. I turn back around and watch, ready to flee or kick or Speak what Words I can, if necessary. I run my hands over her head, her back, her arms, checking for breaks, for blood, and soothing Alis as best I can with my warmth, my scent, my nearness. She sobs and hiccoughs in my ear, shaken, terrified, but whole.

I spare a moment to look down at the battle raging below us. My attention is caught by the spurts of dragon-flame that are burning off the mist in ragged chunks.

"Bradri!" I scream, and another great gout of fire is followed by an acknowledging screech and the snap of leather against the wind. "The hatchling!"

It breaks my heart that I must let go of Alis so soon after getting her back, but Isobin was right. A parent does what's best for their children. Not what they *want*.

In an instant, Bradri, with Caerdac on her back, has scaled the Tower, claws digging into the great bones of her own kind. Caerdac has his hands out, and I shove Alis at him the moment he is close enough. My baby screams again, exhausted and terrified. With another snap of leathery wings—and the whip of a razor-spined tail that I must duck to avoid—dragon, rogue, and child are sailing across the water toward the safe haven of *The Salty Queen*.

Of course, it will only *remain* safe if the Deal-Maker has no opportunity to raise a storm—or worse, a sea monster.

While I have been occupied with getting Alis to safety, Kintyre and Bevel have been engaged in a swordfight with the Deal-Maker. Wyndam and Isobin are squared off against the Viceroy, clearly hoping to distract him long enough for Pip to recover herself and flee. She is leaning now on Isobin, panting and wrecked, half shielded by the pirate queen's body.

And Wyndam is doing his best to keep himself between them. The Viceroy smirks, just one small pull against the corner of his mouth, and then he is moving. He ducks around Wyndam, and snatches the dagger out of the sheath at the small of his back, skids around the women and turns sharp on his toes, the knife raised over his head.

The Viceroy means to plunge it into the back of my wife's neck.

"Pip!" I shout, but my voice is lost beneath the Viceroy's howl of rage.

415

TWENTY-ONE

Wyndam gets there first, thank the Writer, and intercepts. The dagger clangs off his sword. Pip pushes Isobin out of the way of the rebound strike and lunges. The Viceroy, still weakened from his ordeal and now off balance, misses his swing and goes down hard on the floor. His head makes a thick crack sound. Pip lands hard on his chest, but he bucks her off. She rolls to the side, the momentum flipping her over and over. The Viceroy scrabbles to his feet.

He is knocked right back down by Wyndam's well-placed kick to the back of his head. He slams face-first into the stone, and the crunch of his nose is loud even with the thunder churning overhead. Wyndam swings his foot down to land in the exact center of the Viceroy's back, and the villain howls.

The Deal-Maker, overcome with fatigue and grief, crumbles where she is, despite grappling with Kintyre, and falls to her knees.

"Spare him!" she begs, as Wyndam rests his curved sword against the Viceroy's neck. "Spare him, please!"

"Why should I?" Wyndam snarls. "Your son is the source of every evil in my life! If it wasn't for him, my mother would never have met Kintyre Turn! If it wasn't for him, I wouldn't have wanted to adventure with my father so badly, would never have made this Deal with you, or lost my voice, or put my uncle and his family through so much torment! If it wasn't for him, you would never have walked the world and stirred up those Red Caps, or made Lanaea's father send her away. If it wasn't for him, *she would be alive right now!* So give me *one good reason!*"

The Deal-Maker presses her hands against her breast, folds her fingers, pleads even as the tears run out of her eyes, and jewel-blue blood runs out of her wounds.

"I love him," the Deal-Maker whispers. "Please. He is my son."

"He is *evil!*" Wyndam reposts.

The Deal-Maker hiccoughs a soft, sad sob. "And yet, he is still my son."

Pip, limping, goes to Wyndam and puts her hand on his shoulder.

"Do you want to kill him?" she asks, weary. Sore. Done.

"Yes!" my nephew yells. "Yes!"

"And when he's dead, will you be able to sleep? Will you be able to live the rest of your life happily, knowing that you have killed him?"

Wyndam presses his sword closer, nicking the villain's filthy skin, and a bright red pearl wells up against the steel. "Yes!"

Pip releases his shoulder. "Then be my guest."

The Deal-Maker howls, and Kintyre is forced to grab a handful of her hair to keep her from throwing herself between Wyndam and the Viceroy. Wyndam swings his arm back, clearly aiming for a decapitating blow. He lets it drop, and then... halts.

He hesitates. He draws back again, but now his sword is shaking.

"I..." he says, grinding his teeth, snarling, frustrated. "I... I can't..."

"The difference between heroes and villains, Wyndam, is what you do when someone is at your mercy," Pip says softly. "It's okay to not kill him. It just means you're the good guy."

"But they killed Lanaea!"

"They have killed many people," Pip says. "Will you add bodies to that pile, too?"

Wyndam drops his sword to his side, arches back, clenches his fist, and screams at the sky.

Above him, as if terrified of his rage, his newly returned ability to make *noise*, to *be heard*, the storm boils and thunders, and then shrivels up and evaporates. The Deal-Maker collapses onto her side at Kintyre's feet.

Pip limps over to him, and holds out her hand. Kintyre deposits the phial of Deal-Maker blood in her palm. She kicks the Deal-Maker, forcing the witch onto her back so she can meet her eyes, and then cleverly steps back, staying out of grabbing range. I finally feel it safe enough to edge closer.

"I was willing to Deal with you. Squarely. *Fairly*," Pip snarls, absolutely no-nonsense. "And now, I will force it on you." She lifts the phial of Deal-Maker blood. The Deal-Maker's eyes widen with dismay. "So here is the Deal you are going to *take*. You and your bouncing baby boy will be stripped of all magic in this world, and you are going to promise me that you will return to the farm where he was born. You will live a quiet life there, together, where you will harm no one ever again, either by intent or by accident. You, Deal-Maker, will be fully human, and fully mortal. And you, Viceroy, will never again have access to the magic in your blood."

"And in return... you will make my final act as a Spirit to sacrifice all that I am to return you to your world?" the Deal-Maker sneers.

"You know what?" Pip says. "I don't actually trust

you to keep that Deal. Especially since we're not exactly your favorite people right now. Forsyth and I will find a different way back. Or, failing that, we'll bargain with a Deal-Maker who isn't a total cunt."

"What are you asking for in return, then?" the Deal-Maker snarls.

"In return? You get to keep your lives." Pip looks pointedly over her shoulder at Wyndam and Kintyre. Father and son have never looked so much alike as they do now, with their swords and teeth still bared.

"You are being too compassionate," Kintyre says.

"Maybe," Pip says. "But this is a vicious circle in these books. There's been enough violence. Enough dead people, don't you think? I'm offering you a chance for redemption, Varnet. And I'm offering you, Deal-Maker, exactly what you've been wishing for—the rest of your life with your son."

The Deal-Maker is silent, staring. Her expression is filled with hunger and resentment in equal measure. And then, slowly, just once, she nods.

Pip reaches down and shakes her hand.

As soon as her hand is released, the Deal-Maker and the Viceroy vanish. And with their disappearance, the Deal-Maker blood in the phial boils away. Pip uncaps it swiftly, and a small puff of swirling blue steam glitters and winks in the weak sunlight before it evaporates entirely.

Pip stumbles backward, surprised.

"Did it work?" Wyndam asks. "Do you think it worked the way you wanted it to?"

Pip nods grimly. "It has to. I believe it has to."

"Why?"

Pip turns to him. "Because we are the family of Kintyre Turn. We are the heroes. And heroes always win."

Wyndam's posture relaxes, and he lets a small smile

curl over the corner of his mouth. "I hope you're right, Aunt Pip."

Pip grins back at the honorific. "I hope I'm right too, Nephew Wyndam."

We all slump and curl in on our hurts now that the danger has passed. Isobin goes immediately to check on the small gash on her son's temple. Hands shake as the leftover adrenaline burns off, fingers are flexed, eyes scrubbed. Gusty sighs ring out through the tower as we all, nearly as one, yawn. It is like a glass of cold beer, this frothy, intoxicating sensation of *relief*. From below, there comes a great cheer of victory from the crew of *The Salty Queen*.

Even the sea is calm, smooth as the surface of a looking glass, and just as quiet. Sunlight sparks off the few remaining ripples, throwing up diamonds.

But we still have to make our way down the tower. And back onto the ship. And then all the way back to Lysse. Blast and drat. Even the *thought* of moving exhausts me. But I make myself move, anyway.

I move just enough to curl myself around my wife. My beautiful, strong, incredible, clever wife.

My wife, who lifts her face and smashes her mouth against mine, kissing me like she could swallow me whole, pull me into her, hide me forever within the space between her heartbeats. And I kiss her back in such a way as to say that I would welcome it.

"You're safe," I moan against her lips as we catch sips of air. "You're *here*."

"Shhh, *bao bei*," she soothes, petting my hair. "I'm here."

"I was so scared," I sob, and suddenly I am crying, clinging to her, dropping to my knees and burying my head against her stomach, weeping with relief and burning-off terror.

"Me too, *bao bei*," she says, and crouches, pressing herself into the space between my thighs, under the warm shelter of my arms, protected by the canopy of my torso. "God, I thought I'd never see you again. I thought I'd have to... to *kill* myself, to keep him from... I love you. I love you!"

"I love you, too," I whisper.

And while my wife and I reassure one another, I trust my brother and brother-in-law, my nephew, and his mother to keep watch over us. I trust my family to care for us as we celebrate, and comfort one another.

≈≈≈

Another hour sees us all safely back aboard *The Salty Queen* and sailing north, toward the Icedance Sea. The pack ice will be breaking up soon, and it will only take us a week to sail around the northeast passage, stop in Erlenmeyer to resupply, and make port at the very small sliver of land in Lysse where our Chipping abuts the Sunsong Sea. From there, we will dispatch someone to fetch the cart out of the Stoat Forest, if it is even still there to fetch.

Isobin's first mate willingly gives up her cabin for Alis, Pip, and I, and we share a warm, tear-filled and sleep-framed reunion. Caerdac and Bradri keep to the deck, with Wyndam and Capplederry. The bo'sun informs me the next day, when my little family emerges in search of food and what Pip gamely calls an after-action debrief, that Kintyre and Bevel disappeared somewhere below decks yesterday, and haven't been seen since.

"Though," she informs me with a salacious smirk, "we 'eard an awful lot of bellowin' and gruntin' down by the powder storage, didn't we, wenches?" A bawdy roar of agreement rings along the deck.

I pinch the bridge of my nose, hold up the hand that

doesn't have Alis tucked pliant and sweet against my ribs, and say, "And that is the precise limit of what I need to know."

The bo'sun laughs, tosses hair the color of carrots over her shoulders, and saunters away to share her saucy gossip with the pilot.

Our group slowly congregates in the captain's cabin over the course of the afternoon. First Pip, Alis, and I arrive to find Wyndam already seated with his mother on the daybed, chatting affectionately. Kintyre and Bevel follow in after the food when the cook brings it in. Word is sent to Caerdac and Bradri, who promise to come as soon as the dragon has finished washing away the blood on her scales.

We are picking at our mostly empty plates and indulging in Isobin's fine, pilfered Brystalian wine and crisp Gadotian ale, when Kintyre asks, "So, what do we do now? What can we do, I mean? About..." He gestures between Pip and I, and it is clear that he means to ask how we intend to return to the Writer's realm with no Deal-Maker blood to strengthen a Deal enough to do it.

"Nothing," I admit, and the words are ashen in my defeat. "Absolutely nothing."

"So, what will *you* do, then?" Bevel asks. He is tucked as close to Kintyre as he can be, and while I can see that Isobin is amused by it, that she thinks he is being jealous of Kintyre's attention and demonstrative in his claim, thinks that Bevel is unnerved by *her*, Bevel's unease actually stems from how close we came to losing Alis. Though I often compare Bevel to a bulldog or a hedgehog, when it comes to children and families, he is rather more like a dragon.

"Now?" I say. "Now, we return to Lysse and research more Deal-Makers, I suppose."

"And sleep," Pip adds. "I am so done. I personally

would like to sleep for at least about, oh, another *week* before we start on another adventure."

"Another adventure?" I tease, pulling her close against me and relishing the feel of my whole family in my arms. Pressed between our chests, Alis is still and soft, radiating happiness and clutching at both of our collars. "Surely it will only be the denouement of this one."

"I'm never sure anymore," Pip says into my neck, her free arm slipping around my waist to hold me tight. "Even the Excel didn't really help this time. So much for my hundred thousand dollar education. What a waste of wealth."

"Your *what?*" Isobin asks, startled.

"It means... well, a hundred dollars is roughly equivalent to a gold coin, so it... it's quite... er... *expensive*," I finish, lamely.

"For an *education?*" Kintyre boggles. "Sister-in-law, what is it that you are trained to do that is so *dear?*"

"Well, ah, it's kind of like, um, what Forsyth did, but on a... you know what? Never mind," Pip says. "Let's just say I paid a lot to be a clever clogs."

"Very well," Kintyre acquiesces, and with no little reluctance.

"But did you get to *choose* it?" Wyndam blurts suddenly. He has been mostly silent until now, packing away what food he could get his hands on and gazing longingly at the ale when he thought no one else was looking.

Pip swings to face him, blinking, startled. "Of course I did," she says, sounding baffled. "Why would I pay so much for something I didn't enjoy?"

Wyndam looks down at his plate and marshals a few remaining crumbs into a regimented line with the tip of his knife instead of answering. A thoughtful, resentful sneer in the corner of my nephew's mouth as he ponders over what he wants to say reminds me, startlingly and wholly, of my father.

"Come now. Out with it then, lad," Kintyre says gruffly.

Wyndam starts, looks up and around at all of us waiting for him, and then clears his throat. He is, of course, out of practice at speaking, and his voice makes several crackling noises that might have embarrassed him if he was less eager to say his piece. All this time, I had imagined my nephew would have the same deep baritone voice as his father, but it is more in the tenor range. And his accent and cadence is definitely like that of his mother.

"Not sure I should say anything," he mutters at length, after several grunts and grumbles. "Won't much matter, I don't think."

We adults exchange glances around the cabin.

"We're glad to have you be part of the conversation again, Wyn," Bevel says, clapping the boy on the shoulder. "Don't mute yourself now."

Bevel hands Wyndam a cup of ale and bids him to drink up. It is a solemn gesture of import—Bevel is making a point of offering Wyndam the alcohol, of treating him as a man, after his adventure. It is a deliberate show of considering Wyndam an adult. And thus, an invitation for Wyndam to speak his piece equally. It is the kind of subtle cleverness in emotional manipulation in which my brother-in-law is so excellent, and yet he is so oblivious to his own prowess. Just as Elgar Reed wrote me as the consummate spy, he wrote Bevel as the ultimate diplomat. He has to be, as Kintyre's walking apology. No one else would be so fine a match for my brother.

The ale finished, Wyndam visibly girds his loins and says: "As long as you actually *are* listening to my part of it, old man." He is trying to make light of it, to fracture his own tension with laughter. Bevel chuckles obligingly. Good. For all that my brother-in-law has always been quietly desperate for a baby, I think Wyndam has always been desperate for a father. And in Kintyre's absent and casual affection, he has genuinely tried to find one in Bevel.

"Yes, er, about that..." Kintyre begins.

"Didn't ask you, Kin," Bevel interrupts his trothed. Kintyre snaps his mouth shut. He huffs, then quaffs his own ale mutinously. Well, now, it seems that with Bevel's talent for handling pouty Turns, I should be glad he never deemed my foul moods worthy of his attention.

"It's just that... well, did anyone bother to ask me what I wanted?" Wyndam grouses to us all. "That's what I wanted to say. Aunt Pip is a *woman*, and she got to spend all her money on an education that probably a lot of folk might say she got no right to. But I was a prince! And I didn't get no say at all!"

Isobin draws herself up, taking a breath to argue, but I hold my palm up from the table, a subtle and small gesture that she nevertheless catches; a quiet plea not to interrupt Wyndam. We must hear him out.

"No. Ma wanted me to be a landed noble, when I used to be a *prince*," Wyndam says, arms thrown skyward, exasperation flooding out of him, along with the crashing waters of his long-damned confession. "Father wants me to be Lordling Turn, and I don't know nothing about it, or why it even matters! Bevel wants me to be a son and child for him, when I'm seventeen already. Pointe wants me to be Sheriff! Aunt Pip can do anything she wants, but I'm a man, and I'm a Turn, and I'm a lordling *and* a prince, and I still don't got a say at all! Uncle Forsyth is right—you've all just treated me like a convenient prop! What about what *I* desire? What about—"

"Well, then," Bevel interrupts, striking at the heart of the matter. "What *is* it that you desire?"

Wyndam blinks at him, his tirade cut short by the straightforward inquiry. The wind goes out of his sails, and he slumps in his seat, the anger-induced flush retreating from his cheeks.

"I... miss being the Prince of Pirates," Wyndam says softly, swallowing his words in his sudden shyness, embarrassed that he must be so *blunt*, so *honest*, in front of so many.

"But you cannot," I say softly, and they look up at me. Wyndam gestures for me to go on. "Queen Isobin allows only women on her ships. Unless you care to unman yourself?" I ask archly, trying to bring the conversation back around to humor to give my nephew the opportunity to regroup.

"No!" the lad protests, covering his crotch hastily, as if fearing I would descend upon him immediately with a pair of garden shears. "No."

"You *could* still go back to sea, if you miss it," I say. "If you choose to go as Wyndam Turn. I know the king could be talked into commissioning you. Or, if you prefer to go as the Pirate Prince, I know there would also be those lads who long for a life of adventure on the high seas, and who would help you man the first ship of male pirates." I frown meaningfully. "Not that I approve of that sort of behavior, of course."

"I don't want him on the water," Isobin says, voice rough. "It's too dangerous."

"But surely it's *his* choice," I counter gently. "And he has more than proven himself in battle."

Isobin looks away, chewing on her bottom lip.

Wyndam shrugs, temporarily and voluntarily voiceless in his desire to not contradict her. But the silence strings out as we wait for him to find his words. He has demanded to be given space for his voice. We are giving it.

"I don't know if I really want to go back to sea," he says at length. "It's just that... my opinion hasn't mattered."

"I suppose there wasn't much consulting with you in regards to your own wishes," Isobin says at length. "And I suppose I'm another of those who failed to *ask*. For that, I'm sorry."

Wyndam crosses his arms, mutinous, his lashes spiky with moisture that he most likely does not wish to shed in front of his family.

"You just packed my sack," he crackles. One of the tears escapes, and he dashes at his cheek angrily. He is filled with a rage I remember well from my own youthful years, when everything felt dire and people still treated me as a child, though I thought myself a man. "You handed it to me and chucked me into the catboat, and when I got to Turn Hall, no one *talked* to me!" he hisses. "Everyone talks *at* me!"

"Are we talking at you now?" Bevel asks.

Wyndam blinks some more, and scrubs at his eyes, and says, sullenly: "No."

"Well, then."

"I just..." Wyndam stops, and looks over at Kintyre. "I just wanted to be like you. Everyone talks about you; you're a hero. The great Kintyre Turn."

"And what did you think of this adventure?" Kintyre says softly. "Is it everything you dreamed?"

"It was awful," Wyndam moans, miserable.

"They always are," Isobin admits. "You were always too young to realize it before. But as thrilling as it sounds on the page, hardly any of it is actually fun."

"Not even the girls?" Wyndam asks.

"Not even the girls," Bevel jumps in, hastily.

"Well..." Kintyre begins, and is drawn off into laughter when Bevel pounces on his trothed and slaps a hand over his mouth.

"Don't you say another word, Kintyre. You got all the fun parts of bedding without wedding, but it was me who had to sort out the hurt feelings after. So you just hush!"

Instead of hushing, Kintyre palms the nape of Bevel's neck and kisses his trothed quiet. Isobin erupts into uproarious laughter at that.

"Oh, ew," Wyndam says, and shuffles closer to my side of the table.

Both of us resolutely decide to focus our attention on the way Alis is battling sleep so valiantly. Her head keeps bobbing, and she is smacking her lips, trying not to yawn. She is also making little sniffly sounds, and I hope against hope that this is more symptoms of exhaustion and not a cold. But she has been in the cold and the wet for *hours*, and we haven't any of Pip's marvelous medicines here. A fear surges within me. After everything I have endured, might I lose my child to an illness that could be easily managed were we back in the Writer's realm?

No. No, I will not stand for that.

"You know, nephew," I venture in a whisper, shoving down the ball of fatherly panic. (Surely I must be all out of worry and fear. *Surely* I've used up my allotment for the day? Writer, being a parent is *exhausting*.) "There is a great tradition of the heir to the Seat of Turnshire going off on adventures before the lordling settles down to his post."

Kintyre must have heard me, for he looks up and shoots me a dirty look. I simply grin back, blithe and benign. I shoo him back to his occupations "You are the son of Kintyre Turn," I say with as much warmth as I can possibly infuse in the assertion. "The Writer will let no real harm come to you. You would be like a grandson to him; the child of the main character. Either on sea or on land."

The truth of that sinks home, and I feel, for a moment, a hot shame building in my breast. Elgar Reed has been alone, save for his cat and his characters, his whole life. While I cannot praise him for everything he has created, and all the sorrows he has wrought on my family in the process, I must also accept that he is the author of many of my joys as well.

And that I have pushed him away, cruelly, and wholly, and perhaps even unfairly. Like Wyndam Turn, Elgar Reed is just desperate to belong somewhere. To have something to call his own.

Something that, in my righteous anger and fear of my creator, I have denied him. I am so willing to think that others can change, that they are *good* and *honest*, as the Deal-Maker Spirit taunted me, and yet, I have extended none of that benefit of doubt to my creator. In my own terror of the truth of what I am, why I was written, I refused to believe the best of my Writer.

How petty of me. How small.

How shamed I feel.

"The Writer's grandson," Wyndam echoes, awed. And thoughtful. Whatever it is that he decides he wants to do with his life, I do not doubt that the choice will be well considered.

"Yes," I say. "But be aware that those around you might suffer by their association to you; especially the women. Let no one harm them only to punish you." I reach out and wrap my arms around Wyndam's shoulders, and he allows the embrace, albeit a bit reluctantly. "And know this, Wyndam Turn: if you love, love well, and love bravely. Do not be a coward like your father."

"Father is no coward," Wyndam protests, but presses his forehead to my shoulder all the same.

"Then why did it take him fifteen years to confess to Bevel?"

"Fifteen years?" Wyndam asks. He snorts a laugh when I nod. The mantle of gloom has evaporated, and his laughter is a fresh breeze, blowing away the last of the miserable, damp fog of uncertainty. "What an elfcock."

"Agreed," I say.

The cabin doors open then, and the last two heroes enter. Bradri slides into the room up to her shoulders, neck resting curved up so that her head is level with my shoulder. She smells briney, but it is fresh and not altogether unpleasant. Caerdac, knuckling his eyes and wiping away sleep, stumbles over to the table and fishes around for a fresh cup of tea. Wyndam pours him one and presses it into his hands. Caerdac offers him a sleepy, pleased grin.

Oh, dear.

I ponder the look the rogue had sent in Wyndam's direction when they first met. My nephew can't be more than two or three years the junior of the rogue, and I wonder, suddenly, if Wyndam's romantic inclinations run more along the lines of his father's—no care for physical sex or gender, and only for the person themselves. Wyndam watched Lanaea the way Caerdac is watching Wyndam now, and I wonder if Wyndam notices.

Bradri peeks over my shoulder and offers an inquisitive chirrup.

"The hatchling is sleeping," Bradri says, and she sounds slightly disappointed.

I look down, and yes—Alis has fallen back into her exhausted toddler slumber, clutching Pip's finger in one hand and the buttons of my shirt in the other. "She is," I say.

"Oh."

"You can visit with her later," I promise the dragonet, and Bradri's ruff wriggles, the sails of skin between her horns flushing a happy indigo.

And for a moment, just one hushed, peaceful moment, I feel content. My family is arrayed around me—intimate, extended, and adopted alike. We are safe. We are happy. We are together.

Things are *good*.

"Well, then," the dragonet says, and then turns her attention to watching Wyndam carefully, covetously. Apparently, this dragon has collected a second human into her hoard.

"Did we miss much?" Caerdac says, hauling the last remaining chair up to the table by hooking his ankle around the leg and making a horrific scraping sound. "Are you all in here having fun without us?"

"Fun," Wyndam snorts. "Oh, yes. Heaps of fun. You'd be so jealous." He shrugs stiffly, nursing his left shoulder, cradling the arm he had been yanked down into the Rookery with, the one he has just wrenched again in battle.

"You'll have to fill me in," the rogue says, setting down his teacup to prod at Wyndam's shoulder, earning a wince and a sharp intake of air, and then a relieved groan as the rogue's fingers find the right spot. "*After* Master Turn tells us what he meant by offering us a manor in return for our help."

"A manor?" Kintyre asks, and there isn't any true worry that I have offered the lad Turn Hall reflected in him. Not really. I think.

"And a sheriff-hood, don't forget," I add. Of course, I had done no such thing. Not out loud, at least.

Every pair of eyes swing off Caerdac and onto me, widening in surprise.

"It is the perfect answer," I say, feeling slightly defensive at the looks of disbelief on Kintyre and Bevel's faces. "The Sword of Turnshire oversees the sheriffs of the whole of Lysse Chipping, and he is sore stretched without help. There is a house, a serving staff, and even a large space for Bradri to call her own, though Pointe will need to find somewhere else to practice his swordplay." I focus on Caerdac and Bradri. "Does this interest you?"

"But what about Wyndam—" Bevel starts, but Kintyre quiets him with a hand on his arm.

"Wyndam does not want the posting," I say. "And I believe he communicated this to you many times before his voice was lost."

Wyndam nods emphatically and crosses his arms, resolute. Then, seeming to remember that he can speak again, says, "Right!"

"I... I need to think about..." Caerdac hesitates.

"I don't!" Bradri says. "Our answer is yes!"

"*Dearest*," Caerdac moans, but looks happy to be defeated.

Wyndam laughs, and in revenge, Caerdac pinches his shoulder, hard, earning a jerk and a gasp, and then another softer, fonder chuckle from Wyndam.

Amused, Isobin nudges Kintyre away from the private conversation he was whispering with Bevel and indicates the two youngsters. Kintyre scowls and huffs, but Bevel rolls his eyes and pinches Kintyre's side. Kintyre yelps and jumps.

"What was that for!"

"Nothing," Bevel says, smiling. "Just... Wyn's *definitely* your son."

"Oh, that?" Kintyre says, waving a hand at Wyndam and Caerdac's tête-à-tête. "That's all his mother. Ouch!" he yelps again, as Isobin gives him a matching pinch on the other side of his stomach. "Leave off, you two!"

While everyone else is engaged in their own little worlds, Pip leans over to me and whispers: "I've been thinking about, you know, the mother thing. The overarching theme of this adventure, this novel. You know? And it occurs to me... that Deal-Maker... did we even know her name?"

"Her name?" I whisper back.

"I mean, we knew Neris, but this Deal-Maker..."

"No," I admit, realizing it even as I say it. "I don't think I ever heard it. No."

"Jesus, Elgar," Pip groans, and slaps her forehead with her palm. "The mother of the most powerful villain in the books, and he doesn't even give her a damn name. Ugh. I think our whole adventure just failed the Bechdel Test."

"Spectacularly," I agree, frowning in distaste. "How annoying."

TWENTY-TWO

When Wyndam Turn steps off of *The Salty Queen* this time, it is by his own volition, and with the blessing of his mother. We thank Isobin and her crew profusely for their generosity and hospitality as we disembark, and if we do so mysteriously lighter of a few coins and some relatively unimportant jewelry, well... pirates will be pirates.

Wyndam takes a private moment to say a meaningful and heartfelt goodbye to his mother, and they arrange to meet again in six months' time, in this same spot, for a bit of family catch-up. It is heartening to see how well loved he is by the crew, and the bo'sun cannot stop sobbing into the chief gunner's shoulder, wailing about how grown up her little boy has become.

If traveling out of Lysse with a cart, two horses, and a giant cat was a spectacle, returning without the cart but plus a young lad riding a scarlet dragonet the size of an elephant brings even more curious farmers and townsfolk to the side of the road to stare and holler welcome to the adventurers returned.

"There are hatchlings!" Bradri chirrups, as three bold, wee things escape their mother's skirts to dance in the shallow, curving furrow her tail sweeps into the dirt of the road as she walks. "Hello, hatchlings!"

"Hello, hello!" the children laugh as their mother collects them, fear in her eyes.

"All is well," Caerdac assures the mother, craning around from his seat between Bradri's wings to smile at her. "Dragons love children. They're really very peaceful, clever creatures. They would never harm someone unless they were attacked first."

"They also don't like being talked about as if they are not there," Bradri complains, and bucks and tumbles her rider into the dust.

Caerdac laughs and lets the children help him up.

Our return to Turn Hall is hailed by Pointe, who is startled and pleased in turns to be introduced to Caerdac and Bradri, happy that if we were not successful in our quest to find a way to send Pip and I home, we at least found out what had happened to the stars and brought him a new apprentice.

"Lewko's missed Cap," Pointe says. Wyndam tugs Capplederry's ruff possessively, clearly determined not to be parted from his new friend. "Ah, well," Pointe sighs, amused. "A dragon should make up for it for the wee fellow."

"You have a hatchling, too?" Bradri asks, ruff perking upward, and I foresee Pointe being in quite a lot of bother chasing after the two of them in the near future.

"Dearest," Caerdac admonishes. Ah, at least Pointe will have help in keeping the peace.

When all the sheriffs have left and all the Turns are safely inside Turn Hall, we each take our weary turns with the large bathing shed out back, rather than waiting for the indoor copper tub to be filled, and shuffle ourselves off to bed.

When Alis is in her crib, sound asleep, Pip and I fall into my mother's bed together, too weary and road-sore and happy to be on a real feather-stuffed mattress, to do much more than wrap ourselves around one another and hold on tight.

"Forsyth?" Pip asks, and it is not fear in her eyes that I see when they meet mine. No. Not fear, but a deep and bottomless worry that carves chasms into the skin around her mouth, paints lines of white in her hair where no twenty-seven-year-old woman ought to have them, and makes her clench her jaw as if she could hold back the tide by simply holding her breath.

Three weeks ago, I had stood in my mother's bed-chambers in Turn Hall, attired as a gentleman of my station, and begged my wife to stay here, in this, my homeland, with our child. In my elation to be home, I had dreamed of fetes held in honor of my daughter, the ease of a life led as a nobleman's younger brother. A life where taking up the hated task of paperwork, and visits to our tenants and people, from my brother would both free him to spend more time with his own newly forged family, and make him grateful and gentle toward me. A life where my wife could teach at the Free School, and my daughter could learn to ride a horse and draw a bow, and where I could aid Bevel in his work as Spymaster for the King without having to go out and become one of the Shadow's Men myself. Where the good, honest work of the Chipping, and the good fresh air of Lysse, would serve us all well, and my family would grow hearty and rosy-cheeked and happy.

But in that intervening time, I have remembered the cruelty my creator has inadvertently written into this realm. Children die every day, all across Hain, for want of simple access to clean water. Fevers, and runny bow-els, and a wound succumbing to sepsis and mortifying from something as little as a paper cut kills thousands. A fall from a horse is nearly always fatal. Education for the peasantry, where it happens at all, rarely goes beyond the basics of reading, writing, and sums, used to ensure that they aren't cheated at market and little else. The woods are filled with monsters, the seas even more so, and the towns and hearts of men even more than the rest.

This place is a world where a woman had been imprisoned against her will, bound to a man who had stripped her of all her power and agency, and had tied her to him as his wife for no greater reason than his own bestial lust. A world where, to punish the woman for the sin of being a woman, my creator had sold her child into indentureship to a cruel old warlock, and separated them forever.

And then he'd had the temerity to call that child evil, and a villain, for trying to tear the world apart for that injustice. Had the gall to make that woman hysterical and ungrateful for wanting to murder her warden-husband and win back her son. And yet, also, to fill both of those characters with such blind *hate* that they could never comprehend the hurts they were doing to those around them.

No.

No, this is not the sort of world in which I want to raise my child.

"Let's go," I answer Pip, though she has never truly voiced the question. "Let's go home."

"Are you sure?"

"Yes."

"I just..." She rubs her face against my chest, an adorable, frustrated gesture. "I need to know. Before we go back. Do you really resent having no place? No prestige?" Pip asks softly.

"Do you really regret asking me to be a part of your life?"

Pip looks away, biting her bottom lip, and I decide that if this conversation is to happen—and, I feel, it *must,* or else it will ferment and ooze between us—I must be the brave one and go first.

"Yes, a little," I admit, and before Pip has the chance to misunderstand my honesty, I add: "But you must understand, Pip, that I also resented being tied to my lands here, as well. It was difficult to see the freedom of the world my brother had, and have no measure of it myself."

"But as Shadow Hand..."

"The lion's share of my duties involved sitting on my arse in my study parsing missives. I traveled to the capital as Shadow Hand only rarely. And when I went as Lordling Turn, it was only when I was bade come by the king or for the annual oath-renewing. Which, in itself, was a chore for one who finds crowds, drunken revelry, and excess as unappealing as I."

"I guess, I just... all those times you said you wanted to work for the Canadian monarch, or that you hated how long it was taking you to find a job that challenged you..."

I run my hands through her hair, gentle, thoughtful. Soothing. Petting. "In ultimately understanding that I could not find one, I made one for myself. I am a self-made man in your world, my darling. And is that not the height of respectability there?"

"Well, yeah," Pip says. "I just... I don't know. I feel like I haven't been fair to you."

"And was I fair to you?" I ask in return, gently, sweetly. "Can you tell me there were not days when I frustrated you? When my lack of knowledge, of understanding, my inability to answer the phone or drive a car didn't simmer inside your heart?"

"Well, yes," she admits.

"And I know that our individual opinions of what a marriage should and shouldn't be clash sometimes," I point out.

Pip's lips curl upward. "That's true."

"But we have worked that out, have we not?"

"Yeah. And the make-up sex is pretty spectacular."

"And so, could I not be optimistic that these other small issues will also be worked out? I felt rudderless in your world, but I am coming to love and understand it. And our adventure has taught me that the idyll of the world I left behind was more fantasy than I remembered."

Pip smiles and tucks her arms around my waist, leaning up for a kiss that I am happy to bestow.

"There are things about being the Ladyling Turn that I know I'll miss," Pip admits. "Though one of them will not be the silly honorific. But I see how much family means to you now. Not that I didn't know how much you loved Alis and I, but, well, I won't be so quick to pooh-pooh you when you talk about your brother or Pointe anymore. I promise."

Another kiss, and when it has come to its slow, syrupy stop, as all kisses naturally do, Pip adds: "I didn't get it before, why you were so resentful of Elgar Reed. I was afraid of what he would do to Alis, but I didn't think about your fear of what he could do to you—or what being around us might encourage him to write about Kin and Bev."

"And Wyndam, now," I say.

Pip leans away, so as to be able to meet my eyes. Her expression is all concern. "Do you think he'll write more?"

"Honestly?" I say, "I think Elgar Reed will never put quill to parchment ever again."

"Hmm," Pip says. "On one hand, that's a shame, because I really did love his work when I was younger. On the other, though... god, it's just so problematic. His work is really derivative and misogynist, and honestly, if the rules of the magic he created really are so perfect they made themselves real, then I don't want him to have the power to hurt anyone else."

"And do you suppose that, without his interference, every person and creature in Hain will now live an idyllic life of happily ever afters?"

"I can hope?" Pip says.

"Then I shall hope as well."

Our discussion is broken up by Alis's piteous wail of, "Daah daa mama ma!"

I fetch her out of the Turn family cradle, and Pip goes to the credenza for the ever-present bowl of porridge. It is still warm, so Alis is happy to settle on her father's lap and allow her mother to persuade her to accept the spoonfuls. We had been discussing the transition to more solid foods back before we came here, and Alis had often expressed an interest in what we had on our own plates, eating little pieces of naan and peppers, and making faces if she didn't like our selection of condiments. Now, I envision her learning to eat with the crumb of Cook's fine white breads, and the soft goat cheese that Turnshire is known for, the stone-fruit jams, and the ginger sweets, and the braised venison of my own childhood.

"This isn't so bad," Pip allows, as we feed Alis. "I mean, I'm not ready to give up trying to find a way back, but this... for now, this isn't so bad. Your world during a peacetime is pretty relaxing."

"Oh dear," I tease. "I wish I had my smartphone so I could have recorded that."

"Shut up," Pip laughs at me.

"Shut up!" Alis echoes, gleefully, and we all laugh together then.

"Hmm," I say instead, and duck down for a kiss. "Well, until another option presents itself, you shall simply have to put up with being an idle, pampered Ladyling."

"I think I'll survive," Pip says. "Do you have any other options in mind?"

"I don't," I admit. "It is true that we could try another Deal-Maker, but it's in their nature to lie and find ways to make the Deals go sour. I do not think I would trust ourselves to another."

"No. No, there has to be some other way. We just need to find it," Pip says.

I can't help but grin. "Back to the Library, then? Is that what you're proposing? Because I must admit that I am curious about how Saetesh is faring."

"Careful, *bao bei*," Pip teases me, eyes glittering. "I might get jealous if you're much more obvious about the fact you're crushing on his big fat brain. And then the fans will start slashing you."

"Hmph," I say. "They cannot. *You* are my only romantic interest. I have found my very own OTP already."

"Softy," Pip whispers against my mouth, and then kisses me sweet and dear. "And oh, how very little you understand fandom, my hubby."

TWENTY-THREE

nother three days pass in the domestic familiarity of Turn Hall, in which none of the household really rouses themselves much further than toward the kitchens or the nearest privy. I am quite content that Kintyre and Bevel's rooms are in a different wing than our own, for there are noises that a man does not need to hear coming from his own brother's quarters. Nor have him hear from his own.

On the fourth night, Caerdac, Bradri, and the Pointes come to dinner, demanding a recounting of the adventure. Dorthi spends an inordinate amount of time remarking upon how much Alis has grown since she was last seen, and how many new words the little lady has added to her vocabulary, and Alis absolutely delights in the attention.

We are all dressed in our best, and I feel quite myself again in my Turn-russet trousers, a matching waistcoat of floral brocade, and a mustard-yellow frock coat the color of Forsythia, a blossom from Pip's world which she says does quite well for my complexion and gray eyes. She is dressed in another of my mother's old gowns, a gold similar to the thread of the embroidery on my waistcoat, but with more flowing, swirling fabric in the skirts than Pip really knows what to do with.

It is now warm enough to take our meal outside,

and so we all crowd around a table in the rear courtyard, beside the kitchen garden, and watch the sun set as we regale my friend and his family with the tales of our adventure. Bevel has a small stack of parchment with him, and makes notes in pencil as we talk, making sure to get all the details correct. He can probably never publish this story, but he can at least record it for posterity. For the Shadow Hand who succeeds him, if no one else.

No additional lights rise in the sky, as they have not since the night the last star went out, and when the sun sinks behind the horizon, we all watch the veil of the heavens for several silent moments, waiting... hoping... but no. Nothing appears.

The moon, solitary, lonely, is the only light.

Pip remembers the stories, perhaps not as well as I, but that has not returned the stars to the sky. The realms, the books, are still destroyed. We may never get them back.

That puts a somber shade over our merrymaking, and Pointe and I excuse ourselves to take a turn about the fishpond, watching the fireflies and the fairy lights dance above the water. Moonflowers speckle the boundary between the lawns and the covey forest with a soft, yellow-white glow.

At least here, below, the little lights of the world still twinkle and shine.

"Is it selfish of me to be pleased that you didn't just vanish at the end of this adventure?" Pointe says as we wander close enough to the forest for a pair of foxes to stop and chatter at us with laughs that sound almost human.

"And a good evening to you, too," I tell them, for one can never be sure which animals have human comprehension or not. Then I turn to Pointe. "It is not selfish. Did you think I would?"

"You did the last time."

"And for that, I am sorry."

Pointe shrugs and says nothing for a while.

"Are you leaving, though?" he asks.

"Pip would like us to."

"And you?"

I look up at the starless sky and wonder if this is the beginning of the end for Hain. Without Elgar writing new tales, will this world fragment and collapse, like an old book falling to dust in the back of the returns bin? I fervently hope not. And yet, I cannot help the selfish thought that if it *does*, I do not want to be in it. I do not want Pointe and his family, nor Kintyre and his, in this world when that happens, either.

But no, these books are too popular, too well-known. If books live on in the hearts and minds of Readers, then this world, *my* world, will live on for another thousand years.

"I think perhaps I would like us to go, too," I venture gently.

Pointe nods as if this is no surprise to him.

"It is only that, with the heir in the family seat, what is there for the spare to do?"

"There's lots," Pointe says, and he doesn't mention charity work, or my free school, or work as one of the Shadow's Men, or how King Carvel sent a letter to Turn Hall the moment he learned I was out on an adventure, and that his messengers have daily been nagging me to move to Kingskeep and take up an official post as his advisor, or any of the other opportunities and good works that I would surely find to fill my day should I stay. But we are both thinking about them.

"All the same," I say. "I think it is important to raise my daughter in Pip's kingdom."

"You mean the Writer's realm?" Pointe asks, and

when I shoot him a startled look, he grins and gives me a little shove. "Yeah, I would want my kid raised there, too, if I could swing it."

I am about to reply that it would also be my dearest wish when a sharp flare of light above my head catches my attention. At first, I think it is a fairy speeding across the field, but then I manage to pinpoint the source. It glimmers and twinkles, and is soon joined by a second bright, popping flare, which condenses into a dazzling, diamond-like glow, a pinprick of white light far above our heads.

"The stars..." Pointe breathes.

"The stars," I agree. And then, a sudden thought occurs to me. "Oh, god, Pip!"

I turn and dash back toward the house, Pointe hard on my heels. Pip is already halfway to us, Alis clutched tight in her arms, and the rest of the dinner party, servants included, are not far behind her. We collide in the darkness with a deliberate, joyful embrace, followed by a swift kiss.

"The stars, *bao bei*!" she crows. "It must be Elgar!"

"Do you think?" I ask, cautiously delighted.

"Yes!" Pip shouts. "See? Look!"

And there, not five paces away, the sky fills with the sound of the world shattering and a flare of light so brilliant that we must all shade our eyes. After-images dance in my vision, and Alis is giggling and clapping.

"Is it safe, do you think?" I ask, as Pip leans toward the rip in the fabric between the realms. "Does it lead back to Victoria?"

"Only one way to find out!" Pip enthuses.

"And if it's not?"

"Then what's one more adventure, *bao bei*?" Pip asks, windblown and grinning, and by the Writer, do I love my wife.

Caught up in the current of her enthusiasm, I can only let myself drown in it, and grin. "What, indeed?"

She leans up to kiss me, and as we part, she meets my eyes very seriously, asking without words.

"Yes," I say. "Yes, of course I'm coming with you."

"Then, this is goodbye then?" Pointe asks, sticking out his hand. I bypass his arm and hug him instead.

"You could come."

"What, and leave the dragon and the kid in my place? No. Lysse would be on fire within the hour." He says it with joviality, but it is forced. He blinks, hard. "Take care of yourself?"

"Yes," I say. "I will. And you take care, too. Fare well, Rupin Pointe."

"Fare well, Forsyth Turn," Pointe says, his voice tellingly thick beside my ear. "Thanks for taking the time for goodbyes this time."

"Thank you for being here for it. I am so glad you got to meet my family."

I fear the portal will close quickly, so the rest of our leave-takings are swift and, though tear-filled, also triumphant.

I hug Kintyre last, and he squeezes me tight, lifting my feet off the ground as he grunts, "Be well, brother," in my ear. When he sets me down, he dashes at his eyes and turns away. I therefore cannot see his face when he says: "I'll miss you, bookmouse. I... lo-love you. Go'wan."

His confession raises such a lump in my throat, so that I can only croak: "I'll miss and love you too, you oaf."

Pip and I are going home. As one, we stand before the rip, Alis snug against my hip, and clasp hands.

And then, through the portal, the whole of the crowd can hear the thud of someone dancing triumphantly, the sound of a proud Writer crowing: "I did it! Ha ha! I am a genius! I did it!"

Laughing, filled to the brim with bubbling joy and a sort of desperate relief, Pip and I step through.

~~~

The light flares and fades, and I open my eyes to find myself flat on my back in my living room, wedged between my coffee table and my sofa. I touch the back and sides of my head, but I seem to have fortuitously missed both surfaces on my way into my swoon.

"Did what?" Pip asks, as soon as the vertigo has cleared enough to allow us to sit up. Pip climbs to her feet and makes such a muddle of her skirts as she does so that she nearly falls down again.

"Look! The books! The books are back!" Elgar Reed says, pointing with pride at our bookshelf. "And I'm the one who did it!"

"How?" Pip asks, depositing a startled Alis in her playpen and wobbling over to where Elgar has thrust a much-inked sheet of paper at her.

All around my reading chair, there are balls of paper and the corpses of used-up pens.

Pip takes the paper and reads aloud:

And though the author did not know why the other works of fantasy and science fiction literature were vanishing, he was confident in the great workings of his own world, that the magic inherently perfect within it would bring them back. He toiled to find just the right words to invoke the magic and reverse the slow drain of wonder in his own realm.

Then, having found the perfect Words, the author invoked the spell which brought all the stories back into the world.

The pleasant side effect of which was that a portal
~~~

opened between the realm of his imagination and the realm of his reality, allowing Forsyth Turn, Lucy Piper, and Alis Mei Turn Piper to return to the author's world. This portal opened a mere five feet away from them, and was bespelled to remain open until all three had come through. It was exactly the same as the portal which had taken them there in every respect, except for the direction it traveled.

When the erstwhile travelers returned home, the portal closed, and every book, poem, play, screenplay, comic, fan fiction, or other sort of writing and story that had vanished from the Writer's world had been restored to their proper places. And no one in the author's world ever remembered that they were ever gone—except for the author, Forsyth, Alis, and Pip.

The End

"Well then," I say, coughing, a little choked up. "Bravo."

"What were the Words?" Pip asks, eager.

"That's the beauty of writing," Elgar crows. "I have no idea. But I don't need to know. I can just say that they were perfect, and they are." He laughs, spreading his arms. "I tried to find the perfect words, and then I remembered that you said that Readers can't *hear* Words of Power, and bam! Nothing I could come up with would be as good as just *saying* they were perfect."

"That's some lazy-ass storytelling there, Elgar Reed," Pip says, but she does so with a smile, and embraces my creator with an enthusiasm that startles both of us. With a wide-eyed glance at me over my wife's shoulder, Reed tentatively returns the hug.

"How long were we gone?" I ask Reed, when Pip pulls away, and he shakes his head, still startled.

"Uh... about eight hours? Maybe nine?"

"About the same amount of time as it would take you to read a *Kintyre Turn* book," Pip says, voice breathy with awe. Then she blinks, and looks back down at the paper. "Wait, it took you *nine hours* to come up with three paragraphs?"

"Hey," Reed says, shifting, defensive. "Writing is *hard*, okay?"

Pip laughs, and hands the paper over to me so I can read for myself the spell that has brought us home. I have never seen Elgar's handwriting before. It is cramped and scrawled. No wonder he preferred to compose on a typewriter. Or, now, a laptop.

Pip wanders over to our bookshelf, hugging her elbows, looking pensive.

"I can't believe I forgot all of these stories," Pip whispers, staring in worshipful awe at the books. It is once again jammed near to overflowing. It is evidence of our success, and the dusty jumble that usually fills me with consternation at its disorganized tip, fills me instead with pride and the satisfaction of a quest well completed.

While it is the books that mesmerize my wife, I cannot stop staring at the paper in my hands. So easy a thing, so small a gesture, and so profound a change it has wrought in its Readers. Is that what being a Writer means? Not the creation, but the way that others are affected when they are done reading what you've toiled to create?

If so, I cannot fault Reed for his drive to create, to write me and my whole world into existence.

"Do you want to go back?" Reed asks, breaking into my little daydream, voice small. "Did I... are you mad at me?"

For a moment, I consider it. Mad? Perhaps a little. I would have liked a better leave-taking, but at least this time, I was able to see Pointe and his family one last time. This time, I did not vanish from the lives of those I loved dearest with no warning, and no explanation.

But do I want to return?

No.

No, my life is here now. What the Deal-Maker Spirit did not understand when she taunted me with my own fears was that now that Kintyre is Lord and Bevel the Shadow Hand, all the meaning my life once held has been stripped away. True, I have my family still, and my friends, but I cannot stand to be idle. And to be the spare to the heir is about as idle as a person could be in my realm.

"No," I answer, and for the first time, I feel the whole truth of it in my heart.

Elgar deflates, a tension I didn't realize he was carrying dissipating. "Well!" he says, clutching his hat. "That's... ah. That's it then. Yeah? Day is saved, and all of that. I should... ah. I should go."

"No!" Pip says, turning around suddenly. "No. No, we still have that wine you brought at Solsticetide. Come on, we'll open it."

"Going to tell me another story?" Reed asks, alluding to the first time I met him, in the bar of a hotel at a science fiction and fantasy convention. His face fills with a hope that I hadn't ever expected to encourage in him again.

"Yes!" Pip calls as she gathers up her ridiculous skirts and goes into the kitchen.

We both watch her go.

"That's a pretty dress," Reed says tentatively.

"It was my mother's," I explain.

"Ah. I guess... you don't want to talk about... um, family? With me."

"On the contrary, actually. While I was there, I realized something," I say, reaching out and offering my hand to my creator. "I should like to forge a peace with you, if I am able. It will be... shaky, to start. But I think, perhaps, in time... we could be friends. We could be family, if that is what you want. I will shut you out no more."

"No more?" Reed echoes, hopeful, his hands tightening around mine.

"No more," I say. "You see, I always wanted my father to... well, to be short-winded about it, I have shut out the very thing I have been longing for, and I regret it. I hope you will forgive me, as well."

"Yes! Yes, of course!" Reed gasps. Delighted.

"And you will work with me to attempt to mend this rift between us?"

"Of course!" Reed says again, and begins to pump my hand. "It's a deal!"

"Ah!" I say, and draw my hand back quickly. "Maybe... perhaps, we should not use *that* particular phrase."

"Oh. *Oh*," he says, jamming his hands into his pockets, startled and worried. "Right, yes, of course. No deals. Of course."

"Of course."

"Though I... you must understand that I have to draw the line at calling you fa-father," I caution him.

"Right," Reed says, sweating, nervous. "Right, you already had one of those."

"But friend," I say softly. "Th-th-that I can call you, if you l-l-like." I hold out my hand again, a truce.

And cautious, hopeful, but still nervous, Reed takes it.

BLOOD

"It is a Deal," the woman-shaped thing says, and takes the man's hand to shake.

It is warm, and firm, and she locks eyes with him because she knows that this Deal, this magic, will be the last she ever does. The task he asks is too great, requires too much. She will not survive it.

Not a third time.

It is only because of the Deal-Maker blood in his veins—veins he opened for her to drink from—that she is able to revive her dormant power enough for her to perform a magic so great. And with him gone from her, parted this time forever, she does not *wish* to survive it.

He holds her gaze as well, for he is a master warlock. He knows the checks and balances of magic, and he too knows that his revenge will cost her life. The power in his blood is locked away, but that doesn't mean he can't take what's left of *hers*. They were each barred from accessing their own magics, but nothing in the Deal said that they could not use the other's. As he opened his veins first for her, he now drinks from hers. Gulp after bloody blue gulp, teeth stained and smiling.

Behind him, the tear waits. When she is a husk, desiccated and fatigued, he presses a gory kiss to her forehead, and stands. Just before the white light envelops him, whisks him away from this world forever, he smiles.

"Thank you, Mother," he says. "Goodbye. I will revenge you."

"I know you will. Farewell," she croaks. "My darkling boy. Take what is owed to you."

The sky shatters, and white light fills her vision. She dies by inches, with the last image of her child in her mind and a smile on her lips. She thirsts. She dries. She can feel her remains evaporating.

Now that she knows that the Writer is real, and that he has finished her tale and placed her book on his Shelf of the Complete, she wonders if the rest of the stories are also true. That she will be given the chance at a final conversation with the Writer once his Pen is laid down.

If she is, she plans to save her final mouthful of moisture so that she can spit in his face.

ACKNOWLEDGEMENTS

My very great thanks to:

My Reuts Team—especially Kisa—who originally loved this world enough to ask for more than I had
planned to write. This was never meant to be a series,
and having the opportunity to return to Hain has meant
the world to me. Also, thank you for being patient while
I juggled, jumbled, changed honorifics, and generally ran
around like a crazy person while I tried to do some extra
worldbuilding to support the arc of this extended narrative. Sorry I keep changing the timelines and titles!

My inexhaustible beta readers: Jason (who helped
smooth up the poetry wonderfully), Ashley, Sunny, Ran-
dom Nexus, and Devon.

Aunt Brenda and Dennis, in whose Sauble Beach
bunkhouse a majority of this book was plotted and written.

Heather Emme, who came up with the name Capplederry.

Adam Shaftoe, who came up with the name Saetesh.

Devon Taylor-Black, who came up with the name
Caerdac (though I changed the spelling).

Stephen Tassie, who came up with the name Bradri
(though I really changed the spelling).

To Stephanie, Ruthanne, Jason, Sunny, Ashley, Adri-
enne, Mags, and Alexis, who put their heads together and
helped come up with the series name.

Christopher Winkelaar (www.eyelessmax.com), my
former roommate and, in no small way, part of my inspiration for both this world and for Forsyth. Chris and
I were roommates in University, and he introduced me
to D&D and fantasy RPGs; it was clear who the obvious

choice had to be when it came time to commission the map at the front of these books.

Devon, Gavin, and Taran Taylor-Black, who provided lots of amazing feedback on the books, who created the marvelous D&D 5.0 compliant mini-campaign set at the Lost Library that you can get for free on Elgar Reed's website, and who put up with me coming over to their house to play with Baby Taran as he grew older so I had a pattern for Alis.

Mom and Dad, who let me move home and take over the spare room for an office so I could follow my dreams as Forsyth follows his.

And of course, thank you to you Readers, peering beyond the veil of the skies into the worlds and lives I've Written, and loving them. I cannot express how humbling and wonderful you are.

ALSO BY J. M. FREY

(Back)
Triptych
City By Night
The Dark Lord and the Seamstress, a coloring storybook
Hero Is A Four Letter Word,
short story collection
"Whose Doctor?" in *Doctor Who In Time And Space:*
Essays on Themes, Characters, History and Fandom,
1963–2012
"How Fanfiction Made Me Gay," in *The Secret Loves of*
Geek Girls
"Time to Move," in *The Secret Loves of Geek Girls*
Redux
"Bloodsuckers" and "Toronto the Rude" in *The Toronto*
Comic Anthology vol 2
"The Promise" in *Valor 2*
"TTC Gothic" in *Amazing Stories vols 1-4*
Lips Like Ice, as Peggy Barnett
Time and Tide

The Accidental Turn Series
The Untold Tale
The Forgotten Tale
The Silenced Tale
The Accidental Tales,
more stories from the Accidental Turn series

The Skylark's Saga
The Skylark's Song
The Skylark's Sacrifice

ABOUT THE AUTHOR

Photo by Marion Voysey

J.M. Frey is an author, actor, and professional smartypants. She's appeared in podcasts, documentaries, radio programs, and on television to discuss all things geeky through the lens of academia. J.M. lives near Toronto, surrounded by houseplants because she is allergic to fur. She's a tea and wine nerd, and her life's ambition is to one day set foot on every continent (3 left!)

Her debut novel *Triptych* was nominated for two Lambda Literary Awards, nominated for the CBC Bookie Award, was named one of *Publishers Weekly*'s Best Books of 2011, was on *The Advocate*'s Best Overlooked Books of 2011 list, received an honorable mention at the London Book Festival in Science Fiction, and won the San Francisco Book Festival for Science Fiction.

www.jmfrey.net

PACK ICE
ERLINMEYER
ICEDANCE SEA
PERMAFROST LINE
PIRATE ISLE
SUNGSONG SEA
HAIN
TURNSHIRE
TURN HALL
KINGSKEEP
THE VICEROY'S CASTLE
SALT CRYSTAL CAVERNS
GWILFIFESHIRE
MOONCALL SEA
LOST LIBRARY
LONG POND
VALLEY OF TOMBS
STGAR FOREST
URLAND
THE EYERIE
SWORDS HEARTH
GADOT
CINCH MOUNTAINS
CRONN'S NEST
SKIPPING LAKES
BRYSTOL
QUEEN'S DREAM
RAINSLEEP SEA